CHA

MW00874920

Benjamin Peter Green
New York, **Two Years Earlier**

jOurnAL eNtry ~ nOon, fEbRUary 5[16]

Let'S hAVE a GOoD ol CHinwAg abOuT growING up.

AnNuaLly, thE miNutE I wakE uP aNothEr yEAr oLder, it'S aS iF thE worLD exPECts Me tO haVE fiGUREd ouT anOTHer RIDDle oF thIS liFe...

ya know, tHaT thINg i nEVEr aSKed foR. uNDer nO cirCUmsTAnces haVE i evEr unDErstooD WHY i HAVe bEEn forCed iNTo celeBRatinG aN exISTEnce i DIdn't siGn uP foR in THe fiRSt plaCe... I hAd nO saY in ThiS. JesUS ChrisT hiMSelf diD nOT aSK foR mY perMissiOn bEFORe POOFING mE inTO mY mothEr's woMB –

gONNa haVE a propEr chaT witH him, oNe dAy.

dOEs anyOne eVEr asK themSELves why wE ALL SCrEam and CRy bloODy murDER whEN we'RE RELEased intO ThE worLD aS BAbIEs? *PERHAPS IT'S BECAUSE NOBODY REALLY*

---

[16] *Welcome to the journal entries! Fun Fact: I was originally going to write all of these and scan them into the book...but my writing is as illegible as hell. So I found a font close to it, but still readable.*

WANTS TO BE HERE. ToTS proBAblY haVE SOme sorT of sIxTH SENse upOn poPPing out Of theIR motHER'S vAGgIe...bUt theN wE aLL geT braINWAshed tO beliEVE we HAve a REAson tO be hERE, THUS we'RE froCED to discovER it, anD tHEN TRApped Like LITTle micE unTIL thE goOD LORd ComES baCK TO saVE uS.

If he does.

onCE we GET OLDer, everYTHiNg comES back fuLL circLE, AnD we cRY agaiN beCAusE We'RE ALive...
excEPt foR mE, I nevER crY.

toDaY jUSt sO haPPEns tO bE mY 16tH bIrthDaY. I'm iN mY roOm, the ONe wiTH tHE vieW iN tHE corNEr oF oUr qUAInt nEw yOrk fLAt, sIMPly drEadINg goINg inTo tHE KiTCHEn TO gREet tHE daY, aLthOuGH ThE sMELL oF mUms cHOcoLAtE cAKE iS haRDcoRE teasINg mE bY wAFTIng iTs waY iN hERe... so i fANcy i wONT bE aBLE to withSTand iT muCH loNGer. iT's noT thAT i loATHe biRthDay's enTIREly, i juSt dONt uNDerSTand thE celEbraTORy fACTOr oF gETTinG olDEr. bEinG aN eyEwitNEss iN thiS houSehoLD tO thE curSes oF adULthood hAS maDE mE lONG tO stAY yoUNg foREVEr.

iF oNLY it WerE poSSIblE.

buT aLAS, thE dAy-oF-biRTh-faiRiEs hAVE neVER beeN
thE leaST biT faVORabLE to mE reGARDing mY wiSHEs
thROuGHOut thE yEARs, sO i guESS i'M stILL shiT ouTTA
lUck wIth This One aS welL

welp. muMa's SUMmoNIng.
hAPpy FUCKING birthDay to me.

    With slight reluctance, I end the one on one
conversation with my journal, who is practically my best mate
(I know, fucking sad, innit?), and tuck it…*him? her?*…securely
under my firmest pillow. Standing up, I squeeze my shoulder
blades together with my arms bent at my sides, performing a
stretch that opens up my chest.[17] But of course, as usual, I get
interrupted by my pussy lungs and therefore am forcibly
erupted into a violent cough that sends my chest into panic
mode. I tell myself to chill, and slowly clear them up the best I
can. Even though this time I don't need my inhaler, I still have
to hunch over to catch my breath.

Having asthma plus being addicted to cigarettes on top of it
bloody sucks.
I do not recommend.

    Once I'm stable and breathing more properly, I
carefully assume the same stretching position once more.
Tilting my head back toward the ceiling, I roll my neck to and

---

[17] *RANDOM Fun Fact: This paragraph haunts me, because the night I*
wrote it, at like 3am, a car smashed into the wall by my house and
exploded, quaking the shit outta my room…scary.

fro until it satisfyingly cracks, silently appreciating the grace
of getting to catch up on some much-needed shut-eye. On
special occasions such as today, mum is more lenient and
allows me to sleep a bit longer than usual, granting me the
morning off from chores and errands. It's grand for a change,
though sometimes I feel guilty because it then causes her to
have oodles more on her plate since there's no way in hell
Colin will assist her...prick.

But who am I kidding,
Selfish as it may be, I have more energy than I've had in
months.

I throw on a clean black t-shirt and my dark green
hoodie. My old black jeans are a bit faded and I presume will
soon have holes in the knees...but I consider that stylish and
roll them up a few folds to show off my navy blue,
well-ventured Converse. I slide on my silver rings, complete
some basic hygienic shit, then I'm off toward the aroma of
cake.

The toeboxes of my battered shoes bend impressively
as I creep down the wooden hallway and peek my head around
the corner to scope out the scene in the kitchen – I just want to
get a feel of the afternoon vibe, that's all. Though I attempt to
be stealthy, the wood within every inch of this small apartment
deafeningly creaks with every step, and after a few squeaks I
hear my mother chuckle,

"You'd be a very poor thief, Benjamin."

I roll my eyes playfully and accept my defeat,
"Mornin, mum." I kiss her on the cheek. "You alright?"

"Just fine, dearest." She wipes her hands on a
dishtowel and holds my face gently. She's full of grace as
always, though looks worn out, like she too could use a day or
two of sleeping in. It makes me wonder when the last time she
had that luxury was. "A very happy birthday to you, my love."

Mumma kisses my forehead so softly, it has me presuming she believes if the gesture is too hard, I'll crumble to pieces. I sit down to a gorgeous piece of chocolate cake and tea for my brunch, and scarf it down as if this will be my last meal.

"Mum?" I say with a mouth full of silky buttercream.

"Hmm?" She hums sweetly in response to me.

"Will you ever tell me the secret to the perfection of this devilishly divine cake?"

Her entire expression ruthlessly taunts me then, "I should think not!" Lifting the cake batter-covered spoon to her mouth, she takes a lick and audibly moans with pride at the taste. How elegant yet absurd this woman can be *baffles* me. "Just know the main and most crucial ingredient is love, and the rest I shall take to my grave."

I shake my head at her playful impertinence behind my tea cup as I lift it to my lips. Beginning to put clean dishes into the cabinets above her, my mum's sleeve slips up beyond her elbow, and I notice something that causes my ass to spring up faster than a fucking May tulip.

"Good God, mother!" I grasp the drinking glass that aided me to see this monstrosity out of her hand and hold her wrist gently. "What the bloody hell is this?"

"Watch your mouth, child," she reprimands first. "It's nothing to fret over, I simply fell while in the garden –"

"Bullshit!"

"Benjamin Peter!"

"Oh c'mon, mum, I'm not daft." I gently run my thumb over her wounds, "These cuts and nasty bruises are not from a fall, these are from violent hands that meant to hurt you." *I don't want to say these next words, but I have to know.* "Tell me father didn't do this to you."

"Benjamin, you need not –"

"Tell me...now." Her inability to respond immediately tells me all I need to know. I want to be angry, so

fucking enraged that it propels me to take the kitchen knife and hold it to Colin's neck and threaten that if he even dares touch my mother again, it'll be the very last thing he ever does – but instead, all I feel is complete and utter sorrow for the dauntless, yet helplessly delicate woman standing before me.

For a while, it was only cruel verbal abuse and careless drunken arguments that would cause my mother trauma. Being younger and a bit more naive then, I believed her when she said Colin was just stressed because of work, so I didn't defend her as I would now – *do* now. Back then, she was able to stand her ground and fight back without me.

She's a lady but is certainly not a pussy.

However as the years went on, father progressively became disgustingly more violent. The lashes my mother normally would hide were becoming significantly worse and inevitably obvious, and the bruises appeared more and more often – it was heartbreaking when some days, she could barely get out of bed. So, I vowed that if there was anything I could do to ensure that it was *me* who took the hits, I would do it.

And
do
it
I
fucking
did.

Colin didn't stop beating my mother entirely, though he did begin taking more of his anger out on me with pride when, after one brutal injury to the hip he caused my mum, I lashed out and took him by the throat against the wall, threatening that if he ever struck her again, I would gladly kill him. He laughed, spat straight in my face, then socked me on the side of the head until I was out cold. I woke up to blood coming out of my ear, mumma crying on the sofa, and him gone. It mercilessly progressed after that and has never stopped.

"Mum…" I press away the flashbacks and my eyes meet hers; eyes that are distraught and held captive by every emotion she feels prohibited to let out. I squeeze her hand, "I cannot stand for this any longer, and neither should you. We must leave –"

"There is nothing I can do, Benjamin," she says in a knowingly hushed tone as if the demon of my father lingers and listens here while his physical being is at work.

I argue this subject with my mother nearly on a daily basis. She refuses to leave my dad after he threatened that if she dares to attempt such a thing, he will fight for custody of me in court, thus commencing an obvious win due to his superiority in the court system, proceeding then to take me far away to God knows where, never letting me see her again.

An utterly charming man, I know.
So we aren't to even consider sodding off until I turn eighteen.
Until then, we are no more than the broken cottage that never speaks.

"Why can we not run away?" I ask for what seems like the millionth time in my life.

"Because, child," she runs her fingers through my hair like she loves to do, and looks as if she wants to cry, "running away will not change a thing if you are fleeing to nowhere."

She's right.
Plus he'll find us, or send out henchmen who will.

"Happy thoughts, Benjie," she smiles, and I want to roll my eyes into another dimension. I will never understand her optimism in such fucked up situations, but I will forever admire her strength for it. It is unlike anyone I have ever known. I long to be like her one day.

Today is not that day.

"It's just a bit longer." She takes my hand. "We'll make it, you and I. I love you to the sun, the moon, the stars, and back; and farther than that."

❧ ❧ ❧

This evening, I have plans to go to the harbor with some mates I've grown up with to celebrate my turning the big one-six. It was entirely their idea, as no part of me desires to go, but I heard from a little birdie there will be whiskey, so…

Go, I must.

Mother is hardly ever hesitant in allowing me to go out with friends, nor is she strict about curfew, but I promised her I'd be home before nine. Without fail, she encouraged me not to worry, but as usual, it is not on my itinerary in any sense to leave her alone with a plastered Colin parading through the door while I'm not there to protect her…if that duty should so present itself; which, do to the fact that it has not been a stranger to us recently, I know I always am better off safe than sorry.

Father used to come home earlier, but over time, it slumped to later hours in the evening. Sometimes, it got so late, that we thought *(hoped)* he might not return home at all –

Oh, what a marvelous jubilee that would've been.

Choosing my worn-out leather boots for this outing, I pray my lungs will do me a kindness and stay on their best behavior tonight. The cold has been biting like a pack of hungry wolves, so I don't have much faith, but hey, maybe Mother Nature will grant me mercy for my sweet sixteen. I slip a box of fags[18] into my coat pocket, along with my lighter and phone that I rarely use, and quickly kiss my mother on the cheek as I head out the door, already late to my own soiree. I promise her again I'll beat my father home, and before I can hear her response, I take off down the corridor and race down the nine flights of stairs, the echoes of my feet bouncing off the walls. Outside, with record-breaking speed – since I have done this dozens of times now –, I unchain my bike from the rack, run a few steps with it for momentum, and strategically swing my leg over the seat to hop on; beginning to book it down to the docks to a party celebrating a life, that…did I mention I didn't ask for?

Whiskey! Whiskey! Whiskey![19]

⌭ ⌭ ⌭

"Benjie-man!" The moment my tires reach dock territory and skid to a stop across the pavement, I am paraded by the friendly arms of my five mates thrown around me dramatically and the smell of an excessive amount of booze already on their breaths. They know all too well I hate being hugged, but they like to bask in my discomfort as often as they can. "Happy bloody birthday, darling!"

---

[18] *This is British for cigarette, just in case you were alarmed*
[19] *A stellar John Mayer song.*

Charlie[20] and I have been chums for as long as I can remember. His thick Brooklyn accent is so incomprehensible, that I constantly suggest he should just hire a translator to follow him around. Char is quite boisterous and…flamboyant, if you will; the type of bloke that would willingly do a musical, but he's alright. His pasty cheeks are getting redder by the second from the liquor surging through his veins, and he drunkenly squeezes a sloppy kiss on my face, followed by commanding the crowd that I must acquire a drink immediately.

"So," he slurs, "does it feel goddamn beautiful to be *sixty?* Are your joints aching yet?" He slaps me on the chest, "You're getting old, brosky!"

I shake my head and let out a small cough-chuckle, "Yes, mate, time is fleeting. I can already feel my lungs giving out." *Sick joke, Ben.*

"Well," like he's living in a musical and everything happens in perfect timing, a plastic cup filled with cheap whiskey is handed to him on cue, and then graciously he passes to me, "drink up, kid, you ain't gettin' any younger."

Bummer.

After making my rounds, the lads and I board *Molly 2.0,* my infamous lobster boat amongst our small clan that I named after the direly missed-but-never-forgotten *Molly 1.0* I was forced to sell and leave behind in Portsmouth, and I captain us into the middle of the harbor. The winter night breeze is sharp as it breaks through the barrier of my coat with ease, and my lungs silently plead for something warm.

---

[20] *Fun Fact: A lot of random character names in this book are names of members in my family. I wanted to give them little cameos. Charlie is my big brother's name*

Eh, guess Mother Nature doesn't give a shite about birthday wishes either.

I shoot a generous swig of liquid gold, and instantly my insides are given a big hug.

Luckily, whiskey always cares.

When I finally feel a proper time to park and party, the water begins to rock the vessel gently with the ripples our movement created. The air is full of laughter and incoherent conversations of the absolutely smashed, that all just wind up as continuous shouting and crooning. As I observe all of the careless individuals around me, I begin to wonder:

How?
How are they so free?
They don't seem to give a fuck about if they get home before their dad...
or that aging is inevitable...
They're just simply existing...
while I am complexly surviving.

Yanking me out of my yapping head, I hear my name shouted unnecessarily loudly by my mate Sammy[21], "Ben! Have you charged the Lass recently?" He means *Molly 2.0* – we respectfully call her that quite often.

"Mhmm." My deep, deep subconscious knows full well that I indubitably did not, but I don't want them to know that, nor do I wish to fully adhere to the truth yet and accept I was that daft.

"Well, I don't hear the motor running...did you turn it off?"

---

[21] *My other big brother's name*

In response to his panic, I shake my head and curl my lips in, strolling casually over to the stern to find he's right…nothing. *[Pretending to be]* Perplexed, I shuffle back to the small control panel and turn the key in the ignition off, then on again, then repeat the method about five times, to no avail.

Le boat is dead.
Brilliant!

"Well…" I look at my audience piercing me with their eyes, and matter-of-factly say what we're all thinking: "fuck!" I present a toothless, cheeky-lipped smile, and some can't help but combust into simultaneous laughter.

"What are we gonna do?" Sammy freaks as if the Titanic is sinking. I reach into my pocket and check my phone, but the bars are little to none.

This is why I never use this damn thing.

"I'll just swim back." As I look up from the ignition, they all gape at me as if I just said *they* all should swim back.

"Benjie, you'll freeze to death," Charlie tries to rule out the option. "Especially with those lungs of yours – there's no way we're lettin' ya do that."

He looks to everyone else for reassurance, yet no one gives it to him; not even me. We all already inaudibly agreed that *[unfortunately]* I'm the only semi-sober one on this boat who would also most likely be the one bloke out of this group to make it back to the dock alive…working lungs or less than.

"Thank you for your concern, Charlie darling," I mimic my mum's voice and put my numb hand on his cheek. I whisper dramatically, "I'll be back for you."

The group laughs again and Charlie wiggles his tongue at me flirtatiously.

Such a fucking queer one.

I strip off my coat, followed by the rest of the upper half of my clothing, thus causing an uproar of playful shouts and whistles from the boys; then off go my shoes and socks. My lungs already ache from the lack of coverage and just the thought alone of diving into ice-cold water before swimming even a mere mile or so to shore, but I choose to ignore their bitching.

"Be careful, Greenie." I hear a bunch of variations of this phrase as I step onto the edge of the swaying vessel. The water blends in with the night surrounding the boat, making a bit of hesitation creep into my stomach. But before I can let it overtake me further, I swing my arms over my head, clap my hands theatrically, and dive in.

Almost immediately, my entire body goes completely numb. Mercilessly, the icy water lights my skin on fire *(I always found this ironic)*, and pierces it like pins and needles all at the same time. The shock my lungs receive is like a stab in the heart with a freshly sharpened blade, and I can already sense that out of spite, they are going to ensure coming up for air is extra brutal for me. However, despite all this, I forcibly carry on.

Beneath the water, I can't see a bloody thing, so I haven't the foggiest idea where I am. My body begins to give out and beg for air, though as I begin to head toward the surface, the unimaginable happens –

Something,
No...
Someone
with...claws? Or someone in dire need of a manicure...
grasps and sinks into my right ankle.

Treading water, I try to stomp and kick the arcane thing away, but as if I have been magically chained to an anchor, I begin to be hauled under and, actively gaining speed, plummet farther and farther down into the blackness of the water. My lungs burst as I scream, filthy water beginning to fill my chest as I flail about, frivolous in attempting every movement I can to get out of this flagitious grip. My head is spinning with terror as I slowly begin to accept the fact that I'm gonna die –

They're gonna remember me as the poor little British boy...
The one who got pissed and died on his sixteenth birthday, due
to mysterious causes after diving into the harbor.

Mum...will be left for ruin.

Left alone.

No...

I close my eyes and everything happens in slow motion. I whip, stretch, and beat every limb this way and that in hopes of impeding whatever monster is out to end me, and as I start to see ill-lit shapes and spots, believing I am about to fully knock out...suddenly everything comes to an abrupt stop.

No more plummeting,
but also not rising
...just floating.
There is a hand caressing my face...
What the actual fuck, am I alive?

Unsure what the bloody hell is happening and frankly semi-afraid to find out, I manage enough strength to force open my eyes and then freeze as before me, I see the most fiercely ethereal, radiantly dazzling young woman I have ever laid my eyes upon…

A scaly, golden tail is where her legs should be, crystal blue wing-like quills stream around where her feet don't reside, and her hands are half the size of Wolverine's claws. Her luscious, silky silver hair goes on for miles, and hovers around her with such elegance – like each strand listens to her every command. She smiles luminously, and I gasp as her weaponous gray, razor-sharp teeth say hello.

Hey, wait…
*I **gasped**, didn't I?*

And no water entered my mouth
No coughing
No suffering as I had twenty seconds ago…

I can…breathe…?

✐ ✐ ✐

"Hello, darling boy."

The strange, exquisite creature studies me with ultraviolet, iridescent eyes, and I become paralyzed by her enchantment straightway. When she speaks, her voice is an echo of power and though her mouth doesn't move, I can hear her perfectly in my head as if she lives up there as my second conscience. I can uncannily breathe perfectly and take in everything, even though I am far too deep beyond the surface to see its moonlit sky anymore; and although my skin is still quite chilled, the surrounding water around me feels warm and airy. I'm beginning to certainly suppose I'm dead, and that guardian angels are actually, contrary to popular belief, *smashing* sirens.

"You are not dead. You are finally coming alive."

Oh…can she hear me?

*"Of course I can.
Your thoughts are your voice, pet."*

Holy shit.
This is impossible.

"Only if you believe it is."

I do. I'm dead. Or passed out. You're not real.

"Perhaps I can convince you otherwise."

The aura she casts causes a sensation in me I've never felt before, nor did I think I ever could feel. She is strikingly inviting — lucidly sexy. I can smell the faintness of her eucalyptus and sea salt scent as she stretches out her femininely strong arms and draws me into her pillowy, bare breasts. I want to be terrified of this woman, want to escape her hold and be rid of all of the nonsense that is surrounding me; tell her I loathe being touched, let alone even hugged, but somehow I'm the farthest thing from doing that.

She delicately brings her thin, scaly hand up to my cheek and her dagger-like fingernails softly stroke my flushed, frozen skin. Her touch stings, yet slowly lights a foreign fire in me that I don't seem to be in control of –

Who –
or, rather…
What
is she?

I don't know if it's worse that I haven't a clue if this temptress can hear all of the chaos polluting my mind, or the fact I don't care if she can…but regardless, she obviously is well aware of her magnificence and the spell it has me under.

Her fingers generously run through my dark auburn hair and then down the back of my neck, curving around to glide across my shoulder. I shiver at her constant touch and her ever-present, dominant gaze going to and from my eyes, to all the places she's feeling and *wants* to feel, around my body. My curious gaze follows her hand, and I see it has found its way curved around my torso. The siren fervently gapes down at it, and as I begin to pull away, she pulls me in closer like a dance.

I'm wildly uncomfortable, yet I never want it to end.
Sweating, though underwater
Soaking wet, yet I feel warm and dry.
Nothing feels real, yet it's all so bloody vivid.

I can feel…
everything.

Breathing down my neck, she places one arm behind my back holding me close – too close – and with the other free one, petting up and down my thigh along my jeans. I close my eyes to finally accept and take in this intimacy I've never felt, as she paints her own picture on what magically feels like my skin. This whole event envelops me like a potential dream sequence I never want to wake up from…Or, perhaps, maybe a Heaven – *maybe a hell* – I'm riveted to have the key to.

Still wrestling with my thoughts, I'm suddenly thrown off by her hand slithering its way upwards from my thigh. My breathing becomes more and more unsteady as her stare now doesn't leave my eyes, and from the arm wrapped properly around me, she sends her gentle claws playing through my hair again while her wandering one below approaches the most tender part of me. Upon contact, I let out a staggered gasp, and with consolation she hushes me, proceeding. I look down to watch her stroke a part of me no one has ever touched other than myself, and inadvertently several moans escape my throat at the sight – at the *feeling*.

Fucking hell...
Why am I letting her do this?

I am unable to think of anything but the new sensation her hands are creating. Sure, I have jerked off a few times before and it has been easily satisfying, but I'm infinitely more sensitive to this woman's touch happening here and now, that if I were not floating by her magic, I presume I would be too weak to hold my own weight. My breathing is fast now, and though in the deep corners of my mind I am terrified my lungs are going to collapse on me, all I can truly focus on is her mimicking the pace of my rapid and rigid exhalations below. I throw my head back and an audible groan erupts at my body's response to her touch. Before I know it, she begins to glide her hand up beyond my belt with ease, and deep into my trousers...

But before she lays her hand on my actual skin, I freeze at a sound that doesn't quite fit this scene, being pulled out of my lustful trance. My head shoots up to see a shadow of a boat masquerading the light the siren has been producing for what feels like an eternity, and when she notices my distraction, she tries to win my attention back with a touch just above my erect cock – but it only startles me. I grab and attempt to yank her wrist out of my pants, but her nails tear through my skin, and I am then possessed to force her hand out aggressively. Howling in a complete and utter seething pain, my teeth grit, and I am filled with an intense fury and an urge to assert a dominance I didn't know I had. Commanding her eyes with mine and expelling a menacingly sharp, hypnotic green glare, my insides boil with a power I've never confronted. My skin rolls with radical tension, and I don't even have to tell her with words to let go – my newfound domineering mind does it for me.

Straightaway, as if I've cast my own spell, the realm around us explodes in a blinding, glorious, electric green light and deafening bells, coming from nowhere and everywhere all at once, begin to chime. Struck by disbelief, I halt my body's movements, my head and eyes darting in every direction as I watch as the commotion sends the siren cowering from me like a reprimanded dog, screeching something that echos thunderously in my head as she scurries away in fear; thus sending everything to obsidian:

CHAPTER four

Benjamin Peter Green *I'm sorry...*

Back Above Water

"Yo, Ben, stay with us, man!"

As muffled noise breaks through my ear drums, my eyes shoot open to find myself dazed on the dock in a cold sweat, unable to feel my fingertips and toes, and surrounded by harbor security and my mates. Involuntarily, my entire body turns to one side and empties all the water and contents out of my stomach...I think I heave up my fucking lungs as well in the process.

I wish.

Everyone gives me space as I collect my bearings and dare to attempt to catch my breath. I lay on the soggy wood-paneled ground for a bit, trying to think of rainbows and butterflies in an attempt to not burst into sobs as my thigh and lower half of my stomach writhe in pain, as I faintly hear a few blokes giving rough testimonies of the events to some of the head chiefs who came to our rescue. I hear the scattered words:

well, I think...
> *...told him not to!*

> > *drunk...*
> > *...maybe*

...call
> *...jumped in!*   *...to charge the motor*

...green explosion!

...mother, Elizabeth Green

..blood...

Mum –
Fuck, what time is it?

At the mention of her name, my body practically flies up from my fetal position, yet instantly turns into noodles. At the same time, my head does cartwheels, my new wound throbs, and I unwillingly collapse into a bobby's arms.

"Whoa there, bugs bunny!" I recognize the brawly voice ringing in my ears as Officer Kelly's, who's always lurking around the docks ensuring none of us causes any ruckus. We always do, however we usually don't get caught...but tonight, he got lucky. Kelly puts a blanket over my bare back and hands me my dry t-shirt I had taken off before I took a swim. "Take it easy; lose those sea legs. You're sliced up pretty bad."

Thankfully, the dumbshit officers don't realize *how* bad, as I still have my black trousers on *(a lucky duck, I am),* and that's where the real slices are...so maybe I still can get out of this trap somehow.

I feel like complete shit and all I want to do is fall back onto the wet ground, only to then magically reappear back in my warm bed with my mum safely baking cake in the kitchen, and me being granted the birthday wish of redoing this entire day over again as if it were all just a horrible nightmare. I search for an escape route, and my eyes land on my bike a few yards ahead of me. With my vision nauseatingly warped, I do everything possible to center my focus on it.

Bike.

Straight ahead.

My way out.

Straight ahead.

Move, noodle fucking legs, move!

If I can get my limbs to get their act together and make it over there, I can make it back home in the nick of time. Kelly holds me up by the shoulders as I continue to come to, and another bobby is challenging my twisted vision *(and my patience)* by moving a hairy finger side to side, demanding I follow it with my eyes and not my head. He then shines a flashlight in them like he's wanted to do it his whole life, and finally, I pull myself from the burly man's handle on me and demand to know the time. The gentlemen look at me as if I'm asking what year I've landed in, but the flashlight man tells me,

"Quarter to nine, son. You were out like a light. It was lucky we found you when we did, because –"

"Lads, I need to get back!" My voice is hoarse, I'm trembling due to the cold coming from everywhere, and I'm having a gutwrenching panic attack, but I can't tell if it's more so due to the fact that I *potentially* almost just got mystically palm fucked by a mermaid and have no idea what's real or fake currently, or that my mother is less than twenty minutes away from a broken promise that could potentially lead to lethal alone time with Colin.

Definitely a bit of both.

I repeat with more edge, "I need to get out of here right fucking *now.*"

"Oh, no you don't." Officer Kelly loves his job way too damn much, especially when he catches 'hooligans', as he calls us…*but I don't have time for his cockshit.* "We still gotsta ask you some questions, not to mention you and all your little hooligan pals here ain't nowhere *near* twenty-one. Soon as we get the story straight, we'll be handling that business as well. Plus," he points at my torso, "that nasty gash needs medical attention. You'll be here a while, kid. So just relax."

I do the exact opposite and more panic floods my body like the water did while I was drowning.

Chest...drowning...
I gots an idea –

I pretend to begin putting on my shirt, and as I stretch up and out of Kelly's arms again, I begin fake coughing so hard that the officer is forced to step to the side so I can barrel over to drop my hand to my knee for support, my other one gripping my chest. At this point I would've bolted, though now I'm only half faking, because amidst my method *Oscar Award-winning* performance, I genuinely begin to lose control of my breath, wheezing as I realize I am in desperate need of my inhaler, which is in my jacket...

Which someone conveniently hung over my bike.
Ah, I love when things work out like I'm in one of Charlie's musicals.

As bobby man Kelly stares at me dumbly, I try to mime what I am in desperate need of, but instead, my mate Matt[22] gets through to him with the words I can't release. Full of adrenaline, I dash off to my jacket and fumble in the deep pocket for the canister. The moment I find it, I shove the nozzle into my mouth and suck in sweet, sweet, salbutamol, relief flooding my lungs rapidly as I place one hand on my knee and the other on my bike's seat for support. As I catch my breath for what feels like the thousandth time, the coppies pitifully allow me my space –

---

[22] *My brother-in-law's name*

Suckers.

Without hesitation, I limply throw my leg over my bike and pedal like my life depends on it – or, rather, like my mother's life depends on it because it might. Half of my drunk mates cheer at my triumph while the others shout in protest and confusion; meanwhile, the officers blow their whistles and scream curses at me, their fat asses attempting to reach my speed, all to the pot. I feel as though not only am I pumping my legs at the speed of light to get to my mum, but I am also escaping away from tonight…from my friends, from the bobbies, from the docks, from the cheap whiskey, from *Molly 2.0,* and from every single fucked up thing that happened in that Bermuda triangle-homicidal-harbor-nightmare that felt far too real to be a dream.

I pray to anyone listening that it was a dream.
If I had one true birthday wish, that's all I would ask for.

I cannot stress this enough,
Happy fucking birthday to me.

🐚🐚🐚

As I approach the run-down building I live in, due to my break-neck speed, the wheels on my bike create skid marks on the sidewalk as I screech to a stop right before I strategically hop off mid-pedal and heave it into the rack, not even bothering to chain it up. Instead, I scram up the front stairs and in through the rod iron door, knowing full well upon entering the premises it would be far better for *my* well-being if I settle for the elevator, but at this point, what have I got to lose? Especially after that potentially gold medal-worthy

Olympic cycling ride here…My lungs and my oozing wounds
can't despise me any more than they do right now.
Plus, time is of the essence.
*Thankfully, my blood is pumping with so much cortisol that I
can't feel much.*
Though later…I can't imagine I'll be able to say the same.

When I reach the door of our quaint apartment, it is
already ajar, thus my mind floods with the worst possible
scenarios, such as:

What if she's already dead?
What if you're too late?
What if you're stuck with him forever?
What if he's waiting? Run away now!

What if…
    What if…
        What if…

I throw the door open, the force metaphorically
slamming the thoughts out of my mind, and see nothing but
haze. It looks like my brain, personified.
 "Ma?" I call out through the thick smoke. "The fuck
is going on?" The polluted air fills my lungs to the brim, and
at this point, I wouldn't be surprised if the two organs just
decided to move out.
 "Darling, keep that door open, would you? Your
father's dinner was a bit of a cock up and it's looking like your
bedroom in here."

Welp, I guess it's not a secret I smoke after all.
I'm choosing to bypass the statement.

"So he's not home?" My heart rate begins to normalize as my brain starts to remind me that maybe I'm just paranoid about Colin now…

"No, lovie," Mum says, and I finally find her through the fog. "But he will be soon, though…Unfortunately to a direly burnt chicken, which isn't going to be peachy, is it?"

Nope. Not paranoid. Even my mum is worried.

"I'm right here." I put my hand on her shoulder and I can see the anxiety rise in her like a thermometer about to burst. In a normal household, what would be a *no-biggy-burnt-dinner-easily-fixed-sitch,* in this family is a matter of life and…*well, I don't like to think about it.* Instead, I just vow to prevent whatever would come next. "Do you want me to run down to the deli to pick up some grub? I'm sure Buddy won't mind, that fatass always has hidden scraps from the day in the back."

"Benjamin Green, behave!" Mother swats me with her dish towel, though can't help but laugh. As I chuckle with her, my lungs scream bloody murder at me and I truly believe I am gonna cough up blood this time. She performs the classic motherly back rub on me as I'm hunched over trying not to puke again, and says gently as if she isn't bothered one bit by anything in the world, "Thank you, darling, but I can handle your father. You go wash up; get some warmth back in your little lungs. They don't seem very keen on you this week." She then proceeds to give me that *'mom look'* up and down as if she really just looked at me for the first time since I walked in. "Took a little dip in the harbor, did we?"

Something like that.

I muster a smirk and head off to the loo. It's not until now, when the adrenaline from the night starts to wind down, that I begin to truly feel a stinging, burning sensation across my lower thigh and up my waist.

"Bloody hell…" I mutter to myself.

As if my body senses the secluded safety of my bathroom, all at once I am reduced to a subtle yet quick limp to the mirror, and through it I see beads of sweat starting to form on my forehead. I've decided that this frequent sensation of simultaneously freezing my ass off and being anxiously hot is not a feeling I fancy, so this time I'm gonna cut it short. I turn the nozzle to the shower, and as it heats up, the steam begins to calm my nerves and defrost my body a bit. I find myself back at my reflection, wincing as I peel off my shirt that I didn't realize was partially sticking to me, and I half pretend I don't see the start of a slash that starts up my adrenaline like a ticking time bomb again.

No…I wanted it to be a dream…

I want nothing more than to never take off my trousers to see the rest of the damage done to my leg, but they are both still frozen and I need a hot shower more than anything before they fall off.

Taking a slow deep breath, I slide my pants down to the upper half of my thighs, and I stop dead.

No…
No fucking way…
C'mon, It was a dream.
*It **had** to have been a dream.*

Falling against the wall behind me, my breathing staggers the more I eye the wound that I prayed was a figment of my overactive imagination, but was undeniably created by dagger-like claws. I look from my flesh to my reflection so much that it nearly gives me whiplash, and as I gape at the

crusted blood around each lesion and some fresh residue
currently soaking the inside of my clothes on the floor, I want
to pass out again.

It was probably just a rock!

No fucking way a rock makes these kinda marks.

Maybe it was the boat…
Or one of your mates on accident.

No, these are from the nails I saw.
Nails that could have easily ripped my skin apart.
Unforgettable, inhuman nails.
Nails that I was touched by…so softly, then so violently.

And Pan? Was that me she called Pan?

Don't be silly, that was all just a dream…

…

…

Right?

I almost want to cry, but I'm not exactly sure what
for. I'm nearly hyperventilating now at all of the images
forcing their way back into my head – the siren, her sensual
beauty, her touch, the unfamiliar feelings she created in me –
now I really feel like throwing up again. I close my eyes and
turn around to face away from the horrific sight in the mirror,
my forehead and hands propping me up against the wall. I
begin to try and control my unsteady breaths, but my wounds
are throbbing now in the steamy air, and I feel nauseous and
more anxious every time I feel them pulse with pain. I strip the
rest of my clothing off gingerly as if I'll shatter to pieces if

I'm too careless, and begin to slowly slide my hand along the wall, guiding my unstable body into the shower. Even though the scorching water sends seething, raging pain throughout the lower half of my left side, I stand there motionless, allowing it to drench my hair and face and wash away the day the best it can.

My father, in another life, told me real men don't cry. Not for anything, ever. He explained crying makes a man look weak; vulnerable – easily taken advantage of. He said wearing my heart on my sleeve was feminine, and for a properly generous time, I believed him. It was one of the few things we could both agree on, and most days, I admit, still do. So with that in mind, I let the shower storm upon my face and do the waterworks for me, as I do everything in my power to not let my emotions get the best of me. As I finish scrubbing the last five hours off of myself, I hear a panic-inducing noise come from the kitchen –

Shattering glass.
God, please no.
Is anxiety just going to be my new normal?

I turn the shower nozzle off and remain unmoving, my hand still on the mirrored chrome. I listen and hear my mum and Colin's muffled voices, but still can't tell if the noise was an accident, or –

"For God's sake, Colin, I apologize!"

My brain doesn't even process fully as I nearly destroy the shower curtain and wrap a towel around my waist, still sopping wet as I go to open the door.

Then it does.

Well...I can't win this battle naked, can I?
I would've dared to try.

With ease yet haste, I barely dry off and pull on the boxers and sweats my mum must've left on the sink for me sneakily whilst I was bathing. I can't help but curiously yet rapidly glance in the mirror, hoping my shower magically caused my wounds to disappear...

But nope.
Still there, dammit.

I find gauze in my medicine cabinet I once used for sports injuries and whatnot, and doctor myself up the best I can in split seconds before slipping into the remaining t-shirt. With clothes on and without the crusty blood and gunk seeping through, I can at least pretend the gashes don't exist.

Placing the disappointment on the back burner, I pull open the door and tip-toe around the corner, peering into the kitchen to see my mother sitting alone at the table, her head between her hands.

I rush to meet her and kneel, putting my hands on her shoulders, "Mum, what's going on? Are you hurt?"

"Jesus Christ, Benjamin!" She shoots up from her seat, her hands nearly touching my waist but pulling back. "What the bloody hell happened to you?"

I look down and see my gauze attempt didn't last merely a few seconds, as blood is staining through the fabric of my shirt again. I attempt to play it off, "Wow, mum, you turned sailor within the twenty minutes I was in the shower."

She doesn't appreciate my joke. "I'm not chuffing, Ben, what –"

Just then, the devil himself emerges from his bedroom down the hall, gawking at me with glossed-over eyes. He licks his lips, which happen to be the same color as mine.

It pains me how much we look alike.

"Hello, son," his empty voice gives me chills, and he smiles because I'm sure he could see them appear on my arms. "Happy birthday…right?"

"Yeah," I answer with disdain.

"You want a drink or what?"

"No, cheers…I'm alright," I speak facetiously. "Still a few years short, I'm afraid."

"Since when has that ever bloody stopped yeh?"

"Colin –" My mum instantly chimes in, but gets cut off by him.

"I'm serious, Beth." And so, he begins. Never with a warning, always as if it's a side hustle and he's getting paid the big bucks to chew one of us out. "Smoking, slamming down drinks, probably having idle sex with every bit and, let's just be forthright, any bloke he can; and what's next? Gonna be a little druggie on the corner with your chums? Look at your stomach, boy." He gestures to my open wound then. "I can only imagine what kinds of shit you're getting yourself into. Figures as much."

"Colin Green, that's quite –"

"No, mum," I hush her with a sharp raise of my hand as I walk toward my sorry excuse for a father, my tone turning matter of fact, "he's not wrong. Howbeit, he gives me a bit too much credit. I'm no sleazy casanova like he was at my age, I'm sure as hell not gay, and drugs have never touched my tongue – though I can't say it all hasn't crossed my mind a time or dozen…but we know he's right, nonetheless." I throw out my arms like there's a crowd of people in the room, "We *all* know just how much of a total bloody screw-up I am! But

Christ, don't we also savvy that I don't inherit the gene from my mum, oh no, *no."*

Mumma's voice squeals desperately for me to stop, *"Benjamin! –"*

But my face finds itself inches away from Colin's and I hiss,

"I'm

      just   *you done fucked up, bud.*

        like

          you."

At my last word, I get a fist to the stomach from my father's brass-like knuckles, and as I hunch from the impact, a violent slap to the jaw follows. Through the ringing in my ears, I hear my mom's muffled screams at him from behind me, and I take a second to debate whether or not it's worth it to fight back. Likely without thinking long enough, I allow my fist to swing and hit him square in the cheek, then extend my leg to kick him in the hip. A sloppy attempt, it surely was, as the bastard doesn't fall, but instead takes me by the neck and pins me against the exposed brick wall – *fuck them New York interior designers* –; his whiskey-heavy breath wafting straight into my face as he mutters,

"Look, boy," his eyes are a frozen crystal and his tone is in a whisper, yet as sharp as the nails that fed on my flesh just hours ago, "I don't have the foggiest who the devil you think you are, but you'd be a goddamn wank to ever speak to me in such a way again." His voice then climbs up to a sergeant's shouting level as he squeezes the jugulars of my throat, *"Do you fucking understand me?"*

Although feeling the begging of the nerves in my head and eyes to do so, I don't flinch. Rather, I stand straight as an arrow, my breathing cut off, eyes locked on his. I groan between gritted teeth, *"Fuck you."*

Colin sends a knee into my gut, searing pain coursing through my fresh wound as he throws me onto the couch. I choke fiercely as my mother storms at him roaring curses and rebukes, and when I gain the strength to bring my head up, I witness him smacking her alongside the cheek. Mum whimpers in pain as the tender spot turns a rosie pink, and she prudently tries to punch him back, though leaves nothing but a tingle in her vulnerable state. Colin grabs her by the hair and drags her mercilessly over to the stove – still hot from her slaving over it to cook his supper – and dangles her face over it.

"See here, woman," his voice sounds demonic, and his actions are proving the constant satan simile isn't far off. "If you don't behave, you're going to have a brand spanking new beauty mark right across that flawless face of yours. Is that what you want?"

Mum's voice quivers, "Colin, don't do this, please –"

"Oh, Beth darling, begging is *so –* "

Before the bastard can finish, I kick the back of his knees, dead-legging him and grabbing my mother by the shoulders in one swift motion. I hurry her over into my bedroom around the corner, slamming the door before she can get a word in. As I hastily turn, I'm all too promptly greeted by my father's head into mine, being then shoved violently across the floor as my vision blurs and ears ring again. He rushes at me, digging his disgusting animalistic claws through my already open laceration, causing me to yelp in agony.

"You little fucking arse!" Colin spits at me as my blood oozes out, staining the carpet. "Quit playing games, get up and be a man."

"I would rather die," I hiss venomously, "than ever be a man if it means to be half the sadist you are."

"Fair enough," he slurs as he slides an old pocket blade out from his trousers, stomping his leather boot onto my chest so I am paralyzed to heed his authority. "Let's honor that statement, shall we? After all, you may end up *just like me* if I don't save you the trouble, *son.*" My mouth grows sour at the words, and my eyes gape at him in astonishment as he presses the quick-release mechanism, unleashing the sharp, rusted-with-red blade. He holds the tip up to my throat, "Any other smartass *fucking* comments you'd like to throw at me, boy?"

At this moment, I feel like I'm already dead. Colin theatrically swings his arm in the air and raises his knife, aiming it directly at my throat, and I accept my fate as his sole crushes my lungs to near oblivion. Though just when I think it's all over, his head is bashed with a vase full of mum's daffodils, causing him to tumble over me as we both get soaked with week-old water. Mother stands over me with her hand outstretched,

"Fucking run like hell, Ben."

Without wasting any time, I grab her hand and yank her along with me, practically pulling her arm out of its socket as we storm across the flat. I open the fire escape window and help her outside onto the wrought iron platform, and once she is safely planted, I begin to climb out after her. Alas, my split gash and heaving chest cause me to move in half time, therefore due to this lag, in no time I am attacked by hands grasping my waist and nails digging into my skin – *an all too recent and traumatically familiar sensation.*

"Get facking back here, you pussy ass son of a bitch. I'm not finished with her."

"Oh like hell you aren't, you pillock." Like an unfriendly game of tug-of-war, I heave my body forward using the window pane as an aid, then let the momentum of his pulling yank me in, allowing me to forcefully jab an elbow into his nose. He throws his head back, blood trickling down his lips from the impact. "Lay one more hand on her," my words are hoarse, yet cogent and promising, "and I swear to the stars I'll kill you."[23]

He snarls and laughs ferociously, mocking my words as if I wouldn't have the balls. With one hand grabbing me by the neck and the other solidly on my chest, he hurls me toward the granite kitchen countertop, leading my hip to jam into the corner, and me to clutch the quick-forming bruise and fall to my knees like a fucking pussy. Rage overflows every fiber in my being as the serpent slithers swiftly out the window to my mother, who graciously yet idiotically waited for her son. I have no choice but to race after him through my agonizing pain, now pulsating from nearly every area of my body.

Despite her trying to run and flailing about within his solid, inescapable grasp, he holds her by the neck, cutting off her airflow – decidedly his favorite ruse of choice. I am inches away from him again on the wind-swept balcony, baffled as I see my beloved mother's face already turning a ghastly shade of blue.

I surrender to desperation, "Father, *stop!* You'll *kill her!*"

He scoffs at my plea. "Oh, her most *cherished* Benjamin. So loyal and sensitive to his *precious* mumma. Puny mum's boy." He growls these next words, sending wrath through my knackered body, *"When are you gonna grow the hell up?"*

I can't feel my body anymore. My spirit has left, and I am but a soul floating above my tattered skin. Outpourings of a broken roller coaster of emotions and an ever-present will to murder this monster are the only things that reside among me. I screech beyond the wind through any voice I have left,

"At least my mum is *here!* You're a sorry excuse for a father – a waste of oxygen, and a disgrace to the Green

---

[23] *'Touch her and I'll kill you' vibes. One of my favorite lines of the whole book.*

name!" I step closer with a resentful outrage surging through my blood like a drug I'll never withdraw from. "You're never here. And when you are, you still *aren't.* You're a bogging drunk, an undisguised devil, and a fucking coward-psychotic-bloody-*bastard!*" I inhale crisp night air and bark up more phlegm, not even attempting to find my breath again before I continue. I can feel my green eyes electrify the same way they did in the water of the harbor, *"Let her go,"* I say with intensity and finally with clarity as if my lungs know what's on the line and are on my side for once. I proceed, "If you're gonna hurt anyone, hurt me. Destroy *me. Ruin me completely.* Kill *me* and spare her. *I fucking dare you, Colin Benjamin Green."*

I curse and spit at the name that I am forced to carry as my own, and snarl as I pull his arm around to face me. He releases the grip on my mum's throat causing her to crumble to her knees, choking and gasping for any and all oxygen.

The man laughs a hearty, throaty seaman's laugh at me and slurs condescendingly, "Oh, Ben, my foolish son – don't you see? It seems I already have."

With that, he kicks my mother down the iron staircase and her cries rattle the metal as she tumbles with no mercy. I practically disappear into thin air and reappear at the speed of light just as her petite body's momentum has her taking a spill over the ledge. My adrenaline once again assists me in doing the impossible, by firmly snatching her wrist before she plummets nine stories down to the lethal pavement below.

The lurch of her abrupt halt in mid-air yanks my shoulder out of its socket and I nearly topple over with her as she swings back and forth. Although the pain is gnawing and cramping, I completely ignore it as I know it is replaceable – *my mother is not.* My strength can normally easily carry her featherlike weight, but as we are both panicking, our hands begin to dampen, and the traction becomes little to none. I try everything in me to compose myself and recollect my thoughts, as I have a life – *my mumma's life* – literally in the palm of my hands.

I've always needed her…
But now, she needs me more than ever.

I reach down and heave up with my good arm, feeling my side wounds tear even more with the straining. I'm struggling hopelessly, yet managing to disregard the worst pain I've ever felt in my life to ensure this *is*, and will always be, the *worst possible* to ever be present –; to make it stop here in this moment and not suddenly become the nightmare that could befall me if I don't endure the agony and pull my mother to safety.

I haul her arm like an anchor rope, the two of us now screaming in torment, and after what seems like ages, she yells with promptness and anxious defeat, "Ben, you must let go!"

"Are you fucking mad?" I yell through the chaos and gusty wind. "I've got you, now *please* climb!"

"Benjamin, I can't!" Mum begins to sob and my heart wrenches as I am hanging on to her delicate, soaked hands with everything I have. She stammers, "I – I am slipping – I'm – neither of us have any strength left, love." She somehow smiles up at me, her eyes glistening, and it feels like a stab in the heart. "It's okay, Ben, it'll be alright! You'll be –"

"No, mumma!" Now I'm the one sobbing. "I can't lose you – *please!"*

"You shall not ever lose me. *I love you, Benjie. To the sun, the moon –"*

I shake my head and attempt one last vigorous pull, when behind me comes an ungodly yank of my hair, followed by an immediate barricade of two arms around my chest that pull me back to keep my eyes from witnessing the devastating scene. I yelp in shock and pain, but as I draw back, it strikes me like a bullet to the heart –

I
let
go…

My eyes expand as my mouth releases a cry for my mum so thunderous, I swear the world shakes. I break down then – *completely*. I don't give a fuck about crying, screaming, wailing, vulnerability, or being a man. Pure devastation clouds over me and I become it in its entirety. I collapse inside and out with absolute misery and intensity, that I feel as if I were the one who fell from the ninth floor and collided with the pavement, and in this very moment, I want nothing more than to be the one who did.

I fucking let go.
Sending my mother…
My mumma…
My whole world…
Plummeting to her death.

Another shove sends me forward now, "You sorry excuse for a son! *You've killed my wife!*" On my knees, I'm spun around to greet a brutal punch that sends me nearly tumbling down the flight of stairs beside me.

God, how I wish I would have.

I tremble and mutter through tsunami-like tears and gnashing teeth while pointing an accusing, seething finger, *"You –* you bloody motherfucking *maggot!"* I stand, hardly able to look this heartless creature in the face as I begin screeching into the night, *"You – you caused* me to let go! That's my *mother – I was trying to save her –* and *you caused me to let go!"*

"Oh, for Christ's sake, she was already long gone, you weak ass boy! I was doing her a favor cutting her agony off short!"

"Doing *her* a favor?" I am going berserk and it feels like I could murder this vile man right here, right now. The nerve – the *unbelievable* iniquity. "You *watched –* you didn't fucking *help* me *or* her in the slightest – *you…you* killed my mother! *I fucking hate you!"*

"You killed your own fucking mother, boy!" He heartlessly spits. "The blood is on your hands; you're the one who let go, ain't cha? So you're going to have to live with that bloody fact forever!"

I impulsively drive my foot with all of my vexation and outrage directly into his dick, and as he hunches over pronto, he grasps it, nearly vomiting from the impact. I then decide to not waste my breath on him any longer, but instead race down the fire escape stairs, skipping steps and half-jumping flights until I reach ground level. With reality as I know it already entirely numb, I risk taking in the image before me that I know full well will haunt me with trauma I will have to bear forevermore.

all hail character development… </3

CHAPTER five

Benjamin Peter Green
New Jersey, Present Day

After a few days of forced brutal detoxing, I still feel like the bottom of a homeless man's foot. I wasn't planning on having to go through that plot twisty shitshow…*and unfortunately I mean 'shitshow' metaphorically **and** literally*… in the first place, *because I was supposed to die instead*…So I guess this is my punishment for fucking up *that* happily never after.

Ah…that was morbid.
Apologies, depression is not only a side effect of the withdrawals, but also a side effect of…well, Benjamin…and Benjamin still being alive.
…Lol. Clearly I need some help.
At least I'm self aware.

Despite all that, I have been cleared to enter Brand New Life Wellness Home[24] *(yippee…)*, thus after minor preparation and mindless packing of the little to no shit I own, the subway ride to Hasbrouck Heights only took about half an hour. In that time, I got a bit more writing done in my journal trying to regain strength back into my bruised wrist, had the luxury of mulling over my pitiful life choices some more, and then had a cracking epiphany just how much I properly loathe my life – an efficient and productive commute, if I do say so myself. Now, I am off on a cheeky new adventure in New *facking* Jersey, opening up this storybook to page one with me

---

[24] *The church my parents own is called Brand New Life Christian Center, and we change lives of many with addictions, issues, etc. I felt it deserved a shoutout.*

lighting a fresh smoke in my stylishly braced hand as I take in
the exterior of B.N.L.W.H *(bloody long acronym, innit?)* from
the freshly cut front lawn – a favorite smell of mine, so at least
I have that going for me.[25]

Let me paint a vivid image for you, shall I? *Ahem:*
It's a pleasantly grand Cape Cod-style home planted smack
dab in the middle of a quaint and quiet suburb. Secluded by
trees stripped of their beauty from the winter solstice is this
handsome, white staggered shingle siding, two-story house
with a premium brown slate tile roof. There are two grand bay
windows draped in white lace curtains on each side of the dark
brown, wooden front door, three bedroom casement windows
upstairs with black shutter blinds, and a front stoop leading to
a long white picketed porch. It's a lot to take in, as it looks as
if it would be a properly generous size for an average family,
especially coming from a kid who lived in small flats his
whole life that barely had any room to exhale in peace.

I want nothing more than to stand here and look at it
forever so I don't have to go in, but alas, I'm chivalrously
greeted by a roundish Italian man who I recognize from the
article from the website Nurse Clarke was showing me in the
hospital yesterday; his in a pinstripe sport coat making him
look like he snorted a solid amount of cocaine back in his day.

"Can I help you?" His voice is raspy like he smokes
about as much as I do, or maybe he just likes to pretend he's in
the mafia to complete the *Godfather* ensemble.[26]

Who's to say?

---

[25] *It is, indeed.*

[26] *This man is based on my dad. Entirely. From the pinstripe sport coat, to the Godfather vibe, to his name. Hi, dad.*

I nod up at him, exhaling my smoke and quickly puffing out a small cough, but cutting it off as quick as it came. "Cheers, I'm Ben. You Chuck?"

"Ah, yes, Benjamin the Brit!" *Brilliant, I've already got a pet name.* "We've been expecting you. C'mon in."

And thus, I have joined the cult.

He helps me with my small supply of things, and upon entering the foyer, I am greeted by shiny cherry wood floors, high ceilings with a grand chandelier, and a very modern interior design of white marble and wood. To my right is a small step leading into a room with two leather lazy boys, a couch to match, and a few random table chairs that seem to be intended for newbies who don't feel properly 'at home' yet. All of the seats look as if they'd be facing a television set, but instead, face one chair that resembles a king's at-home throne or some shit like it.

To my left, is a small dining room with a 'last supper' looking table, all preset with placemats, plates, silverware, and the lot. In the corner stands a fine china cabinet, plants hanging on the walls, and a large archway which I'm assuming leads to the kitchen. *Now, why from the start have I been giving you this imagery?* Because all this is to say: they've done a proper job making it feel like I'm walking into my own home.

Though the rug below me is quite eccentric with its paisley patterns of dark reds, greens, and browns, but I guess that's just me being critical.

"Well, this is it!" I can tell Chuck is quite proud. He points to the room with the lazy boys and begins a tour I didn't ask for, "There is where we have therapy circle chats. We meet once a day and talk through struggles, wins, thoughts, or whatever one may need to vent about for the moment. It's just a nice time to come together and center ourselves as one for a bit." I twiddle my rings and only muster a nod at this bullshit. He proceeds, pointing to the opposite room, "Then there is obviously the dining area, where everyone eats meals and snacks together – which reminds me, if you have something in particular you prefer or have any dietary restrictions, let one of the staff know – you'll meet them today as well." Chuck is talking awfully fast and so matter-of-factly, I'm almost certain he's given this speech four hundred times. "No one is allowed to leave the table for one-half hour after eating; even the bathrooms are locked during that time."

"Why?" *I'm just as surprised as he is that I asked a question.*

He readily answers, "We have a few individuals with disordered eating, and we don't intend to feed their habits while we attempt to, well, feed *them.*" He chuckles at his facetiousness. What an odd yet sensible way to put that – so I can't say I'm not amused as well. I am, however, taken aback by it all, *considering...*

"Wait, hold on, I thought this was a drug rehab."

"Well, actually, in a way it is. This house is for anyone who has a major addiction, so whether that be food, no food, sex, drugs, *rock and roll*[27] *–"* he half jokes, "you name it – it's all the same here. Whatever an individual's struggle may be, whatever their *'drug',* per se, they can overcome it with one another here."

"Grand." I look around, envisioning the odyssey I'm about to embark on. "A bunch of fucked up kids in one house. Should be riveting."

Fuck me and my poor excuse for a filter.

---

[27] *My dad was the #1 rock 'n roll entertainer in OC back in the day. I felt he'd appreciate the reference.*

Luckily, mafia man nods in agreement with a hearty laugh.

"And you're one of them!" He claps me on the back. "Welcome to the circus."

I'm shown the kitchen, and it keeps the theme of the rest of the place as it has everything a normal house would have from a sink to a toaster. A large marble island sits in the center of the room with stools surrounding it for casual snacking, which I'm assuming doesn't happen often since a bowl of clearly untouched fruit is placed in the middle of it. There's a small window above the sink that overlooks the serene, winter scenery in the backyard, which has a small octagon gazebo and a tree with a wooden swing across from it; and my eyebrows raise at the rarity of a pool that once resided but now has been entirely emptied.

Probably so we can't all synchronously drown ourselves.

This tour is causing boredom and pins and needles to surge through me; my lungs are tired from holding in my hacks, and I just don't give a damn about the rooms I'll inevitably discover on my own. The living room is quite similar to the therapy circle room only with a glass coffee table and a television; on which he mentioned they have movie nights every Tuesday…my brain immediately went to war:

Good God.

                                                                It'll be fine.

Imma off myself on a bloody Tuesday.

                                                                Fuck off, brain.

I'm then finally taken upstairs to the bedroom farthest down the hall. It has two twin beds, one in each corner, although I can instantly tell which bed is mine because whoever is living on the left side of this room has clearly made themselves at home. The worn-in comforter hangs off the mattress as if we're interrupting someone's wake-up time, charcoal sketches of different seasons and other random Picasso-looking pieces clutter the wall unevenly next to the bed, and a few pencils, silver rings, and other random shit lay on the dresser in front of the window. It's like a tornado hit one side of the room, yet didn't come close to touching mine.

"That damn kid," Chuck mutters under his breath. "I told him to clean up before you got here." He shakes his head, but then gives a grand gesture toward my new sleeping arrangements, "Alright, well, make yourself at home. The bathroom is on the right down the hall, and if you need anything at all, our house help will be just downstairs; though, I don't doubt Finneas has already sniffed you out and will take good care of you."

"Who's Finneas?"

On cue, a young bloke not much older than me with wet, jet-black hair and a towel wrapped around the waist lassie's dream about appears in the doorway with a cheeky grin on his face; his copper eyes beaming at the sight of me,

"Ayo, pally. That'd be me."[28]

---

[28] *FINNEAS! Finn is a fan favorite all around the world. He is the best friend I wish I had. I am eager to hear what you think.*

CHAPTER six

Benjamin Peter Green
Brand New Life Wellness Home, **Present**
Day

"Ah, right on cue!" Chuck claps Finneas on his bare back, but the dude doesn't even flinch. I can tell these two have known each other long enough to be buddy-buddy –

And I pray I'm not here that long.

"Finn will show you the ropes," Chuck tells me with a reassuring smile, his hand still on pretty boy's back. "He's a good guy, this one, don't let'm scare you with his gusto. I'll be back at dinner." He looks back to the junior Greek god, "Delfinnium[29], be sweet to the kid, capeesh?"

The black haired bloke's eyebrows furrow into a glare and his head cocks to the side in distress, his shoulders slumping, *"No,* Chuckie, no *never* the full godforsaken name, fuck me."* That *is* a wild name to live with, and I'm glad he said so I didn't have to. *I probably still will. Give it time.* "But comprendé, at ease, sir!" Delfinnium throws his arm up into a mock salute and is plainly nothing short of Brooklyn in the flesh. "I've been waiting for this day for a fuckin' year! This is my time to shine. Take care now, yeah?"

He gives Chuck a nod goodbye and two puckered air kisses, then immediately his intense attention turns to me.

I've never been so intimidated by a lad my age before.

---

[29] *Fun Fact: Originally, Finn's name was going to just be "Finneas", but one day during the writing process, I met a baby on the airplane named Delfinnium, and I was like absofuckinglutely.*

I Prefer Peter

His presence is just very…loud.
Maybe it's the fact that he's half-naked, or the fact that I don't
think this kid has two fucks in the jar about anything.

"So," he walks past me toward his side of the dresser
and pulls out some briefs and sweats, "before your head gets
in a toss-up, my so treacherously given name *is* Delfinnium,
but that ain't flyin'. Most everyone calls me Finneas, mkay?
Mkay. Now! Word on the street is you're my new roomie.
Whattya in for?"

For no good reason, I revert to silence and wandering
eyes as a defense mechanism. I've always had minor social
anxiety, but initially forgot because…*well, drugs*… But in this
present-day shitland where I'm sobering up and have just met
Jack *fucking* Kelly[30] over here, and with no coping tricks up
my sleeve to handle this kind of personality, I'm in a bit of a
kerfuffle – thus, I'm just as frozen as the ice queen of
Arendelle.

"Hello?" He continues as if he's trying to catch a
signal while slipping on his clothes. "C'mon, whattya got?
What's your damage?"

My eyes wander at anything and everything…

Silence…
Wall…
Silence…
String on the carpet…

Fuck me.

"Are ya mute, man?" Delfinnium's got a Brooklyn
attitude, no denying that. "God, been waiting a fackin' year for

---

[30] *Fun Fact: I love Newsies.*

a roommate and they give me a geedamn mute? J. Christ. Send 'em back."

At this, I gain enough vigor to shoot him a glare. I don't want to be here, nor do I need to take shit from a kid who thinks he's the bloody king of Jersey, or this house, for that matter. I scoff at his remark and shake my head, going over to my suitcase to mindlessly unpack. He softens up a bit then,

"Sorry, man…look," Finneas voice lowers nearly three notches now, which is better, but not saying much, "I'm deadass just trying to help. Everyone can use a friend here, ya know?" *Fuck that*…but I let him continue his speech anyway. "See, you don't wanna be here, I don't wanna be here, none of us do. We'll all say we do, 'cause that's what them wardens expect or want us to say, but it's all shite. We're just trying to get by and get out so we can live our lives. We're all on the same side here, aight?" When I don't acknowledge him, he walks over, twists me, and puts his hands on my shoulders… *He's quite the bold one, Mr. Brooklyn.* "I don't know who the hell you are or what your deal is," *and I don't know why you give such a damn,* "but you're with me so I got your back, yeah? However, I cannot be cooped up with a mime. Now c'mon, kid, at least tell me your name."

Finneas' eyes are searching mine and pleading with me now. Maybe this confident seeming son of a bitch really does need a friend. Sometimes the ones who seem the most sure of themselves are the ones who need someone the most.

He begins to shake his head and walk across the room, when finally I remember how to speak, "Uh, Ben." I clear my throat. "I'm Benjamin. Benjamin Green."

"Holy shit, you're a Brit!" This triggered the volume button again. Delfinnium gallops over to me, throwing his arms around my shoulders, skin still damp from his recent shower. "And you *speak*, good God! *Thank God!"* He lets go and takes a step back, his persona changing like someone hit a reset button. "Benjamin, your Highness, happy to make your acquaintance." He bows with one arm crossing his torso, and the other behind his back. "I'm Finneas Scott. Room*mate –"* he chuckles at his witty pun, "that's ironic, ah? And B.N.L extraordinaire. I take the throne of being in the cellar the longest, so I know all the ins and outs, do's and do fuckin' not's. Stick with me, brother, you'll be right as rain." I tighten my lips and muster a nod with a left eyebrow raised in understanding, as I don't think I've spoken a sentence that long, or with that many inflections in my entire life. I am, however, glad to hear the acronym for this place is shorter than I previously guessed. "But seriously, Green," he turns back and walks toward his closet to grab a crimson red *NEW YORK* hoodie, "what's your story?"

Before I can even think about answering, what sounds like a front desk bell is dinged three times from downstairs. I instinctively think aloud,

"The bloody hell does that mean?"

This makes a giddy giggle rise out of Finneas. *It's obvious he's not around British people often.* He runs a comb through his wet hair as he looks back and forth at himself and me through the mirror's reflection, "That, my newest friend, is the ninth circle of hell summoning."[31] I raise my eyebrow again, though this time cocking my head in question. He turns to elaborate further, "It's otherwise known as the daily dub – therapy circle time. It's when we go to that front window room and talk about our feelings and shit."

I shake my head and shoot him a hand gun, "Smashing. I'll pass. Have fun."

"Yeah, nah, you gotta go."

"Nah, yeah, it's not my thing."

---

[31] *An allude to the iconic classic, Dante's Inferno*

"Oh, don't kid yourself, sweetheart, it ain't anyone's *thing*. You don't have to talk, but you'll have to show that pretty face of yours if you wanna get points."

"Points, what points?" I can't restrain the exasperation in my tone, as this place is already causing my stomach to ache and it hasn't even been a full hour.

"When you rack up a certain amount of 'recovery rewards', 'privilege points', 'gold stars', or whatever the hell you wanna call them, you get special privileges. Observe…" he walks over to the dresser and holds up his phone, shaking it for emphasis, "Not only this, but you can also potentially go out for an evening, sometimes get a longer curfew if you charm them into trusting your ass, have an extra special meal, get to pick the movie on a Tuesday night – it ain't too crusty of a deal. The more you get, the bigger the privilege."

"That's dodgy as hell."

"Yeah, word to. It seems shady at first, but the *metaphor* within it, Greenie, is to show you that when you choose to make the decisions toward sobriety, whether that be to help yourself move forward or maybe help out someone else here who's struggling, little by little life rewards you – says *'thank you'*, so to speak, for doing what you can to stay alive and healthy, rather than the opposite; like we've all gotten in the habit of doin'. Which undeniably and oh, so serendipitously, led us here. It's all for the reminder that life is kinder to *you* when you choose to be kind to *it.*"

I caught maybe half of that. "Sure."

"But cha gotta be sincere," he points at my face. "Otherwise, you ain't gettin' nowhere, ya hear me? Why do ya think I've been here so damn long? I didn't figure it out for a long time, pal. Hell, I'm still figuring it out. But at least I'm far enough along to know I ain't packin' up my shit until I get my shit *together,* ya feel me?"

"Sure."

"Not a question guy, I see…Spectacular. You're easy, I like you. Now let's hop to it."

❦ ❦ ❦

Finn and I are the last to arrive downstairs, and I'm relieved to see only four others around my age occupying seats. I'm also quite pleased to see all of the 'coveted' spots are taken because I was already planning on claiming one of the *'I'm new and uncomfortable'* extra kitchen chairs. My new BFF Finneas (BFF*F*), and his motormouth pop a squat on the couch with two guys who look to be in their early twenties, and to my left are two birds *(that means girl, for those of you who don't speak British)* sitting snugly in the lazy boy chairs chatting amongst themselves, both imaginably my age or so. Last to join us is a woman perhaps in her early thirties, though dresses like she's in denial about that, carrying a clipboard and a thermos still likely halfway full with this morning's coffee. She casually joins Finneas' conversation, putting in her two senses and what-nots as if she was involved the whole time, before taking a seat on the throne-looking leather chair to show she's the one in charge now.

"…alright, we'll agree to disagree for now." This is all I catch as she leaves Finneas chuckling and shaking his head in obvious denial of whatever her opinion was on the subject. She tracks on then, speaking to all of us but doing a decent job of keeping it informal, "Alright, let's chat, shall we? How're we doing?"

An awkward silence fills the air suddenly as no one, not even Finneas, wants to speak up first.

We all must be feeling like shit today.
At least I'm not alone there.

I'm still looking down, twiddling my rings, and playing with the velcro of my brace when *of course* the inevitable happens despite me giving hardcore *'don't fucking acknowledge me'* vibes.

"That's a new face." I immediately feel twelve eyes stabbing me mercilessly. Due to the spell that they pull me under, I reluctantly lead with my eyes first and glance up at the woman, tightening my lips as if I were a child caught cheating on a test. "Welcome to Brand New Life," she says in a cautious tone as if I'm a rescue puppy who might bite her if she's too overbearing. "I'm Kelsey, I run the group sessions and, well, mostly everything else too when Chuck is out. Feel free to share whatever you feel you need to in this daily time we have together, whether it be strengths, struggles, plans of reinvention, why you perilously hate life…" she titters, trying to get a friendly rise out of me, but I don't budge.

Sorry, lady. It's too true to be funny.

Kelsey resumes; not defeated, but challenged, "Why don't we all introduce ourselves so we can be well acquainted before we start, yeah?" She gestures for the dude to her right to begin, and he acts caught off guard by this as if he isn't listening even a smidge to what's going on. *I don't blame him, really.*

"Hi," his voice is much higher than I anticipated, and I almost chuckle. "I'm Kyle Henderson; you can call me Kai. I'm bulimic."

"No," Kelsey reprimands him like a gentle mother would. "Try again, from the top."

Kyle rolls his eyes and says to her indirectly *(because he's still looking at me like he wants to kill himself)*, "Sorry. I'm a *recovering* bulimic." He over-exaggerates a smile without showing his teeth, which I did happen to catch a small glimpse of before…and let's just say it made me not feel as bitter about mine being a crooked British cliché. "Welcome, newbie."

I give him a nod and a half-smirk before the room proceeds to awkwardly greet me.

"Well, fellas," Finneas' voice springs up next and is inherently operatic compared to Kyle's, "this *bloke* and I already had the pleasure of getting acquainted, 'cause I'm his new roomie!" He's way too proud of this statement, and I don't know how to feel about it. "In case you forgot though," his attention turns back to me, "I'm *Finneas* Scott; feel free to call me Finn. I'm a recovering coke head comma alchy."

That checks out.

The meathead speaks after Finn, and though *'I'm Nick.'* is all he says...

You know those people that you see and for some *unknown-though-simultaneously-crystal-clear* reason just get the immediate, nearly undeniable urge to punch in the face?

Yeah. He's one of those.

The twat makes sure I know he spells it with a *K* when spelled in full as *Nickolas,* and that his last name is Schmidt, but to be honest I probably couldn't give less of a rat's arse than I already do. He is, however, a recovering druggie like myself, so aye, at least we're on the same crazy train here. Apparently, he almost shot himself in the head last summer, but he didn't go into much detail about that. I guess I wouldn't either.

We move on to the lassies, one of which isn't minging, but looks sort of like she hasn't washed her hair in at least two weeks. The other appears as if she hasn't been bothered to eat merely a crumb in months, maybe longer.

"I'm Cailey Pierce." The blondie with the bad hair is the first one to actually offer up a smile other than Finn, who doesn't truly count because I figure being smug is his default setting. "I'm a…" she hesitates as if this is her least favorite part of the entire day. Her voice lowers as if she's telling me a secret, "a recovering sex addict."

Welp. No one taught me the survival skill of how to respond to this…
Thus all I do is nod politely.

The last bird, though thin as a wafer, is quite peculiarly dazzling. I've never seen anything like her if I'm being honest, and I'm not commonly one to care or notice things of the sort. Not that I'm a fruit…it's just been pretty hellish to look at women at all since the traumatic mermaid thing wrecked my psyche when I was younger, whether it *was* just a vivid dream *or* a brutal reality…Regardless of which, *(I still don't feel comfortable concluding),* refraining from flashing back to that experience whenever I… *'notice'*…a lass is aggressively impossible.

Yes, it was bloody torture at first, but I've gotten used to the bypassing of lust.
So naturally, this took me by surprise…

She looks like death with pretty eyes – though the word *'pretty'* is an insult. They are a radiant cerulean contrast to her bittersweet chocolate brown hair and drawn, porcelain skin, through which I would be able to make out every vein, bone, and mark if she weren't wearing proper winter clothing indoors. She looks extremely delicate, startlingly so, even; though still, she somehow manages to look quite lush.

But whatever.

"I'm Maya Sexton."[32] She waves her hand throwing up a peace sign-hand gun sort of thing at me. "Sorry, Cailey, I know my last name triggers you." Cailey shakes her head and replies with a generous smirk. It makes me wonder if they're close, or if Cailey just has thick enough skin to take a joke. Maya continues, "I'm a recovering anorexic[33]," she then motions to her body, "if it weren't obvious enough. I also have a severe, rare Asperger syndrome, i.e. God forgot to create me with a filter; so if I offend you, I only half meant it. Probably."[34] Her facetiousness is stronger than she is, and I get a kick out of it. However, she catches me off guard with her engaging lean-in, causing her flannel to slip off her shoulder and showcase her protruding bones. I hold back a small gasp and grind my teeth, as it looks quite painful, but I don't think she notices because instead she calls me out, since no one else did during this time of getting acquainted –, "And who are *you?*" She challenges.

Anxiety shoots through me and when I peer around the room, my mouth becomes dry when I feel all of the eyes impale me once again. My lungs won't let me forget how much they want to explode, considering I've held back several coughs since arriving; not to mention I could hardly pay attention to anyone speaking because the only things constantly playing repetitively in my brain are:

Do not have a panic attack,
for the love of God

---

[32] *MAYA! Fun Fact: I toyed with naming her Mia, because she is loosely based off of me...but that would be hella weird. So "Maya" was the next best bet.*
[33] *Yes I am. I had it for years, and even had to get surgery. I'm pretty okay now, though! - Maya and I have a lot in common. <3*
[34] *This I don't have...I don't think. It would explain a lot if I did...LOL*

I Prefer Peter

Turn the sad boy vibe off...
Give more mysterious, brooding Edward Cullen

I want a cigarette
Or, like, maybe some drugs would be nice

Don't let them smell your fear

I really really really really really really
don't wanna be here

God, she's pretty.
↑ *SHUT THE FUCK UP ABOUT IT* ↑

Now at this thought, I rapidly realize I need to get out of here, but if I'm ever gonna do that, I need to strive to win the Oscar by faking it till I make it.

Make it *out.*
So, blast it. Here we go.

"Cheers," I manage. *Classic start, bruv; because now everyone is instantaneously enamored and bewildered by the surprise element that you have an accent.* I seize the opportunity, "I'm Ben – wait *no –"*

Fuuuuck.
Ijit.
You ruined it.

Everybody then, including myself, simultaneously makes more or less the exact same puzzled face.

"Do you not remember your name?" Recovering kill-myself-druggie Nick says sympathetically. "It's okay, I've been there, buddy."

"No, no." I hardly glance at him, because I *will* punch his face if I look at it for too long. "I just –"

"Is your name *not* Ben?" Tiny Maya snarkily taunts more so than asks.

"No, it *is*," I declare this a tad more crossly than I initially intended to, stabbing straight into her blue eyes with my own of dark green, and though she doesn't cower back because of them, she surely stiffens. I can tell she didn't notice they are just as vibrant and enticing, yet equally as empty as hers are, until now. I think my eyes are one of the only things I don't unreservedly, mercilessly hate about myself. "It's Benjamin," I explain, "but **I PREFER PETER.**"[35]

Reinfuckingvention plan commenced.

Before anyone gets too confused and asks the dreaded question *why*, Kelsey saves me, "That's your middle name, right?" I see she has my paperwork. Quick, solid system they've got goin' here.

"Right," I nod, picking the skin on my left hand.

"Is this part of your reinvention?" She plays therapist now. "Choosing to leave Ben in New York, and bringing Peter here instead to discover the new you?"

Fucking hell, what bullshit, but I'll bite.

"I'm just hoping Peter's a little less fucked."

---

[35] *THERE IT ISSSSSS! It's funny, I had no idea this was going to be the title of the book when I wrote the line. Once I came across that journey, I was reading through and tried to conjure up something original...thus, I Prefer Peter was born.*

I originally meant to *think* this, but how matter-of-factly it spilled out loud abruptly causes everyone to come alive for the first time since we started. Their laughter is pleasing, but I wasn't the farthest bit joking.

I sincerely hope Peter doesn't suck.

After what feels like centuries, we finally start coming to an end of the session once finished discussing everyone's plans of progression for this week, and also strengths and weaknesses from the previous, thankfully excluding mine altogether. Some things I had the pleasure of hearing were,

"I can't sleep at night"
and
"I hear cruel voices constantly"
and
"I see dead people" (Just kidding, no one said that)
and
"I had an Oreo yesterday then cried for forty-five minutes."
and
"I touched myself in the shower and thought of Kurt Cobain"
...
I'm a tough nut to crack, but I had to think of dead puppies not to die of laughter with that one.

When therapy concludes and Kelsey leaves the room, no one moves from their chairs, but instead, we stretch and let out long exhales of relief as if we all were collectively suffocating ourselves this whole time. I crack my stiff neck and continue to observe the others quietly, and I can't help but notice the only one who isn't buying into my silence and keeps glaring at me as if I'm the devil in disguise, is Maya.

"So I'm curious, Ben – no, forgive me – *Peter,* " her tone is heckling, "what makes *you* fucked like all of us?" She badgers, turning the heavy back on. I don't say anything, nor do I flinch at this kind of behavior; so I only give her a curious eyebrow questioning her meaning. She elaborates, "It takes a pretty shit sitch to get into this place. Why you? Why are you here with all us clusterfucks? Why are you wearing a brace? What's your story?"

Damn, she's more mouthy than Delfinnium.

"It's not a competition, lass." This is the first time I've spoken in about an hour, and my voice feels out of place here. "But you can be more fucked if you want, by all means. Let's be real, with a last name like Sexton," I turn my head briefly to blondie, "apologies, Cailey;" then return my gaze to Maya, "you're off to a bloody brilliant start."

This causes the room to chuckle tensely, but she skips the chuckle herself and just gets pissed off. Her imbalanced psyche and my sardonic tongue don't seem like they'll be a tasty cocktail when mixed together.

"Follow-up question:" she speaks rather speedily, "How'd you get to be such a giant dick?"

Kyle the *(former)* bulimic chimes in sharply, "Maya, let's take it down a notch, yeah?"

"Sorry," she says, clearly anything but, "I'm just curious to know this brooder's story. He hasn't said a word since his mind-blowing revelation that changing his name might change the fact that he's a freak stuck in this shitshow, when, *newsflash,* it won't."

"Eaaaaasy!" This is the first time I've heard Finn miffed. "Heel, Impossible Burgers, for the luv'uh crud."

I scoff internally.
Allow me to inform you:

Impossible Burger
A hamburger that's not really a hamburger =
So nobody really likes them.

Maya Sexton
A lass who's not really herself & says mean, impulsive shit due to
impossibly vile aspergers =
*So nobody really likes **her.***

+ Finneas plays on PURGER, making it BURGER.

Maya Sexton + _Impossible Burger_
A girl who has impossible Aspergers
Therefore, she is: *An Impossible Burger.*

A fucked up yet clever way of telling her through 'Finneas
Math' that she's speaking out of her ass and to shut up.
But I already caught onto her unfiltered opinions and chatter,
so now I'm just biting back.

Good idea?

Perhaps not.

Will I do it anyway?

Course I will.

"I have my methods," I say to her, the corner of my
mouth peaking as I throw in a dash of charm, "as far as having
– I mean *being* – a giant dick is concerned. But hopefully,
Peter won't be too *hard*…on you."

Maya deafeningly rolls her eyes, though everyone
else can't help but nearly explode with giggles at the profane

joke. As the blokes tease about cocks, and sex addict Cailey across from them is convulsed in a *[probably horny]* cackle, Maya and I, however, are on a completely different page as we quizzically study each other. We are both fully aware from the bullshit I'm oozing that *"Peter"* is no less of a proper cock up than Benjamin, and her blue pixie eyes tell me that quite clearly.

"But hey," my cunning eyes reply, *"maybe I'll score some kiss-ass pro-recovery points or something for trying."*

"I'm a drug addict, by the way," I verbally add as the chaos quiets down, still peering into her hypnotic eyes. "I'm not doing the 'I *was* a druggie' thing because I've been here for what, two hours? Yeah. Not quite on that level yet." I forcefully jolt away as I unwillingly cough, either because she just cast a spell on me or due to the fact that I have been suffocating myself by holding it in for an excruciatingly long, bloody time.

Who's to say?

Either way, It doesn't go unnoticed, but mercifully it cuts off quickly. I crack on as if spewing out my grocery list, "Also manic depressive, chronically yet stealthily anxious, I have asthma though I'm addicted to the bitter, slow suicide of cigarettes," they easily understand the hacking now, "and I also have this unruly revelation every night that most of this world doesn't give a fuck if I'm alive, which works out because, well, I bloody hate *being* alive…so." I look up at Tiny then, "But again, birdie, you can keep the whip if you wanna be the ringmaster of this circus here."

Finneas' lips are pressed so far into his mouth it looks like he may swallow them, and everyone else's expressions are just about as apprehensive to what could be coming next.

Maya covers her bony shoulder then and leans back in her chair, arms folded.

She smacks her tongue, "Overachiever over here."

"I don't like to brag."

"So tell me, have you ever considered maybe you're the problem?" *Cor, this chick is ruthless.* Cailey tries to intervene, but I hold up my hand to halt her cause I'm insatiably curious about what else Sexton has up her XL sleeve to attack me with.

I respond, "No, actually, that concept never crossed my mind. Please – Mia, was it?"[36]

"Maya," she practically calls me a tosser with her tone. This lass is feisty, yet she's noticeably easily miffed.

"Right, yes, my mistake; of course. It isn't like I hardly know you or anything," my sarcasm makes her blood boil and I take delight in it. I clear my throat, *"Please, Maya,* enlighten me, would you, on how *I* am the problem."

"Well," she doesn't even hesitate, "you have this absolute and final conclusion, or *complex,* that everyone hates you, or wants you dead; or doesn't care about you or whatever…right?" I'm assuming this is rhetorical, so I just bite the corner of my bottom lip. "But have you ever considered the fact," she proceeds, "that maybe you just loathe yourself *so* much that you've tainted your mind into assuming that everyone else *must* hate you the exact same way that you do? Or rather, maybe you just candidly handle your insecurities by tearing yourself down first, believing that if you make your flaws openly known, other people won't get a proper chance to judge you. Therefore, it causes your brain to figure that if *they* know that *you're aware* of your flaws, it'll make them shun you less, thus making you more comfortable

---

[36] *THERE I AM! I made a cameo.*

because the anxiety of *'what the fuck are they thinking?'* isn't quite as resounding... am I close?"[37]

An impenetrable silence fills the room. Kyle, Finneas, Nick, and Cailey all eye the tacky carpet while I stare open-faced at Maya, my elbow resting on my knee while my hand loosely grips around my mouth. All of us register her hypothesis of the inner workings of my brain, and I'm not one to ever get offended, mind you – but I *am* one to get pissed the hell off at one time or another. Maybe it's the fact that this bint doesn't even know me, yet she saw right through my bullshit and now I feel hella exposed to her, or the fact that I can't quite discern if any of her pratings were accurate or not...

How am I to know?
I've never dug that deeply into my own psyche.
I've never known my bloody self that well.
Maybe once...but not anymore.
Or, perhaps I never actually did.
But I intended to eventually discover it on my own.
*But nooo...she's evidently got me **all** sorted already.*

The truth is quite ghostly, so what she blabs immediately ties itself into the tightest knots imaginable around my mind, my stomach, my lungs, and then every other part of my being until the chair I'm in feels like a death sentence.

Being interrogated and bulldozed is quite a rarity for me...
Sure, I know she's ill, and half of what she says comes out of her little ass...so I can take it all with a grain of salt...
But right now, she's speaking what she believes to be the solid cold truth...
And the worst part is, I don't think I particularly disagree.

---

[37] *...exposing myself here*

And she's a fucking nightmare.

Not to mention she ever so graciously shared her theory with the rest of the class, and now I feel completely bare – naked – in front of complete and total strangers who I never wanted to meet in the first place.

My temper writhes within me and I feel it screaming in my ears like a piping tea kettle, "Ya know," I start eerily calmly, knowing I probably shouldn't say this, but…[38]honestly *fuck her,* "I wouldn't be so hypocritical and smug blabbing about how *I* care what people think about me, which, frankly, I don't give one flying fuck." I lean in at this and my eyes meet hers for the first time in a bit, leading her to turn a shade paler. "Howzabout, Maya, you come talk to me about the art of not giving a damn when you can eat half a piece of toast in the morning without worrying the world is going to think you're fat. Or, pardon me, let's dive into that, shall we? Perhaps, rather, it's the sense of being in complete and utter control – though, considering you can't stop and you've wound up here, you're, in fact, not *in control,* are you? Which is why you've ended up here…" I cross my leg over my knee as I switch intrusive thoughts, "Or is it the fact that you believe you take up too much space? Or rather you're just extremely caught up in the punishment your illness thrusts upon you and you believe that you don't deserve to get better because that would make you a *'bad anorexic',* or so the cruel voices in your brain tell you?"[39] She looks like she's about to cry, slit my throat, or both. I didn't think all of that would projectile vomit itself out, but alas, anger is a vile thing. "Whatever it be," I conclude

---

[38] *This is the name of my poetry book! It's available on Amazon!*

[39] *Since I am a recovering ani, I knew exactly what NOT to say to someone who has an eating disorder…thus I made Peter say it. Crazy how much power a writer can have.*

hostilely, "here's a friendly word of advice: before you even dare psychologically assess *my* baggage, I'd check your own. Alright, darling? I'm done here." Her lips form a straight line as she grinds her teeth and digs her nails into her palms, holding back wrath as best as she can.

Everyone's asses are glued to their front row seat of the shitshow, while I keep Maya's stare as I stand, disengaging when I head for the stairs to isolate myself to my corner bed and my journal again.

CHAPTER seven

Peter Green
*Brand New Life Wellness Home, **Present***
Day

jOurnAL eNTry ~ 9Am, FebRUAry 21

FuCK mE, i DONt knOW hOW i'vE noT kiLLeD mYseLF yEt.

iTs bEeN a weEK oR so noW sINCe ivE sTARted mY ruTHLesS adVEntURE HEre aT BNL, aND to bE fRANk, it's pRopER shIT. sURe tHE withDRAWalS frOM thE laCK of drUGS iN my sYSTEM aRE noWHERe nEAR as BRUtAL aS theY weRE, buT thEYre defINITely STILL lINGERINg lIKE liTTLE evER pRESent DEmoNs. I'M sTILL naUSeous evEry IS minUTES, i gET chILLS liKE a bLOODy mANIac, anD my muSCLES AND JOINTS ARE sTiLL slOWINg caTCHIng up wiTH thIS CHange – BloodY HEII, it's PAinfUL to EVEn hoLD a peNcIL, buT i suRE as ShiT AM noT goNNA talk abouT thiS wiTH aNYOne iN thE 9th cirCLE of HEII.

Due TO THE lAck oF sUBstaNce ASsIsTANce, My drEaMS aT niGHT Are viCIOus viviD niGHTMAres oF saDIStiC siREns, mY lUNGs arE tHeIr oWN WARzoNE wiTHIn me, mY anXieTY (whiCH maKES breATHIng jUST thaT mUCH morE impOSSIble) aND dePRESSioN hAVE gonE frOM a S to a BRooding 9 – aND iT aLL hASn't goNE withOut noTICe. I gET constANT cheCK ins frOM THe stAFF, HAVE to tAKE certAIN naTURAL suPPLemENtS evERY houR, aNd aLWAys gET trEATed liKE a bomB reADy to exPLOde.

bUt perHAps that'S fair, SincE i DefiniTEly feEL like ONe.

tHE pEOPLe herE ARen't toTAL toSSers, hoWEvER theY aRe quiTE STraNGE, aND we'Re definiTEly noT cloSe bY anYMEAns. tHE laDs anD lasSie's who ruN BNL tOoK MY phONe, buT jokEs oN thEM caUse it'S jaNk, sO theY Did mE a favoR; mY cOPy of *The Outsiders*, because thEY thOughT it wAs a 'Bad INFluENCe' oN me iN My stATE riGHT now (fucK thaT buT ok) –, tHey evEN tOok my glaSSes rePAir kiT becAuse it hAd a ScrewdrIVer in It, iN whiCh theY presUMEd i maY stiLL haVE tenDencies to ofF mYselF wiTh it or SOmething.

WelL, mIss AMY[40], taKE mY ciGareTTes awAy neXt, anD i juST might.

i tHOught FinnEAs waS halF kiDdinG abouT THe privLEdge poINts thing...but FUCK NO. it'S hELLA botCHed doDgy coCkass buLLshite.

---

[40] *That's my mom's name.*

speaKINg oF thaT bAg of beaNS... hE aND I gEt aLOng alRIght. tHE kid's a HANDfuL, buT hE bUys me fAgS whEN hE GoeS ouT, sO we'Re tighT. they lEt yoU smOKE heRE, whICH doESn't mAKE muCH seNSe to mE, bUT iM noT gONna quEStioN tHE luCk. evERYone elSe i DON'T fanCY, aND i suPPoSE thE FEEling iS muTUAL, bY diNT of lAST week: DICKnick aND I goT in A tuSSLE oVER noTHINg — reALLy. nOTHing. I tEND to KEEP TO mYSElf, aND someHOW thIS oFFEndeD HiM, oR mADe hIM aSSumE i WAs siLEnTly juDGinG evERYone (i wasNT. mOStly juST him. :))...anD he stARteD puSHIng mE arouND ANd throWINg ouT inSULTs. So, i gAVE hiM quiTE ThE shiNER to gO WITH hiS douCHEy fACE.

I FInally goT TO punCH iT — ha. *i'm noT sorry.*

He gAVE mE a NICe poP to thE jaW iN reTUrn, aND it's still a bit sore, buT thOUGH he suREly holDs a Lot of GAme in hiS talk, he canT mereLY paCK a punCH tO cOMPensaTE.

MAYa iS still a mYSTEry. iM geTiNg paSsed tHe faCT tHAt sHE reMInds mE of thE pRovOKIng mErmAID; nOW shE's juST a ~~preTTY girl~~...i thiNK...sO THAts a gOAl achIEved. shE loST poinTS cAUSe hEr weIGh iN wAS a COCK up, aND thOUGH moST pEOPle arE miFfEd to geT poinTS deDUCTEd, shE waS certainly proUD. I thINK it

Was the fact That eVEN though she lost points, she also lost weIGHT, which in HEr eyeS, iS a reAL priZE to gaIN. iT's faSCinatinG, innit? no mATTEr hOW mANY EYEs aRe watChing hEr, shE StiLL maNAGEd tO fiND a loophole to fEEd heR addICtioN. iM fairly jEALOus, i Wont liE – id DO anYThinG foR a xanny oR juSt SOMETHING otHEr thAn NICotIne anD mY suPPlemEnts frOM whOLE fOODs to tAke tHe edGe off..

iT's TAkinG EveryTHINg iN mE tO muSTeR UP thE strENGth to gO DOWn to BREAKfast thIs moRNiNg, aND if iT weRE a choice, I WOUld hAPPIly deCLINE EveRYTimE. ALaS, wE doNT geT MAny choICEs herE AND i juST goT a FUCKin WarninG fROM onE of tHE warDEns (sheS actuAllY a rAtHEr niCe lADy, buT ya KNOW), sO cHEErS foR nOw.

I sluggishly slither out of my – well, I guess it isn't *my* bed, but the bed I'm currently residing in –, pull on a sweatshirt, and trudge down the cold, wooden steps with bare feet. The roasted aroma of coffee boosts my serotonin a smidge, and when it hits my lips, it sends a warm embrace through my body that it so desperately craved.

At least they can't restrict me from my caffeine addiction.

I peer over from the coffee pot to the dining room table, and through my glasses *(yes, piss off, I look quite posh with four eyes),* I see I'm the last one to join and that there's an open seat next to porn prob Cailey. I inch through the kitchen, casually eavesdropping in on the conversation, which is a debate about why Finneas believes the Earth is flat.

"You ever actually seen someone discover the curve?" I don't even have to see him to know that he's enthusiastically talking with his hands, currently motioning the shape of a half-moon with his cupped palm, "It goes on forever. For all we know, if you just keep on goin', you'll plummet over the edge at some point. There's no solid proof *what* we're floatin' on. Life is a simulating illusion of sorts." He sips his coffee...*Seems like either a total black-for-the-blend type of guy or a 'more cream than coffee' drinker. No midway.* "Whatever the fuck that means."

"So everything they taught us about the solar system in school was a lie?" Kyle's groggy voice tells me his brain is still too tired for this.

"Everything is a lie, babyface." At these words, I enter through the archway, and Finneas' infamous cheeky grin paints his face a rosy pink. "Well, top of the mornin', sunshine! Your jaw is healing nicely, wouldn't yah say, Nicky boy?"

"Unfortunately." DickNick doesn't even look up as he shoves a piece of toast in his mouth and chews violently, his eye seeming to still be a nice multicolored piece of art I've created.

"Good day to you too," I say to him aloofly, my eyes averting his person and eyeing the nosh spread for the morning. "The fuck is this?"

"The fuck is what?" Kyle says, slurping discolored cereal milk from his bowl.

"What literally every single one of you is scarfing down like Christ made it for you." They all drop their spoons and eye me like I've admitted to murder.

"You kidding me, Brit..." Finneas raises his eyebrow at me and smirks, astonished. "You've never had Cheerios before?" I shake my head and shoot them back a glare of amused curiosity.

"You say it every goddamn day of your life and you've never heard of them?" Maya deadpans, single-handedly keeping the British stereotype alive. *Love to hear it.*

"I'm not an old man with a monocle," I take my seat next to Cailey, who studies every inch of my every move precisely...*I've learned to ignore it,* "I don't say *'cheerio!'*. Though, I've been in America since I was a lad, so yeah I'm *familiar* with the heart-healthy crunchy that helps lower cholesterol...but no, never had 'em. Is there a reason why you all are cultist-ly munching the same thing?"

"A new rule has commenced, Greenie. Monday's we all get the same thing for breakfast." Finneas sips his coffee and uses it as a tool for painting emphasis in the air, "Chuckie claims it *'helps starts the week off in one accord with each other'* or some horsey shit."

That's stupid as hell. "Right." I narrow my eyes at the cereal, then at him, then back at the bowl. "And why Cheerios?"

"It's always gonna be something simple, I'm assuming. Less scary for the foodies." He whispers the last bit referring to the not-so-foodies, Maya and Kyle. I peer over at the gal's bowl, which is empty not because she's finished, no – but because she's barely filled it.

"Fascinating," I respond aloofly, looking from her bowl to meet her sleepy eyes – *which are clearly stating they want me to drown in a lake* – offering her snarky smirk. I think I already drowned in the icy blue lake her eyes ever so diabolically pulled me beneath, but I ignore that sappy shit as quickly as it foolishly entered my thought stream. Regardless, for some reason I can't help but antagonize the hell out of her – it's like a virus.

"Sorry, Your Highness, is that not good enough for you?" Maya folds her hands in a mocking, pleading apology. "What would you rather have? We'll send a waiter right over."

Cailey chuckles and lets out a small snort. I turn to look at her, and since she looks rather embarrassed, I wink as if to say it was a darling little sound she made.

She nearly orgasms.
These people are so easy.

I turn my attention back to Maya, waving my hand, "Pish posh, love, don't go calling the help on my account. I'm sure your Cheerios – or lack thereof – " I gesture at her floating, soggy few, "are splendid, but I'm fine with coffee and a cigarette. I think I've had it for breakfast for the last five years."

She doesn't look up from her spoon of mush. "Wow, how edgy," her monotone way of speaking makes Finneas sneer, "we're all inspired."

"Thank you, it's my aspiration in life to dazzle." This makes him laugh out loud. He told me recently that he's never laughed more since I've been here.

I still don't know what to do with that statement.

My usual morning inclination decides I need a cigarette right fucking now, so I push out my chair, grab the pack out of the pocket of my sweats, and begin to repeatedly pound the bottom of the box onto my palm.

"If you're addicted to cigarettes, you should be trying to quit here. Plus, didn't you say you have asthma?" Kyle believes his epiphany is resounding.

I look at him as if he's solved world hunger, "I'll keep that in mind." My facetiousness is cut off rapidly as a cough viciously attacks me because my lungs have a mind of their own. He scoffs and shakes his head before munching on another bite of his breakfast, while Finneas and even

DickNick begin to tease my misfortune and threaten to hide my inhaler if I don't quit soon.

At least the blokes here can handle banter.

At last, I catch my breath, and I sneer and shake my head at the boys. Hearing no laughs of mockery coming from her way, I glance at Maya, but her eyes are still locked tightly on her uneaten, nearly now disintegrated meal. The sorrow and desperation in her eyes are evident, so much so that I can almost hear the screaming, brutish voices that are in her head inside of my own. In the short time I've been here, I've noticed that as damn cool as she constantly is – or at least makes herself out to be –, her inner demons torment the shit out of her, and it's blatantly obvious.

At least to me...
I know the feeling all too well.
It's bloody brutal, to say the least.
Damn, what I would give to perceive that fucking cool all the time.

As Kyle and Cailey stand to bring their bowls to the sink and Finn starts an open debate on why flying is the best superpower overall *(I agree, but no way in hell am I joining that kerfuffle)*, I make my way around to Maya's chair and since everyone is too busy disputing to notice, I kneel beside her. Though she doesn't willingly acknowledge me, I sense her tense up which ignites a certain pride within my gut. I quickly whisper,
      "There are one hundred and forty calories in a cup of Cheerios, therefore less than *five* in that one tablespoon you have there – well, likely in your whole breakfast, really...considering that coffee is black, and finishing all of

the cereal milk isn't mandatory. What I'm saying is: you've got this." I tip a fake top hat and wink, "Cheerio."[41]

Her head swiftly turns to me at the exact same time I make my way toward the foggy sliding glass door that leads to the snow-blanketed backyard; just a bit too late for me to see her initial reaction to a genuinely nice gesture from me for once. As I slip on shoes, her eyes burn through my back until I'm out of sight and puffing away on a smoke, lightly swinging on a damp wooden plank with worn rope stretching high through holes on both sides and tied securely around the girthy tree branch above me.

Exhaling, I think of the conversation from the guys inside, and how I wish I could fly. I've written it in my journal once or twice – that I'd give anything to soar high above the trees and sing with the birds; touch the cotton candy clouds at sunset and watch the sky change scenery with a front-row seat – damn, would that be something…something that would make this dismal life a whole lot cheerier. The closest thing I ever got to flying was getting high off my arse, and now that I'm trying not to do that anymore…

Guess I'll have to come up with another tactic.

As I play Dragon's Breath, a smoke ring game that I made up when I was twelve as an early closet smoker,[42] I hear angry boots trudging toward me through the snow and a dainty yet sharp voice shout,

"Hey!"

I don't acknowledge the exclamation right away, but she knows I heard it. Instead, I finish my game by blowing a large ring of smoke around a smaller one lingering in the air and watching the vapors dissipate satisfyingly. *Then* I look

---

[41] *AAAAAAAAND I'm in love.*
[42] *See pg. 25*

over to see Maya with her arms crossed, shivering like a chihuahua in the Arctic, and staring at me as if I'm completely bonkers.

"Hi," I say plainly, which I can see makes her temper rise, *that* which makes me amused.

"What the fuck was that?"

I stop swaying and tangle the ropes to face her, "What was…?"

"That shit charade you pulled inside."

"Fine. The milk adds maybe eighty more calories, depending." I inhale smoke and attempt to hold back a cough, failing as the frosty air bites my chest. I choke out, "But you already knew that."

"Fuck, can you turn the prick side of you off for only fifteen seconds at a time?"

"Oh, contrary to popular belief," I untwist, no longer facing her, "I *have* a sweet boy bone in my body, but alas, it's a small specimen, so…yes."

"How did you know all of those facts?"

I shrug and puff more smoke, looking at anything but her, "I'm psychic."

"*Damn it* – look, Green, for two seconds *please* stop pulling shit out of your ass." Maya stomps in front of me then and grasps the ropes of the swing, trying to halt the swaying I resumed. She's too frail, so I assist her with my feet. Her desperation demands, "Answer my question."

"Look, I'm not big on chit-chat."

"Bullshit, you have a bigger mouth than Finneas when you want to."

I chuff at the bold opinion. "Alright, well, I prefer to be alone."

She grabs my shoulders now, assumingly trying to shake the coldness out of me. I'm obviously not cooperating, and truthfully it's not that I don't want to, it's just that I don't do well with face-to-face empathy. That part of me shut down a long time ago, and she's becoming uniquely vulnerable, leaving me uneasy.

"Peter, for the first time since I've been here, finally somebody has come even a centimeter close to how I actually feel. Del is willing to listen, at least, but he can't fully comprehend it –"

I interrupt, "Who?"

"Ugh, *Finneas,*" she grunts in utter frustration. "I call him Del – it roots from Delfinnium. But *don't* call him that, only I can call him that – capiche?"

I nod.
But that's all I do. She's scary.

"Good. Now look," she continues, "during therapy circle, I let it go believing you were just being an overly sensitive dipshit who knew eating disorder stereotypes and listed them off to get a rise out of me…" I tighten my lips and subtly raise my eyebrow to show I'm following, and it propels her to crack on, "I mean, they're fairly easy to recite – hairy arms, infertility, shitty digestion, body shutting down, yaddah yaddah yaddah. I've heard it all." *Damn, I wish I were that nonchalant about my issues.* "But then you go and shoot out all of those facts about a goddamn cereal I didn't think anyone else gave a shit about, and you even sounded moderately compassionate. What gives?"

I desperately need a way out of this. I run my numb fingers through my dampening hair, "Look, Maya, I'm –"

"Peter, please. It's just us out here, and I know we're not *chums*, as you say," *I don't say that,* "but you can go back to your cold exterior, fly on the wall, *'I'm all fucked up'* persona later. Just do this for me, this once. Please…"

Sometimes it's difficult to remember that Maya doesn't intend to constantly say the first choice of words that pop into her head, nor does she mean to be offensive…not *always*, anyway… it's just who she is. Most would consider her brain's forced lack of filter a fatal flaw, but in actuality, what they don't realize is that it's just a quirk that's merely beyond her control. So when I look into her longing eyes, I try to see what she wants me to see: a girl who just wants to be heard; to not be alone – to be understood. Therefore, despite myself, I give in.

"I don't normally talk about this. I left it in my past, and I fancied it to stay there…" I glare at her, hoping she'll retaliate against her wishes, but her eyes are still round like a small puppy's. *I really, really don't want to talk about this. My stomach is turning.* I sigh in surrender, "I went through the same thing." Maya's hands loosen from my shoulders and then fold around her own, her face growing the color of the snow beneath us. I stand and gently guide her to sit on the swing, flick my fag bud into the snow, and take as deep of a breath as I can without choking. I pace uncomfortably while biting my thumbnail, and continue,

"Earlier on, when my family life started turning to total shit, I exercised for therapy or whatever – to keep my brain occupied, ya know? It kept me moving. But, I would forget to eat constantly. Before long, my body got leaner and I actually looked quite young – young*er*, anyway. It was almost as if I were aging backward. People called me *Benjamin Button* as a joke." She smiles at that, and it warms my heart a bit that she knows the classic film.

I don't want to tell her that also, the less I ate
and the smaller I got…
The less I resembled ***him***.
I don't feel like sharing that.
I don't feel like ever saying that out loud.

I crack on, "Before I knew it, it became a game. It was the only sense of control I felt I had in my life when really, it was controlling me…I would never admit that to myself though. Counting, weighing, portioning, running, losing, depriving, *repeat* – it was a year and a half of torturing myself to…well…death, nearly." I push away the morbid memories the best I can, and I can see from my peripherals her nodding in comprehension, relating to my words, though I can't seem to face her. Rubbing my eyebrows with my thumb and middle finger, I press on, "Eventually, I was bloody tired of feeling not only mental but overwhelming physical pain, as well as the guilt that came along with it all. So, in order to not feel *anything* by any means, I switched gears to drugs, and eventually the eating sort of fixed itself, in a way. I only liked myself when I was on the drugs; therefore they allowed me to like myself enough to eat. It was a lose-win situation…a new addiction just aiding the old one. But again, the admittance never surfaced." I sit with that for a moment, as I have never blamed myself out loud for my drug addiction before…*Fuck this girl.* I sigh, "That's how I know all that stuff."

When I look over for the first time since I began speaking, I can tell Maya hasn't taken her eyes off me this entire story. I'm taken aback by their color that fits in so properly out here in the cold – she's a winter by nature, no doubt. I quickly look back at my Converse, now soaked and causing my feet to go numb, and bite the inside of my lip. We both silently mull over everything I just word-vomited out into the open air, and within those few moments, I realize…

*Not only did I openly admit it to her **and** myself…*
*I've never told anyone **any** of that before…*
What does that even mean?

"I know I can't fix you…" I conclude before I think of the revelation any longer and spiral. "Clearly, I didn't even truly remedy myself, damn it, so I wouldn't dare try *you* out of regard for your future wellbeing…" I chuckle melancholily, and she copies in agreement. "But I can say: I hear you. You're not alone, alright?"[43]

Without a second thought and fully ignoring my un-huggable persona, Maya ditches the swing and tenderly throws herself around me. My arms fly up in a startled reflex as hers wrap around my waist, squeezing me into a hug as tight as her frail arms will allow. For a moment, I freeze, unsure how to respond.

Hug her back, ijit.

Just this once, hug back.

Before it's too late, my arms find their way around her upper back. Her long, soft dark hair brushes against the cracked skin on my hands and smells of cashmere and rain. Even though I'm uncomfortable, I can sense she needs this more than she wants to breathe…so I lay my cheek atop her head, and we remain there for a moment. The world is quiet despite the winter birds humming and the breeze blowing through the wind chimes near the patio next door. Her breathing is unsteady and out of sync with mine – like we're two opposites desperately trying to connect – failing, but doing our best. Regardless, she doesn't seem to mind…

And I guess neither do I.[44]

---

[43] *Reminder: You are never alone. <3*
[44] *One of my favorite quotes in the book, and also one of the first I ever posted!*

"I thought they didn't have Cheerios in England."

For the first time in what seems like ages, an actual laugh escapes my throat. I pause in wonder, unable to remember the last time I heard the way mine sounded...it's bright, unusual – unfamiliar. Even she gives an awkward smile as if she didn't expect this reaction. I step back from the hug abruptly then, snapping myself back to her observation referring to the heart-healthy calorie facts I spewed earlier.

"Right..." I recall for a moment, "Those numbers may have been an estimation based on the similarities of the cereals we have back home, or, ya know...me living here in America for six years may have helped." Her perplexed look at my sarcasm is adorably deafening. I smile knowingly, "I fancy you were too hyper-fixated on your breakfast to remember I mentioned that earlier. Nevertheless, give or take a few calories...the effort was there."

She smiles at me. "Well, thanks." This time her eyebrow raises, "This is the most I've ever heard you speak...You're really not that horrible, are you?"

I scoff and roll my eyes, the hostility from before rushing back through my veins like a safety vest. "Ask me again in ten minutes."

CHAPTER eight

Finneas Scott
Brand New Life Wellness Home, **Present**
Day

Welcome one and all to my fuckin head! It's a circus up here,
so try to keep up, yeah? I talk funny.

After another breakfast goes by featuring me winning
a debate with Nicky about some rando thing that no one else
gives a rat's nut about, I head upstairs to find Greenie in his
natural habitat: the right corner bed hovered over that diary of
his. I gots no idea what the hell he writes in that thing, but he
has more chats with the inanimate object than he does with
any real person, and to be quite frank, I don't think it's
healthy.

"Yo, Petey –"
"No." *because of this, I named my puppy Petey!*

He doesn't jack the new nickname I so generously just birthed
for him.

"C'mon, kid, is you gonna write in that thing all
day?" The little prick doesn't respond, as black ink jots down
illegible words while his braced fingers somehow bend up and
down so quickly, he looks like Shakespeare crafting his latest
masterpiece. I wait a few more seconds to spare him a thought
or two, then do what must be done: with lightning speed, I
waltz over and pluck the pen he's so aggressively writing with
out of his grip.

"What the fuck, Finn?" He's more annoyed than
usual, and that's saying…well, a helluva lot, 'cause he's
always trippin' about something.

"If you're gonna talk to someone," I cross the room and pop a squat on the edge of my bed, "I don't recommend a pape, Pete, it ain't gonna give much crack back."

He huffs a shallow breath, rolling his eyes as he straightens up, "I think I'll get more help from a pen and *pape* than I will from anyone else in this fuckhouse." He opens his palm, expecting the pen back because he thinks he's just insulted me.

Funny he thinks he can come close; I don't think he remembers whereda hell I'm from.

Without breaking eye contact, I flick the pen out the open window like an ax and scowl, shaking my head. His eyes grow wider than I've ever seen them as he springs toward the window faster than a jackrabbit, attempting to try to catch the pen but nearly tumbling over the dresser, plummeting after it.

"FUCK." Peter slams his one unbraced fist on the wood so violently, that a nest of birds flee from their tree outside the window sill. He holds his head like I just threw a hammer at him, "Would it kill you to be normal for five *fucking* minutes?"

"Yes." I nod, the answer to his rhetorical question coming out way too matter-of-factly for Peter's liking. "It's strictly against my code of conduct. You were being a dub. What's your damage, man? It's just a pen, go get it."

As Peter gazes out and down through the window that's bringing in the frosty air, his breathing begins to stagger and I can see the chills his skin begins to form like a rash. He puts all his weight in his hands on the top of the dresser in an attempt to hold him up steady, though quickly plops to his forearms when his elbows give out from underneath him. Then, as if the floor turned into a Greenie magnet, his ass collapses onto the carpet with his head clutched in his hands.

It deadass looks like he thinks if he doesn't hold onto his noggin securely enough, it's gonna pop off and roll away.

"Whoa, Green, what's going on?" I dart the few inches it takes toward him and lean beside his tense body, now practically in a fetal position with his eyes squeezed so tight, it almost looks painful. I shake his shoulder, "Talk to me, kid, you alright?"

"Shutthefuckup," he can barely get this out in one breath. Beads of sweat are starting to appear across his forehead and the back of his neck, his skin turning red as if he mysteriously just got poisoned by a damn good stealthy assassin. He lets out a few hacks that make me reach for his side of the dresser to retrieve his inhaler, but he grabs my arm and brokenly chokes, "Finn – don't –"

I grab it with haste despite his demand. I can see the veins popping out of his forehead now, and it looks like a scene from a horror movie I wouldn't even think to buy a ticket for. "Green, for all I know yur dying right before my eyes, let me help you, dammit!"

"It's – when the – pen – *fuck."*

"What?" I'm mid-hollerin' now. This dude is scaring the daylights outta me, and don't get me wrong, I like the guy, but I don't need no blood on my hands today. *"Pen,* what pen? *That* pen?" I shoot my arm toward the window, "Itta magic wand or somethin'?[45] The fuck does it have to do with –"

He cuts my words off by violently snatching the inhaler from my grip and sucking in every bit of oxygen he can. Tossing it aside, he hunches over, clutching his chest for dear life as he gags and chokes as if he had just been strangled by a rope.

I watch him as I sit stone still. "What happened?" I don't know what else to say, and though I'm not scared anymore since he obviously ain't croakin', for some reason I

---

[45] *I have a pen on my website that says this quote LOL!*

still feel like I should be. This kid is as unpredictable as a fucking storm in the Pacific Northwest.

His breathing slowly starts to come to, and he paces every sentence like his air is limited to none, "The pen...my mum...gave me that pen."

"Alright..."

"And when you threw...out the window...and I wasn't able...save it from falling, I –"

I can't make out what he's trying to say, but his voice trails off like he's recalling a distant memory, or maybe a nightmare that he had once. His eyes are somewhere far, far away, and the chills on his body are still protruding like scales. When he tries to hide his tremulant hands, I pretend not to notice that he's doing a shit job...but I think he and I both know there's no hiding the aftermath come-down of what he just experienced.

Not that he needs to anyway.
We're all a little fucked up – c'est la vie, baby.
Hiding it will make it worse.
I told him I had his back, and damn straight I do.

"Hey look, man, you don't have to explain." I hold out my hand for him to take, and lift him to sit on his bed. He nearly collapses again when I let go, so instead I wrap my arm around his back, securing him in my grasp as I take a seat next to him whether he likes it or not.

Dude needs a fucking hug.
Or like...75 o'them.

"Scary shit happens to our brain when you're comin' off whatever the hell we took." I try to hold him tighter to ease his trembling body but to no avail. Poor kid is like an autumn leaf, so I try a different approach, "Really, I'm just happy I didn't have to perform an exorcism on you or somethin'. Think I would get enough points to take a trip to the damn moon for it, though." He chuckles a bit at this, and it's like a sweet symphony to my eardrums. The small chime of it's like a release mechanism to the locked-up muscles all over my body, and I let out the breath I didn't even know I was holding. I can tell whatever the guy just relived was hella traumatic, but it was almost as brutal on this side to watch him suffer. "That happen before?"

"Once or twice," he sighs, and I know by the depth of it that he's totally pullin' a fast one. It goes without saying that it's happened more than enough times that him saying *'once or twice'* and pushing the intrusive memories of them aside to avoid the soup-ta'-nuts conversation, is now a natural reflex. "But never while I was awake."

"So, what, like a nightmare thing?"

"Mmhmm," he hums, pulling his weight back now and holding his own. "More like a night terror. It's realistic enough that I can see, hear, and feel everything as if I'm there. Or there *again,* in some cases." He gestures outward as if this was one of those times. "Sometimes I can't quite grasp what's real and what isn't. *It's fun."* He smirks at me to break the tension, and I think it's the first time I feel any sort of emotion other than anxiety in a hot *minute.* This kid's smile, on the rarity that it presents itself, has a way of making a light turn on inside of you.

"Well, don't worry," I break my cutesy observations, "I'll go get the damn pen back for your troubles. But first, I think I gotsa proposition for you."

His smile breaks, leaving him unenthused. "What might that be?"

"Come out with me tonight."

"Where, to the fucking living room?"

"No, Greenbean, on the town! I gotta'nuff points racked up to go out for one...*semi monitored*...evening, and I can bring a plus one. Congrats, you are the lucky *bloke.*"

"No."

"Yes."

"No."

"I ain't taking no for an answer."

"*Hell* no."

I stand, my arms stretched out in a plea, "C'mon, pal, you gotta get out of this prison of a bedroom and let that icy air put some hair on your chest. Ya know, before the cigarettes get to it first."

I crack a smile at him, but he looks more anxious than reluctant in giving into my proposal. I can't ever read Peter, and I doubt he'll be one I ever wrap my head around, but I can't help but try for some goddamn reason. There's something behind those jungle eyes that is so provoking, no matter how much he gets on your fucking nerves, ya still can't win.[46]

"I can't leave." He shakes his head and crawls over to his journal, closing it and placing it under his pillow like a molar for the tooth fairy.

"Why? I thought you were dying to get out of here for even a night."

"I am, indeed." Peter's eyes are fixated on nothing on the floor, but still stick there loyally, nonetheless. "But if I leave out that front door, good luck getting me to come back in." He apprehensively chortles, and my mind spins with an idea so wack, that I can't help but blurt it out the second it skims my brain.

"Then fuckin' don't..."

---

[46] *Finneas has some of the best perspectives on people than anyone I've ever met in my entire life...and he ain't even real.*

The kid snickers as if I'm fibbin', though curiosity subtly sneaks up behind his gaze, "Sorry, what?"

"We'll leave," I move in closer, switching to a secretive tone, "and once we're goin', we'll just *keep* goin'."

"As delightful as that sounds, there's no way we can pull that off."

"Why not? Check it, Green, they're just *people* who run this little house; out-smartable people who trust my hot, sorry ass. If I, a seasoned patron, take you, a newbie who's too *precious* and, well, green – no pun intended – to do shit in their eyes, to a movie or whatnot; with that moment of liberty, we can catch the next train to Christ knows where. It's an easy out."

He studies me like I'm telling the grandest lie in history. "And why now?" He rubs the eyebrow he always raises with his fingers. "You could've gotten out of here ages ago with a plan like this. Why tonight?"

Something in me is tugging at my vocal cords to blurt out that it's because I hadn't met him yet – that nothing has made me want to leave this hell pit and go live my life again than the magical aura of this kid for God knows why... But I refrain because it sounds...well, fruity as hell.

"It never felt right," I choose instead. "I always had something, or someone, to take care of – and I think the best way to take care of *you* is to get you the hell outta here. Bringing me along is just a bonus for both of us. Tonight could be the night if yur in. Are you game?"

Peter glances up at the ceiling as if asking for its permission, then rests his elbow on his knee while he rubs his chin and holds his mouth in thought. He surrenders his hands up in defeat, "It's a date."

"Fuck yeah!" I playfully hit him on the shoulder and my wheels start churning. "Alright, here's the dealio: fill a backpack with whatever's small and importanté. We don't got a lot, so that should be a piece of cake." Petey cocks and nods his head in amused agreement, and my brain twists some more, "I'll let the wardens know I'm takin' you, and – wait, *fuck.*"

He looks at me with a raised eyebrow, "What's wrong?"

"You've been here for what, a few weeks?"

"Right, yeah, why?"

"Problem is, you gotta be here at least a month in order to gain the access to leave; it's a weird ass rule. They think after a month or so, we're ready to be introduced back into the world or some doggyshit like that."

His face narrows, "Well that's bloody dodgy, innit?"

"That's the most British fucking thing you've ever said. But yes, dodgy indeed, Greenie. We need another plan."

Rolling his eyes, Peter stands up and looks out the window again, his thoughts now brimming along with mine. Snow is starting to fall in little flurries from the sky, and it makes my mind pivot, making me miss home a little…or, what it used to be, anyway. A lot has happened in the last few years, and Winter seems to always remind me how much has changed since I was young. I'm not too sentimental, but there's something about how life used to be that I always recall being so damn beautiful…until I went and *beautifully* screwed it up.

Perhaps one day I'll letcha in on what I mean. Snow just always seems to do this to me.

Peter's snapping fingers and firm voice rip me from the reminiscing. "Take Maya."

"Why the shit would I take Maya?"

Before he can respond, his eyes dart up and above my shoulder as a snarky little voice in the doorway beats him to speaking, "Cause *Maya* has a car."

CHAPTER nine

Peter Green
Brand New Life Wellness Home, Present Day

The nightmares are going to devour me whole.

Of course it wasn't enough that they happen at night and I haven't slept since I was sixteen…but now since I've stopped attacking most of them with drugs, they're happening in broad *daylight*, too?

Fuck. Me. Seriously. Fuck me with a power saw.

Finneas got the minor details of what they entail, but I couldn't go much farther than that. Not only does opening up to someone by letting them sieve through the inner workings of my unconsciously psychotic way of thinking an absofuckinglute ticking time bomb…but in all sincerity, it's hard to explain what's going on in your head when you can hardly understand it yourself.

Once the trigger is pulled, whether it be a word, phrase, picture, or even an action – *like someone throwing a pen out the window that you failed to catch, which brings you right back to your mother's plummet to death…* – whatever it may be, it starts with a haze, and then my vision goes dead black. As if there's a projection screen behind my eyelids, random, horrid memories play in vivid sequences, forcing me to remember every detail and feel every emotion as if it were all happening directly in front of me again. If it isn't a memory, it's an illusory vision of sorts – ones that make my skin crawl and my stomach ache; ones that create a myriad of mystifications that rise in me, driving me to wonder if any of them really *did* happen...

They can be gruesome, perplexing, somber, disturbing –; they can be whatever they want to be. It is something I have no control over, and that fact tears me apart every millisecond I'm alive.

You know that moment when you're near falling asleep, and suddenly your body jolts awake as if you were pushed off of a bridge? It's like that. Only I keep falling.

Down.

> *Down.*

> > *Down.*

Sometimes I'm drowning and my lungs are about to combust, but I never break the surface even though it's an arm's reach away.
Sometimes, I'm stuck in a hole, but the farther I climb, the farther away the top becomes.
Sometimes mumma is alive and we're far away from Colin – happy like we always dreamt of.
Sometimes I'm much younger and my tongue disappears, making it impossible to scream for help when I'm being taken away to an orphanage...
Sometimes I catch on fire from the fury I have erupting within me, but no one is there to extinguish the flames.

It's all...strange.

And now that they happen when I'm already awake, I don't know how to make them stop. My eyes don't simply shoot open with my body rising in a cold sweat – no, I don't just *wake up*. Just like when it's night, no more do my lungs ache with screams until my mumma sings me sweetly back to sleep, causing sweet relief to engulf me with the reassurance it's all over…

Now, I have to fully live through it. Entirely. Coherently, randomly – viciously. *Alone.*

The nightmares felt…*feel*…so real. Sometimes, I could swear they were…*are.* I can still remember nearly every one of them in broad detail as if they all happened yesterday…

It's fun.

Not even the drugs aided the madness. Sure, every now and then I was too high off my ass to know what was real versus imaginary anyway, as I was constantly seeing weird ass shit…but when night fell and it was time for dreaming, it was like the devil offered me a bed every night and I accepted without reluctance. Mum did the best she could, since we couldn't ever afford doctors'…but no matter what, all in all, my brain just never became my friend.

And I don't know if it ever will.

The invite I received from Finneas to *'go out on the town'* with him tonight has me mindlessly detaching and reattaching the wearing out velcro on my wrist brace…it's honestly bloody unnerving. The last time I hung out with a friend, I almost died…and if that won't trigger a raging terror of some sort, I don't know what will. *But,* however, if it means potentially getting the fuck out of here…

Carpe fucking diem!
C'est la vie!
And all of that blah blah bullshit.

Maya overhearing our little plan of escape obviously narks the hell outta Finn, but consequently, I'm intrigued... She's different...and hella fun to tease the daylights out of.

"Whaddya want, Half-Pint?" In the short amount of time I've been here, I've caught on that Finneas talks to Maya as if she's his annoying little sister, and I can tell it drives her mad.

Bravo, Delfinnium.

"The walls are thinner than I am, gents, so I overheard your little escape plan," she scolds in a motherly hush, though still as if catching us was a part of some heroic significance. Her tone is hushed as she enters, and her arms cross as if she is now a part of a secret society that owes her a comp for her knowledge. "I want in."

"What?" Finneas snorts with distaste. "No, girlie, we ain't babysitting. Three's a crowd, now scram."

"Wait, mate..." I loosely hold up my hand and walk toward the lass. I can see the tense shift in her eyes as I approach, but before I get too close, I pivot back around to Finneas and continue, "If you say you're going out with *Maya* tonight, there's no reason why they'll even bat an eye. That's your ticket out."

"Alright, sure, but where does that leave you?"

"He can sneak through my window," I turn as Maya passes me to sit on my bed. Even just standing in one place for a significantly short amount of time leaves her winded. "There are a few lattice panel trellises that make up the side of the house that can act as a makeshift ladder."

"Uhm...there's a whosie-*whatnow?*" Finn's head bobbles like a resin figurine. "Why girlie's always know the two-bit details of useless shit, I'll never understand."

"You'll figure it out," she directs at me about the… lettuce…trolly?…*lattice*…? things, rolling her sleep deprived eyes and leaving Finneas in his minor state of alpha male driven hostility.

"And why do you suddenly wanna tag along, Impossible Burgers?" Finn runs his fingers through his hair, clearly miffed his dynamic duo became the three amigos. "More importantly, what's the catch?"

Maya glances in my direction, as if her answer's reasoning has something to do with me, but she *subtly* lets her eyes wander to the carpet instead of landing. "You think you two are the only ones who want to escape this asylum? Don't flatter yourself. My reasoning is purely based on selfish ambition."

Bullshit.

"Fine." Finneas is already pulling out an empty backpack from the closet and tossing it onto his bed to fill with essentials later. "But we leave at 7pm sharp, chick. Wear somethin' purtty."

It felt like an eternity for night to roll around, but at last, Finn and Maya are dressed like your typical cliche first-movie-date-couple, hence the plan is now commencing:

ESCAPE PLAN:

7:00 pM — FinN aND mAYa lEAVe foR "moVIE"
♪ iF SOmeonE askS whAT fILm, fiNN saYS itS a
"SuRpRISe" & maYA canT KnOW TILL THEY GeT THERe

7:05 Pm — I esCAPe THROUgh MAYAs wINDOW & tRY nOT tO kill
MYSeLf clIMBIng tHE pLANT WALL laDDer thING♪ dURIng tHIS,
MAYa AND fiNN drIVE "awaY" But JUSt drIVE aroUND tHE
blOCK onCe — OR unTIL mY Ass mAKEs iT To gROUnd lEVeL

AsSUmiNG I DOnt dIE oR Get caUGHT, iLL Leg iT To tHE
BACkseAT aND we drIVE oFF aND liVE haPPiLy eVER fuCKINg
aFTEr :)

      Now it's 7:03, and I'm wandering aimlessly around Maya's room, glancing along the walls at detailed sketches of skeletons embracing and surrounding a hollow shell of a girl's body, all which I presume to be alluding to her own. The woman in the various drawings sobs and pleads *'let me eat'*, while the death figures say *'no'* with clear depiction of malice and sadism. *They're disturbing yet beautiful, really.* Next to them are torn out pages from classic novels, such as *Catcher in the Rye, Fahrenheit 451, The Outsiders,* and *The Great Gatsby,* among some others that have various lines highlighted, or blotted with ink for the creation of blackout poetry.[47]

I knew she was an enigma.
I can't lie, too, that she has good taste.

---

[47] *This used to be my wall*

I Prefer Peter

I'm thoroughly impressed.

thanks, Peter.

On her bedside table, a few photo frames featuring her and her family are neatly aligned. She never talks about them, or at least there are no instances I can recall...and I guess I don't blame her, since I don't talk much of mine either...

And I shan't for good reasons.
I wonder what hers are...

Frozen in time, she seems quite happy. There isn't one photograph where she holds back her pearly white Cheshire cat smile; not one where her eyes, let alone entire being, look as hollow and empty as they do now.

It's a rare sight for her – the smiling, I mean. I'm so calloused to seeing her default, seesawing cold to warm*(ish)* persona, that I never seemed to picture her not sick – I still can't – even though it's clearly displayed right in front of me in four black frames. I can't quite fathom that the lass in these wholesome pictures is the same girl who cried over Cheerios the other day.

I wonder if she misses being normal.

Was she ever normal?

But then again...is anyone ever?

After glancing at Maya's clock, I see it's time to start sweating my balls off trying to figure out a way down the side of this house without the open invitation of death. Just as the lass said, the lotus planters *or whatever-the-shits* are built like a ladder up the side of the house's wall, though what she failed to mention, was they seem flimsy as hell...However, I don't have much time, so before I can overthink myself out of it, I swing my leg over the windowsill and carefully begin my descent.

The trellises creak as I step down, and of course, due to the increasing declination of my luck, a wooden splitter jams itself straight into my left forefinger. I jerk my arm back like a pussy, causing my fucked up wrist to lock on me and my grip to falter to the hilt. All of my awkwardly placed weight sends not only the stupid vertical garden, but also me, tumbling down off the wall and onto the patches of dirt and pointy pebbles several feet below with a loud ***THUD.***

"Fuck me." I sit up and carefully crack my tweaked back and neck, turning as Maya and Finneas slowly pull up in the knick of time with no headlights. Through the foggy window, I catch them laughing as they seem to have had a front row seat to see my lack of ninja-like qualities coming to fruition, though I'm not complaining; twas a jolly thing, because I wasn't about to sprint far after the way I landed caused a garden gnome's green pointy hat to give me a good ol' spike to the dick.

Just as I'm about to stand to my feet, I hunker back down as the house's side lights flicker on. I'm momentarily blinded, though I shoot an anxious glance in Finn and Maya's direction, and when my eyes adjust, I make out their arms eagerly motioning me to run.

The window rolls down with a squeak, "The fuck you nappin for?" Finneas speaks in a hushed tone yet it's still loud enough for the neighbors to hear. "Get your ass in, Greenie!"

Despite the pain in my left nut, I haul ass and leg it to Maya's junker Ford Falcon's back door. I nearly throw it off its hinges as I swing it open and launch myself onto the torn cushioned bench seat, pulling the door closed behind me as if I'm being chased by a serial killer.

"Step on it –" I begin demanding with haste, but before I get the last word out, Finn is already out the long driveway and making his way down the street.

We're out.
We fucking did it.

"Well, that's a new look for you."

I look up from the seat cushion when my celebratory thoughts are interrupted and once I conclude I am in the clear, catching Maya's crystal eyes peering down at me, glowing along with the passing golden streetlights as she smirks teasingly.

I prop myself on an elbow, "What, *panic?*"

She laughs, "God, no. Panic is your natural scent, you're just good at hiding it exteriorly." *A psychoanalytic brute, this one.* "I just didn't know you were capable of wearing something not from the grim reaper's color scheme."

I look down and eye my old forest green long sleeve shirt, which is a fair contrast to the usual black or gray that have dominated my wardrobe for years. My first presumption was that it would help me blend in with the bushes if need be, but considering the majority of my escape plan was replaced with seething masculine pain and frantically sprinting into my getaway car, I guess it was more of an A for effort.

"Is that your attempt at an insult?" I sit up then and roll my sore wrist. I look up from it to meet her stare, which instinctively makes her body stiffen like I pulled her straight up like a puppet on a string, or just stuck a stick up her nonexistent ass. This happens so often now, that I'm starting to think I'm *Avatar: The Last Mayabender.* "At least my clothes fit. You're drowning in cheap polyester."

Her eyes become slits. "Remind me to start doubling my meds so I can tolerate being in a car with you."

"Triple them, maybe you'll go *sleepy.*" I wiggle my fingers at her, smiling facetiously.

She turns her back to me and slouches in her seat. Darn, I must've offended the poor lass. "You're such a prick," she says through gritted teeth.

"Really brings out my eyes, doesn't it?"

"Alright, children, enough!" Finneas mocks his best dad voice and waves his hand at Maya and me. "Half-Pint, you're here by default due to the generous sacrifice of your vehicle, so I will tolerate you and your sass. Petey, it was your idea to bring her, so you'z better behave or I will turn around and bring that dick-pricking gnome with us instead."

I catch Maya peer over her shoulder and send me a sneer, so I respond back with a roll of my eyes so piercingly loud, it may as well have cracked the windows. She huffs, thus I, satisfied, shimmy down until my head reaches the back of the seat, fold my arms, and close my eyes. "No promises," I simper.

CHAPTER ten

Maya Sexton
*Somewhere ... **Present Day***

Two days. It's been two days since we escaped the fiery gates of BN*hell*, and I can honestly say, I'm scared outta my batshit fucking mind. I thought I would be hella stoked, but once the adrenaline wore off, my best friend named anxiety reminded me that I have no clue where I'm going, no telling if these two pussy lickers are going to rape the daylights out of me – *sorry, please get used to my sporadic way of thinking, that filter thing I'm bred to have is long broken and is unrepairable* – and that either way, there's no turning back now.

Not that I would ever want to go back...like, don't get me wrong, Brand New Life was a nice refuge and all, but being trapped within the walls of a home that isn't yours to call your own, with a staff of men and women monitoring your every waking move, and a point system that determined whether or not you were worthy enough to leave and live your life?

That place was a twenty-four hour nightmare.
*Ironically, it made Finn **feel** the need to drink.*
*It made Kyle **want** to vomit.*
*It made Cailey **crave** porn.*
*It made me **still** try to starve myself.*
*It made Nick **want** to shoot himself.*

Now Ben – I mean *Peter* or whatever, I can't speak for due to the fact that we hardly speak much at all other than to bicker, aside from that once upon a time he had his nice guy panties on...but otherwise, I don't know many of his opinions on, well, anything…but I can only assume he felt the same. Right now, he's sitting in the backseat hunched over that beat up leather journal of his, writing what looks like a novel long doctor's note.

I.e., his penmanship needs some work.[48]

I turn around from the passenger seat and watch him for a brief second. I say, "Hey."

…He doesn't even flinch.
It's as if my existence is purely illusory.

Finneas lets out an airy laugh through his nose, as if to say *'classic'*, and I try again, "Hey, Edgar Allan Poe."
Peter wets his full lips and his head slowly rises then, his intimidating green eyes making my body feel like someone stuck a wooden plank up my non-existent ass. *I feel like he knows it too.*[49] "Good one," he grants, but his attention immediately reverts right back to his illegible pages.
"What're you writing, your suicide note?"

Damn…I say some awful things, don't I?
Fortunately, he's not in the least bit sensitive and does the same nose laugh thing Finn did, though without looking up at me.

He follows it with a plain response, as if bored with me, "Just writing."
"No shit, Sherly. Writing what?"

---

[48] *Same. My teachers used to send my written papers back because my writing was bad.*
[49] *He does.*

He shrugs. "Just stuff." The vagueness that comes from this kid, along with the lack of ability to genuinely hold an actual conversation, is mind-bendingly agonizing.

"What *stuff?*" The volume in my voice raises to an irritated growl through gritted teeth, and he smirks cheekily, knowing all too well that he's annoying me, which *clearly* and thoroughly amuses him.

I don't know why he gets under my skin...
And I don't know why I let him.

I'm normally pretty damn great at keeping my cool and at least *acting* like I'm the shit...but his *'pretending not to be an insecure fuck up'* game is far more believable than mine, and it infuriates me. I keep staring, and finally, he huffs, flicking his drooping hair out of his eyes,

"Well, if you must know," he looks out the window as he speaks, "I'm planning to overtake the floating, rotating orb that is this god-forsaken world we live in," he turns his regularly startling green gaze to me then, "and you're the first person on my hit list. Sorry love, I didn't want you to find out this way, but you asked."

Finneas lets out a tickled ha-ha, and I roll my eyes, shaking my head in annoyance for what I assume is going to be the first of many times I do this today.

"Petey talks to his diary like it's his therapist," Finneas' smart-assery flows about as naturally as his hair.

"Delfinnium talks to his dick like it's his pet."

"Hey, *never* the full name. And leave Richard Dickson out of this."

Peter shakes his head, eyes once again glued to his book though reluctantly surrendering a smirk as Finn reaches behind the seats and makes a jerking off gesture in his face.

Del either reminds me of Joey Tribbiani from *Friends,* some sort of main greaser plucked out of *The*

Outsiders, or an up-in-coming star from post-World War II Hollywood who would do almost anything to make his showbiz dream come true. He'd be the classic charmer who got fawned over by every horny whore back when Los Angeles wasn't yet a total shameless freakshow. His hair is always perfectly slicked with the exception of one small strand flying loose around his honeysuckle eyes, of which he attempts to flick away every ten seconds by a jerk of his neck, but never to any avail. He keeps his focus on the open road and sucks on a lollipop that he got at the gas station a few miles back, meanwhile, Peter looks like his Ponyboy sidekick in the backseat with his messy *'I tried to look like I didn't try'* styled burnt auburn hair and round, gold rimmed glasses as he writes his life away and chews a stick of spearmint gum. Though, despite it, he's lighting cigarette after cigarette like a chainsmoker, which completely defeats the gum's purpose…but he doesn't seem to give a flying fuck.

But, if I'm being honest, Peter strikes me more as the main character type…
I just don't think he knows it.
Or at least doesn't want to admit it.

But, God, these two.
What I would give to look this fucking cool all the time.

     "You know you're fucking killing yourself with those things, right?" Despite my brief moment of jealous admiration, I don't know what propels me to constantly nag Peter like it's my nine to five…It almost feels like some sort of new festering addiction. Before I know it, I'm gonna be thrown into the next nearest psych house for *'Pick on Peter'* syndrome.
     "Oh, brilliant!" He hardly looks up. "Perhaps then I can come back to haunt you with all the other little demons in

your head." He sucks in smoke to his already poor excuses for lungs, blows half of it straight into my face, and then the rest out his nostrils like the devil's little apprentice. Swatting away at the air around me, I grunt in frustration and he chuckles, but then chokes because karma's a bitch and I'm her favorite.

"You'll be dead before you're forty."

He smirks, "See you in hell."

"Alright, cats, *settle down;* come up for some air." Del snaps, not hiding the fact that he's over his two unsolicited children. Though I have a tendency to get under his skin, I will say a particularly positive thing that came from the torturously claustrophobic walls of BNL was meeting Finneas, who happened to take me under his wing like the angel he is, and infallibly become my big brother, friend, and somehow father figure all mashed into one person. He reminds me what it is to be sane; *human* – even though I am fully aware he isn't much more lucid than I am. Nonetheless, he keeps me grounded. He's a good one to have on your side. "I gotta pull off to top off the tank," he groans. "Think you can refrain from murder till then?"

Neither Peter or I respond verbally, but mentally it's unquestionable that neither of us are promising anything of the sort.

There are times, several instances a day, in fact, I would happily stab Peter in the emerald green eye with one of his old, dirty heroin needles and feel nothing but pure and utter pleasure while doing so.[50] Perhaps it would do him a favor, even. He always hints at wanting to kick the bucket anyway…it's actually kinda sad.

But still, he infuriates the hell out of me and drives me crazy…
Though the strangest thing about it is…
It's enthralling.

---

[50] *UNHINGED AF. I love.*

I can't fucking stand it.
Yet, I can't get enough of it.
It's contradicting and absolutely maddening.
Is this what his drug addiction is like?
...whatever.

Thankfully, the off-putting scenery outside pulls me from my intrusive thoughts of the pesky boy in the backseat. A bit after Finn exits the highway, it's almost as though some sort of hidden, eerie magic suddenly made the road disappear and become a treacherous sea of bumpy dirt and gravel.

My face scrunches. "Where the hell are you going?"

Del doesn't look at me. "Don't worry, chick, your captain's on course."

"Well, did you two *change* the course to the middle of buttfuck nowhere and forget to give me the intel?"

"I did what the damn sign told me, Maya."

"What sign?"

"Well if you weren't munchin' on Greenie's ass every forty seconds, perhaps you would've seen it."

"I don't even see the road anymore..." Anxiety seeps into my stomach out from my veins, through which it's mass produced. "I hardly see anything, this area is so –"

"Just relax, front seat driver. Be a little more like your sleepy bestie back there."

I half turn around to see Peter passed out with his pen behind his ear, and his journal open face down on his thigh.

He's so peaceful when he's shutting the fuck up.

Although, jokes aside, how he can manage to successfully fall asleep on an *Indiana Jones Adventure-esque* ride like this, is absofuckinglutely wild to me – and so quickly, for that matter. He seems like the type who could make a nest anywhere and sleep like a baby.

I can hardly fall asleep in my own bed.

Not only that, but everything in me wonders what he could possibly have written in that book of his, and why he guards it as if it's The Ark of the Covenant. I don't have a clue what Peter values, but I sure as shit know if anything happened to that journal, he'd flip his lid. So with that tempting image in mind, I hold my breath, stretch my body, and reach my arm out toward the book.

As if his spider senses just tingled, Peter's hand smacks his journal down so hard in one fluent motion, that my arm snaps back as if it's almost been devoured by a mouse trap.

"Nice try, luvie." He doesn't open his eyes when he chides, but his lips form that infamous, infuriating smirk. "Touch it, and you gain fifty pounds."[51]

I ignore the heinous made up punishment. "Sorry, I just can't imagine you writing anything worth reading. I had this presumption you were mildly illiterate since you hardly speak, so I just wanted to confirm my suspicions."

"Why would I speak to someone who doesn't value anything I say? Much rather talk to myself. I'm clever. *Brilliant* even."

Everything Benjamin Peter Green says makes me want to punch him in the mouth. Or rip my ears off. Anything to stop hearing the snarky vibrations that come from his throat and out of his pie hole.

Apparently, the backseat child decides sleepytime is over, cause he leans forward and rests his forearms on the bench seat in front of him and turns his attention to Finneas, "So uh, where's this gas station?"

---

[51] *I'd shoot him.*

He must not have been that fast asleep…
I should've talked more shit on him.

"We shoulda been there by now…" Finn squints aiming to see through a mist hazing over the windshield, that I definitely don't remember being there two minutes ago. "Where da'fuck did this fog come from? Or am I trippin?"

"It rolled in about a half mile back." Peter is looking out the backseat window now, and turns to peer through the trunk's as well. "Can't see a bloody thing on all sides."

"Maybe…maybe you should turn around…" I trail off because I can't decide if what I comment is a question or an unease ridden suggestion; and regardless, I am fully aware it's a shitty idea…but I just don't see how proceeding forward could be better anyhow. The snow blanketed trees, dead grass, and all land that was surrounding us not even twenty minutes ago, is now engulfed in a gray sheet of thick nothingness. When Finneas doesn't respond and keeps driving onward, heebie-jeebies build in me as the air gets thicker and everything looks like something out of a horror movie. "You must've taken the wrong exit."

"No shit, Sherlock," Finneas' tone is aloof now, as all his focus is pinned on the road, *or lack thereof*, ahead. "I'd turn around, but for all I know, we could be on a motherfuckin' bridge and plummet to our death's if I spin this wheel more than a few inches."

As untrue as *[I hope]* that is, I can almost feel the illusion of swinging to and fro on a rickety bridge while my car slowly and chillingly guides us onward. Nausea fills my stomach, so I open the window to lean out and grab some needed outside air.

"Fuck," I'm caught off *all* guards, "it's hot as hell out here…" It's as if we've suddenly gone from being in frosty February to sticky, humid mid July. "What the hell is going on?"

Peter rolls down his window, sticking his scarred hand out into the open. Wavering my hope that I'm just losing it, his brow tightens. "Finneas," his voice is mildly apprehensive, which doesn't aid my panic due to the fact that Peter is rarely ever openly nervous about anything, "you need to turn around."

Finneas takes his turn then feeling the blazing heat out his window, and immediately the vehicle comes to an abrupt stop, jolting us all forward.

"What the shit?" He snaps his arm back into the car and rolls his window up as if an animal is trying to get in. "Alright, kiddies, buckle up. We're haulin' ass back."

Finneas hits the gas...
Nothing.
Zip. Zero.
The engine revs, but the car doesn't move an inch.

"Put the car in drive, you ninny." Peter leans over the seat and freezes as his eyes land on the gear shift. "What the..."

Even though the Ford is in drive and still has enough gas to go a few more measly miles, it stays completely stagnant. There is no muck or mud to get stuck in, either – it's simply as if the car is actively saying *no*. Finneas slams his foot on the pedal as though stomping on a bug, and still we remain S.O.L.

"Fucking piece of shit car!" He slams his hands against the wheel, and shifts the gear to park...*not that it would make much of a difference either way.*

"Excuse me, this is *my* piece of shit car," I defend it automatically despite the harsh truth. "Maybe it just died –"

"The ignition wouldn't be on if the car was dead, you ijit! Use your brain." Peter irritatedly taps his temple as if reminding me where said organ is located, and narrows his eyes at me with distaste. I'm not in the mood for his shit right now, but at the same time, he's right about the ignition thing, so I don't rebuttal. He hisses, "I'm getting out to see where the fuck we are —"

"Oh, no, no, Greenie." Finneas looks at him through the rearview mirror. "You don't know what the hell is out there."

"Well then let's make some chums, shall we?"

Disobeying, *per usual,* Peter throws open the door and steps out of the car, his feet hitting the gravel beneath him with a soft crunch. He dizzily stumbles at first, unable to grasp his bearings; be it from being cooped up in the backseat for days, or, after what I saw after being at BNL with him for quite some time, his withdrawals are still really taking a toll on him.

Serves him right.

Whoa, wait, no!
*Maya, you bitch, who are **you** to judge **him**?*

I'm no better…
Fuck, at least he's actually trying to sober up.

Ugh, not that I care.
Maya shut up.

"Well it's bloody hot!" Peter hollers to us as if we didn't already know. He immediately pulls out and lights a cigarette somehow graciously even with his braced hand, adding more haze to the already polluted air.

"Thank you, Captain Obvious." Finneas opens his door now and steps out to meet Peter, stealing a cancer stick from his box. I guess Peter is feeling generous for once in his life, because if anyone else would've laid a finger on his cigarette pack, he likely would've either cut off their hand or chivved them almost immediately.

Finneas scrunches his nose at the dire heat that hits his olive skin, and then shuts the car door, leaning his back against it and taking in the eerie gray around him as he puffs. I don't have even the slightest desire to leave this car, but it seems I'm outnumbered; and if it magically wants to take off, I'd rather not be the sole victim inside.

"Wait, so how long were we driving after you exited?" I hear Peter question Finneas as I walk up behind him.

"Couldn't have been more than twenty minutes or so... it all looked the same after a while, and that clock she's got on the dash ain't worth shit."

"Mate, why the bloody hell did you even drive blindly for that long? You shoulda just turned the ship around!"

"I needed the fuckin' gas! I don't know, *mate,* if you're so British and *brilliant,* as you so boldly declared, you drive next time. Oh wait, that's right! Ya can't, can you, baby greens?"

Peter rolls his eyes so intensely it looks like it might've hurt. He does that a lot. "I'm the one who actually *can,* Alchy Ann, so cool it before I report you. But until then, what're we gonna fucking do, Brooklyn? Take charge, Jack Kelly. Seize your fucking day." Still puffing his cigarette, he shoves Finneas' shoulder as if he's ready to rumble with him like they're back in New York.

"Ladies, please!" I interrupt them by pushing Peter into the car – or trying, anyway...I don't actually cause him to stumble. Rather upon my impact, he humors me and takes a few steps backwards, snickering at my attempt as he 'falls' against the car. As Finneas joins him in the tittering, Peter's green eyes sink into me and say...*something...probably dickish...*so I give him a sneer as I turn around to take my turn

in surveying the area. "Do either of you have service on your phone?"

"I wouldn't know, chick." Finneas' words make my heart crash into the deepest pit of my stomach. "It's as good as dead, and your doozy Ford ain't got an aux to help it for shit. Petey?"

"Well, the wardens stole mine, so..." Peter slides his sleeves up past his wrists, revealing a myriad of scars that my eyes automatically, ruthlessly attack. When I catch my mouth falling ajar, I look away as quickly as possible, licking my dry lips as an attempt to appear as if I just momentarily spaced out and accidentally *happened* to land on the ever-present reminder of his past demons...Though, alas, I know he half noticed, because Peter's leer that's fixed on me turns subtly cynical, as if he's speaking to me purely from the castleton green within his eyes. However, he deadpans in between slow puffs all the same as if the nonverbal exchange never happened, "Getting it back never made my honey-do list."

"Well that's *perfectly* convenient for clusterfuckery horror movie shit to start happening now, isn't it?" I snap, equally avoiding the touchy scar subject. *"We're all gonna die out here!"* No matter how many times my head shoots in all possible directions, I see absolutely nothing – it's like opening my eyes under dirty water without the burning sensation of chlorine.

The sun isn't even quite peeking through the fog, but I can still feel it beating on my fair skin and I can already tell I'm starting to burn on my arms and the back of my neck. Being out in the open air only reminds me how fragile I am, and suddenly all I want to do is be back in my front seat. Though right before I give in, a small, blinking, golden light catches my eye in the distance through the haze. I point, though both boys are back to being besties and are too focused on their weird ass fucking smoke ring game to notice.

"Yo, tweedle dumb and tweedle dumber! You see that?" They snap out of their playtime and follow my finger. "It's like a…signal light or something."

"Probably just a windmill, IB, or water tower or something."

I hate when Finneas calls me Impossible Burgers.
It would be like me calling him coke-a-holic or some shit…

…who am I kidding,
I should've started calling him that ages ago.

Peter ugly coughs and nods his head in agreement with Finn, "No way I'm Great Gatsby-ing it across a fucking pile of God knows what to God knows where."

"Maybe it's someone –"

"Sorry, didn't finish – *to God knows who.*"

"Just get back in the car, girlie," Finn dismisses me. "Let the men finish their ciggies, and we'll hit the road."

Fucking pricks. "Need I remind you *men* that the car has magically decided to turn against us?"

"Eh, I'll whisper some sweet nothings into the engine. She'll purr." He rolls his tongue at the last word, and Peter lets out a chuckle-hack as he throws down his addiction and steps on it with his black leather boot. Disgusted, I shake my head and start for the passenger seat.

"You both are sick."

"Oh, chin up, buttercup," Peter practically ballet leaps after me and grabs my shoulders from behind, whispering in my ear with his warm, cigarette breath, *"we all are."*

I shrug him off and keep walking. He snickers again and begins to assume his position in the backseat, but just before he does, a gold beam erupts into the sky and oscillates like a cinema searchlight where the signal had been seconds ago.

"The fuck..." Peter mutters behind the car door as if using it as a shield. "That can't possibly be meant for us," his tone is unsure of whether that should be a question or a statement.

Finneas puffs his cig one last time before flicking it into the void. "Nah, no...it's just a –" But before he can finish, the light splits into three. Now they look like they're waving – one for each of us – summoning us to come closer. The two boys and I gape blankly at the peculiar sight, stiff as wood...or as Finneas when he hears someone mention *City of Angels* on Broadway.[52] He clears his throat after about ten seconds and begins lowering his body into the seat, "Alright, well, we ain't gettin any younger."

"Whoa, now wait a second!" My body heats up forty degrees at the audacity of him even beginning to consider exploring this idea. "Are you genuinely thinking of going toward that death trap?"

"Oh, I've already done my thinking, princess, and I'm going. This is the most excitement I've had in years. Petey, you in?"

"I was in when they split in three."

"Atta boy, atta boy!" Finneas smacks him on the shoulder, and they both practically dive into the Ford. I stand next to it, eyes fixed on the dancing lights as my seething skin begs me to get back into the vehicle. My heart races at the thought of going anywhere near what may be lying beyond this point, but once again, I'm clearly overridden.

"Hey, Sexton," Peter pops up from across the car's hood and signals with his head for me to come join the party. He adds tauntingly, *"Adventure awaits."*

---

[52] *If you don't know, Google it.*

I'm pretty sure he winks then before disappearing, or maybe I just imagined it...But nonetheless, it instantaneously sends an electric spark through my spine. I really don't care to decipher whether it's based on anger, desire, or beguile, especially right now...

So instead:
Fuck him.
Fuck this plan.
Fuck today.
Fuck everything.

I sit my ass on the seat and close the door, accepting the fact that dying may just be on my to-do list today. As soon as we're in and ready, the car is geared into drive again, the wheels turning as if they never stopped.

CHAPTER eleven

Peter Green
*Before the Wrong Exit ... **Present Day***

joURNAL ENtrY – iTs FEbruAry somethiNg

i goT no ~~fUCKing~~ blOODy FUckiNg iDea wheRe we ARE or whAT daY it is, buT we'VE beeN home FREE ouT of BNL foR tWO dayS noW, AnD thiS craMPeD, shittY backSEAt iS beGInnINg to fEEl raTHer tRIumpHANt. bUT I wonT fiB, aS thRILLeD aS i Am to BE ouT of thAT priSOn, i CAnt sAY mY anXIety haSnt bEEN eVer PReSent conSIDering i HAVe alMoSt notHINg to Take thE edGE oFF (i nEarly finIShed mY pacK of fAGS – im nEar deatH), aND i hAVe nO blooDY clUE wheRE 'Ol cAPTain FinNEas iS eN rouTe tO.

buT whaTs lIFe wiTHOuT a liTtlE advEnturE, riGHT?

SIDENOTE – SExtOn wOnt stOP peEking baCk hEre anD ruNNing hER boNEy jaw. sHe's sEEminGly IMpossIBle to husH up! I hAvEnt a huNch aS to whY shE's sO inTRiguEd bY me... :) gUEss iM jusT sO daMN chaRMing.

sHe'll alWAyS be a mYStery, thAT onE.

We biCKEr noNstOP aND honEStlY, it's RatHER heLLA amUSIng & ~~a bit adorAblE~~ thE waY shE geTS so inFURiateD whENever soMEthinG, QUItE litERAIIy anYTHInG at aLL, comEs ouT oF mY mouTH. frANkLy, iT seeMs ALL i hAvE to Do is lOOK aT heR aND shE begINS PLotTinG A nEw blUEpriNT of MY seCREt mURder.

thOUGH i KNow shE NEVEr wouLD.
SHE's oBVIOUSly obSESSED witH me.

iT's faSCinaTING.

anyWay, On A TOtAL OpPOsiTe NOte, iVE ReaLIzeD AGAin On thIs eXCURsion THAt iM preTTY damN gooD at hidiNG whEn iM anXIous, esPECially THANks to THIS herE jourNAl AND iTs aBIliTY tO hELp mE esCApe witH its SafeTY blANket—likE tEndenCies, or emOTionaL supPort Dog vIBes, or SOMEthing. iM fAIR at supprEssiNG anY emoTIon witH it, in ALL honESTy. "fEElinG" iS juST NOt someTHING i oFTen mUSter uP thE enERgy foR. I watchED my parenTS givE into emOTIons daily, anD well...it obVIOUsly diDnT geT theM far.

goD, i MISS my mum.

STOP, BeNJAMIn, jEsuS.

sEriously, It's eaSIEr juSt to Not caRE abOUt anyThing.

to noT feEl.

thAT's whY i miSS druGS so Much.

buT All in ALL, i quITE fanCy tHIs thRILling impROmpTU roADtriP. perHAPS a fresH starT is neeDed... I duNNO. sURe whAT kelSEy sAID aBOUT "reINVENtioN" waS COMplETE aND totAL hoRSEshIT, buT i WONT lie... i woULD fanCy if "pETEr" goT someThing a Little grANDer thAN mErelY surviVing liKE "bEnjaMin" did hIS whOLe lifE. inDEED, we'rE thE samE bloODY perSON, buT fuCK man...iF i doNT CAtch a bREAk sooN, i WILL shOOT mySelf iN...tHe someWHeRe. anD thaT's a PROmise.

pROBABly.

I DonT knoW. iVE beeN saYinG thAT foR a loNG tiME now.

i'm a coward.

mY heaD is juST so SUFFOCating; I coulD swear i liVE underWATEr. I coNSTAntly feEL liKE giVING in aND LEtting thE phleGM of mY lunGS droWN me – i haRdlY evER comE up FOR aiR anyWAy – thE surFACE is nonExiStent. iF God doEs exist, hE forgot to creaTE me witH a clEARing evERY onCE in a WHIle, anD it iSnT faiR...

sO what'S thE issUE WIth holDINg mY bREAth a LITTLE lonGER tiLL i 'accIDENtally' faLL inTo thE voiD of OBlIVioN? MAya AlrEADY ASKed iF i'M CoMPilINg mY ofFIng noTe...wHAt's tHE hOLd up?

PeteR, stop. No, no, no.

Sorry.
iM jusT TIred.
I JUSt wanT thIS worlD to stOP so I can geT off.

YA knoW whAT WOUld bE niCE?

MY OWN WORLD!!!

A plANEt iN whICH I RULE, oR evEn a fuCKIng iSLAnd wheRe I caN EScape thE totAL, heINous exisTENce of HUMAnity – It DoeSNT MaTTer! i DOnt giVE a damN whAT or WHERe it is, jUSt AS loNG as iT's nOT in MY heAD anYMORe.

WHENeveR i UsED to gET higH in mY rooM, i WOUld gO to a plACE wheRE i wAS in CONTRol of anYTHINg anD everyTHIng. whERE realitY DidnT fuckING exist becAusE honEStly, what EVEn is 'reAL' anyway? RealITy is a CRimE – coMPleTe and uTTEr bullSHIte – thE THEIF anD

DEstroyER oF joy. AS MLKjr SAid: *"thE WOrLD oF REaliTY haS LimiTS; ThE worLD of IMAginatioN is BOUNdLEss."* ...

IM SICK OF BEING RESTRICTED TO THE GLORY OF EVERYBLOODYTHING THAT COULD POTENTIALLY MAKE ME THE LEAST BIT FUCKING HAPPY

tHIs worLD is aLREADy An illusion, anD i cAnt stAND thE fact thAT iM here – aND aloNe, aT that – whEN i didNT sign uP foR it. I HavENT ONCE haD a SAy iN thE stOry Of MY liFE's sCRipt sinCE beiNG vaGINAlly shovED INTO thiS univERSe...and That's fucked up.

I'vE ALwayS WANted soMETHING of mY own. soMETHING I created. I wanT tO be aBLE To telL the SUn When to riSE, thE rain whEN tO fALL – i WANT thE grass To bE a PErfect vERidiaN and the SKY is tO bE ROYAL Blue – FUCk thE duLL 'skY blue' THat evERYboDy preTEnds iSnT caKEd in SMOg aND fuMEs – I ALWAys thOUGht iT waS obSCEnely ovERRated.[53] I WANT thE floWERS to bE DREAmliKE, anD thE aIR TO be pLEaSaNT. I WaNT it to FEEL liKE i'm FUCKING HIGH ALL THE TIME aND sEE a supERLatIve, aLTEred VErsioN oF reaLIty wiTHout A sinGLE drUG polluDIng mY syStem. a WORLd whERE i CAN just bE fucking happy... AND i wANt iT tO be, moST

---

[53] *Welcome to my unpopular opinion of the sky*

impORTAntly, wHERe nO onE evER diEs bECAUSE growINg up isnT eveN an aftERTHOUght – gETTinG oLDER wouLD bE FUCkinG bANnEd. I NEVEr goT to enjoY mY youTH becAUSe of cockin (coLIn) GreeN, anD i WANT It bAck.

I DESErve it BAck, dONT i?

suRe, i CAnt ever trULy geT it back... hEr back.
aNYThing back.
buT i cOUlD surelY crEAte silhOueTtes of it aLL aGAIn.
sOmethIng beaUTIful tO carRY aloNg thE REst Of mY LiFe
– makE up FOr LOst tiMe.

Im SO usED to BEINg in this ~~goDdaMN~~ geedamn gray aREA, thAt i THINk it BECAMe my autopiLOt.
sEEms i JUST realized I'vE FORgoTteN what It feelS likE to be aN actuAL huMAN beinG, aND FOR thE lonGEST timE ivE beeN okay witH it... maYbe i STill am. perHAps it'LL just alwaYS bE thiS way.

Or, mAYBe i CAn chaNge it...
who'S tO saY?
bLAst it ALL... anyWAY. iM geTTing thE long wiNKS anD thE withDRAWL SYmptOms aRe kICkinG in AGAIN. uGh IM LIKE a FuckinG pregnaNT lady oR someThing.

I Prefer Peter

sweEt dreaMs.

CHAPTER twelve

Finneas Scott
*Somewhere ... **Present Day***

I took the wrong fuckin' exit, man.

I gots no idea how I managed to do it either! I was looking at the damn road ahead of me the whole time…it was almost as if something took over the car and it got off the highway on its own…

I believe it. Deadass.
It's a shitty ass car, it's got nothin' on a ghosty.
I mean, it died and resurrected like Mr. Christ…
Only in this story, when the spirit believed we were deep enough into the adventure to never look back, it supernaturally died on us again…Now Peter and I are sweatin' our nutsacks off, and Maya, her…itty bitty titty sacks, I dunno.

Sometimes I conclude we live in a simulation and we're actually not in control of anything, ever.
What even is reality, amirite?
Anyyyway…

Of course I had to tell the two **bickerdicker's** that I totally uppin' meant to take the exit when I did, but nah. Total *cock up,* as Petey would say…Even so, I'd never give them the pleasure of seeing this here captain's true fault – especially because I gots no fuckin' idea where I've stranded us. Now here we are, walkin' toward a creepy as shit moving light show that may or may not be signaling us to our death's. So, if we do so happen to kick the bucket, I'll allow them to die without them knowing their pal Finny was the prime culprit.

"Do you carry that diary everywhere with you, Anne Frank?" Maya gestures to Pete's ass pocket, which indeed is stuffed with that leatherbound bestie of his.

I checked twice to be certain.

"Are you looking at my ass because you're jealous?" Leader Peter doesn't even bother turning around. "Your eyes have been burning a hole through my trousers for ten minutes."

"What do you even have in that thing?" She ignores his true statement.

"Free therapy."

"Touché, pally," I can't help but say. I know this kid is fucked up in all the wrong places, but I've decided he's cool as hell. I sure hope he catches a break soon.

After some brief *(too brief)* quiet walking, the only noises being Maya's heavy breathing and the sound of gravel beneath our feet, the girlie speaks up to break the hush-hush,

"Is it just me," *an opinion...surprise, surprise,* "or is this thing getting farther away the closer we get to it?"

"What're you talkin' about, Half-Pint?"

"Like…" she pants, "the more we walk toward the searchlights, the longer we're taking to actually *reach* the searchlights…logically, we should've at least been halfway by now."

"You just gotta build your stamina, chick. A wise man once said food is the gasoline for your machine[54]…or some shit like that. We haven't even walked –"

"It *is* like it's backing away from us, innit?"

---

[54] *If I'm not mistaken…I made this up. I am that wise man.*

Well saw me in half and call me Isaiah.[55]

Peter catches not only me, but also Maya off guard because this is the first time these two have genuinely agreed on something…at least with a witness. He glances at her with his eyebrow raised knowingly, and she simply and silently nods. I wanna say something so fuckin' bad, but I may taint the tender moment – so instead, ladies and gents, mark this brief moment in history in your booky's, cause we may never witness it's sheer and delicate brilliance ever again.

I ain't gonna lie, my silence is also due to the fact that I too now start to notice this wild chain of events that Maya was babbling about. As we trail forward on the gravel, the lights pull away from us. Once we all agree this could indeed be a vicious, never ending treadmill, we eventually stop to reassess.

"This is fucking deadass sketch, kids," I say as I feel the ghosty vibes kicking in again. "I say we bounce."

"You're the one who was a gung ho curious kitty before; why are you being a pussy now?" Maya is just bitter she's more outta breath than both of us guys, even with Peter being a fucking asthmatic chain smoker.

"Yeah, well now I'm *curious* what tomorrow will bring and I'd like to live to see it. Let's turn around while we have the chance."

"Hold on…" Peter steps forward while Impossible Burgers and I keep still behind him. "Is you lot's seeing this?"

He's so British – that was just as bad as any fuckin' grammar I've ever used. "Seeing what?" I've yet to see Greenie this interested in anything – he's been quite the surprise today – I'm flabbergasted.

---

[55] *Clearly Finn went to Sunday school LMFAO*

He turns to look at us, "They stopped moving when we did."

Simultaneously, Maya and I switch our focus from Peter to the searchlights which did, in fact, halt as if they were never moving at all.

"What the shit?" I take a step forward, and immediately when I do, the lights lunge back as if I startled them. "Whoa, wait, did you –

Maya and Peter give me a baffled *"yes"* at the same time, their eyes buggin' like one of them squishy, kiddie toys.

Safe to say we're scared as balls now.

"Alright, well," Peter claps his hands, "I need a cigarette, and my lungs ain't thrilled about this heat that's about as dry as DickNick's personality, so I'm scramming."

He starts back toward the car, but then another wildly impossible thing happens that sends Maya and I just about shitting our pants.

"Peter!" I say with a force that presumes if he takes another step, the ground will eat him up whole. "Wait, keep walking…"

"I intend to…" He says smartass-ily, giving me a snide expression before trucking on. Sexton and I stare in awe at the light fixtures as Peter moves.

"Holy hell…" Maya's face turns whiter than usual as she races to him and grabs him by the neck of his shirt, "Green," she whispers as if the lights will hear her, "it's *you.*"

Peter's face twists. "The hell d'you mean?"

"Walk forward, but look behind you."

Peter keeps his hard expression, but does what Maya says. As he places his steps, the lights move along in our direction with him, as if pleading with him to turn around.

"Fuck, Pete…" I say in astonishment, "It's like you're their leader Lord, or somethin'…"

"No way I'm doing that…" he claims, assuredly. "One of you bring your arse's over here."

Maya doesn't volunteer, so I move toward Peter with haste. The lights don't follow me an inch, thus sending my brain into more complete and utter interest, so I then take it upon myself to move in the opposite direction again toward 'em –

Low and behold, the lights move away.

"Benjamin," the real name pops out because this is serious business now, "the lights ain't givin a damn about us, they're sure as piss is yelluh following *you.*"

"Well, *Delfinnium,* that's cockshit." After this blasphemy, Petey continues walking toward the car, though it's evident the kid's in denial and doesn't want to look back cause he knows full well what he'll witness. It's fucking impossible, but it's happening, *damn straight.*

"Peter," Maya's voice is faint due to the unforgiving heat and her unruly ability to become dehydrated as quickly as a small puppy dog, "please, for the love of Christ, just walk toward the thing."

Baby greens stops dead in his tracks and whips around as he speaks, "Have you both gone mad?" *He sounds so fuckin' British again.* "It's bloody blazing, you're even more near death than before," he points at Maya, "there's a freakish circus-trick-illusion-or-whatever trying to fuck with our minds, and you both want me to *follow* it?"

"If you don't, it's sure as shit gonna follow you." He looks past my cheeky smirk and sees the lights have drawn nearer as he drew farther. "Fuck it, right? You wanted adventure, there it is. Seize it, sweetheart."

Peter gives me a stone cold glare. He hates being tested, and I know it full well…which is obviously why it had to be done. Thanks to the peer pressure I have provided, the kid storms past us, thus taking the position of captain reluctantly. As he does, the lights become closer and closer as Maya and I follow sheepishly behind.

Carpe Diem, bitches.

CHAPTER thirteen
Peter Green
Somewhere ... **Present Day**

I wouldn't dare say this out loud, but something about this charade sends electricity up and down my spine. It's an unfamiliar, forgotten sensation, and I can't decide if I enjoy the fact that I'm getting more and more intrigued as the mystery gets infinitely dodgier, or if I instead loathe the potential reality that something may be genuinely exciting to me. Seems I've suddenly become even more of a walking contradiction than I already am...

Didn't know that was even possible.

I've always adored fantasy...and I won't fib that I wished, throughout my entire young existence, for some sort of *fantastical* adventure to fall into my lap some way, somehow...but as much as I fancied the pipe dreams, they never seemed to fancy me back. Reality shocked me out of believing in magic a long time ago...and that was that.[56]
So, all things considered, I seal my emotions tightly in the bottle of my soul, per usual; claim I want out of this expedition to Maya and Finneas, and begin to walk brutishly back toward the car. Though, despite that, I strangely begin to notice that this all has a similar feeling to the euphoria of slowly getting high, and I won't lie...

It's teasing me...
and it's fucking wicked grand.
It's the best I've felt in a minute, and I can't shake it.

---

[56] *A harsh truth for many people. We must change that.*

So...I guess what's the use of hiding it?

Be that as it may, due to my raging pride, I disregard the blissful feeling I've longed for for months, and make believe it doesn't exist.

Why am I like this?
Why am I so damn embarrassed to feel?

Before I spiral, I immediately channel the foreign elation to questioning: I don't quite understand any of what's going on, nor the feelings behind it, and the constant state of the unknown is adding to my chronic anxiety and bloody gnawing at my core. I can't help but wonder *why* the hell these lights are following *me*, and more importantly *how* the fucking fuck the lights are following me. Is the heat causing us to go absolutely mad? Is the lack of drugs in my system finally pushing me over the edge?

God, what I would give for a hit of something –
Anything –
Right now.

All at once, my inability to function without the sheer splendor of nicotine kicks in, and if this sham continues any longer, I may just explode. Therefore, I make the executive decision to head back toward the shit mobile, but I am stopped yet again before I do, noticing the impossible legitimately *is,* in fact, happening right before my eyes no matter how hard I dare try to pretend it isn't. Finn and Maya are standing in a daze, gaping at me as if I turned into some sort of flesh eating goblin, because blimey...

*I **am** making the lights move.*

Finneas says something, but I can barely make it out through the pounding pulse and voices in my head. I phony that whatever he claims is fucking wack, howbeit I can't escape the feeling that I *need* to move forward...

So move forward I do.
And my two little sheep follow me.

Onward we carry ourselves, the lights drawing nearer as we go, and I continue to hide the fact that the sensation in my stomach becomes more of an elation in my chest, and when the illuminations start to burn into my eyes, my heart jumping into my throat. I haven't the foggiest what I'm expecting, but I am starting to fancy my soul knows something I don't...

And I'll be damned if I let this high go.

Us three amigos keep our heads low and our breathing as even as we can as the heat becomes thicker with each cinderblock-like step. I stare at the uneven gravel as we track on, never understanding why watching one foot step in front of the other always seems to make trudging through the sun's blazing rays a little easier.[57]

"Yo," Finneas breaks the gnawing of my inner voice, which is ruthlessly attempting to coach my lungs into not disintegrating, "check out the sky..."

Both disoriented, Maya and I look up, and despite the fog, the sky above us has discreetly transformed into a gorgeous array of deep purple and burnt orange. Hints of pink that streak above remind me of sweet cotton candy, and the traces of what was once a dull sky blue are now dreamily

---

[57] *Does anyone else feel this?!*

sapphire and highly saturated. It's as if Jesus Christ himself is painting a portrait right in front of us.

"So what?" I say, though my eyes don't match my tone…*I don't think anyone notices though.*

"That ain't normal and you know it. The sky ain't capable of that on a damn doozy day."

He means on a normal day.
I'm starting to speak Finneas and it's riveting.

"My mom used to tell me when the sky turned that warm shade of pink, Mrs. Claus was baking cookies up at the North Pole."[58] Without looking at her, I can hear the smile on Maya's face as the memory slides off her tongue. "I would always think, *'No wonder Santa is so fat; Mrs. Claus bakes him cookies every single night!',*" she giggles like a small lassie. I look up at the sky again, squinting my eyes at the gleam as I try to imagine a young Maya with her mum, admiring the colors above and childlike fantasies, though still worried about calories even if they weren't going into her own system. I don't know much about her past or where she comes from, but with a memory like that, I know one more thing Maya and I have in common –

We both miss our mother.

Finn chimes in too, and his tone is more melancholic than I ever thought possible for Mr. Smug, "My ma used to tell me during a storm that when the lightning struck, Christ was bowlin' and had just nailed himself a strike –; thunder was a spare. I always thought to myself, *'damn, this Jesus guy is pretty fuckin' good at this game, no wonder everyone hung*

---

[58] *My mom used to tell me this!*

out with him!'."[59] He chuckles at the memory and smiles brightly while he reminisces. "She was mad brilliant with them stories, lemme tell ya."

This is the first time I've heard Finneas mention anyone in his family...for all I knew he was an orphan, due to the fact that he commonly strikes as the lone wolf type. But cor, when he spoke of his mum, I didn't even have to turn around to know that his commonly intense eyes were completely softened, and the usual confident way he carries himself was totally humbled.

It's amazing what a mother can do.

I toy with the idea of bringing up my own mother, but when I feel my skin tingle and the burning of tears sting behind my eyes, I simply go with, *'It is quite nice.'*...even though *nice* is a bloody understatement. *Astonishing, dazzling,* even *magnificent* could be of proper description; but even though I could write a novel and a half about the gorgeous sky and all its glory, I have one other thing tugging on the strings of my brain...

Or rather, my nostrils.
What the hell is that glorious smell?

"Are you lots getting a whiff of that?"

"Oh, thank Christ," Finneas exasperates. "I thought I was trippin balls. Smells like cinnamon rolls or somethin' or other."

"It smells like a bakery on the golden streets of Heaven." I didn't realize how starving I was until this smell filled the humid air. The further we walk, the more the sweet, lucious aroma suffocates us in the most superb yet torturous

---

[59] *Hehe she used to tell me this too!*

way possible. Maya doesn't say much, as I presume even a sniff of food makes her anxiety off the walls, but there's no way on God's decent Earth that any human being could withstand whatever gracious nosh we're *[hopefully]* about to stumble upon.

"Whatever it is," Finn's speed picks up a tad, "it better be fuckin' edible and not some candle or spray scent fabreezie shit, because I'm about to eat one of ya."

"Choose me," my tone is only half kidding. "Neither of us would survive off the birdie." Maya's eyes roll at my ~~[truthful fact]~~ insult, but no words tumble out of that unchained mouth of hers.

No backbite? That's new for her. "You alright there, lass?"

"Tired," her voice is dry and I can tell the heat is starting to attack her brittle bones. To be frank, I don't really feel bad for her...I mean, she did this to herself. *But,* then again, I can't heartily judge her, can I? Though entirely poles apart, we are, at the same time, downright equal.

Ugh...

Therefore, I can't help but *[selfishly?]* think that if one of us guys don't do something, she is gonna fall over any second and then we'll have to fucking deal with it. Thence, due to the fact that I am a fine gentleman, I stop, squat, and sigh,

"Hop on." She halts in her tracks with a look of pure confusion, as if I just spoke Animal Crossing[60]. I explain, "You ain't gonna help us get to this mystery whereabouts if you're dragging, now are you?"

"Ben, I'm fine –"

---

[60] *If you don't know, Google it LOL.*

"Ben," I interrupt with a slight raise in volume, "would probably agree; ah, but alas, *Peter* is feeling a little more chivalrous; tis your lucky day. Now, up you go!"

"Peter –"

"Now." My eyebrow raises, and holy hot fuck my legs are burning in this plié.

I notice she's a bit taken aback by this authority and bites her lip so subtly, that if I hadn't been paying attention, I would've missed it. Even Finneas turns back with a cheeky grin on his face –

What did I do there...?
She must have a thing for dominance.
...I choose to ignore that observation **entirely***.*

"Okay," she surrenders, on my back she goes, and thus we press onward..

...Yup.

Maya is as light as air and I'm no empathist, but fuckin' hell is it concerning. If I don't hold onto her tightly enough, I'm almost positive she will fly away like a fragile leaf in the wind. I refrain from saying anything, though there are moments when I have to look down and ensure she's still there.

I'd let her eat me first. *how sweet.*

"Alright, kats," Captain Finneas, now leading, breaks the silence, "what's the plan once we get to this freak show?"

"Ask for a cinnamon roll," I straight-shoot.

"Word to, Petey. Word to. Follow up question: what if they kill us first?"

"Del!" Maya's strained voice rings in my ears.

"Sorry, girlie, I'm just creating the battle plan here. All signs are pointing to the fact that we're moving toward our sweet, sweet burials, so any way we can make it less horror more snorer, I'm all for it."

I chuckle inwardly at his rhyming wit. "We'll cross that bridge when we get to it," I retort.

"When...?" I can feel Sexton's icey eyes stabbing the dip of my neck.

"If," I reassure her. Though, it's more a manifestation for her convenience, rather than the complete truth.

Subsequently, however, I wouldn't mind either way and somehow she reads this on my face, giving rise to her pain-in-the-ass-burger tongue, "But you wouldn't care if you died, would you?"

My defensive sarcasm word vomits as it does, "You mean I would jump at the opportunity of a potential storybook ending of heroically and willingly sacrificing myself for you blokes if it came down to the merciless, inevitable cyclone of death? Yes, indeed, I would. What a way to go. To die full of pride."

"It's like you romanticize death."

"Death is the biggest adventure I haven't tried yet."[61]

"Bruv," Finneas' head whips around to me, "those are some gnarly last words right there." He warns next with his hands, "Don't say nothin' else just in case we *do* die." Maya scoffs at the sheer insensitivity, but I shake my head in amusement at the morbidity of his humor. "What a deadass profound P.O.V...*Fuckin' legend,"* he finishes under his breath.

Finneas develops a small spring in his step, and I will admit, though my potential last words do sound rather badass as hell and would look mighty sexy on a headstone, my heart breaks a bit at the fact that I meant every bloody word.

---

[61] *One of the best quotes. Ever. I want it tattooed.*

However simultaneously, I, by some means, feel the slightest bit of validation whenever somebody thinks I'm a *fucking legend* for being so welcoming to the thought of eternal sleep. It's like I have a praise kink for death...

What a fascinating epiphany I've just uncovered about myself.

Right, okay, it's not that I'm not grateful to be breathing, even though it's pretty half-assed at this point *to no fault other than my own, I know*...But when I look around at all this nothingness we're walking through that nobody knows is here, I can't help but feel a sense of belonging – familiarity; as if the gravel and dirt know more of what it means to be *me* than *I* do. The solidarity and loneliness that engulfs an area like this is haunting, and to feel inside myself the same way that all of this vast nothingness appears to the eye, is maddening. It's hollow. Every second that I look around, it gets wider, making me feel more lost – alone. It's like the walls inside me are closing in, creating a claustrophobic hostage house like no other, and at the same time everything is broadening. It makes you want to gouge your eyes out and then blow your head off.

Do you see what goes on in my head?
It's sad, for lack of a better synonym.
So, would I mind death? Not really.
I believe it's a friend that's just misunderstood.
It's better than the debilitating existence that my brain forces me to live in now.

"Peter?" Maya breaks my spell.

"Hm?" I hum back softly, still in the trance of my own inner monologue.

"Your hand..."

I look down and notice I've unconsciously let go of
Maya and started prying at the skin on my left hand with my
right. My nails scratch the surface of my fist, peeling away at
skin and picking at scabs as I drown in the oblivion of my
thoughts. The dryness of the air has sucked the moisture out of
every part of me, so breaking the skin barrier is too easy, thus
making them bleed and tear rather noticeably.

"Shit, oh…shit," is all I say. I wipe the small bits of
blood on my jeans, and switch then from my nails to my
calloused fingertips and begin to rub my stinging cuts.
"Do you do that often?"
"Varies. It's a bad habit. Like your tics, but more
normal."
"Fuck you." I can tell she doesn't mean to say this in
the tone that her brain chooses, and when she follows the
words with a guilty smile, she immediately confirms my
suspicion. The difference between what Maya *says* and what
she *wants* to say, are two entirely different things. One may
not notice, but her true speech is less abrupt and forceful, and
she is actually quite pleasant to listen to.

Ya know…when she's not being a cunt.[62]

"What other bad habits do you have?" *Small talk?
This is a one off. Let's give it a go.*
"Oh, ya know, the usual. Skimping on sleep, not
drinking enough water, smoking *and* being unequivocally
fucking good looking while doing it."
"Huh," she chortles. "I haven't noticed that last one."
I let out a small wave of air through my nose to let
her know I appreciate this sarcastic remark. "What're you

---

[62] *YOU WERE SO CLOSE TO BEING NICE, PETER.*

talking about? I smoke all the time," my mouth forms a line and though she's still on my back, I feel her face twist.

"Cocky motherfucker," she says under her breath; but it's audible enough for me to catch because she totally meant it this time.

"Sorry, forgot to mention that one too."

The smell of cinnamon rolls is now overwhelming our senses, and the lights are nearly blinding, even in direct sunlight. A strange fog still surrounds us and it is as thick and dry as a noose around our throats, and the farther we walk, the harder it is to see each other...yet Maya, Finneas, and I press on. I would've missed the small, peculiar knick-knack placed almost strategically upright on the ground, had it not been for the fact that I've been looking down at my sides constantly to ensure Maya hasn't fainted and wafted away without me knowing.

"Wait, *no!*" I abruptly command, nearly dropping her to throw my hands into Finn's chest before his giant black boots destroy the object. "What the bloody hell is that?" I point at what appears to be a figurine of a man about the size of a chess piece, sending Finneas bending down to retrieve it, and Maya hopping off my back to join the investigation.

"It's a shirtless mini man holdin' a knife or some doohickey." Finn brushes the dirt off of the trinket, spits on it, and shines it with his shirt to reveal all of the details and carved features. Without the dirt and grime, we discover he isn't really a man at all...can't be much older than the three of us. "Good lookin' motherfucker, isn't he? Must be some Dungeons and Dragons shit." He studies it more, "Christ's abs, medieval leather pants, slicked back hair, chiseled jaw – fuck, this toy is better lookin' than I am!" Chuckling with amusement, yet the slightest bit of hostility, he hands the mini statue to Maya. "Is this our bait for the death trap?"

"Well it definitely seemed to lure you in. You just snatched that cheese faster than any mouse I've ever seen." Maya surveys the thing like a puppy would do to a small bug crawling across the floor. She crosses her arms and pops her knee as she leans all her weight *[or lack thereof]* to one side of her body, "Mhmm, he's a looker. So, yeah, rest in peace, bitch."

She tosses it back to him and as he catches it, he creates a swift mockery of his head being snapped by a mouse trap and it sends a shiver up Maya's spine. A small line forms across my face, causing him to smile at me with his pearlies that are whiter than the Swiss Alps,

"Ay, Petey, take a gander."

He tosses me the mini bloke, and I catch it with ease. The black, faded ivory is so smooth on my palms and fingertips, and the small, carved eyes peer into mine as if he's actually alive. As if he…

Just blinked.
The fuck?

"Oy, did you –" I stop myself when I realize what I'm about to ask them. *Did you see the inanimate object blink?* Of course they fucking didn't, because it didn't actually happen. The heat must be messing with my contact lenses…

Is that a thing?

I peer down again and examine the figure, and can't help but think I've seen this person before. The familiarity of his features are present and nudging at some part of my brain, but I just can't put my finger on it.

Speaking of my finger…
Fucking hell…

Fucking hell…

My face forms a grimace at a sharp pain like someone is shoving a thumbtack into my right thumb, and when I blink, I clear-cut witness the mini person's knife rise and jab deeply into my skin.

"BLOODY FUCKIN –"

I pull the chess piece out of my flesh and launch it through the air. Finneas and Maya rush to me and as they go to grab my hand, I pull it back and suck the blood that begins to seep out in a small stream down my wrist.

"The fuck happened?" I can't tell if Finn is genuinely concerned or amused. "Did it have a bug on it or some shit?"

"Was it chipped?" Oppositely, Maya's apprehensiveness is clear. "Did it prick you?"

"No – *fuck!*" I'm in minor hysterics as I search for the devil dude on the far away ground. "That bloody thing is alive!"

They look at me in disbelief, and I expected that after what I said aloud rings back into my eardrums. I sound as crazy as I feel, but that doesn't retract the fact that what just happened, in fact, *fucking happened.*

"What?" Maya glances in the direction I'm looking, and then back at my hand. "Are you saying that thing *stabbed you?"*

"Like, with its tiny-man knife…?" Finn finishes, refusing to spare the satirics.

"I know it sounds mad, but I saw it happen; I *felt* it happen!" I hold up my crimson-stained hand. "That thing –"

"I think the heat is getting to your head there, pal," Maya snickers as she steps away from me like I suddenly developed a contagious virus. "Or maybe it's the lack of nicotine in your veins. Congrats, these are normal signs; you're on your way toward recovery."

I roll my eyes aggressively, not only because this bitch reminded me of how much I need a cig, but because now upon her facetiousness, I look down to see the wound genuinely got bigger, and is spreading all the way down my hand and wrist, burning like someone poured a thick layer of salt on top.

"You think I'm making this shit up?" I throw my hand in their faces so that my oozing slice is directly in front of both of their eyes – *let the wankers see for themselves.*

Finneas takes a stifled breath and shakes his head, "You're just buggin, kid." He swats my hand away, "But get that nasty ass shit away from my eyes, it's a queezer."

"You know by bits and bobs I'm deadass, but fine."[63] An argument with these twats would be of no value. "I'm going back to the car to remedy this before it gets worse, you two stay here."

"Nope – no way," Maya bites, strutting on ahead of me. "I've wanted to leave since we got here, and I am *not* missing my boat."

I call to her, "Sorry, love, can't leave Delfin alone."

"Yeah," Finneas mocks drolly, "there are monsters out here."

She hisses back, "Then you'll have something in common."

Stellar wit.

For a moment, Sexton turns and walks on, though she quickly stops dead in her tracks as if she forgot how to use her legs.

"Peter..." she nearly whispers, "which way is the car?"

---

[63] *I try to say this every day of my life.*

Aloofly I answer, looking down at my seeping hand again, "The opposite way in which we came."

"Screw you, Sherlock, I *know* that," she snaps, turning back to me. "Let me rephrase: do you fucking *know* which way to *go?*"

"What d'you mean? It's right over –" Pushing her aside, I point directly in front of us, only to realize I am directing our eyes to absolutely nothing but near darkness. Unfathomably contrasting to the hazy, translucently gray fog in the direction toward the lights, the sight behind us became so bloody dark and thick at some point that I can hardly see two feet in front of me. If we were to start walking, for all we know we could be walking into Satan's clutches. How we failed to discover this sooner baffles all three of us – it's almost as if an invisible magician created the illusion not twenty seconds ago *literally* behind our backs, knowing we were gonna turn around to try and go back.

With my finger still outstretched, I peer around at the mirage of the vastness around me, *"For fucks sake."*

"Great." Maya bites her lip as I can tell her anxiety isn't giving her a break anytime soon. "We're gonna die out here."

"Settle down, let's not panic," *I'm totally panicking, but they don't need to know that.* I wrap my bloody hand in the fabric of my shirt, "Are there any landmarks on the ground that could help us retrace our steps? Footprints, rocks, anything?"

"Guys…" Finn's voice springs up out of the mist like a ghost, or rather like he's seen a ghost, as he points down to our left, "isn't that…"

To all of our horror, upon the ground sits the same figurine I threw with all my might into the nothingness. We freeze, as if one move will set the world on fire.

The only thing that moves, though just barely, is Maya's mouth, "How could you possibly know it's the same one?"

"It's clean," I answer shrewdly.

"What?"

Finneas continues, reassuring me that I am on the same page as he is, "I used my shirt to clean it off and there's no way in the deep, dark depths of hell that anything out here would be clean; and that, Sexton, is *squeaky.*" His voice is frantic yet he is unmoving, like someone is pointing a gun at his head. "Petey, didn't you –"

"Rocket launch the fuck out of it? Indeed I did."

"So how did it get back to…"

He trails off, and none of us dare speak – only stare at the uncanny mystery that is this chess piece thing. I told them that it was alive, and I truly didn't want to believe it as much as they didn't believe me in general, but now…

Now this is fucking enthralling.

I'm terrified, yet so insatiably curious that it's suddenly eating me alive, so I break the spell we're all in and head straight for the little cursed statue. I pay no mind to the warnings and shouts of caution from Maya and Finneas, who clearly must believe what I saw now, and I bend quickly to pick up the figurine. I turn it so the bloke's face is turned up at me, and as I hold it in my hand, immediately the black ivory is painted with my crimson blood.

I study it closely,
and just before I look away,

He smiles at me.

CHAPTER fourteen

Peter Green
Somewhere ... Present Day

Instead of dropping it, I stare into the little fucker's carved out eyes with the same electricity and fierceness I presented the mermaid back when I was sixteen, and peak my trusty eyebrow with authority. The peculiarity of this situation is abruptly euphoric again as I hold this mini treasure in my hand, which appears as if I stuck it in a pail of red paint as my blood soaks every inch of it now.

When I do break eye contact, it's to anxiously take in the space surrounding me as the entire earth begins to rumble ferociously. Even the heavy rocks beneath recreate the weight of light dust in the sudden heavy wind, and I shield my face as it all engulfs me like a tornado of sharp gravel. Sound fades and muffles, and before I can turn to Maya and Finneas, I feel my chest contort and my breathing become heavier; and little by little, damn near impossible. I've felt this feeling too many times now in the recent months, and I'm beginning to wonder when it'll be the last and my lungs finally concede.

Terrifyingly too soon, it becomes laborious to make out even one mere coherent thought, and my insides begin to feel like Hercules is slowly ripping them apart little by little, from my organs to my bones. My eyes roll back in agony and my ears ring like they're made of liberty bells...but still, I dare not let go of the mini man...

I can't let go.
I want to...hell, I even try to...but something won't let me.
My fucking soul won't let me...
What the fuck is happening?

Cryptically, as if the sun decided to retire, everything around me goes completely black, and once again, I could swear to God I'm dying. The fact that I am completely aware of every sense during this potential death sequence is bloody petrifying, and to be completely blunt, not the way I would've chosen to go in the slightest. The air around me turns crisp, sharply biting at my skin and inner chest as it completely differs from the sticky humidity seconds prior. My pupils frantically dilate as they try to conform to this abrupt change of scene, and my ears ring intensely at the deafening silence. I try to call out to Maya and Finn, but it's as if my vocal chords have been cut out – no sound escapes my mouth. The more I try to speak, the less I can breathe. It's almost as if I'm…

Underwater.
No. No. No.

It's not until I finally come onto this epiphany, that I feel the sensation of my limbs frantically treading water inadvertently. In the deep depths of a pitch black, undersea abyss, I am immediately transferred back to the dreaded night at the docks on my sixteenth birthday when I was attacked – softly then savagely – by a…*something.*

'A something'…
*I say that as if I'm not **damn certain** what it was.*

To this very day, I have kept that mysterious and impossibly sensuous experience closeted *entirely*. Even as much as I try to tell myself it never happened, the permanent scars that are carved into my lower abdomen make it pretty damn difficult; not to mention, this here all too similar drowning palooza happening right now is making it rather hopeless to ignore the trauma even more so.

I flail my legs and arms, and do everything humanly
– *and what feels like inhumanly* – possible to break the
surface, but it appears as if I'm stuck in a bubble, a hold, or in
a forcefield of something or other. I can't help but scream
inside as the same vicious thought pollutes my head like a
broken record:

*How much longer do I have until my lungs give out and
disappear; and I with them?*

Low and behold, just when I feel like things couldn't
get any worse…

Of course.
Just my luck…
I don't want to admit it, but it's inevitable.
She *is inevitable.*
Her grace and beauty is unmatched.
There she fucking is.
The something…
The siren.

✏ ✏ ✏

she's bAAAAaaack

"Hello, darling boy."

My chest immediately begs for the last of the air I
was desperately holding onto for dear life as it is mercilessly
yanked away from me at the sight of my lifelong demon
temptress placed in front of my very eyes again. More than
anything, I want to pretend she isn't real – to deny her
majestic ability to lure my eyes to places they shouldn't go,
but I can't…and worst of all, she knows that I'm thinking it
too. I never had to physically speak for her to hear my every
word, whether I liked the concept or not.

It's always been the latter.

Selfishly, I use the mystic grace her aura provides to steady my batshit breathing and, closing my burning eyes securely, yell through my mind and imaginary gritted teeth,

Leave me the hell alone.
You're not real.

> *"You know that's not true.*
> *Dearest, I come in peace."*

Bullshit. Rank at its finest.
Just tear my skin apart again
and then my soul while you're at it.
I fucking dare you.

> *"I suppose we got off on the wrong foot."*

You don't even have feet.
Oh, and you mean when you seduced me
against my will, and then attacked me
when you almost got fucking caught?
*Yeah. I'd say the **wrong** foot definitely*
checks right the hell out.

> *"I never meant to hurt you."*

I scoff.
Classic line.

> *"I assure you, your grace, I was not*
> *aware of ... of whose presence I was within. "*

I Prefer Peter

What the hell are you getting on about?

> *"I feel unworthy*
> *to forbear the tale,*
> *but let's just say*
> *you are among the*
> *chosen, boy."*

Piss off. Stop talking to me like that.
Leave me alone, siren.
You've done enough –

> *"If you choose to hold unbelief,*
> *Uncover the truth yourself."*

All at once, every single part of me explodes in pain. I feel like the strongest men alive are taking hold of both my arms and legs, and stretching them out like taffy until every tendon is where it shouldn't be. My lungs writhe and my head spins until I feel like I may be sick. The water I'm immersed in grows somehow ice cold and scorching hot all at the same time, bubbling and boiling as if I am a raw veggie on a stove being turned into mush for a soup, and making my skin feel like it's melting and seizing simultaneously. Once again the space around me goes dark and silent, and I'm not sure if I'm just blacking out or if I'm about to meet my Maker, but what I do know for certain, is that right now, I am completely alone.

CHAPTER fifteen

Peter Green
Somewhere Over the ?

The warmth of a new sun attacks my sleepy eyelids, and if you were to ask me, I would swear on my life that I am five feet away from the bloody thing. I lift my arm and bend it to shield my face, shading my eyes and squinting them open to get a view of where the fuck I am. Once they adjust to the light, my brows are practically sewn together at the obscene sights producing all too bonafide flashbacks of being high as shit...

The Earth's sky, as society knows it, is a clagged, faded baby blue, crowded with cumulus or cumulonimbus clouds that we shape into animals or other common nouns in a casual game of iSpy, right? Or, in other cases, some may refer to them as 'cotton candy' or 'whipped cream' *(at least I do)*[64]...But upon opening my lookers, I become overwhelmed with the rarest, most exquisitely vibrant royal blue sky I could never have even imagined – it was as if the sea was taken and glued into the air, and then God went in to do some edits and bumped up the saturation. Mingling with the same vibe, the clouds among them are not only white as snow, but so damn fluffy, that I'm certain I could jump up and take a cat nap on any one of my choosing and have the best sleep of my life.

....But then this is where shit gets weird:

Just as a cloud may well-nigh resemble an elephant, a rabbit, or what-have-you, what I am taking in *genuinely* could

---

[64] *At least I DO...*

have been cut out with cookie cutters to be the spitting images of a full ass moving animals. To my left is a school of birds soaring beautifully in the sky, a turtle gliding to the breeze's rhythm, a rabbit hopping along a stratus shaped cloud while a dog wags its tail as he watches, sharks and fish doing flips and twirls as if they are dancing with each other in the water – *I could go on for ages.* It's like an animated picture show is happening right above me, and as completely bonkers as I sound, *it's impossible to make this up.*

What's more, is that the tree above me is not just a lemon tree – it's a *lemon tree.* Instead of branches and vines, I am shaded by the freshest, ripest, brightest yellow lemon slices I've ever laid my eyes on. All of the slivers are arranged in such an artistic way, but they all have a place; and it appears each of them knows exactly just where that place is. The fragrance is fresh and therapeutic, and it isn't until the aroma hits my nostrils that I realize I am laying in a field of tall green grass and lemon halves masquerading as flowers. As I peer around, I also see the same thing with other fruits, such as limes, oranges, apricots, and some fascinating fruits I have never seen before.

Afraid I may be making lemonade with my ass, I shoot up and see I somehow haven't damaged even a small itty bit of the section of grass and fruit I was laying in – it's almost as if I hadn't been there at all. Curiosity getting the best of me, I decide to carry on and make my way around the girthy tree trunk, only to stumble upon what has to be one of the trippiest things I have ever seen…

*And I have gotten stoned **a lot.***

More than a thousand different colored eyes, some colored in a hue I have never even conceived before, are burning their way into my soul as they make up an ascending glass staircase leading up to God knows what.

*I guess you could say...it's a **stare**-case...*
If this is a trip, I'm fuckin' hilarious.
As they blink at me in unison, I blink back at them.
They blink twice more, I swallow hard and blink three times.
This pattern continues for the longest fucking ten seconds of
my life.

I look around me for reassurance that what I'm seeing is, in fact, reality, though there is no one to gather reassurance from.

"Finneas?" My voice sounds foreign in this unfamiliar place, though it's all I hear echoing back through the variety of citrus trees. "Maya?" The breeze tussles my hair and I sigh as I run my fingers through it, feeling the warmth of the sun's rays heating up every strand. I am completely alone in this wonderland of curiosity, and I have no bloody idea where this tornado of a day has blown me ...

But Toto, I don't think we're in Kansas anymore.

I'm assuming there's nowhere to go but up, because The eyes brood at me with uncomfortable anticipation, so I begin my climb up the stare-way to Heaven...or hell – *who's to say, really?* – and I feel my knees quaking beneath me with every step. The transparent glass steps are thick and sturdy; a glossy, crystal overcoating added for support, though my overactive mind can't help but imagine one of my treads being a little too heavy footed and the whole staircase shattering and plummeting. The higher I go, the more the stare-way extends behind me, as if it's convincing me it's far better to continue upwards than to trudge all the way back down. I see the earth below me become farther and farther as I ascend, and my god-forsaken lungs heave with anxiety.

I've never been afraid of heights – or of many things, for that matter – but the more glimpses I catch of the far away surface below, the more ants that crawl along my skin. My entire body begins to shake, and my heart pounds like a heavy metal kick drum in my throat. My breathing escalates into a minor hyperventilation as the vertigo kicks in, and everything my eyes are perceiving starts to stretch and distort around me. My brain fogs and begins to spin like a broken carousel, and all at once my eyes force themselves shut and I fall.

Down.
Down.
Down the glass steps to what I believe will be my death...
But then I *stop.*
Seriously, I am so unkillable.[65]

As if I've reached a platform landing, my descending body comes to an abrupt halt. I hold my head to keep it from falling the fuck off, let out a few hacks as my lungs feel they've tripled in size and are suffocating me like I swallowed a stuffy, and I gather my bearings before opening my eyes to witness that I am flying...sort of.

I look down to see that I have landed on a small slab of emerald green grass just big enough to hold me, which I assume was ripped out of the ground upon lift off. It smells so strongly of lemon that it's almost as if a cleaning product was used to water it, and it's solid despite floating in mid-air. Still, the vertigo and obnoxious scent is mercilessly causing me to tremble like a winter leaf and allude to soon becoming high.

Not complaining about that second one, though.
I could use something to take the edge off.

---

[65] *You're welcome, buddy.*

The stare-way has gone from its normal thirty degree angle to looking like one of those *moving-walkway-flat-escalator-things* you see at the airport that make you feel like you're walking at the speed of a baby cheetah...

Except made of eyes and glass, of course.

In fact, unless it's my lack of vision and oxygen deceiving me, I'm almost positive it is one of those bloody things.

Unable to shake off feeling like I've had seven straight shots of vodka, I begin crawling, allowing the see through conveyor belt to carry my weight high above the ground. Unfortunately, looking down is inevitable in this position, so due to the fact that there are no railings and I would honestly rather jump to my death than touch one of these eyeballs, I soon revert to closing my own eyes, more scared-stiff than I've been in ages *(and that's saying a lot in lieu of recent events)*.

I huddle down on the glass rectangles, "God..." my voice shakes as I pray foolishly to someone I'm not quite certain gives a shit about me, "either take me now, or *please* get me the hell out of here."

A few minutes that feels like a few hours go by as I revert to my painful yet strangely comforting coping mechanism I've developed to ground me in stressful situations – scratching my left hand to death with my right's nails – and all too suddenly, I feel my stomach begin to meet my chest.

We must be landing.
Thanks, Big Man.[66]

---

[66] *Jesus always has your back, friends.*

Reluctantly, I open my eyes and look down to see the most fascinating town I have ever laid my eyes on, and then I'm descending before the world turns black again.

CHAPTER sixteen
Finneas Scott
??? ...

Where the goddamn fucking shit am I?

I wake up in a bed that definitely ain't mine, but I will say, it is mighty snugg. I sit up to not only discover I have spent the night in a very bougie ass lookin hut, but also catch Maya sleeping like a curled up kitten in an identical bed across the room. After stretching my limbs out, I snatch my phone from my pocket so I can do a little testie-test to see if it's got any juice left so I can try and get a clue of where the hell I am…but alas, no dice.

Sketchy af.

I swing my legs over the side of this queen size bed of royals, and am quickly attacked with goosebumps crawling up my shins and thighs as my bare feet hit the cold, dark wood. I don't recall taking my shoes off, so the services here must either be high stars, or extensively into feet…

I tiptoe over to Half-Pint, afraid if I make too much noise some sort of warden will come and take away my new bed privileges, and I place my hand on her delicate shoulder and shake her gingerly,

"Maya…" I whisper with haste, "Maya, wake up."

She budges not.

Due to being in a house with her for years, I am well aware that this chick sleeps deeper than the fucking Atlantic ocean, though my eyes still circle their lids and I silently make my way back over to my socks neatly laid next to my bed and bring one directly in front of her itty bitty button nose.

Maya breathes in the sweaty scent of adventure my foot has seeped into the cotton while tucked inside my leather boot,

"Jesus Christ –" She scurries back as she covers the lower part of her face with her hand, inches away from taking a plunge off the side of the bed.

"In the flesh! And a good morning to you too, dollface!" I present her a handsome, radiant pair of pearly whites as I shake my sock in the air before tossing it back across the room onto the floor *[semi near]* where I found it. "Though, if I were the Son of God, I think I would have some idea of where the fuck we is."

Maya scans the room and I can see her sleepy head's wheels beginning to churn. The mighty many hairs on her arms that her body constantly supplies to keep her boney ass warm stand up like porcupine quills, and her long skeletal fingers run along the back of her neck.

"Did we get kidnapped?" Her voice is barely audible, so I practically have to read her lips.

"Hell if I know." I look around again as if to find a clue of some sort. "My phone is a bust, and unfortunately, Martha Washington, you don't *have one."*

She defends herself in a harsh whisper, "Social media and the calculator app were detrimental to my health, you dickshit!"

"Yeah, well, so is your brain, but don't go smashing it with a hammer like you did your main source of communication to the world, mkay?" She narrows her face at me, and I begin walking toward the tent's exit.

"No!" Maya's *tentative-but-louder-now-whisper-scream* causes me to turn back to her. "You have no idea what's out there!"

"Couldn't be any stranger than what we've endured already, can it?"

And yet, before my hand reaches the curtain to pull it back, the sunlight blinds me until my dilated vision settles and allows me to make out a pair of piercing, sterling silver eyes. As I blink profusely, my own lookers dart to and fro as I realize I am face to face with a fox, who happens to be standing up straight like a man and dressed in a full suit. Every part of my body freezes, as I take him *(...it?...them? the pronouns are still uncertain...)* in.

"Ah, nice to see you're awake," his voice is smooth and hospitable, like a good guy character you'd see in *Narnia* or some shit.[67] He's got an accent from somewhere I can't pinpoint, but it's sure as shit ain't from anywhere close. He continues speaking *(speaking!),* "The third of you is in the courtyard, but I'm afraid he's a bit disoriented and could assuredly use a familiar face. I don't think encountering a talking fox was on his to-do list today."

At the mention of Peter, my body tenses and the hair on the back of my neck stands, as I register we haven't seen him since the entire world went completely dark. Not assisting the anxiety coursing through my veins, Maya screams like someone just told her she ate twelve hamburgers in her sleep, practically flying her little body over and into the beautifully carved, victorian style armoire on the opposite side of the room.

Clearly, seeing an animal-man today wasn't on her to-do list either.

---

[67] *Narnia has been my favorite thing since I was a kid. If it weren't for that franchise existing, I would've never taken fencing, which nearly took me to the olympics; nor would I have learned how to do a British accent. So cheers to that.*

As for me, I am too stunned, spooked, and yet simultaneously too hella curious to move, and though I wanna scream like she did, it's as if I've forgotten how to function completely; so I just stand there gaping at this creature with my heart practically pounding in my eyeballs.

His soot gray suit is tailored perfectly to his slim size, the color bringing out his animalistic yet synchronously welcoming eyes; and due to the fact that his head, hands, and feet are also that of a fox's, I can't help but wonder – *in the most respectful and not 'I'm envisioning this animal-man naked' way possible* – if the rest of his body identifies as the same.

His sport-coat covers an Italian silk, buttoned up baby pink vest, coating a white tuxedo collared shirt; and like a pretty present to hold everything together, a bow tie is fastened perfectly around his neck to complete the ensemble – *it ain't one of those clip on piece of shits either.*

His burnt sienna hair *(or...fur...)* is coiffed as if he's got a team of girlies brushing it back into place every time the wind blows, and the rest of it all over him is finely trimmed and smooth.

This fox must have regular appointments at the groomer or somethin'.

"You're a fox…" Is all I can manage to yank out of my vocal chords.
"Thanks, and you're not too bad yourself."

Why the fuck did I just blush.

He continues, and the reality of this situation becomes more strange and impossible the longer I bask in the wild presence of this…wild animal, "My name is Felix

O'Carson, but please call me Felix.[68] If you would be so kind as to come with me –"

"Hey, whoa, whoa, time out, zippy canine man," I force my voice not to shake and pretend I'm in a video game or some shit where this could be potential normality. "It would *be so kind,*" I mock his foreign accent, "if you would tell us where da hell we are first, for *fox* sake…" I trail off a bit at the end, cause I gots no idea if this animal is tame or would claw my eyes out despite his friendliness thus far. Nonetheless, I couldn't help the pun, even though I'm sure he doesn't hear the end of that joke.

To my relief, Felix gives a chuckle to my witticism and eases my fear as he slightly bows, "My utmost apologies." *I refuse to show it, but I shamelessly forgive him immediately.* "Welcome to Paragon. I'll be happy to answer all of your questions in due time, as I'm sure you will have quite an ample amount. Might I ask your name before we set out?"

"Fuckin hell…" I absentmindedly ignore his question and lean in to check if what's appearing in front of my eyes is, in fact, real, "how the shit are you talking?"

The fox chuckles as if he isn't phased by my curiosity, but amused. "Your vocabulary is quite colorful, Mr…?"

"Scott. Finneas Scott," my name slides off my tongue like a slutty used condom.

"Finneas," but my name slides off his tongue like honey butter. "Like I said, all your questions will soon be answered, but you just have to come with me for the sake, or, should I say the *'fox sake'* of your friend." *What a card.* "It

---

[68] *Fun Fact: When I first started writing this book, I promised my boyfriend at the time I would name the talking fox after him…and so I did…But you never hear the last name said again. I'm a woman of my word.*

will be more beneficial to explain everything to you all at
once. Agreed?"

Before I can agree or disagree, Maya's voice erupts
like a volcano, though it is semi comically muffled behind
closeted coats, "Why in the ever flying *fuck* would anyone in
their right mind follow a fox, let alone a *talking* fox,
anywhere? What is this, the fucking *Chronicles of Narnia?*
Who the hell do you think we are? Fuck off, rat face!"

Least we're in the same headspace with the Narnia thing.

I assume Felix is used to this kind of first impression
meeting, because he lets out another small snicker and runs his
hairy fingers through his coif. His teeth are sharp and
surprisingly pearly white, and it isn't until now I notice his
nose is wet like a healthy pup.

Are we in Heaven?
Maybe hell?
I don't remember learning about fox men in Sunday school.

"That's Maya..." I use my thumb to point behind me
toward the closet. "She's not much into the *Stranger Things*
shit that's been happening to us in the last 24 hours."

"Well," he whispers, "unfortunately for your friend, I
likely will not be the strangest thing she sees all day." He runs
his hands along his jacket, which is somehow in no need of a
lint roller whatsoever...and looks past me at the Maya filled
armoire. He then meets my gaze again, "How about I step out
and let you two take a moment, and I'll be back in five.
Agreed?"

I nod, taken aback at the gentleman-like hospitality of
some stranger who hardly knows us two juvenile scumbags. I
mean Christ, we basically just treated him no better than a
Jehovah's Witness coming to our door, and yet we're still

yapped to as if honorable guests of some sort. Felix gives one more quick glance at the closet, offers me a slight nod and a friendly smile as if to say *'best of luck with her'*, and then turns and makes his way through the curtain.

Feeling like I just got punk'd,[69] I keep my eyes fixed on the same spot the fox was standing as if he's still there. "He's gone," I say, and I hear the closet door creak open.

"Finneas, we need to get out of here," Maya squeaks, still in whisper mode.

"Yeah, no shit…" I finally unglue my gaze from its spot at the curtain's opening and approach an *even more traumatized than before* Half-Pint. "But where is *here* though? I have no clue where the fuck we is, let alone where to turn tail and run. We could be anywhere on God's green Earth right now." I run my hand along the new growing stubble on my chin, and then tightly along my eyelids until I see stars. I'm too fazed to think of a plan, so I accept my fate. "Look, I mean, he seems like a nice guy –"

"He's a fucking *fox,* you dickshit –"

"But he's got Peter," my harsh whisper cuts her off. She shifts her weight back and forth between knees, apprehension radiating off of her like a virus. "I don't care if he's Pete Davidson, I'm following that animal man."[70]

"Why? It's not like we owe Peter anything."

This chick.

I gape at her and inwardly scoff at the audacity of her words. "You seem to be regretfully misinformed, but I owe this kid my life, if not at least a kidney…or a lung, in his case.

---

[69] *Anyone? The MTV prank show with Ashton Kutcher? Are ya too young for that?*

[70] *I don't have much more to say about this.*

He may have halfway been the reason we've gotten out of one hell and into another, but shoot, this is the most alive I've felt in God knows how long." She stares right through me like she's still waiting for an answer that solidifies my point. I sigh, knowing there ain't nothin' I can say that'll hit this stubborn ass's target, so I try the one thing I know she doesn't want to hear, "He's one of us, girlie. We'z a team now. He's the closest thing to family we've got." She looks at nothing particular on the floor, and I assume I tugged at some sort of string in that lukewarm heart of hers because the tension in her shoulders lets up a tad. She knows I'm right…and that Petey is one helluva son-uva. "So!" I clap my hands, causing her to flinch out of her sea of thought. "I'm gonna head out with mister fox man to salvage what's left of Greenie while I still can, cause I ain't attempting to escape this potential eternal damnation without him. Whether you pull up your saggy big girl pants and join me or pussy out is up to you, doll."

I didn't notice until now, but the gloss in Maya's eyes has thickened as I've been blabbin', and as it hazes over her pupils, tears begin to stream across her lower eyelid. She's trying everything in her being to hold them back from pouring down her cheeks, and my heart wrenches at the thought of her being scared shitless into silence, especially as someone who physically can't ever shut the fuck up.

"Aw, heya now…" My tone shifts as I gingerly put my hands on her shoulders. "Know this, kid: no matter what happens, I gotchu, yeah?" At that, a single tear rushes down to her chin. I know she despises crying, so to savor her pride, I pay no mind to it with words but still swiftly wipe it with my thumb to comfort her subconscious. Maya puts on a strong front on the daily, but she's a fragile thing, this one – she'll die before she admits it though. "I won't let anything happen to you, sis. Without you, I'd have no one to rag on daily." She subtly smirks at me because she knows it's true, and that the feeling is mutual. "Now let's get Peter so we can get the hell out of these wherezabouts."

I playfully lick my palm and go to fix her bedhead, and though she instinctively ducks away from me in disgust, she can't help but surrender a small giggle as well. We lace up our shoes and head out the curtain with Felix the Fox, with the warmth of the sun baking our skin and guiding us into a whole new fucking world.

CHAPTER seventeen

Peter Green
I DON'T FUCKING KNOW

I keep waking up like this...

When my eyes shoot open again, I wait for the blurriness of my vision to clear as the murmurs swimming around me filter from a muffled tunneled haze, to obnoxiously chaotic and directly above me. I think I'm sitting on a bed of multicolored peacock feathers underneath a massive umbrella...*(and I say 'massive' as in the size of an 80 foot white oak tree)*...but oh, no sir, it isn't an actual tree. It is, in fact, *a literally fucking umbrella* in it's entirety, shading me as a tree *should be.*

A plethora of different accents from somewhere I couldn't pinpoint if my life depended on it fill my ears, and right now as my vision finally fully focuses, I'm beginning to think that it might.

"He's so gorgeous!"

"Where did you find him?"

"Ditch the intruder!"

"Mommy, can we keep him?"

"He looks so...used."

"How did he get here?"

"Someone go find Gideon!"

"He smells like an ashtray."

"Is he a corporeal?"

"Are there more of them?"

My mind twists as I find myself surrounded by the most peculiar looking creatures I have ever seen in my life, and I immediately wonder if after all of the jokes and alludes, I somehow 'Jobed' my way into hell.

There is an elephant peering down at me with not a single wrinkle on her leather skin. She is smooth and frankly looks rather expensive, if I must say, like her skin may have been handmade from a skilled craftsman in Italy or something. Not only that, but a brown bear with a top-hat is cleaning an old fashioned monocle with the hands of a human, peering down at me through the foggy circular glass. His feet are that of a human's as well, but the animal's eyes that blend in with his coat of fur do not look in the least bit threatening...rather almost concerned...compassionate, even.

I've been high before, but shit...
Not even my altered brain chemistry could make up madness such as this.

There is a baby pink pig with featherlike wings hovering directly above my head with a puzzled expression as if *I'm* the strange one, and a woman whose skin is so powdery white, I could swear she is a vampire without her even opening her mouth to grin. There is a nearly transparent younger boy to my right, who I wouldn't have noticed at all if it weren't for the fact that his 1920's style clothes are fully perceptible, and that there is a brilliantly illuminated ring floating above his head like some sort of halo. Another similarly see through small lass stands beside him in the same old fashioned clothing, though slightly older; a halo also resting just above her tangled *'all play, no work'* curly golden hair.[71]

I have no doubt these odd people-or-whatsits read the racing thoughts I had no problem etching with bold lines across my face, because a woman who appears as if she is a living, breathing porcelain doll that would shatter the second she moves, smiles at me with tiny cupid lips and candy apple cheeks as she expresses enthusiastically,

"Hi! Welcome to Paragon!"

And, like any normal human being would, I scream my fine, bloody ass off and scurry my aching body as far up the feather bed as I can. I curse and scream until my lungs feel like they disappear, and some of the creatures hold their hands *(and when I say hands, I also mean hooves, paws, stubs...etc)* over their ears and roll their eyes, while others try and do their best to hush me gently, assuring me there's *'no reason to be frightened'*...

Oh is that right, woman with an actual button for a nose? I can give you some fucking good reasons to fright.

A hipster looking man in a tailored suit who is discombobulating my entire depiction of reality as he is appearing to have the head and limbs of a humanlike fox, calmly strides up to the scene and whispers something in the doll's ear. His storm cloud eyes meet mine, and somehow they don't quite get me caught in their cyclone, but rather intrigue and welcome me.

---

[71] *The people of Paragon were so damn fun to create – their strange world, too. It was a wild brain exercise for me – thinking, 'how far can I stretch my imagination for this story?' and I would do my best to exceed my own expectations*

His smirk is all humane as he speaks, "Easy, easy." He reaches his…*paw*…out to me, and since I can't be pressed up against the *umbrella-tree-trunk-pole* anymore than I already am, I freeze, hoping the infamous *'maybe if I stand statue-still, they won't see me'* method is a success. I stare at his outstretched gesture like it's a gun pointed straight to my chest and his finger is on the ready trigger.
Alas, my body trembles, and they can all see me clear as day.

"We're not gonna hurt you, boy," the fox reassures me gently. "You can trust us."

I look around again at all of the strangeness that simply has to be a hallucinatory episode, and a small bear cub with a backwards baseball hat and a sweater vest peers up at me smiling. He nods in reassurance with the fox's words, and every bit of my sanity seems to vanish into thin air. I attempt a smile back at him, but I think I look like I'm about to barf because he backs away to his mum fairly quickly.

My voice is raw and it feels like a million tiny needles are clawing up my esophagus, "What in the *fuck* are you?" I loathe appearing weak, but I am outnumbered and frankly, scared out of my ever-loving mind. "What're you gonna do to me? I don't have any money, I'm just passing through, I –"

"Whoa, easy now! We're good guys, we mean no harm!" The fox's tone is insistent; his arm is still extended. "Apologies if I am mistaken, but you are not alone, are you?"

I catch my breath briefly, trying to push down the bile rising in my throat due to extreme anxiety and attempting to excuse the fact that an animal who is obscenely better looking than most men I know is speaking to me. "No, but I lost my –"

Friends?
Are they my friends?

*Fate really had to choose **this** very moment to make me determine this factuality?*

I brush off the hundredth momentary mental conversation with myself and continue, "I lost 'em (*I go with "em' to be safe*) a while back, but to be honest, I don't remember much or how long we've been separated." My breathing quickens again, and my mind shifts immediately – it's doing loop-de-loops with my stomach. Again I ask breathlessly, "What the fuck are you?"

> "I'm exactly what I look like."
> "A fox?"
> "Ah, so you've heard of me."

Cocky, pricky thing, isn't he?

> "Once or twice…Don't recall the ability to talk being in your anatomy, though."
> He smirks. "Your friends are housed comfortably in one of our finest yurts," *I guess he took the load off me and decided they are my mates…alright then.* "Allow me to retrieve them and we can all get acquainted."

I don't have the foggiest what a yurt is, but at least Maya and Finneas are alive. He walks away with haste, and I sit up to a massive distortion of my vision as my stomach churns and chest dry heaves. I cough for what seems to be the first time in God knows how long, and it definitely does not go unnoticed by the crowd around me. The things of all kinds step back in caution, as I throw my head forward to unleash the phlegm that has been piling up while I was knocked out. Thankfully I don't vomit, although I really want to.

Gotta keep it classy.

After a centauric hybrid of a stunning naked woman with stripes on her skin, a perfect feminine torso transitioning into a lower half mimicking a beautifully groomed tiger, and fiery red hair flowing down past her hourglass hips brings me a jug of water to ease the burning in my throat, my heart rate mildly slows and the sweat on my forehead begins to dissipate. Though I'm still feeling aftershocks of distressing panic, the symptoms are beginning to decrease as I gulp down the liquid. The water is sweet as it touches my chapped lips, as if it has a hint of honey or was infused with ripe fruits I've never tasted. It tingles my tongue and feels like pure magic as it slides down my throat, first with force, and then with ease as the dehydration begins to quench.

"Thank you," I finally croak as I hand back the empty pitcher. I clear my throat again, "What happened? Where am I? What are –"

"All your questions will soon be answered," the tiger lady says, gently pushing my shoulders so I lay down. "Just try to be still and rest. You took quite the dive back in the garden."

"That was *real?*" I say this more to myself than anything. I could swear I've been dreaming this entire chaotic cycle of events like some sort of manic fever dream…and I'm going to believe that for as long as I can.

"Everything is more real here than anywhere, boy," the sophisticated bear says in an indistinguishable accent. "Look around yuh. Pinch yourself, if you need."

"Can I pinch him?"

A hearty smack from what I assume was a mother bear followed this small, distant lassie voice, and I chuckle for the first time since waking.
It feels out of place mixed with all of the emotions swirling through my gut…but refreshing, nonetheless.

I look around, trying to fully rationalize my surroundings and guess what year everything is set up to be portraying…but I quickly conclude it's utterly impossible. Pinpointing one specific era is clearly not the vision whoever designed this place had in mind.

Fine, luxury tents – which I take it are the *yurts* – line up in the distance; though neighboring them are what look like exquisitely built 'tiny houses' like the ones you see on HGTV. I spot a well near a lake for what seems to be for washing clothes, but not far from it is a small theater that looks like it was plucked directly out of the 50's. It's not a massive town, though I can tell by the looks of where I am currently, it isn't very tiddly either…

Everything seems to contradict itself in an almost comedic, whimsical sort of way; or as an alternative, be excessively literal, that it's perfectly absurd.[72] From all of the weird-ass shit altering my brain chemistry right here, right now; back to the *stare*-way, the *lemon* tree, the cookie cutter clouds…

It's like I've stumbled into an alternate reality.

So…do *some* use technology, while the others by contrast light candles and use a pony-trolly service for communication? Do they have telephones? What is their main source of transportation, if any other than walking? Are children addicted to their iPads and parents constantly checking their emails, or is that outdated? Or not *even* dated yet…? Are they aware of my world, and what goes on in it? Or does it stop at the newest landmark here?

---

[72] *I got a lot of the inspiration for Paragon from Big Fish and Miss Peregrine's Home for Peculiar Children*

SO many fucking questions; my head is whirling.
This place is all sorts of mismatched.
It's like everyone had a say in what got built, and everyone
agreed on whatever the fuck it was.
It's like a plethora of generations shoved into one quaint town.

Reclaiming my attention is the dapper fox man
making his way back toward the group I'm shamelessly still
cowering from. Finneas and Maya timidly walk a few inches
behind him, thankfully *not* giving the impression that they've
been tortured and/or bitten by these wild beastie nightmare
ordeals, so that's *jolly good.* Ignoring the nausea and warping
vision; relieved to my core and without hesitation, I spring up
and practically fly over to my *friends* at supersonic speed...

I nearly reduce myself to hugging them.
But I do not.
For I do not ever hug.

"Thank Christ, Greenie." Finn knows full well I'm
not a hugger, so he pats my shoulder and holds my face in his
hands in a motherly manner. *Good chap.* "You alright?" I
don't know how to respond to this question, so I just nod; but I
have no doubt my eyes aren't matching my answer.
"You look like hell," Maya can't help but point out,
and normally I would counteract with a brilliantly witty and
superbly sarcastic remark, but I can't help but agree with her
for once.
"Nice to see you too," I blankly retort instead. The
sun begins to mercilessly attack my pale face, as I am used to
feeling thin, icy air this time of year, and I anxiously look
around us as my mind riles up again, "Tell me, lads, are you
high as shit right now? *Please* tell me I'm high as shit right
now because I *think* I am, in fact, high as *shit* right now!" I let
out a strained, semi-maniacal laugh as I tear my fingers

through my tangled, wind swept hair. Maya bites the inside of her thumb and nods frantically in response, as if speaking will cause her to dissipate into thin air.

"If we are," Finn whispers, "this must be a pretty gnarly trip, man, I just saw a zebra with polka dots and a leopard with stripes screwin' in the lemon fields."

I let out a hushed, rebutted guffaw at even the sheer thought of that. Everything that is happening is so unhinged and unbelievable, that the three of us *all have to be* tripping off our tops right now...or we have heat stroke...*or both.*

"Glad to see we are all reconciled," the friendly fox man breaks up our druggy pow wow. "The journey to Paragon can be arduous for outsiders, and I have no doubt you three have oodles of questions...as do we," he says this last part under his breath, yet smiles and puts a hand...*paw?*...on my back. "Shall we?"

He guides us back to the peacock feathered bed I woke up in, and as spaced and cocked-up as I and everything is...to be honest, I'm just happy I'm not alone anymore.

CHAPTER eighteen

Peter Green
Paragon....?

"Is this some sort of L.A.R.P thing you freaks have going on?" Maya is not only keeping her cool, but also her bearings still on the ground somehow, as she rubs the fur on the ears of a runted bear cub with a sweater vest and round glasses. The lass is completely oblivious to the mumma bear eyeing her every move with high alert, but favorably it's obvious enough to the mother that she means no harm in her delicate touch. Frankly, I can't gather if Maya's just busying herself and trying to withhold a panic attack like Finn and I are, or if she genuinely believes these are just average people with an expensive hobby. "I've seen better," she shrugs, "but kudos on the realistic costumes and for getting the kiddos so involved – I'll at least give you that."

She seems to send the *apparently-not-L.A.R.Pers'* into utter confusion, and it's quite clear they have become offended – it appears as though she just insulted each and every one of their intelligences all at once.

"I beg your pardon?" A momma bear nearly roars from behind the little cub.

"Well, c'mon," she retreats back in our direction near the bed and looks around, gesturing to the massive group apprehensively, "you're furries or some-shit, right?"

It was then I truly realized that the ability Maya has to both purposefully and accidentally piss off an entire room so damn quickly, is beyond comprehensible.
A superpower at this point.

Thankfully, Felix gives her an amicable chuckle instead of burning her at the stake or performing some sort of role play blasphemy ritual. "Why don't you sit, sweetheart. You're gonna eat your tongue *and* your foot if you keep going."

"Ooh, that'll be her first meal in weeks!"

A hyena to the far left, or might I say *high*-ena, considering he looks like something out of the alleys of New York where I used to roam, derangedly roars with laughter at his jibe and I have to say, it took everything in me not to join him. Maya glares at him and forms a shot-gun with her fingers and mimes shooting him in the scruffy face.

"Hush now, Henry," a burly, commanding voice fills the air, resulting in giggly Henry Hyena cowering away like a guilty puppy who just peed on the rug. Honestly, I would've done the same if my mind wasn't spaciously wondering if all of the creatures in this place I'm fever dreaming have alliterations for names. Though, pulling me from my thoughts, eyes as black as the night nearly tear the soul from my body as they look into mine. I notice a golden ring around his pupils, and the longer I stare, the more his eyes look like a planet I've never seen, but wish I lived on.

Damn my overactive poetic brain, shut the fuck up.

"Now, Benjamin, was it?"

My eyes dart up and down the creature as I attempt to take in everything that he is without blacking out, yet nearly fail to do so entirely. I must have told him my real name for safety purposes as if I were five and my mum was here instructing me to do so, so I nod like a bat out of hell and go along with it. I turn to Maya and Finneas, who are equally at a loss for words, and I can't help but hope they're experiencing the same rollercoaster ride of emotions as I am.

Magnificently grand, this fascinating creature wipes away all of the rest of my depictions of reality, whereas if someone told me I died and went to Heaven and right now I am meeting Jesus Christ, I would believe them.

Snow white feathers and a mirage of smooth scales parade a massive dragon-esque frame like a luxuriant winter coat. Ferociously grand wings sit gracefully yet powerfully on his back, speckled in gold to match his eyes, and encompassing the most marvelously majestic eagle you surely have *never* seen, nor imagined. His breast is coated in a vibrant array of inconceivable colors, and the presence he brings is so loud, it makes all creatures, big and small, halt in the utmost respect. I'm not quite certain how long he stands on his hind legs awaiting my answer, but I choose to forgive my hesitation as I like to assume he's used to this kind of first impression.

"Benjamin." I've never heard my name said with such vigor – such weight. For the first time since the last time my mother uttered the name, I felt respected as Ben – *valued.* "Might I ask where you found this?"

The eagle-dragon hybrid holds up the mini statue man that I picked up right before all of this chaos unfolded. I look to my hand, remembering the pooling of blood that tiny thing caused, and see that it's now nothing more than a paper cut.

I muster up the courage to answer, "I found that in the middle of nowhere when we got lost…right before we wound up here. Is it yours?"

"It's certainly Paragon's." He has a perplexedness to his tone that unsettles me in more ways than one. Multiple times, the eagle looks back and forth from the chess piece, to me; as if he's a goon checking my ID, before setting it on the ground far, far below him. As the black ivory touches the earth, I watch in a vast mixture of awe and horror as the figurine detonates into light fixtures so bright, they remind me of the sketchy ones that lead us here. The orbs begin to encircle the trinket, pooling around it in hypnotizing streams until a burst of light explodes in a blinding green hue – the small treasure turning into a life-size statue. I swear my heart stops, and I'm safely going to assume my chums' did as well, as their faces are whiter than the giant bird man's coat.

Unfazed, the creatures around us smile with delight to see their beloved sculpture back in its presumably original state and paying no mind to our undisguised flabbergast, the eagle-dragon tracks on as if nothing out of the ordinary happened. "Our world is not known to the corporeals, or *humans*, as you say; normally rather solely the Peculiar, such as we." He gestures then to the fantasy-like things around him and explains the unique peculiarities of nearly *every* single one surrounding us, including himself – an Avidran.[73] It's a complicated concept to fully comprehend, but in the simplest terms, Gideon is a dragon bird.

What the actual fuuuuck, man?

"Your world? Whuddya mean *your world?*" Finneas' eyebrows furrow as he cuts off the creature, and I can see the sweat dripping down the back of his neck.

"We have been here for centuries, though hidden for obligatory reasons," the beastie says, recalling a distant memory as he stares longingly at the magnificently carved likeness of a man. "No one can get to Paragon unless they are, in fact, *Peculiar...*" he then somehow looks at all three of us at once, "so, be that as it may, how did *you* all get here?"

---

[73] *This is a word I created. It's a mixture of greek words, all to literally mean what Gideon is: a dragon bird. Avidran just sounded way more badass.*

"By car," Maya says matter-of-factly, embracing her annoyance. This sends the eagle into a small chuckle, which isn't very small at all…however, all the same, for some reason it's still quite comforting.

"And you are?" His giant head bends down to meet Maya, making her look like a hamster's itty bitty nose compared to his obnoxiously humongous being, and it's no question that she feels like it too the second his eyes shift to her.

"Maya…" She is practically inaudible. "Don't eat me, I'm lean meat."

Though petrified, she's still batty as ever.
Hella with it, this lassie is.

"Welcome, Maya," he gives her a nod of his beak. "It isn't often we get visitors, so allow us to accommodate you three the best we can while we sort things out. I am Gideon[74], current keeper of the town –"

"What's there to sort out?" Finn stands, his normally hang-loose body tense. "Where's the *way out?* I ain't staying in this *American Horror Story: Freak Show*[75] episode waiting to get eaten in my sleep."

The Avidran smirks, "I understand you may be overwhelmed…"

"Finneas. The name's Finneas."

Gideon nods comprehensively at the fact. "I understand you may be overwhelmed, Delfinnium, but –"

Mr. Brooklyn's eyes bug out, *"Whoa, no! Big no-no* there! Look, big G," *Delfinnium losing his chill? What an*

---

[74] *Gideon is very loosely based off of my grandpa, Gus. The authority he holds and the power of his presence reminds me a lot of him.*

[75] *My greatest fear happens to be clowns, so I couldn't watch this season. One of the greatest fuckin' shows ever, though.*

unheard of concept... "first of all, however the fuck you knew my full name is beyond me, but it's Finneas to all o'ya, and I ain't scared'a nothin; let's just get that spotless. Second, this…" he looks around wide-eyed, gesturing at the quaint and colorful town around us, taking everything in once more and still being left dumbstruck, "is all thoroughly impressive, dead ass. But I'm not interested in joining your theater club or your cult thing, yeah? I'been held captive in places I didn't wanna be for too long now, so no-thank-you-very-much and take it easy, we'll be on our way."

Felix then perks up quickly like a little fox – *go figure –,* behind Gideon. "I'm afraid…" he clears his throat nervously, "I'm afraid leaving is not an option." This tumbles out of his mouth like great balls of facking fire, which propels me to stand and assist Finneas in spewing more obscenities, and Maya to nearly gnaw the inside of her thumb raw.

"What are you getting on about?" I finally ask clearly once I have a moment to break through the hubbub.

"Well, you see, there's a reason why you're all here," the giddiness in the fox's tone makes me uncomfortable, and I can tell he's trying not to frighten us more than we already are, but frankly, he's doing a god-awful job. "Just as Gideon said, you would not have been able to enter, let alone *see* Paragon, if you were not…well…special, in some way. At least one of you." He looks over at the statue again, and I don't like the vibe I catch from the act in *any* sense in lieu of prior pricking events…thus, I choose to disregard.

Maya scoffs haughtily, "Well, I can assure you, *your majesty,"* she mocks toward the winged god and the hipster fox, "unless your definition of *special* is mentally challenged, you've got the wrong three amigos."

This sparks some giggles in the sea of middle-aged creatures, but Gideon and Felix evidently ignore the remark. "Benjamin," Felix continues to look at me in wonder, "you said you found the statue in the form of a trinket in the middle of nowhere?"

I more-or-less whisper, "Yes."

"Can you remember what happened after that?"

Through the ever-present fogginess of my mind, I blink back and try to put myself back within the events from before. "I remember...I remember throwing it as far as I could, but it still somehow ended up back at my feet."

"Then he claimed it bit him." Maya interrupts, fidgeting with her nails and smirking toward the grassy ground.

I roll my eyes so loud I hope she can hear it. "Not *bit,* you git – it fucking *did stab me –* "

"Wait," Felix cuts me off, "it pricked *you?* "

I only nod in response, as I realize my disregarding of said pricking has now been cut short...and also upon remembering once again that I am having a conversation with a fox, who may, in fact, believe me, and have a reasoning behind it.

One that I don't particularly want to find out.

"I'll be damned," he furrows his brows at me. "Where did you say you were from?"

"East," Finn chimes in. "Whatsittoya?"

"I'm not sure yet..." Felix looks at the once-trinket man and rattles his head as if trying to shake out the excess confusion polluting his brain. "Alright, I think that's enough questions for today. Why don't we settle you folks in and get preparations ready for supper? It's been quite some time since we had dinner guests! Chef Dalia is making the sweetest cinnamon rolls; her special recipe!"

The three of us eye each other with the same look of unnerve as the crowd hoots and begins scurrying off to start their missions. Though, one particularly unusual-looking lass stays put, surveying us with an inquisitive tiger's eye colored iris' and flawless porcelain skin – aside from the burn scars on her left shoulder. Her white blonde hair is tied up into a loose top knot, and the olive green and purple mini dress she wears is *[purposefully]* revealing some of her best qualities.

"Evangeline!"[76] Felix claps his hands together as if she is an answered prayer, and Gideon nods at her with approval as a father might, and I learn quickly that it is so. *A dynamic duo, no doubt.* "Would you be so kind as to show our new friends around?"

"Pleasure's all mine." When she speaks, the girlie bird looks straight into my eyes instead of at the fox, as if she's doing me the kindness I'd been begging for. Her dusty black leather boots crunch the earth below, intimidating every blade of light green grass in her wake. She simpers at me, "Hey there, freak."

I cock my head, "I'm the freak, am I?"

"A corporeal in a town of Peculiars? Yeah, I'd say you're practically bigfoot." She pushes a loose strand of hair behind her ears, and it's then I notice the tips of them are pointed like she has freshly sharpened daggers for hearing. I've only ever seen fairies in movies or read about them in books, so I don't doubt my astonished eyes grow five sizes. "It's rude to stare, boy," her recurring smirk still lingers, and it sends goosebumps up my arms. "As you heard, I'm Evangeline, but call me Eevee."

"Are you supposed to be a fairy?" Maya seems incredibly irritated and bored by each and every one of these 'L.A.R.Pers', but most especially this lass. She walks up to the blonde bird and feels the fabric of her dress, "Charmeuse. You freaks really go all out."

---

[76] *The fun has arrived. Also, Fun Fact: I've always wanted to name my daughter this, ever since seeing Nanny Mcphee when I was younger, so...there's that.*

Eevee scoffs in transparent disgust, "Paws off, earthling! I don't know where your hands have been; this dress is older than you and half your ancestry." Finn and I chuckle for the first time since any of these things showed up as Maya jerks her hand back; her face painted with sheer annoyance. "I'm a pixie;" she states with pride, *"massive* difference, like you and me, or night and day. Understand?"

"Yeah, fairies aren't as bitchy…" Maya disregards the rhetoricality of the question and muddles under her breath not quietly enough, though I assume that was the point. Evangeline simply leers at her like a Cheshire cat, seeming to be no stranger to the reputation she has created for herself.

"So, sweetcheeks…" Delfinnium turns up the charm once again – even in a town we aren't truly sure isn't a complete and total cock up of our imaginations, he's a classic, smug bastard, "Evangeline, is it? Crazy how *ANGEL* is literally in the middle of your name, ain't it? Bit like magic, to say the least. Might I say, you are the finest piece of first-class –"

"That's nice, Ponyboy,"[77] Evangeline cuts him off like a hardass, placing a hand in front of his face. Pressed down but not crushed, Finn backs away with his hands surrendered and snickers. "Look, newbies," Eevee bends down to tie her shoe, grasping the undivided attention of male creatures in the surrounding area, "we've got a lot of ground to cover, and I should tell you I'm *not* interested in humans. So come, come!"

She turns and begins to skip, practically floating as she gestures for us to follow close behind. Finn stares wide-eyed at her ass as she carries on down the path, still half

---

[77] *The Outsiders is my favorite book of all time. I sign everything with "stay gold" at the end! Can you count how many references are in this book?*

shocked he was shot down more violently than a deer during hunting season.

"We need to get *out* of here," Maya stresses, looking to me for any sort of help that she and I both know I cannot give. "I'm *not* following that bitch."

"Green is not a very fitting color on you, lass." Even in the midst of all the obscenity, I gladly squeeze in room for chaffing. *Spoiler: She doesn't appreciate it.*

"I'm not *jealous,*" the birdie snaps, "I'm *trying not* to die!"

"Yes, you are following this bitch, bitch!" Evangeline shouts to Maya from up the path, supernaturally catching our conversation with her outrageous pixie hearing. "Scoot your no-boot!"

CHAPTER nineteen
Peter Green
Paragon

With hardly any time to stop and breathe, which is vital for me, Eevee shows us Paragon and its entirety as if she created the damn place. From its waterfalls with diving boards, to crowded bars with *bear*-tenders, and even down to a communal shower with a massive, artistically tiled floor in the middle of the dark green forestry and flowers with the colors I've never even attempted to conjure in my mind. It's the warmest spot in the town, and year-round perfect temperature water constantly showers down above it like rain from nowhere.[78]

It's absolute witchcraft. Or magic. I don't know yet.

"If bathing in the lake isn't for you, this is where we wash up," Evangeline gestures to the glorified shower and to the open gazebo area meant for drying off; which is neatly organized with wicker baskets of folded towels, beautifully crafted bars of soap, and some way too puffy things I'm assuming are loofas. "Also, the hirelings could tell you were lacking in the luggage department, so they're already fetching fresh clothes for you. Don't sweat about whether or not they'll fit – they always will; even if you stuff your face like a piggy piñata. This is Paragon, after all."

None of us know how the hell that checks out, yet we nod as if it's as common to us as it is to her, and let it slide. We've been doing that with most of the shit this fairy chick

---

[78] *I have a whole deleted scene set around this shower...should I release it? LOL*

has been blabbing about since she forcefully started showing us around this crazy town, and even if 'cottage core-esque' clothing isn't quite our style, we'll take what we can get.

Though not able to stay silent for longer than the average person, Maya gabs in unhidden annoyance, "Hey, take a step back for me, elfie." She holds her hand up in hopes Eevee will stop speaking, and though granted with a nasty stink face, surprisingly it works. "What if neither taking baths in murky lakes or having a group shower orgy are for us?" Maya crosses her arms over her torso as if trying to hide in her own embrace.

Eevee titters girlishly, "Well that's too bad then, because you could use a good clean up." She touches Maya's semi-matted, dry hair that hasn't been washed since before we hit the road, and takes a swat to the hand like a little fly. "Plus," a glint appears in Eevee's feisty, cat-like eyes, "it gets pretty steamy when the Leon brothers come to play."

"Who the hell are they?"

"The most fuckable sob's in this town."

"Sob's?"

"Sons of Bitches," she rolls her eyes as if it were more obvious than breathing. "Now granted, there are plenty of gems around, but with them animals…shit, you're in for a wild ride."

"Goody, seems we've found the town whore."

Finn smacks Maya on the arm and curses her under his breath, but Eevee doesn't seem bothered by her comment in the least; rather oppositely, seems to take pride in it. Seductively, she roars and winks at Maya, following it all with a smirk because she knows all too well that she is most definitely making the poor lass obscenely uncomfortable.

Fortunately, I am gifted in hiding any and all emotion, thus I shield the pleasure and satisfaction this pixie is providing me.

"So it's a co-ed shower?" Finn's voice strains not to shake in…excitement? Fluster? *Who's to say?*

"Way to keep up, Sodapop.[79] Now c'mon, I want to show you all the mating cove and kitchen!"

Without even a millisecond to take in what she said, Finn is stuck to Eevee like a leech, and I too begin following closely after them; curiosity being the gas needed for my feet to carry on. Noticing there's no shadow behind me, I turn to catch Maya picking the already raw skin on the inside of her thumb and not moving a muscle, and well…

The empath part of me is a bit dusty, so I'll bite.

"Oy," I whisper, as if I may frighten her if I speak too loudly, "she's just trying to cheese you off. I don't think she caught that we're not into bestiality."

She generously snickers at my remark, but rolls her eyes, "Please, it takes a bitch to know a bitch. I'm fine." She moves forward a bit more, but her feet shuffle along the dewy grass as if silently pleading with her to stop.

"Is it perhaps the fact that we're about to walk into a seemingly magical kitchen that's likely packed with infinite loads of food?"

This triggers a lever I didn't intentionally want to pull. "You know what's *fascinating* about you, *Benjamin?* One second you don't give a flying fuck about anything, and the next you're riding on my ass pretending to be kinder than *we both* know you, in actuality, are. So, respectfully, *fuck off,* mkay?" She walks away as if I just told her I killed her cat on purpose. I rattle my head in slight confusion, trying to remember that her emotions are slightly uncontrollable, and I follow her…*very far from her ass, needless to say.*

---

[79] Another *Outsiders* reference.

"Hang on, hang on…so you *do* believe the earth is flat?"

Finneas is somehow having a blast and a half here at dinner, but I just can't seem to get past the fact that we are sitting at a mile long wooden carved table of more-or-less fairytale creatures. I thought at first there were at least hundreds of twinkling lights illuminating the forest around us swinging from one tree to the next high above the table, but the more my eyes adjusted to the radiance, the clearer I made out little fireflies dancing and filling the space with their brilliance. I must say, it's simply lovely, and the grub doesn't look too shabby either.

"Here's to our new guests!" Felix raises a chalice of some sort of purple liquid that's in all of our cups. Glasses clink, and hoots and hollers arise for Finn, Maya, and me for God knows why…I've never had a dinner party thrown in my honor not having a single clue as to what I'm celebrating. Meanwhile, the *almost-one-and-a-half-year-sober* Delfinnium fixes his eyes on his drink, stealing quick peeks of hesitation at the lass and me.

"If it's a mystical magic land, can I bippity boppity bang this into being non-alchy?" Finneas waves his fingers like a wand, "Bippity boppity *booze!*" He snickers at his own joke and even gets me to crack a bit. He and I seem to be easing into accepting this cockamamie fever dream, though Maya, on the other hand, cannot wait *to wake the hell up.*

"You fucking imbecile – it's probably poisoned!" Her whisper is frantic. "One drop of that and you're lunch tomorrow. Plus, are you really gonna potentially take the chance and ruin your new life of sobriety after some rando fairytale fuckers grant you a purple potion that practically says *'Drink me I'm liquid death'?*"

Finn and I look at each other. "Kinda," he says to her matter-of-factly, though doesn't break my eye contact. This immediately sends Maya scoffing and shaking her head, so he attempts to reassure her, "Oh, c'mon, doll, I'm just yankin' yur chain! I'm sure it ain't alcohol. Whatza town fulla magical whozits gotta get sloshed for anyway? They already live the way we try to feel when we drink the shit." He lifts his cup to his nose and sniffs a whiff. "I mean hey, it doesn't *smell* toxic to me; and *real talk,* that kinda smell is quite familiar to this snuffer…and I mean that in more ways than one if yur pickin' up what I'm puttin' down."

She practically chokes on his riddle. "You're a pig."

"Oink oink." His smile blends in with the brightness of the fireflies, and without any further ado, he sips his chalice like a god.

I bite into my piping hot bread that's nestled on my plate beside what looks to be some sort of roast, partnered with potatoes and fresh veggies. It doesn't even need butter to melt in my mouth, and I just about moan with pleasure as I realize when the flavor explodes on my taste buds just how absolutely starving I am.

"Need a room, Greenie?" Finn simpers and mutters through a mouth full of mixed food. I crack back, licking the middle of the crumb sensually staring into his eyes, sending him into a cackle and nearly a blush; which I would've called him out on if it weren't for Gideon *the bloody* Avidran barking my name, his voice oozing interest,

"Benjamin, you look very familiar." The rest of the table joins in the conversation, nodding in agreement and admitting to having the same opinion. "Where did you say you were from?"

"New York." I chug my drink to wash down my mouth full of food. "But I'm no heavyweight. I don't even have an Instagram."

None of them know what that is.

"That accent definitely doesn't say New York."
Eevee looks at me knowingly, her gaze searing into me and
reminding me of when I met Maya for the first time in the
therapy circle.

I hold her fiery eyes, "England, originally.
Portsmouth, before you ask. I'm a proud mut – but that life is
behind me."

Murmurs ring throughout the table like a game of
telephone, and the three of us *corporeals* shift on our asses
uncomfortably. Finn's eyebrows furrow, "You folks gotta
problem with the Brits or somethin'?"

"Not in the least, Delfinnium." Finn's back arches
and he cranes his neck to ease the tension his name
immediately fills him with. The side of my lips can't help but
rise a bit, and I listen to the eagle as he continues, "The creator
of our world and the sole reason why all of us are alive today
was a chosen hero from the great city of London."

"Who was the creator? Christ's little brother John,
'cause the Big J. Man was too busy? C'mon, pallies, we don't
have time for this shit."

"It's a bit of a long story," Felix finally takes a breath
from inhaling his roast, disregarding Finn's Brooklyn attitude.

"Well, by the looks of it, we *do* have some time," I
counter, secretly in serious need of a distraction of literally any
sort to aid the hoopla going on upstairs. *My mind feels like one
of those sketchy-ass, ruthless, zero-gravity carnival rides gone
rogue, and I would really like to get the hell off for a round.*

*Cor blimey, those things are barbaric, spinning death traps
from the deepest pits of hell.*

Gideon wipes his beak and the feathers around it with
a linen napkin, and it's at this moment I realize the beast has

arms. Just about pissing myself, I take my cup and wash down the clod of lead in my throat with as many hits of this purple shit as it takes. *This chalice never empties...it's bonkers.* "If you must know," the eagle-dragon hybrid composedly begins, "long ago,[80] there was a nation here called Parathem. It was indeed a beautiful realm, filled with a race of Peculiar people who all lived in harmony, despite certain varying beliefs – similar to that of your world, I suppose. Pétros, our King and overseer, was a nobleman; a sovereign ruler for centuries, with power unlike anyone else – not even the Royals who lived within the city gates were of any match." The Peculiars around the table listen with the utmost intrigue, as if this isn't likely the four-hundredth time they've heard this story. I fancy they enjoy listening to tales about themselves...

Conceited twats.
Just kidding.
I would too.[81]

The Avidran carries on, "The Royals were ethereal beings; magical, though less powerful than the King when it came to Parathem. Pétros had a precise legerdemain for taking care of his prized nation, whereas the families were mainly looked over by one head Ethereum based on their distinct gift... The Spauldings, known as the family of the most renowned Warlocks, were covered by Clyde; and the Sinclaires, better known as the Wonderers, dabbled in the art of dark magic of the mind and were oversaught by Silas."

---

[80] *Here begins the history of Paragon. World building was probably the most difficult part of the entire book...I'm proud of what I was able to accomplish so far though, & I'm excited to see it evolve. Kudos to those like Gerald Brom or Brandon Sanderson who can do it in their sleep. I long to be like them one day.*

[81] *Hehe. How Peter Pan of you.*

"Well, I sure as shit never heard of 'em. How come the realm isn't on the map, huh? How come you and your *precious* rulers aren't anywhere in the books?" Maya isn't one for fairytales or perhaps even *based-on-true-story-tales,* for that matter, and I can tell by the bags under her eyes she's had enough of today.

"We are all hidden with a deep magic only Pétros and his fellow sovereigns had access to," Gideon explains. "Corporeals cannot see us nor visit our world…*in most cases, of course…"* he gestures to us and I can tell he still is quite boggled with the fact that we stumbled upon their apparent secret hideout somehow, "and we cannot join you in your world."

"Okay, so where the hell is Pétros now? Where did *'Paragon'* come from?"

"Well you see, Miss Maya, one season our King wanted to expand Parathem; hence he began creating a new realm from the ground up. He was admired for it, praised – so much so, that the Royals began to get greedy, and claimed that if Pétros created another portal under his domain, he would need to choose one of them to rule Parathem – but Pétros refused."

"Why? Because he was a power-hungry prick?"

"Enough of that," Felix barks. "Sir Pétros was omnipotent – no one else, whether mere mortal or celestial being, would've been able to overtake Parathem and ensure it survived. The magic and wisdom he bore for the kingdom was too deep to just simply withdraw and replace."

"Okay, chillout, foxy, don't shoot the inquirer. What did he do instead?"

"His refusal made the Royals green with jealousy and wrath," Gideon resumes the story. "The Spauldings and Sinclaires began to wreak havoc among the peaceful Parathem by performing assassinations among the townspeople, harsh kidnappings and rituals of sacrifice in the name of threats, thieving the Peculiar artifacts and Paradust that would strengthen their magic – the realm soon became divided; and what was once harmonious place, became a land full of evil, democracy, and destruction."

Maya's face sours. "What assholes…"

Gideon nods in agreement, then raises a talon, *"But* Pétros wouldn't stand for it. He called a meeting amongst himself and the two families, and made a deal that involved him creating two differing realms to the Spauldings and Sinclaires for their own ruling – Paratoze for Clyde, and Paradmir for Silas; as long as they took their allies and left what would soon then be known as Paragon, stopping the chaos for good. The people could commingle under fae surveillance if they happened to be separated from their families due to conflicting political parties, but still, the wars would cease and be kept within the designated realm barrier, making Paragon a refuge of peace once again."

"Sounds complicated, he should've just offed 'em…" Finneas murmurs ever so quietly, smacking his second helping of meat.

"Oh, but it wasn't that simple, Delfinnium." *But clearly not too quiet for Gideon's profound hearing and to-a-tee-provoking technique.* The way Finn chokes sends me into a chuckle as the gentle beast proceeds, "The Spauldings and Sinclaires agreed to Pétros' proposition, or so our King thought. By nature, due to the Royals being status-seeking megalomaniacs and prideful bastards who thrived on brutality and ruthless acts of violence to gain magic, power, entitlement, or whatever it was they desired; they joined forces and sought to kill Pétros and overtake Paragon, as well as keep their reign over Paratoze and Paradmir. Anarchy erupted again and our King was helpless since he was a god of peace and his distinct bred magic didn't stand a chance alone. Therefore, knowing he was bound to die, he cast a spell which sacrificed himself and his reign, giving it to a future generation he prophesied would come –"

"He must've been *so* powerful then," Maya scoffs crudely and crosses her arms.

"Oh, my dear, but he was," Felix chimes in, seemingly understanding her mocking, but not giving into it. "But when the entirety of your former armies and allies come against you and know your weaknesses and inabilities, what can you do? Each one of them – Clyde, Silas, and their families – had a distinct type of magic…Pétros was a god of peace, with power perfect for keeping Parathem and the people within it alive…he didn't stand a chance against the Warlocks and Wonderers solo."

I shake my head, trying to understand, "Well bloody hell, if you knew that, why didn't any of you help him, for Christ's sake?"

"Well, Mr. Benjamin," the fox sighs, "the factions erupted into sheer havoc…we were bunkered down and fought instead for our own lives…When gods go into battle, that's all us Peculiars and other creatures can do to survive. The magic that they contain was…is…far beyond what any of us contain, if any at all…" Felix's head hangs and he seems saddened by this, as it's no doubt being of little help in the war for the life of his King is a sensitive subject, though he seems seasoned in answering the guilt-ridden questions.

Not to mention, they are the faction of peace and harmony and whatnot…

Guess that came to bite them in the ass, didn't it?
I choose not to point that out.

"So kinda like *Clash of the Titans* or some shit?" Finneas makes literally every Peculiar furrow their brows and cock their heads in confusion, so I quickly take over once

more to save them the description of the action/fantasy remake
film they will never see,

"Okay," I shake my hand so they avert their attention
from Finn to me, "so what happened when he died then?"

"Pétros knew he couldn't leave Paragon to get
overthrown, so his inescapable magic locked the Royals into
their designated realms, unable to be let out without a spell
only his lineage would have the knowledge to cast. The tether,
however, occurring when Pétros died and Paratoze and
Paradmir split and were locked, was that the magic was cut off
short and ceased since then to flow properly into Paragon.
Pétros has not been here to feed it to his marginalized realm,
and the portal he was creating became locked and empty, and
will remain so until another of the bloodline should come and
take it over..."

"So Paragon is dying," I interject.

"Correct." The eagle-dragon's spirit falters. "We have
no way to go through the gates to ask the Royals for mercy,
nor do we have enough magic or Paradust left to thrive
forever." His tone is ominous, sending a twinge of unease up
my back.

"He just left you here to die?" I ask, disgust oozing
from my tongue.

"We believe a savior may be on the way, since there
has been life activity in the forbidden realm. So he, as well as
all of us, had to believe in the magic of fate to bring another
Pan[82] to us before Paragon vanishes. However, it's been so
long, we fear Paragon will cease to exist before our deliverer
comes."

"Though we are hopeful!" Felix interrupts, omitting
the morbidity with glee. "Indeed, we long for the day of
revival when the magic is reinstated and a savior returns, but
until then, we are persevering!"

---

82 * *wink wink* *

"For not much longer…" Evangeline confides through a mumble.

But I heard nothing after Gideon…because at the all too familiar name, I choke on my purple drink and mentally scream at my lungs to calm the fuck down so I can get my question out, and when I finally do, my voice is hoarse and everyone is staring daggers into me, *"Pan*…who's Pan?"

"Pétros Pan – god's rest his soul;" Felix, as well as the rest of the creatures, cross their arms over their chests in some sort of allegiance, "the mighty force that held our people together, and yet also separated us for our wellbeing. He was the chosen *Paragon* of, well, Paragon," he laughs at the irony, "and was once the most respected overseer of our world –"

"Until the rest of the bastards got greedy," the monocle bear from earlier says under his breath between gritted teeth. He obviously doesn't want to hear the *ever-so-exulting* story of their seemingly failed King again.

"So this was all *centuries* ago, yeah…?" Finn speaks up through a mouth full of bread. "How old are you fuckers? Who are the other realm rulers now?"

"Time is a construct, there as age is withal,"[83] Gideon smiles a non-toothy grin. "Complimentarily, if the lineage is still up to date, then we could have estimations, and therefore presumptions…however, time moves differently in all of the realms. Ergo, it could very well still be Clyde and Silas, or perhaps an auxiliary extraction of the Spaulding's and Sinclaire's, or it could just as surely be another. Whomever it may be, they could, in a similar fashion, be evil; or rather peaceful – maybe perfunctory, *though that is unlikely…"* he grumbles this last tad as if sending a secret wish to someone he hopes is listening. The Avidran sighs then, "Alas, no one can know for certain."

---

[83] *A MUCH more badass way of saying "age is but a number" and that time is an illusion.*

I Prefer Peter

"Pétros as in Peter?" My ears seem to have shut down as I still haven't heard anything more than before. My mouth is dry despite all the liquid that I have been guzzling, and indeed, I am fairly certain the beverage doesn't contain alcohol, but my insides are feeling pretty pissed and wonky right about now.

"Congratulations, you know your Greekology." Eevee lights a cigarette and smokes it at the table. *God, what I would give for one of those right now.* "You kinda look like him, by the way."

I already know the answer, but I ask adversely anyway, "Look like who?"

"Peter Pan. Keep up."

The table nods in unity, some pointing at the nearby Pétros statue and making comparisons, and some continuing their meals like it's just another conversation. I can't hear the rest of the jabber due to my heavy metal kick drum heart blocking my eardrums, and all at once my mind hightails it every which way until I feel like I might vomit.

"Benjie, you alright?" Through the haze and murmuring, I hear Finn's voice break through to me, the name *Benjie* searing into my flesh like a hellfire-hot rod iron. On top of that, bile crawls up my stomach like an avalanche of acidic anxiety as I recall and mull over the familiar name *Pan*.

I stutter, "Yeah – no – *excuse me…*"

I untuck my legs from underneath the table and throw them over the seemingly mile-long wooden log bench my side of the dinner party dines upon. I make haste to the small yet quaint single yurt I was so graciously given and collapse on the bed with my birling head in my clammy hands.

Benjie…

Mumma…

The siren…

I Prefer Peter

Pan

Pétros

Pétros Pan

Peter Pan

The name and everything that adds up *to and* with it
sends imaginary red fire ants up and down my body. I grab my
journal from under my pillow and flip to an entry I made when
I was only fourteen:

jOUrNaL eNTrY ~ apRIl 3rd

mARK mY worDS – One DAy, bENjaMIN grEEn wILL ceaSE
to exIst. bECAuse of Colin BenjAMin GREen, mY gIVen
nAme wiLL forEVEr bE a sYMbol oF pUre evIL, anD I
refUSe to carrY it on. iF anYOne shoULD asK, mY MUms
NaME wiLL bE mY fORever titLE, and thE GReEN lEGAcy
wiLL Be NO moRe – iT oFFicialLy diEs wiTH me.
oNE day, I wiLL bE knOWn, aNd onLY knOWn, aS
Peter Pan.

As my eyes marinate and burn into the page over and
over again, the words begin to jumble – and I mean deadass
CGI-like shit is happening right before my eyes, not some
on-sight sudden dyslexia. As if mimicking a bowl of alphabet
soup, my scribbled letters swirl together and dance
synchronously; light emanating through ribbons of teal,

golden, and white as they teacup-twirl round and round, sparkling like something out of an animated princess film. The streams of magic float from the page and into the air in front of me, then parade around my head like birds do a coo-coo man. I slam the journal shut, and my head darts every which way as I follow the magical dust until I become dizzy – but as soon as I do, it halts directly in front of my eyes.

I want to avert my gaze due to the bright light, but something won't allow it…so I keep my stare, squinting my eyes as if I'm looking directly into the sun as it's two feet away from me – when *there, right there – I see an itty bitty…face.*

It's a petite feminine smile – welcoming and exceptionally excited to see me, as if I'm a lifelong friend she hasn't seen in a decade. The tiny thing beams at me with an aura just as bright as the magic that surrounds her, and just when I presume she's solely apart of the light, she explodes out of it like a hummingbird on cocaine and swarms my head like a halo – though instead of creating those kill-myself buzzing sounds that a fly would make, she tinkers…be it the sound of tiny bells, or perhaps mini murmurs of a foreign language I've never heard…I can't quite tell. But what I can easily identify without her having to communicate through words, is that she's incandescently happy she's here with me.

Wings no longer than my cigarettes flutter about like a new-age dragonfly, and I come to terms with the fact that I am seeing a real-life fairy for the first time. *Unless Evangeline can do this too…fuck if I know. Fuck if I believe it, for that matter…* I don't believe it in the *least,* as it has to be the purple mystery juice going to my head…So, in an attempt to stunt her in place for even a measly second, I try to ninja-pinch the wings together; my fingers acting as chopsticks – but this only perturbs her. She pokes my nose with her practically *grain-of-sand-sized* finger, which impressively actually packs quite a pinch, and then lands delicately on top of the worn leather of my journal. I dare to study her so intensely, my eyes begin to cross…Though no bigger than a Polly Pocket, she is as dazzling as snow on a sunny day all the same.

Her arms cross over her chest like the Peculiar's had done whilst discussing Pétros, and my hypnotic spell is broken immediately.

"No, no! I'm not – …*blast,* what *are* you?" I ask, feeling foolish but still letting curiosity lead. "What do you want from me?"

She doesn't answer, only smiles a beaming grin that sends goosebumps up my arms. The fairy flies from the book into my direct line of sight, and out of her minute palm, she blows a mix of emerald green and pure gold dust into my eyes.

I yelp instinctively, "Blasted little *bitch!*" …But to my surprise, my eyes don't burn. Contrastingly, when I open them, I see clearer than I have in a long time, metaphorically speaking…and it scares the ever-fucking shit out of me; thus, I ignore it altogether. The small winged creature lands on the bed, instructing me with expressive hand gestures to bend down to her level. I do so, meeting her lilac irises.

"Do you trust me?" Her bells chime and though her mouth doesn't move, I *understand her.*

"FUCK…" I hop back and scream, slamming my braced cupped palm against my mouth.

She giggles, tiny flecks of gold pooling around her while she does. *"Do you trust me?"*

The fairy reaches her little arm out, her hand outstretched like she's ready to make a deal. I half expect her eyes to beg me to oblige…but it's quite the opposite, actually. It's almost as if she expects me to say yes…like she knows I will.

But I'm fucking losing my mind.
I have to be.
So I will not say yes.

I Prefer Peter

I refuse to believe any of this is real.
I'm drunk.
Or high.
I've relapsed.
I've overdosed and died.
This is an angel taking me to Heaven.

"Do you trust me, Peter Pan?"

At the use of my once written name, I forget to breathe and suddenly, I can't. It's as if someone stole both lungs from right under my nose, and as I grasp my chest and heave, the glinting fairy disappears, and an explosion of tintinnabulation and mirages of luminescent particles swirl around me once again. Overwhelmed and disoriented, I gasp for any and all breath refusing to make its way into my lungs, and before I have time to react, the glitter-like substance shoots straight into my mouth and slithers down my throat like a poltergeist possessing the main character of a horror movie. Hot like fire and burning like whiskey, I create a necklace around my throat with my hand in hopes to soothe the blistering pain; but to no avail. Dropping the journal onto the cold floor, I follow suit as I collapse to my knees and try to cough, but nothing exits just as nothing enters. Dark spots begin to attack my vision, and all that echoes in my head is that blasted bloody last name, along with blurry images of the sultry siren who once said it, a statue of a man who passed it, my mum who co-owned it, the fairy who knew it, and a boy who's now cursed with it. Without thinking, my body automatically curls into a fetal position while holding my head, losing and regaining consciousness with each passing moment.

I guess I'll just die here then...

*(In all honesty, I don't know if that's more of a statement or a
question, so the punctuation following it is subjective.)*

  After what feels like centuries of torture, a plot twist
ensues and I feel an arm wrap around me and pull me upright
against the bed, my body drenched in sweat and limply
hanging like a wet rag doll. I feel a familiar object shove into
my mouth and shoot in a thousand lost breaths, and as oxygen
begins to flood my chest, I topple over onto the savior of the
hour,

  "Breathe now, freak, I know you can," the voice is
calm despite the name-calling and coincides with the breaths I
need to keep awake right now. I force open my eyes, and
though my vision isn't clear yet, I can still take in the sage
green dress made of leaves I saw at dinner, and hair pulled
back into the same messy top knot.

  "Evangeline?" I wheeze out, but it hurts like bloody
hell. I cough so violently that I'm pleasantly surprised when I
don't hack up blood like I'm dying of tuberculosis in the
1800s. *"What the – what the bloody hell just happened – what
– what's happening? –"*

  "Settle down," she gives me space by scooting away
like I'm the plague personified, "I don't need blood on my
hands tonight; metaphorically or physically." When I reach a
state of staggered yet semi-controlled pants, she helps me onto
the bed and I clench my eyes shut to regain my bearings. She
banters awkwardly, "I'm glad I came to ask if you wanted
dessert."

  When I open my eyes a few ticks later, the pixie has
my journal in her hands and is peering through the pages like a
book in the library she's highly considering checking out.

  "Hard no." I grab it with ninja-like speed and stuff it
under my pillow again.

"Aw, I can't read your diary?" Her sunset eyes mock me in new ways I've never even realized I didn't know how to handle.

If that makes any sense at all.

"It's a load of cockshit that you probably couldn't make out anyway," I sound like I just ran a nonstop marathon without water. "My penmanship is that of a doctor writing his seventh prescription in the ten o'clock hour."

I make her laugh with my strange way of speaking, and it's a melodious sound. Eevee doesn't seem like one to get a genuine laugh out often – the hardness behind her eyes is telling, but telling *what* I'm not sure yet.

"So, the part of your name being Peter Pan is a load of cockshit?" I hold her stare and bite my tongue, attempting to figure out how she managed to know that within seconds of flipping through incoherent pages...but I'm at a loss. I also assume my face is as white as her porcelain skin because in half an instant her mysterious eyes switch to an all-knowing stare. I don't think I can lie my way through this one, so I give in.

"What's it to ya, pixie bird?"

She chuckles at the improvisational nickname. "You've had a long day, freakshow. For now, just get some shut eye." She gets up to leave, nearly fluttering as she makes her way to the yurt's curtain; but that could just be my overworking brain imagining things. *Who's to say?*

"Wait, wait!" I spring to my knees. "What happened with the fairy thing? Good God, she's not inside me, is she?"

Eevee laughs again. "Goodnight, freak."

Normally I would argue, but having several near-death experiences in one day really takes a lot out of a guy. I rub my eyes until I see stars, and reach across to my nightstand for my glasses, but my hand shoots back as if I got electrocuted when I see a perfect slice of chocolate cake sitting beside me nearly exactly like my mum used to make, next to a golden fork and a note:

Welcome to Paragon, Peter Pan.

My head shoots up and I see Eevee staring at me through a small opening of the curtain. She winks with a cheeky little simper tugging at her lip, and skips away. I don't have the foggiest how she did that or how she got this cake to taste eerily similar to my mum's, so much so that I couldn't eat more than a nib or two, so instead am saving it for Finn to scarf down for a midnight snack –

But I do know somehow in the seconds she had it in her hands, Evangeline read my journal in its entirety, if not most of it…
And now this pixie chick knows way more about me than I'm comfortable with.

CHAPTER twenty

Evangeline
Paragon

Weird fun fact: this was the last chapter I finished!

I feel bad for him, I do.

That kid has gone through more shit than the pipe of a toilet in a Taco Bell bathroom, and yes – I know what that is, don't ask me how.

Pixie's like me were bred with an averse yet tantalizing power to absorb details and emotions from events we weren't even present for. When I merely got near that journal of his…the choke hold it had on me was nearly physical…

And not in the good way.
Peter – *Benjamin Green* – is not just a corporeal…

He's special.
Yes, shards of a broken boy – completely shattered, even…
But extraordinarily special.
You could make a mosaic out of those broken pieces.
*He's a motherfucking **Pan**.*
And he doesn't even truly know it yet.

That's the crackpot thing – he may be aware he possesses the regal last name, but he doesn't have even the slightest clue who the shit he *is*. I'm sure all that beautiful, naive little twat thought, *according to his journal,* was that his mother's maiden name was Pan and that he was gonna take it in spite of his father being a total micro cock, thus refusing to continue the legacy of the Green's…*and that was that.* But he must know by now he *is* related to the former King…

I mean, the slutty siren he wrote about when he was sixteen was a dead giveaway...

The fish intended to do what siren's like her are known for: stalking their prey, luring them in with their undeniable, sensuous, surreal feminine beauty, then having their way with their catch...Likely, this is then followed by murdering them for shits and giggles once getting bored, getting a good fuck, or receiving whatever it is they desired.

Instead, after Peter came in contact with the slut-sack, the magic lying within his veins began to resonate. Thus, he made himself damn well known by...*accidentally, considering his control is zero to none...*exploding into a green luminescence and asserting the dominance inside of him without even knowing, prompting the siren to flee.

So I repeat: the kid has to have an inkling by now he is **something,**

Plus, if the statue of Pétros pricked his finger, Paragon must have known somehow halfling blood was approaching...it was essentially a DNA test. Once his Peculiar data matched with the Paradust, *poof...*his fine ass crash landed here.

I know it's him.
If any Peculiar has been paying attention, they should realize it too...but shit, everyone is in their own wackadoo heads to notice anything other than how good the damn food is here. Nevertheless, I call bullshit if Peter claims he doesn't believe it, **especially now** *after what happened with the fairy.*

He accepted his sovereignty – there's no other way someone can be blessed with the gift of their full, true divination. The fairy in his bedroom that night was able to give it to him because even for a mere second, he genuinely believed who he was. The magic has been in his blood from birth, but dormant – no kid can simply meander around in that mainland of his with live supernatural powers, that'd be obscene. Therefore, once a man or woman learns of his or her authority and accepts it, the Paradust can be granted to them and awaken the sleeping magic inside, thus granting the evolving process of their abilities to begin.

Peter is phenomenal at pretending he doesn't buy in.
But that fairy wouldn't have done shit if he didn't.

That means now, there's genuine Paramagic growing within him like a little damn baby. Hell, that boy has no fucking idea how unstoppable he could be if – when – he learns his true potential...

*Shit, **he's** been the one creating life in Pétros' forsaken realm*
with that little book of his...
He could open the gates.
He could find a way to the pocket realms and save Paragon.
Fuck, he could create anything he wanted and more.

*He – **maybe...we** – could rule all of Paragon and beyond.*

For as long as I can remember, I too have craved a realm – a universe – of my own, similar to his...one where I can start from the first flower and build up from the roots to create something perfect – something *mine*. To find someone who longs for the same thing is a dream I thought would never come true – a vision that I have been lusting after for what feels like centuries...

Probably because it has been centuries.

I Prefer Peter

I look pretty damn good for my age.

When I held that book in my hands, I was shown a goldmine of opportunity desperately waiting to happen. The desires and yearnings Peter has sketched and scribed for a land of wonder; beauty…

…a place where dreams are born and time is never planned…
A place created with the heart…
A place where you can be everywhere, anywhere, and nowhere all at once –
That's his world. A world that's forming as we speak.
A world we can rule together.

Even though the prognosis was it had to be a member of Pétros Pan's lineage to open and enter the secured realm, the Peculiars of Paragon searched for hundreds of years for a key to it. Like…what were we supposed to do? Just sit like useless footstools and *wait?* Lives were at stake and there was no way to journey to defend ourselves against the Royals in an attempt to gain our magic back and get it flowing again…We were in despair.

After a span of searching, and when our so-called savior never came, we all damn near believed the true answer didn't exist and therefore, due to that fact, accepted we all were inevitably going to die off slowly one by one…

Left with nothing.
Just the same old, same old, for centuries.
A slow burn disintegration.
We failed to understand why Pétros would do this to us, but eventually had to always pin our hopes on it being a part of his master plan.
Because what's living without hope?
…We put so much faith in that bastard.

I began to assume the worst and swallow it was all for not....

But *then,* this anti-hero complex kid with a tranced journal shows up, and there had to be a reason why. Thus, the newest conspiracy finally began.

But no one is doing anything about it, go figure.
So I guess it's up to me.

If that journal has as much power as I felt surge through my veins when I held it for even a few measly seconds, then there's a supernatural force that I need to dive into like…*yesterday.* Paragon has been stagnant for god's know how long now, and as the days go by, we become more desolate and desperate. So the fact that finally, when we're on our last legs, this earthling rando shows up unannounced with a mojo that has been unmatched for centuries and due to his presence, the realm comes back to life…

Not to mention, to tie it all together with a pretty bow, he carries the same fucking name as our former King…just as the prophecy claims…

Jinkies, bitch.

Who's to say that Peter *and* his book aren't the *keys* I – *we* – have been long without for countless years? Perhaps the solution isn't purely one specific thing, but rather also the person it stems from…

Perhaps Peter is the key, and the journal is merely the true gate.

If yes, I can take that journal and open the unfinished realm Pétros left with my Paradust, and from within its poetically

written pages, concoct the home I – *Peter* – has been
searching for since the day he started writing in that weathered
little shit log. The empty world can become everything I – *he*
– *we* – want.

Sure, he came here to save Paragon, open the
Pararealms, and take back reign *and whatnot*...but what's the
harm in a little pleasure in the meantime?

Shit...imagine that.
We could fix everything.
Be so dynamic, that we'd overcome it all together.
Be heroes.
Have everything we want, and nothing we don't.

I'll train him. Mold him.
God's, he'll be my little halfling prodigy...It'll be
supernatural.

Now I just need to get his diary in my hands long
enough to work some pixie magic. I don't want him to know I
took it though, because there's no way he'll put his trust in me
anyhow...he already got hella unhinged at the fact that I
simply *held* it, and even though I did *[semi accidentally]* read
the thing front to back...*hehe*...my eyes didn't have to scan a
single page to know full well that the freak has trust issues.
Thus, I have to work discreetly – which is going to be damn
near impossible considering he guards that thing like he's a
safe lock personified. But the one thing he failed to note was
the giving away of his special hiding spot under his pillow,
and if that is the tooth...

Then here comes the motherfucking tooth fairy.

CHAPTER twenty-one
Finneas Scott
Paragon

"Man, what the hell happened?" Plopping my ass on the Ritzy bed of Greenie's, I try to make him out between the pillows and blankets nearly suffocating the dude to death. "You ran outta there like your asshole was about to erupt."

"I'm not in the mood, Delfinnium."

I cringe, but him calling me by my given name has me presuming he is, in fact, in the mood for a little tiff. "Now, Benjamin, we can do this the easy way or the hard way."

"How about the *go away* way?"

"And leave the comforting presence of this luxurious five star yurt and your sweet, sweet company? Hard pass." I hussle over to the hidden body of his I found and yank the seemingly mile high duvet off of his body.

"Jesus Christ!"

"Everyone seems to think so," I say as he tries tug-o'-waring with me for the covers back. I win, due to his borderline youthish frame, and sit beside him as he stares at the ceiling in defeat. I say rather gently, "You have one of them day-terrors again or somethin'?"

I half expect Petey to scream at me for mentioning the day I threw his pen out the window and he almost seized in front of me, but instead he looks at me with crystalized emerald eyes of surprise, raising that infamous left eyebrow. Bet he didn't think I was fazed by that event, but hell nah – I deadass thought I was gonna be charged with first degree manslaughter that day...Oh, right, not to mention *I also fuckin' care for the kid...sue me.*

He licks his dry lips, "No, I...no." Then his eyes quickly move away from mine and onto nothing in particular

on the comforter as he fidgets with the wearing-out velcro on
his brace. I can tell he wants to genuinely thank me for the
compassion and mother-henning that effortlessly oozes outta
me, but meh. We'll work on it. There's no missing what he
reluctantly says through those transparent eyes anyhow, so it's
the assumable thought that counts for now.

"So then *what* the shit went down just now?" I press.

He takes a shallow breath, easing into the deepness of
it to resist the urge of hacking, as he so often does; and
scratches his left hand with his right. *I don't know how this kid
has any skin cells left there.* "You know that guy they were
talking about at dinner? Pétros Pan?"

I nod, "Mmhmm…the mythical overlord of this
place."

He briefly absorbs my characterization. "…Right,
yeah, okay. Well, we have the same name."

I furrow my brows at him. "You mean the name that
has averaged the list of *'top 50 most popular boy names'* since
the 1940's? So what?"[84]

He shakes his head and lets out a tested breath. "Be
that as it may," he finally sits up, "it's not the first name that
I'm getting on about. It's the last name that's the kick in the
nuts."

"I ain't followin' you, kid. Your last name is as Green
as your eyes."

Another huff of annoyance erupts outta him. "That's
because my *father's* last name was Green."

Sidebar: I don't know anything about Pete's ol' man,
but he damn sure looks like he's gonna spit fire over the name,
so I assume the *'was'* ain't because he kicked the bucket, but
instead was intentional for some other underlying shit…

---

[84] *This is a true fact, by the way.*

*I almost ask, but we'll cross that bridge when...if we ever...
get to it.*
*Signs...and his sharp gritted canine teeth...are pointing to a
fat nope.*

Since my brain is elsewhere *and he can damn well
tell...Sorry, pally...*thankfully, he explains, "I swore to myself
when I was a small lad that I was gonna change my name to
my mum's maiden name once I turned eighteen. Due to
circumstances being the way they are in my god-forsaken life,
it never happened, and all my documents legally still read
Green..." I must still look like a dumbshit, because he inches
closer to me as if telling me the most obvious fact ever yet
simultaneously the biggest damn secret of all time, "My
mother's name was Elizabeth Pan. *My name is Peter Pan.*"

Unsure how to take in everything the kid's saying, I
bite the inside of my lip and let the wheels turn in my head.

Feels like they haven't fuckin stopped all day.

"So all that mystical, magical shit...we thought it was
poppycock, right?"
"Poppycock, affirmative."
"But now me and the ancient ruler not only have the
same name, but the statue that has an uncanny resemblance to
me *pricked my fuckin' finger* whilst in its mini form, thus
granting us access to the realm...*What if it was like a blood
test thing and I passed?* What if this *is* real life and it ain't
some acid trip?"
"Alright..." I slowly play catch up in my head, "as
trippy as that is, so what if you *maybe* are related to the
Paragod?" I inwardly chuckle at my knee-slapper pun. "People
are related to powerful, ancient deceased people all the damn

time – that's what that *ancestry.com* shit is for. For all I know, I could be a descendant of Mary the Mother of Christ."

Peter rakes his fingers through his sweat-damped hair, "Sure, perhaps it means nothing and it's just a fun party fact I can tell at kill-me-now social gatherings. But in this case, it's a bit lopsided due to the fact that only Peculiars can enter the Pararealm's, and apparently *only a Pan can truly save Paragon*, and I am, in fact, *a Pan.* If it were as plain and simple as me being related to Abe Lincoln or whomever, we wouldn't have just poofed up here. Pétros is made of magic – *true, deep* magic – according to what they said out there," he points to the direction of the table, and I can see his hand is scratched bloody raw. "So if this is all real and I *am* somehow a part of some ethereal family tree..."

"Holy shit then *you're* a Paragod, man..." I keep my voice at bay, even though I want to shout so Maya can hear it in her yurt next door. "Youz must be the Christ they've been waiting for, cause there's no way in hell it's Half-Pint or me – not a chancy-chance. That little chess thing must've known it too, cause our blood wasn't tested for nuthin'. So *you*...youz probably got some wild superhuman shit going on inside ya! Baby greens, you could be the one to open the realm gate or whatever theyz were all jabbing about, find and defeat the Royals, and get the magic flowin' again so none of these weirdos die! *Shit!* I knew there was somethin' off about you, Petey!" I smack him in the chest and he coughs brutally. I hold my hands up in surrender, "My bad. Though if you learn your superpowers, maybe your lungs won't be so trash."

His face contorts, "Doubtful. I'm not a Paragod. I'm just..." I grant Peter an ever so gracious judgmental glare, and he stutters, "Look, I – I don't know what I am. Regardless, I couldn't save their realm from dying if I were trying to in a fucking video game. I don't even know *how* to open the forbidden realm, let alone if I did, how to reach the Royals through it to what...beg them for mercy?"

"No, no! No mercy. We both know you are way too cool for that, man. You would fight to the death."

He narrows his grape-colored eyes at me. "As-if. I don't know anything about being…well, anything, Finneas! If I somehow figured it out, the moment I open the realms they've been locked in for centuries, those mighty motherfuckers are gonna take me out first, then bring everyone down with me and conquer what they've been trying to do since Pétros' fall. I'm too weak – too vulnerable and inexperienced, and I'm not afraid to admit that. I'm *fucked!*" He says the last word with a distressed laugh.

"Peter, you may be ignorant of yur abilities and the stairway to victory *now,* but –"

"I wouldn't even know how or where to start with them!" He interrupts, not listening to a word that slides off my tongue. "Even if I am a part of the *bloodline*, there is no way in hell I have even the slightest dribble of magic in me, Finn. It just doesn't check out. I would've cast a dozen spells ages ago that made me not want to jump off a mega building every waking moment of my existence, or to feel high all the time without drugs, or to…I dunno…be taller."

Tomato Potato.[85]

"Well you've seen them movies, man, you need all the training first. Gotta learn to control your abilities and all that shit in rookie-god boot camp. All that power is just chillin' like a second spirit inside you waiting to be liberated! I have no doubt them Peculiars know what to do – especially that majestic eagle dude if you just tell *him* you're part of the Pan clan –"

---

[85] *I try to say this everyday.*

"No way," he barely lets me finish. "Telling anyone here, *especially* daddy Gideon who I *may* or *may not* be is the last thing I should do."

My eyes practically bulge out of their sockets, "Why the hell *not?* They all know something's fishy with us anyhow, and right now they're practically drug dogs yappin' and sniffing our old inner jean jacket pockets!" The kid starts on his hand with his wolverine nails again. "They already half assume one of us is the chosen one or some bullshit, so maybe you being the long lost Messiah is our ticket *outta here."*

A voice breaks through our inner circle wall and is so out of place it almost slices my eardrums to pieces, *"Or* it's our way of never leaving." Maya's already halfway across the room by the time she finishes her sentence; hair up in a messy bun and looking like she's ready for gossip at a slumber party. Peter points to her words as if she took them right outta his mouth, and I roll my eyes in detest. "Gotta be careful," she continues, "they may strap you up to a stake and burn you, or drain you and use your power for all of their long awaited desires."

"The fuck did you come from, mole?" I snap as Peter stands and pulls sweats over his boxer briefs outta respect for the lady.

Whatta chivalrous lad.

"We may all have our own bougie tents now, but even *'magical'* curtains are thin, boys," she mocks the word with jazzy hands. "Plus you two gossip as loud as middle school girls in a P.E. locker room."

"So I'm assuming you heard everything?" Peter tiredly sits on the bed and rubs his face.

"I have ears like a moth." *Weirdest shit I've ever heard.*[86] "He's right, though. We may never get outta here if he says he's a Pan." *She must really think so...she only admits his justifications when she has to.*

"Why, cause they'll *worship* him?" I say facetiously, turning to the newest found 'almighty'. "Are you *not* okay with saving and then *ruling* this, and potentially other Pararealms, thus resulting in these creatures treating you like their head fuckin' honcho?"

His face pinches, "Do you even know me? There's no way that's going to happen. I'll get killed if I agree to do this." *This kid has worse imposter syndrome than anyone I've ever met.* "Not to mention, it sounds like a lot to adopt...I can barely remember to eat in a day."

"Amen," Maya deadpans and doesn't even look at him when she says it.

I let a puff of frustration out of my nostrils like a damn doggy. "Look, kids, would you rather go back to our sick, mundane, prison break-like lives, or potentially partake on one of the grandest damn adventures of our existence?" *I don't know why the shit I even have to convince them which is the right answer.* "We escaped Brand New Life *so that* we could start none other than our brand new lives. So, lets fucking *commit,* bitches! Carpé that fucking diem. Peter, for Christ's sake, you may be more powerful than any character in those goddamn books you and Sexton read and be right on the brink of unimaginable welly! And you, little chick...well, you'll burn more calories than you'll know what to do with."

Petey gives me a half shrug and shakes his head, "You're a damn loony. If they kill us, know it's on you."

---

[86] *Fun Fact: Moths have some of the best hearing out of any animal/insect...weird, right? I learned a lot whilst writing this book LOL.*

"Atta boy!" My heart leaps. When it comes to an adventure, he's an easy bloke, that one. "Impossiburgers, are you in?"

The look on her face is unreadable, but it seems Peter ain't as illiterate as me. He nods at Maya and says something to her with those eyes of his without saying anything at all.

"Fuck you, idiots." She looks away from his trance and turns to me, inhaling deeply before exhaling with the words, "I'm with you. But if I die, I'll come back and haunt your asses until I personally see you in hell."

"Deal." I give her my devilishly handsome grin. "Get some sleep, beauties. In the morning, the brand new life begins.

CHAPTER twenty-two
Peter Green...Pan? TBD
Paragon

jOurnAL eNTry ~ goLDen HouR iN paRaGON ~ iDK whAT dAY it iS anyMOre

i gUEss GOod nEWs TraveLS fAST hErE in tHE biG P, bECAUSe reGardleSS if i hAd oR hadNT cHosEn tO waNt eVEry cREaturE aND theiR motHer tO knOW i Am a poTEntiAL desCEndaNt oF pETros PaN, IM tHE taLK Of tHE towN RIght nOW... i takE it EevEE iS quITe tHe DadDy's GiRl.

iM nOT quITE cERtain whAT i WAS exPECting, bUT it surEIY wasNT GIDeon, tHE drAGon—eAGLe AKA AVIdrAn myTHIcal wONDer, sUMMonINg tHE toWn tO hAVE a fEASt iN mY hoNOR aND a GOOd oL' FAShioNEd KumBaYA aROUnd tHE troU—De—LOup..

tHat'S whAt tHEy cALL tHE mASSive boNFire piT aREa heRe.

I DidNT asK whY, NOR WILL i.

It'S rATHEr okAY – a RAt pLAYs tHE guiTAr anD eVEN thOUGH we ALL hAVE tO bE quIEt as HEll tO heaR hiS liHLE soNGs, tHE CALm oF soRTs fOr a biT, conTRAry to tHE eCcEntRICity hAPPEning hEre noNSTop, iS quITe nICe.

BUt toNIghT, THE RAt dIDnt play.
aLL eyeS weRe on Me.

LOads OF QuesTIOns weRe thrOWn onTo me aS if I beCAMe an oVErniGHT seNSAtion AND no One woULD stOP uNTIL THEy couLD haVE theiR inTErview. I defINiTELy doNt fEEL differEnt — I answeRed thaT onE NEarly 90 tiMEs. I DoNt KNow whAT iT meANS to haVE [accidentally] accEPted tHE magic, whaT tHE heLL to Do witH iT, oR whAt to do NExt; anD franklY, i DOnt wanT to knoW whAT thesE peoPle haVE in Mind on That MAtteR...CausE SOmethING teLLs mE tHEY haVE bEEn creatiNg a GAme plaN For loNGEr thaN I'vE bEEN alive.

AS i Was oN a WAlk in The woODs to catCH a BReak, I stuMBled upON tHE taLLest trEE i HAd evEr seEn witH staIRs (nORmal StairS, nO blooDY EYES THIS TIME) leaDINg up to gOD knoWs whaT. sO, oF couRSe, I clIMBed thEm... oDDly enOUGh, mY lunGS didNT giVE me aS kILler of a TIMe aS I imAGIned, bUt iM chalKINg thAt up TO coinciDEnce. iT led mE to a TREehouSe, whICh seeMEd to havE beeN uNoCCupied foR somEtiME duE to The coBwebs aND duSt; sO i tOok thAt aS my INVItation to

265

stay aWHIle. TherefoRE, riGHT noW, iM saT iN a tREEhouSe iVe clAimed As My oWN, smOKing a FAg i StolE frOM aN upRight STANDIng sALAmandeR whEN hE waSNT looking, oVERLooKINg PARAgon aND iT'S enTIREty WhiLst trYINg to finOOGLe mY waY ouT of tHIS 'PetER pAN' situAtion.

I HaTE to conSTantLY be THAt annoYIng clicHé, bUT SERIOUSLY: iM nOT speCIaL – theRe's nO daMN waY i AM oR evER HAve bEEn, anD i dOnT wanT thEse peCULIar creATUREs to beliEVE otHERWISe eVEn foR a sPLit secOND. pERHaps we'rE reLATEd iN somE way, pEtROS anD I, bUt no...noT by 'choSen oNE' magIC herO buLLshiT tHAt onLY hapPEns in mOVies anD boOks. iF thESe pEOPLe exPECt mE to tAKE thEM unDEr mY wing anD sOMehow unLOck theIR forBIdden pOrtal, thUS settinG oUT on a perilOus quESt to gOd knowS WherE to fiND The dYINg magIC; deFEat tHE roYALs anD tAKE poSItioN oF RULer oVer aLL THe PARAwhATEVers befOre thEY caN smiTE EVeryoNE – *inCLUdinG me* –, aND oN tOp oF aLL of iT, connECt thEM weIRdos bAck witH theIR *deaResT* loVED onEs iN onE PiECe?!

...Lordie, theY havE a bIg stoRM coMIng – becAUSE i CAnt. I genuinEly juST cannOT.

I donT knoW how, anD i doNT wanT to trY to figURe iT ouT, thUs caUSing theM anY morE HEartAche aND disAppoiNTment thAn they'VE ALREady EndurED whEN I faIL thEM....becAuSe i Will. I knoW i wiLL...

I'm nOT a savIOR — i nEver haVE beeN.

I coULDNT even SAVE MY OWN MOTHER.

FUCK ME.

WHy shOuLD i eveN begiN to beliEVE I could saVE a wholE realm — leT alone tHREE of them, aND evERYone withIN thEM?

i dONt.
I WoNT.
thEY'LL haVE to fiND someONE elsE, caUSe I surE as heLL aM not thE onE theY'vE bEEn waiTIng for. Also, SIDenoTE, i'M TAKIng oFF THis blOODy fuCKing briM___

Get it? Cause he got scared and flubbed up with his pen. I always wondered if people got that.

"Hey, freak."
I become engulfed with vertigo as I watch my brace plummet to the far away ground below, and I nearly drop my journal too as I expel a startled yell; my soul practically

feeling like it aggressively ejected my body and flooded back in again all at the same time.

"If you're trying to stop my heart from beating," I try to catch my breath, "you've nearly succeeded, love."

Evangeline smiles. "Nah, that fire stick'll do it for you." She takes a seat next to me, both our feet dangling hundreds of feet from the ground below us. She snatches my cigarette and takes a puff...*bitch,* "You know you really shouldn't smoke up here. One spark and our whole home goes up in flames." She hands it back as she blows smoke into the air, somehow making it look gracious and not deadly.

"Ah, what a sight that would be," I sing pertly; the corner of my mouth twitching upward as I side glance at her. "Trust me, I'm a professional." I inhale in a puff then and blow it out through my nose like a dragon, making her giggle like a five year old. "Plus, from what I understand, it's already on its way out. If anything, I'm just assisting the inevitable."[87]

Her giggling stops abruptly as her expression turns from campfire warm to thin ice. "Decided to be the villain now, have we?"

"I mean, my origin story *would* be one for the films..."[88] I wink, and fortunately for me, she smiles again...something tells me I never want to get on this pixie's shit list. If amber eyes could kill, I'd be a bloody goner. "How did you find me up here?" I switch subjects while I'm ahead. "Following me now, are you?"

"Don't flatter yourself, Portsmouth. I come here to think and write in my little diary too." She winks at me with her gold flecked eyes and looks down at my journal, which I instinctively close and place beside me out of her reach. "Oh, c'mon," she pouts, "I didn't see anything."

---

[87] *Such a dick.*

[88] *Yes it would. It's called I Prefer Peter*

"Not this time," I say accusatorially. "I have to say, you didn't seem in the least bit surprised when your father announced my lineage bombshell to the entire town."

Her eyes narrow at me as she gives me a knowing stare, "Were you casually checking to see if it made an impression on me that you're the town's Jesus?"

Blimey...how many god's do these people have? I can't imagine Christ is thrilled to be one of many...I heard He gets jealous. "Don't flatter *yourself,* pixie bird. I actually just wanted to confirm the fact that you snooped my journal and snitched, and low and behold, fancy I was right. Not an uncommon affair though, quite frankly – me being right and all."

I can't tell if it's guilt or annoyance that strikes her face at this, but she sighs and bites the inside of her plump bottom lip. "You admitted it to me anyway...Take it as a favor I did for you – you should be thanking me."

"Oh, is that right?"

She leans in, "What if I told you I could help you."

My left eyebrow rises like a defense mechanism. "What're you getting on about?"

"Let's just say, you and I want similar things. Our aspirations are fairly much of muchness, to put it plainly."

I've never heard that phrase before in my life.

"Alright...and what *raison d'être's* might you be referring to, Evangeline?" She looks at me with confusion, and I chuckle inwardly. Here I am thinking pixie's were supposed to be well versed in culture. I switch to layman's terms, *"What do you mean, Evangeline?"*

She scoffs. "I know what you said, you sob!" *No, she did not. But I got to rhyme, all the same.* "How about instead of explaining, I just show you what I mean..."

I Prefer Peter

My eyebrows wrinkle for what seems like the millionth time since I've come to this strange place, but I decide to humor her. Stuffing my journal in my pocket, I head for the descending steps, but she chuckles behind me, "A Pan who takes the stairs?" She shakes her head and her earrings jingle like little bells. "You have a lot to learn."

I walk over near the edge and point to the far away earth below us, "Oh, did you expect me to plummet to my death instead? Cause it wouldn't be the first time I considered that, lassie, but I don't think I should revisit those reveries."

"Not jump, you silly ass.[89] *Fly.*"

I scoff so hard it nearly hurts. "I can't *fly*, you ninny."

"Not with that attitude." And with that, she pushes me so hard, I lose my balance and go tumbling over the edge of the treehouse's small porch. I holler desperately, my lungs tearing as I shriek cursed obscenities at the bloodthirsty bitch; though when I look up, she's gone. The treehouse gets higher and higher as the thorny ground becomes nearer and nearer, and as I brace for the impact of the fatal fall, I prepare myself for an excruciating meeting with the possible afterlife. I squeeze my eyes shut and accept my fate, when instead, my falling is abruptly halted by two hands scooping me up from under my arms into their firm grasp and hauling me onward before my brutal crash landing.

My eyes snap open…
and *I'm… flying.*
With assistance, but soarin' high, nonethefuckingless.

"WHAT IN THE FLYING FUCK?" I screech so loudly the birdies flee from their nests around us.

---

[89] *Hi, Tink Easter egg!*

"Something like that, yeah!" Evangeline crows, her voice muffled by the wind attacking my ears. "This pixie bird needs to teach her little hatchling how to fly!"

"You psycho git nearly killed me!"

"Yeah, yeah, well I didn't, did I?"

I crane my neck to look up at her and her raging audacity, but instead I'm taken aback to see Eevee has transformed into the most magnificent bird-like creature I have ever laid my eyes on. Her wings seem to stretch on for miles, casting the most beautiful illumination of bronze I have ever seen, with sparkling streaks of burnt orange, royal blue, and crimson red hues throughout their feathers – *she is fire, personified.* Her petite frame is still the same, though she glows like the sun and I can feel the magic radiating off of her like midsummer heat, warming my skin as she carries me through the air.

We make it in one piece to the clearing near the trou-de-loup, and by now everyone has turned in for the night making Evangeline and me alone. She lands gracefully, clearly a seasoned flier; and though she sets me down gently, I'm trembling so defectively that I immediately sink to my knees when my feet meet the sweet, long-awaited grass.

"What in the bloody god forsaken *fuck* was that?" I snap perhaps a tad too loudly, but waking the guitar playing rat and/or his friends is the least of my concerns at the moment.

"Fun, huh?" She is clearly unfazed by my fury, which makes me even more furious. The pixie chick has returned back to her original girlish form, and though it's easier to feel more domineering over her less majestic state now, she is very much challenging me.

I grill, "What the devil *are* you? An Avidran like your father, or –"

"I'm a phoenix pixie, don't shit your britches." She throws her head down forward, tying her hair into a top knot like she's done it a gazillion times. "A.K.A, the hottest breed of them all – *pun intended* – and I happen to be the last of our kind," she says this with pride, though a hint of something else glints in her eyes that doesn't go unseen by me. Sadness, maybe? Longing? I dunno, but she proceeds before I figure it out completely. "I get it from my momma, bless her soul. She and the rest of my family were killed in the war between Pan and the Royals...Gideon took me under his wing...literally," she titters, "and taught me how to use my magic. So, whenever I please, I am able to shape-shift into a positively gorgeous firebird or, if I have enough Paradust left to spare, really whatever I have a hankering for at the moment. Perks of the crop."

She says this all so damn casually, that it drives me mad. While trying to wrap my head around *additional* cockamamie bits of information, I'm still gathering my land legs from being airborne and also catching the fact that we have something fairly mega in common. I choose not to engage in the subject, as I don't think my lungs can withstand the leaden chat.

"Bloody hell, Evangeline!" Is what I stick with instead.

She smirks, "Were you scared?"

"Was I *scared?"* Of course – *I was damn straight terrified.* "No, I wasn't scared. I was miffed at the fact that you intentionally tried to murder me and are not forthwith apologizing for said attempt."

Her nose scrunches, and she giggles that giggle that makes me want to rip her little laugh box out. "You weren't even close to Grim, you silly ass. I was merely letting you get a feel of Paragon from the most appropriate perspective for a Pan."

"Oh, enough cockshit already." I finally stand, a bit woozy but still steady. "Even though I may be a descendant of the chap, that's *all* I am. I am in no way *Peculiar* the way you all are with your powers and shit, and you know it," I point a finger at her and move in, but she doesn't flinch.

"Of course you aren't."

"Thank you."

"You're much more than that."

"No!" I throw my arms up. "That's not –"

"Peter, face it, if you were a dud, I would know. Pixies can feel magic more than breath itself, and with you, my senses go off like a metal detector in a penny arcade. Moreover, there's more than enough proof that you simply *refuse* to admit to yourself – *you just regularly wear that pride of yours like an ugly sweater at Christmas.*" She mutters the last bit under her breath, though just obnoxious enough to be patronizing, forcing a glare out of me. "If you only knew the power you have that's laying dormant inside of you –"

"I don't *want* to know the power inside of me, do you not comprehend that?" I whisper-shout, tapping my index finger to my temple. "Not that there is any, because I think I would've known by now and believe me, I would've taken full advantage of that shit my whole damned life." She bats her eyelashes a few times, listening. I crack on, "I'm very clearly *not* remarkable in any way, Evangeline. I am only here because I am related to some ancient guy, and for some reason Paragon wanted you lot to know, and *that's it.* I am not capable of any of this," I gesture to her, myself, and the surrounding area and beyond, "for a plethora of reasons, and since you read my journal cover to cover, you'd know that damn well."

"Of course you aren't capable."

I don't know if I should be offended, but regardless I accept her compliance and almost catch my breath. Again I say, "Thank you."

"So due to those facts from your impressive monologue and then some, I'm going to help you."

My face and everything inside me turns sour. My voice squawks, "You're *what* now?"

"With you as my apprentice, in no time I will teach you everything you need to know about magic and how to use it. We're gonna save Paragon *together*. Since it's in your veins already, you just need to learn how to wake it up. You've already started, actually –"

"*No.* That is not happening."

"Oh, you better believe your naive ass it is."

"What do you even know about the Pétros Pan magic I may *or may most likely not* carry?"

"I just *do,* okay? I know everything. It's better to just accept that early on. Now, stop asking questions." She circles me like a hungry wolf, then stops behind me at her second go-round. "Do you trust me?"

"Not at all."

"C'mon, Peter Pan, do you trust me?"

"No!" I genuinely chuckle at her persistence, and at this point I'm going mad as a hatter. I turn to face her, "My answer isn't changing, lass. Discretion is the better part of valor."

"Bummer, Sir Pan. I was gonna give you your first lesson."

I protrude my bottom lip and fake pout, "And what might that have been?"

She points and glances up, and even though curiosity killed the kitty, I follow her gaze. A rumble of thunder shakes the ground beneath me, and I really, really, *really* don't want to believe what I am seeing, but inconceivably *yet so believably,* a vast assortment of cats and dogs[90] are plummeting toward the ground –

Plummeting toward me.

---

[90] *Hehe...it's raining cats and dogs.*

"Bloody…" I look back and forth from the meteorite-like pets, then back to her so many times, I get whiplash. "Shit, no, *Evangeline stop this now!*"

The itty bitty tosser doesn't say anything, yet just looks at me and smiles with her finger still pointing upward as if she's frozen there like a statue. The animals rain down faster, skydiving without a parachute so quickly that I don't have time to think for even a split second. I throw my arms up over my head and shield my body, squeezing my eyes shut, imagining what I simply want – *hope* – the cats and dogs will do and what's been on my mind for the last half hour –

Fly.

The space around me is deafeningly silent then. The roaring of thunder stops, and all I can hear are the blissfully unbothered crickets and critters from the forest. My body tingles with that sensation of warmth I'm beginning to grow slightly fond of, and I bask in its pleasure and the green glow that attempts to sneak through my eyelids for a moment before I open my eyes. When I do, I see Eevee gaping up once again with joy plastered on her face like caked on makeup. She meets my gaze, grinning from pointed ear to pointed ear, and nods her head upward, non verbally telling me to look up.

I do…
And to my ever present awe, see they're…
floating.
Flying.
They've suspended in mid-air as if I hit the pause button on a telly remote.

I'm afraid to put my arms down so I paralyze in place, nearly face to snoot with a Siberian Husky.[91] "Evangeline, did you…?"

"No," she whispers through a smile. "I didn't."

The husky then licks my cheek. He *says,* "Good boy, you passed!"

I yelp in shock, still having not gotten used to the fact that all creatures here can talk, and shuffle out of the way as all of the animals slowly float down to the earth around us. They laugh at my jumpy disposition, yet commend me on scraping through my first unhinged magic lesson that I still don't quite believe was my doing. I stare at my hands, which now don't give me any proof that I did jack squat, as they have gone back to normal temperature and are no longer glowing.

Fucking glowing…

I gently rub the scars and fresh cuts along my skin given by my own nails with my thumb to get some reality back into them. I stretch my naked wrist and shake it out, knowing full well I'm never getting that blasted brace back.

"Alright, scamper on now." Eevee tosses her arm out as if throwing something to the animals, and from thin air, tiny little pieces of some sort of meat fly into all of the mouths of the wild pets. They swiftly scurry into the woods, meanwhile I'm cemented where I stand, my mouth ready to catch flies; completely oblivious to the pixie's itty bitty body shifting and planting itself beside me. "Trust me now, freak?"

I sharply turn to her, eyes stretched wide in wonder and mouth still agape. "No…" I snicker, peering at the tree line of the forest again. "Not at all."

---

[91] *This is my favorite dog breed, so naturally it had to make an appearance.*

She laughs. "I have one more thing to show you, but it can wait until morning. Go get some shut eye – I'll see you at breakfast." She begins to leave, but then turns to me and smiles, "See? You're more than you think you are." Boldly, she rises into thin air to meet my cheek, and kisses it gently. My insides light on fire, and I can't tell if it's from uneasiness, bliss, or both...

Is that possible?

I remain completely stunned, though she walks away lightly as if the most insane things that have ever happened to me thus far *didn't* just happen to me, but as much as I want to, I don't call after her. I instead watch her until she is out of view, and then slowly head for my yurt as I study my hands again. When I think of the flying cats and dogs, a small glow illuminates through my skin and the warmth returns; but as I become tense at the occurrence, it dims as quickly as it came. I touch my cheek, the place where a strange pixie bird laid a small kiss, and I smile – a real, genuine smile – recalling everything that happened tonight.

"I just did that..." I whisper to myself. *"By George,* I did that."

CHAPTER twenty-three
Peter Pan? TBD
Paragon

"Yo, Peter, pass me the buttah, will ya?"

I'm not gonna lie, ever since last night's impromptu training session with Eevee, I'm a little more than terrified to use my hands in any sort of way. From the unanticipated magic to the even more unexpected cheek kiss, I still don't have the foggiest whether or not it was all a wacky dream. She hasn't been around this morning in order for me to ask for reassurance, but the last thing I want is for anything – let alone the butter – to start glowing, catch fire, or some wacko shit making everyone get all gobby about it. Sure, by now they all know that I'm a Pan, but even if I, *even a teeny bit,* believe that there is something, *anything* in me relating to actual magic…

I'm not quite ready for them to know that yet.
If ever at all.
I'm still not quite sure I even completely believe it yet.
I'm okay with being a normal, uncool, blood relative.
Ugh.

I allow my hand to slip beneath the long sleeve of my shirt and reach for the butter dish with the nub I've created. I nearly drop it but luckily, Finn is too busy indulging in the carby heaven of his toast, so I get off the hook this time.

Nearly, anyway.

"Hands don't work today?" Maya sips her black coffee and eyes me curiously from across the table. The facetious comment from her is refreshing, as she's been a bit less obnoxious since coming to Paragon. I've gotten quite used to, perhaps even fond of, her brash, outspoken behavior, and I have a feeling this cold turkey contrast is also eating her alive...so I'll be accommodating and engage.

"If you must know," I half whisper, "I'm actually thinking about getting someone to conjure me up some paws, so I must get used to doing things without thumbs." At this, a literal cat-woman sitting next to me looks down to meet my gaze, and narrows her yellow eyes. I give it a swift apologetic nod and closed, lined smile, then sit forward hoping the awkward moment will pass.

This makes Maya chuckle for the first time in what feels like forever. "Charming," she manages to stifle the giggle. "Really getting into the Paragon spirit now, are we?"

"Well, if I'm not *magical,*" I jazz my hands and mock the whispered word, "the least I can do is try and blend in somehow."

"Well, consider hooves then." She pokes at her uneaten food with a fork. "Or, honestly, any part of an ass would really suit you."

This genuinely causes me to projectile spew half of my coffee out onto the table while the other half burns and shoots up my nostrils. I hold back a phlegmy, cup-o-joe infused wheeze, and the already peeved cat-woman hisses, stands, and struts away slowly with her tail high in the air, which I'm safely assuming is her way of giving me the bird.

At last, I catch my breath. "You're quite the firecracker today, Sexton," I say, wiping my mouth with my sleeve. "Feels like I haven't heard your normally running on mouth speak in days. What's the occasion?"

"Brain was on backorder. My apologies, I didn't mean to disappoint my number one fan." She rakes her fingers through her unbrushed hair and stares at me again, this time with an expression I can't quite read. That's one thing that fascinates me about Maya: either she's a wide open book you've read a million times, or it's like attempting to read a foreign text you've never seen, or better yet, a foreign language yet to be discovered.

"What's that face for?" I ask her.

"Honestly I don't know. You just seem different too today."

Hide your hands, Peter, hide your hands.

I raise my brow in question, "Is that right?"

"You don't look as much like the personified version of death today, for lack of better words."

I suppress a chuckle. "Fancy I couldn't think of better words, truthfully." *Except for maybe 'death with pretty eyes'.* I pull out the fag box from my pocket and pound it against my open palm. "Decent night's sleep, I guess." I gaze at my cigarette and momentarily become tempted to conclude if last night was a dream or not by trying to shoot fire out of my fingertips to light it, but I advise against the intrusive thought. I stick to my trusty lighter and inhale the smoke into my lungs that are, I would say, the *actual* personified version of death…with nothing pretty about 'em in the least.

However, she's practically igniting my cigarette for me with the way she's glaring at it in my hands. Her face twists, "How many packs of those do you smoke a day?"

Not that it matters, but I can't help but perceive that this is the longest conversation she has ever engaged in with me, and I become satisfied with that observation. She notices my inward smirk at the accomplishment and hides one herself as I answer, "Well, after stealing every fag I could find for the last forty-eight hours, and then finding out everything is free here at their general store around the corner…let's just say my dear lungs are gonna *need* magic in due time." I blow smoke out of my nose and shrug, "Shit, maybe then my asthma will piss off too and I'll discover a life of oxygen flow normality…*wouldn't that be bloody brilliant.*" I mutter under my smokey breath.

"Your tar pit lungs are going to evaporate by then, pal."

"Well then, it's a good thing I'm already dead inside, innit lass?"

"A little less than half of you left to go then," she says, not missing a beat and glancing at me from behind the rim of her coffee cup.

I cock my head and raise an eyebrow, "Less than half?"

"Those eyes have been dead since I've met you." *There's the poetic, vile tongue I've missed.*

I sip my coffee, which seems to magically never get cold here, and instead of meeting her eyes, I focus on the steaming dark liquid gold and suppress a smile. "Ditto, love."

If I'm not mistaken, *which I'm positive I'm not,* Maya's cheeks grow ever so slightly pink at this, yet she squashes her tiny smile as quickly as it came as she always does when it comes to me.

But I savor the conversation –
and save her the trouble –   this just always makes my
and pretend not to notice.   heart happy. not sure why.
Because I'm chivalrous like that.

"But, really…" her eyes still don't meet mine as she eyes nothing in particular on the table, "you should quit it with the cancer sticks. You'll live longer, and I think, ya know…" she looks at all of the Peculiar creatures around us and the area surrounding, "you seem to have a lot to live for now."

No…
If anything, this situation in its entirety makes me wanna die…
But I don't say that for fear that I might get flipped off again.

The compassion for Paragon is fairly difficult for me to compute in my current pandemonious brain in general – *indeed, pan pun intended* – especially from the usual she-demon herself. "I am not their hero," I mutter too quickly for her to respond. "And do my ears deceive me, or did Maya Sexton just say something remotely bonny about this place?"

She sneers, "Don't get used to it." Her icy blue eyes finally find mine, and though they seem a thousand miles away, somehow a surge of the energy they carry soars through me and brings me more than any caffeine could ever manage, even in a place of pure, strange magic. "The only good things about this place are that there's no ninth circle of hell therapy circle, and they don't give a shit about how much I eat."

The magic fades and I half sigh at that, biting the inside of my bottom lip. I notice for the first time since sitting that she's eaten less than I have, and all I've eaten is a half-a-pound of smoke and two cups of black coffee. I inhale my cig again and decide against my better judgment to instigate.

"So…" I gently brew, "if you can ooze even the slightest bit of concern about my senescence due to my fatal smoking habit, does that give me the okay to tell you that despite the freedom, you should probably eat *something?*

She shakes her head, "Nope."

Though presumed, that answer was inevitably never going to be accepted.

"I'll make you a deal." My emerald eyes create an indelible teal aura between us. "You eat two pieces of toast tomorrow morning –" *and just like that, instant anxiety befalls her,* "no jam –" I quickly add, "just a little bit of butter *or* I'll even accept plain for this time; and in return, I won't smoke until lunch. How 'bout it?"

Her expression becomes hard. "I feel like that is *not* the equivalent of me eating two pieces of bread."

"Oh, gee, I thought that was a rather long time without a cigarette for me!" I teasingly taunt. "I normally have one or two for breakfast, though I suppose I could go longer –"

"*No,* you British little bitch! Mine is *worse!*"

"Oh, oh! Of course, how silly of me." She shakes her head and rolls her eyes loudly, as I reluctantly half smirk and toss my cigarette butt into oblivion. "Be that as it may, you're tough, at least I think…" Her eyes turn to slits as she worries her bottom lip between her teeth in challenge. "So c'mon, just this once. We're already living in the comfort of uncomfortability, what's a little more to spice up the adventure, yeah? I won't have my usual cigarette and coffee first thing in the A.M, as I've done for years, and you have two pieces of toast. It won't kill me, it won't kill you."

She ponders the challenge, and I'm baffled I even made it this far. "No jam?" She begs for reassurance.

"That's what I said: *no jam.* All I dare ask is for a one time commitment." *For now, anyway, but she doesn't need to know that.*

"Why are you doing this?"

I don't want to go into the sappy woe-me detail about how I overcame my brutal nosh battle little by little, bite by bite, morning by morning, because I know that's a no good waste of time for both of us; and I also don't want to say something I regret in any way. So instead, I simply shrug. "Help me help you, help you help me."

"Again, why –"

"Are you in or what?"

Her eyes dart every which way, avoiding mine as if attempting to find a way out hiding somewhere around us. I think she and I both know full well that this has to be addressed and challenged sooner or later *(more like sooner than later),* thus she surrenders. "Okay – wait, *no, no, I can't...*Okay. *No...Maybe!"* She rubs her eyes until she sees stars, and eventually comes back down to me. "I'll think about it, okay?"

I nod, then wink. "Good girl."[92]

This time she does not successfully hide her beet red face, and before I can ask why she looks like she suddenly got attacked by the sun, *even though I fancy I know why but I can't imagine that is, in fact,* **why**...I jump when I feel a tap on my shoulder, yet turn to see there's no one behind me.

"You okay there?" Maya's brows crinkle in question, as I'm almost positive it looked like I just heard Jesus speak sweet nothings in my ear from behind me.

Before I turn back around fully, I feel the tap again, though just the same – no one is there. "Yeah..." I say, not turning to face Maya and her puzzled expression that I can feel without seeing it. "I'll be back in sec."

There seems to be a recurring theme with this damn table.

As per the right shoulder that was mysteriously tapped, I walk slowly the same way down the cobblestone path toward the lake and peer around, yet see no one.

"Hello?" As I hear my voice echo back at me, I genuinely just feel...stupid.

No fancy words about it.
I just feel dumb. Embarrassed for my own self. That's that.

---

[92] *Hot damn.*

I Prefer Peter

I'm standing here alone, swearing I felt someone tap me, and then following the tap down to the lake for...nothing.
Am I going mad?
Is all of this magic shit already going to my head?

I check to make sure the blades of grass beneath me are not *really* blades, because let's be frank, here it would make more sense if they were than if they weren't. Once I'm pleased to find that they are not hazardous, I plop onto the greenery that is more like a bed, than anything.

A bed of grass.
Go figure.
Cause damn, it sure is uncommonly comfy.

I stare at the moving clouds that I was welcomed with the first time I ever crash landed here, and I count the ones that look like sheep hopping over the moon until I begin drifting.

No, no, stay awake.

A little nap won't hurt.

Get back to the table.

Just five minutes...

My eyes grow heavier and heavier until finally they give in and I fall asleep under the warm blanket of the sun.

✐ ✐ ✐

I Prefer Peter

Shift POV: Maya Sexton

"Finneas, did you see which way Peter ran off to?"

Near the pine tree lined opening of the forest, Finn lights a cigarette in between his lips and hums out an *'uh-uh'*.

I swear to God, sooner or later one of these chain smoking idiots is gonna set the realm on fire.

"Why you lookin'?" Billows of smoke follow his words and I have to swat it away from my face. "Since when have you ever given a monkey about what Petey's up to?"

I don't care...do I?
...Given a monkey?

"Oh, ya know, just making sure he's not close to dying on the yurt floor again or anything."

He chortles at my dark humor. "Our newfound king's always runnin' around doing somethin' now; it's hard to keep track." I almost sense hostility in his voice, but I can't imagine why. Peter is like a god to Finneas, it's as if everything he does is automatically transcendent. He proceeds, glancing at me beyond the bridge of his nose as he tilts his head back, more so occupied with the smoke rings he's blowing out of his O-shaped mouth...a trick he learned from Peter, no doubt. "Did you check with Eevee?"

My face contorts and I may or may not have totally let it. "Why would I check with *her?*"

Huh...I guess I didn't realize hostility was contagious...

Finneas clearly expects the tone that accompanies my response, and thus snorts casually. "Because I think you and I both know that pixie chick totally digs the kid."

"Evangeline? Into *Peter?* Please, she doesn't even like humans, let alone *us.*"

"Easy there, Impossible Burgers," Finn chuckles through his words. "No need to get testy, or all peanut butter and *jelly.*"

Gayest thing he's ever said.

"Do you know where he is or not, Delfinnium?"

His eyes narrow at me with distaste. "Hey now, toots, don't shoot the messenger. Not my fault stupid cupid did you dirty." He runs his fingers through his hair and inhales, then puffs out more smoke like he's posing for a damn picture. "Check the lake."

"Much obliged." I roll my eyes and stomp away with my bare feet in the grass. I've come to thoroughly enjoy walking around here barefoot – it gives me a sense of grounding…pun intended.

I know what you're thinking and no, I don't *fancy* Peter, to use his shit-Brit lingo. To be quite frank, I despise Peter. I can't stand him. He's a broody, loud mouth, cocky, prick who doesn't give a damn about anybody but himself, and uses his mysterious, unspoken past and mental instability as an excuse to be that way. His little journal is just a ploy so he doesn't have to be social or speak to anyone, and not only that, just when you think he *does* care about you, it's all for his own little egotistical show.

Fuck…
I really think that…
↑ *Not sure if that's a statement or a question.*

I Prefer Peter

> Perhaps I'm being harsh.

Does it sound like I'm convincing myself of it all?

> **No,** It's the truth.

Is it?

> Ugh. Yes. Shut up.

Ignoring my brain that will likely never cease to operate at a million miles-per-second, I walk down the pathway leading to the lake. Birds are singing gorgeous songs above me with literal human-like operatic voices, and the light breeze is whistling along with a melodious tune that's far too realistic for my brooding case of denial. Upon reaching the lake, I almost miss Peter laying sound asleep within the dancing brush of the switchgrass and wildflowers with colors I can hardly fathom. It's like he blends in with the serene nature – like he's one with it.

Like he belongs.

I may sound absolutely batshit crazy for this too *(what's new, right?),* but it's almost as if the brush surrounding us is dancing around him, *for* him...as if it's praising him in some way. With my feet barely audible upon the soft grass, I hesitantly start toward him without knowing why I begin to move in the first place. I know I shouldn't wake him because he looks so peaceful, but for some strange reason, I can't stop my feet from being drawn to his peaceful state. My head is furious at me for giving into this so easily, yet my soul is calm...I have no idea what has come over me; it's like a spell or some shit.

It isn't until I almost reach him that a splash sounding like a rather large – too large – fish in the water stops me in my tracks and I find myself gazing upon one of the most petrifying, yet most intriguing things staring back at me from the brink of the lake's inlet. I narrow my eyes and squint to assure myself my vision isn't playing tricks on me, and as I do, the half amphibious creature smiles vile, supremely long, eerily limpid razor sharp teeth at me. Her skin is scaly and soggy, and as she waves, I am greeted by fingers that have death written all over them.

"Hello, darling girl."

At her acrid voice, fear splits my insides in two and before I can think, I'm sprinting back the way I came, away from her deep, sadistic stare, and a blissfully unaware Peter.

CHAPTER twenty-four
Peter Pan?? TBD
Paragon

I wake from a restful sleep that I could swear went on for merely seconds, but seems to have lasted until sunset. Time is such a nonexistent construct here, and I'm afraid my body is already adhering to the fact of it.

The sky is painted again in magnificent hues of oranges, pinks, and purples, and that is one thing about Paragon I have grown exceedingly fond of. It's as if God paints the sky differently every night simply for the realm's enjoyment...*blimey, what I would give to hold this kind of power.*[93] The setting sun still warms my skin as the breeze hugs me simultaneously, and as I gaze upon the open water, I can't help but be brought back to my days on the bay of Portsmouth when I was a young lad. Just *Molly* the lobster boat and I ruling the high seas, as I imagined it. Alone in the stillness, just her, me, a secret cigarette, and a lust for adventure –

Life was so bloody simple then.
Sure, it had its worries; its daily ponders...
Now every time I see water, I see a siren.
Every time I see something fall, I see my mom – the one I couldn't save.
*Every time I look in the mirror, I see **him** and remember why growing up is the foulest curse of mankind.*
Poor young Benjamin didn't realize the storm that was brewing right under his little nose.
For someone who wanted to leave Portsmouth so badly...

---

[93] ** wink wink **

God, what I'd give to have those days back again.

    Days where I would be my own best friend. I didn't have to care about anyone other than myself, my darling mum, and at that time, my so-called *family* wasn't in shambles, so even my father was on that list as well...School and chores were practically child's play; and frankly...I couldn't wait to grow up.

    I guess that's the funny thing – we all want something in this life so *desperately,* and we'll do anything and everything in our being to get it. Then finally one day, *bam! – it's ours*...yet the sudden inherited blessing we longed for, for what seems like our whole lives, all at once feels more like a *curse.*

Perhaps it's because we never truly had the faith it would genuinely happen for us?
Sure, we wanted it, but we never prepared ourselves for it actually happening...

    But then it does.

And so we discover, perhaps we really never exactly even wanted it at all.[94]

    Sitting up, I criss-cross my legs and dig into my jacket pocket for my journal, though my heart stumbles when I feel only the worn out denim material and my pen. I peer around to attempt to find its brown leather peeking out of the nearly neon green grass in case I'd forgotten I had used it as a pillow...but alas. I figure it's safe in the yurt where it should be, so I look around deciphering my next option.

---

[94] *This is one of my favorite passages within the entire book.*

I recall a distant memory from when I was little, of how my mum used to get cross when I would color pictures, mess up, then frustratedly tear up pieces of paper and carelessly throw them into the rubbish bin. She would tell little Benjie that he was *'wasting trees'*...[95]

I still try not to waste paper to this day.

The memory carries my legs to the nearest tree, which must've somehow miraculously read my thoughts because one of the abnormally long branches stretches down, handing me a piece of blotting paper seemingly made from her own bark. I, of course, thank the tree for her generosity and sit under the shade of her full foliage. *The giving tree, no doubt.*[96]

Clever.
Clever and loony as hell.

Placing the paper on my knee, I let loose a breath and begin to write:

jOurnAL eNTry ~ faNCy idK daYS oR hoURs anYmore.

it'S a coMMon affAir iN thIS lIfe i LiVe for Me tO HaVE trouBLE puTTIng mY feElings inTo cohERent worDs aNd/oR PhrASes iN normaL conVersaTion. Tis a DangerOUS, twiSTEd gaME thAT getS me neXt tO buTTfuCK noWheRE...ThOUGh, i reAd SOmeWHere thAT poetS acCUratELy arTIcul/ATE tHE FEElinGs we CANt desCRibe,[97]

---

[95] *My mom used to tell me this hehe*
[96] *Shel Silverstein is one of my heroes – has been since I was 5.*
[97] *Aye, we do.*

oR somE horsEy shiT – sO i'M goNNA tRY to beCome a PoeT RighT now foR thE hELL of iT...foR shiTS aND gigGLes, iF yOU wiLL...tO see iF IT remEDIes mY siTUAtion EVen a Tad:

by PetEr...grEEnpaN:

IF A FACE AS SMOOTH SANDPAPER
AND WITHERING BRITTLE BONES
ISNT ENOUGH TO CONVINCE YOU
TO NEVER, EVER GROW OLD
THAN WHAT WILL?
I HEAR YOU SHRINK?
IM SHORT ENOUGH!
YOU LOSE YOUR STRENGTH?
COR, WOULD THAT BE ROUGH!
BALANCE LIKE A DRUNKEN SAILOR
CAKES AND ICE CREAM
DULLER IN FLAVOR
RESPONSIBILITIES
LOSING YOUR KEYS

SOMEONE, PLEASE
IM ON MY KNEES
LET ME STAY
FOREVER YOUNG

GROWING OLD

Fun Fact: I wrote this poem a while ago, having no idea it would make it in this book, let alone a book in general. It's one of my favorite things ever, & was such a special addition to the story.

I Prefer Peter

IS LIKE THE WORST SONG
EVER SUNG

THEY SAY
ADULT LIFE'S
AN "AWFULLY BIG ADVENTURE"
THOUGH I'D RATHER FEED MY RIGHT ARM
TO A SNAPPISH, RAVENOUS CROC
THAN HAVE SOMEONE CALL ME "SIR"

I CANT COMPREHEND
THE FUSS OF THE "FUN"
WHAT HAPPENS WHEN TIME CATCHES UP
AND YOU CAN NO LONGER RUN?
WHAT HAPPENS WHEN THE LITTLE
WHIMSICAL THINGS
DONT MATTER ANYMORE?
WHERE SILLY GAMES
AND DEEP GRASS STAINS
ALL AT ONCE, BECOME A CHORE?
WHAT HAPPENS WHEN FAITH AND TRUST
TURN INTO LUST
AND THE MAGIC BECOMES A BORE?
WHERE PEOPLE CURSE
AND HEARTS JUST HURT
AND SAD ARE THE NORMAL FEW
MAYBE THIS WOULD REVERSE
MAYBE THEN BE HUMOUREDLY PERVERSE
IF PEOPLE NEVER GREW

OH, TO SEE THE WORLD
THROUGH THESE EYES OF MINE
WHERE TASKS ARE **NEVER** PLANNED
AND PEOPLE **NEVER** DIE
WHERE LAUGHS REPLACE YOUR CRIES
AND COLORS ARE MAGNIFICENTLY GRAND

OH, TO LIVE A LIFE
A LIFE
IN NEVERLAND.

riGHt, okAy. thAt workS.
CheeRs.

❦ ❦ ❦

As I walk back up the way I came, I hear the faint whistle of a flute coming from above in the trees. I look up to see a familiar pair of beat up combat boots, and I chuckle to myself.

"That your mating call?" The music stops and Eevee's face peers down at me from on high. She smiles with her snow-white Cheshire grin,

"Yes, and it seems to have worked quite well."

I shake my head in disapproval of her flirtations. "Tell me you weren't watching me sleep…"

"You're not a snorer, in case you ever wondered."

"Of course I'm not, I'm unquestionably too charming for that," I say matter-of-factly, propelling her eyes to do a roundabout around their sockets. I nod up to her pipe instrument, "What've you got there?"

"Oh, I dabble in the art of the Siku," she says modestly, as if it wasn't one of the most beautiful combinations of tones I've ever heard. "Ironically, it's also called a pan flute."

Go figure. "Oh, is that right?" She throws it down to me and without any challenge, I catch it. I study its small bamboo tubes and strange semi triangular shape, and instinctively, it's like I've played the thing for centuries. My mouth finds the openings of the pipes, and as if I'm under some sort of spell again, I begin to play. It's not too shabby in the least for never seeing the instrument before in my life, and Evangeline seems to concur because she gawks at me in bewilderment, yet simultaneously grants me her infamous knowing cheeky sneer. Warmth surges through every vein of mine as the music fills the air, and my skin casts a golden hue – I look like the sunset.

"Guess I'm a natural," I try to say casually while hiding a prideful smile and forcing the glow to dissipate. I toss it back up to her and try not to have a heart attack.

Trying not to have a heart attack seems to have recently become a regular on my to-do list.

Eevee tosses the small flute back in one quick motion, "Keep it. Seems like it suits you, Pan. Really brings out your magic."

I look at her with soft disdain. "Your generosity overwhelms me. Ta muchly."

She cringes. "You're so British it hurts."

I tip a fake hat, "Cheers."

With that, I begin to walk away, but before I can get merely a few steps up the path, the pixie bird floats down beside me and blocks my way.

"Not so fast!" She hands me a piece of torn fabric that I assume is supposed to act as a blindfold. "I have a surprise for you."

I don't think I've ever liked that phrase. My eyebrows raise as I look at the tan material hanging in her outstretched hand. "Do you, now?"

"Go ahead, put it on."

I shake my head. "I'd rather not."

"Oh what, you're not a bottom?" She says snarkily, and I am taken miles aback in surprise at her forwardness.

"The hell did you say to me?" I faintly smile unwillingly.

"Kidding!" The pixie defends much too promptly. "It's clear you're more top than you probably even know." My cheeks heat involuntarily,[98] though thankfully she isn't looking at me but throwing her hair into a new fresh topknot – her evident defense mechanism. Evangeline tracks on in the midst of her hair just about whipping my face, "But this time, just do what I say and put it on. I'll even say *please.*"

Okay…I don't normally dive into any thoughts or chit-chats in this said genre, but really…

Plainly even jesting I'm a bottom…
Insult of the century.
…even though I would hardly know yet.
Still. The audacity…

Regardless, I put on the blindfold like a good boy.

Wink wink.

---

[98] *Mine too..*

"Alright," I say in complete darkness as I feel the upper part of my brow already begin to moisten with sweat. "Where are we going?"

She holds me by the waist with her super-nonhuman strength. "You'll see." I can hear the grin in her voice as we take to the sky.

CHAPTER twenty-five
Peter Pan? TBD
Paragon

Flying with a blindfold on is disorienting as hell, I'll tell you that much. I had to stop myself from upchucking nearly a dozen times, until finally we landed in a seemingly open place that smelled of pine and sweet water, with songs of birds coming from every which way.

I hack out phlegm that was compiled in my lungs from miles high, and run my fingers through my now sweaty hair. "Might I take off the bloody blindfold now?"

"In a minute," her voice is insistent. "I don't want you to ruin my surprise!"

I'm beyond cheesed off by all of this, but I humor her little game. "How do I know the surprise isn't you threatening me with a special pixie weapon of yours and then stealing my magic for your own selfish purposes?"

There's a small pause as she fidgets with something I can't make out, and then she scoffs. "Quite the imaginative one, aren't we, Pan?"

"I dabble. I'm also gonna pretend you didn't hesitate. My utmost apologies if I foiled your master plan."

"Oh, yes...*Shit! How could you?"* She teases frivolously. "Well lucky for us, I have a master plan B."

"And what might that be, Evangeline?"

Causing me to jolt a bit, she takes me by the wrist and opens my palm, placing something all too familiar in my hand. She says, "Remember when I accidentally read your journal...then accidentally stole it again?"

Accidentally is a mighty strong word. I still my entire being as my voice becomes heated, "Been doing some more afternoon leisure reading, have you?" I try to seize the rage boiling up inside me.

"Trust me on this one –"

"Trust you?" My voice raises and echoes throughout the area I still can't see. "You must be dead ass bonkers! I trust you less than I trust the small invisible boy in town at this point! Who the blasted *fuck* do you think you –"

"Shut up for a second!" She sassily cuts me off and practically speaks at the speed of light. "When I was overtaken by the emotions and longings you scribed in that book, it was no secret anymore that you and I dream of the exact same things. You longed for them back in that god-forsaken real world you live in, and I've eternally wished for them in mine." Though simmering with fury, my ears are attentive to her passionate tone. "Not only that but when I held that journal in my hands that night, I was shown –"

"Hell?"

"Freedom."

"Come again?"

"Peter, amongst all of the nightmares, trauma, and sheer darkness that soaks that book nearly cover to cover, you wrote about a land of wonder, beauty –"

"A place where dreams are born?" My tone is mocking this entirely.

"Exactly –"

"Evangeline," I pinch the bridge of my nose, "that was just some metaphorical poetic bullshit –"

"A place created with the heart," she recites. "A place where you can be everywhere, anywhere, and nowhere all at once! A nearly perfect place – your own land – where you'll *never* have to grow up. Somewhere that feels like when you were back with your mother –"

I compulsorily cry at the mention of her, *"Evangeline! –"*

"A *home!"*

I lose my breath at her uttering everything I wrote, verbatim. My body heats as even the poem from earlier is coequal with her words, as if after courteously conjuring paper for me from within their stumps, the trees whispered my secrets like I was solely tea time gossip....*so much for 'the royal treatment'.* I set my hands on my knees and cough at the thought of my mum, her image vivid in the blinding darkness.

Though now, honestly...I don't know whether to be outraged, or rather pleased to be...heard.

"Look," she proceeds gently, knowing she crossed a bold line, "for as long as you can remember, you have wanted a realm – a universe – of your own. One where you can start from the first flower and build up from the roots to create something perfect – something *yours.* Now to find someone who wants the same thing is a dream you likely thought would never come true – a vision that you have been craving for what feels like centuries. Am I wrong or right?"
"Eevee –"
"Am I wrong or right?"
I sigh so deeply, it hurts like hell. "You're right."
"Peter," she pleads. "I know what I've done seems like an invasion of privacy –"
"It was," I retort, as if she had asked a question.
"Fair. But…" She grunts in frustration like a child, "Just let me show you why I did what I did, alright? I needed your journal again to be certain…Listen, my theory was correct. Everything you've written in that journal is *there –"*
I'm assuming she's pointing, "just between and beyond those two twirling, intertwined oak trees in the once empty realm Pétros left behind. I saw it with my own eyes, but I couldn't step through without you. With certitude, I can say you inherited that book for a reason, and with it…and a little bit of my Paradust… you'll not only be able to have your dream

world, but save Paragon and everyone in it as well…We'll be a perfect team. Just, *please,* trust me."

I feel her tiny hands grip the back ties of my blindfold, and as she unloops the knot, I am met with the all too bright sun attacking my light eyes, even in the dim of dusk. Her ablaze eyes search mine for understanding, and as my vision adjusts, I just can't hold her dodgy stare. I stare at nothing in particular on the ground and heavily contemplate turning and storming away as fast as I got here. Want to take up all the magic in my innermost being that I have no fucking idea how to use, and fly far away from this…pixie bitch.

But even if I could, I don't know that I would.
I don't know why I feel propelled to trust Evangeline or anything she's saying…
Perhaps I'm as naive and juvenile as I perceive myself in my own head…
*Because my journal **isn't** enchanted – it's artlessly a collection of unhinged thoughts and unrealistic expectations –*

'Let your imagination and soul run wild, my dear.' …[99]

Unless…

"Then prove it."

"Really? –"

"Show me *now* before I change my mind; you don't have long." My speech is short. Excitement blooms up in her like fresh flowers in spring, and she hops next to me, planting her feet in the ground beside mine.

"If you don't mind, I need you to hold up your journal."

"Why?"

---

[99] *Pg. 32 - Do you think Elizabeth knew? Who's to say…*

"Just do it, freak." I tilt my head toward her and give her a glare, not appreciating the ever present attitude if it isn't coming from me at this point. She offers back a puppy dog lip, *"Pwease..."*

Unamused, I dig my journal out of my jacket pocket again and raise it into the air. "Now what?" I look down at her and ask, annoyance seeping off my tongue.

Though unexpectedly, she closes her amber eyes and inhales a deep breath, facing forward with her shoulders straight and head high. She holds out her hand with her palm facing the sky as she recites:

> *"And now we bring the one atone,*
> *So bring us land, a land of own.*
> *An island of dreams, from heart to bone;*
> *A never-land for us to roam."*

From the tiny pebbles to the insects alike in and on the dirt around us, all at once they begin to rise. The earth beneath our feet begins to tremble, as an orb of emerald green light, similar to the color I glow when my so-called magic presents itself, appears like a mystical bubble out of Evangeline's palm and floats delicately in front of our very eyes. With hers still tightly closed and my lookers the polar opposite, she guides the orb with the twisting and turning of her nimble fingers out far enough away from us until her soul is content with the distance, and once she is confident, the pixie extends her arm like a wizard without a wand as she calls out with gusto,

"Ánoixe i CHORA tou pote!"[100]

---

[100] *This is Greek for "Open Neverland".*
Anoixe = Open + i CHORA tou pote = Neverland.

Ready or not, Eevee seems to vanish into thin air as a cyclone erupts around me. Without warning, I'm aggressively launched and slammed onto my back by a gust of wind that doesn't feel quite like a common breeze, yet more equivalent to a massive, angry, invisible giant shoving me and knocking all of the air out of my chest with his burley hands. I cough forcefully, my lungs unable to find oxygen without my inhaler, and definitely not accommodating anything, an unforeseen electric shock follows the blow and I feel as though I am fried from the inside, out…yet the warmth that I can't seem to run from simultaneously engulfs me completely…it's an all too contradictingly overwhelming sensation of peace and sheer torment. I lay there submissively until the jolts and the cyclones cease, and for what seems like the trillionth time, I fancy I'm dead.

When I finally look up, I counter maybe a trillion and one…

I shoot straight onto my feet as I take in what appears to be a small-looking glass-type portal to another dimension between two parallel mile-high trees. I can practically feel the breeze from the other side of it greeting me, welcoming itself into the realm I'm frozen still in. Temptation radiates from its outer reflections along with the light of Paragon's setting sun, and in the middle of the gleaming borders lies a gateway to a world I've never seen, yet only forever dreamed of in vivid delusions and wild imaginations. Assuming it's a trap, my mind hesitates, though amongst all of the impossibilities that have deluged me thus far, I figure:

What the hell have I got to lose?

I carry my legs to the opening of what I'm presuming…*semi hoping*…to be my long awaited awfully big adventure. The scent of fresh pine, as well as wafts of vanilla and lavender fill my nose immediately; goosebumps covering me from head to toe.

Terrified yet full of wonder, I step through.[101]

---

[101] *At ONE time, I was going to end the book here...then I realized how fucking stupid that was...so I did not do that.*

CHAPTER twenty-six
Maya Sexton
Paragon

It's breakfast time again and for the third day in a row, I'm sitting here with some mighty petrifying, yet looking toasted to perfection bread, with no one to stare at in distaste whilst I may or may not eat it. Peter's disregard for our vow hurt at first, but now I'm just pissed the hell off. I hope the cigarettes he's likely devouring shrivel his pathetic excuse for lungs.

Finneas pops a squat in front of me, his plate filled to the brim and his mouth nearly salivating like a wild animal. I look up from my carby demon dish and ask, trying to sound as casual as possible,

"Have you seen Peter?"

His eyebrow arches. *"Peter* Peter? As in *Pan?"* He teases, but I'm not in the mood. Not even in the general vicinity of it. Yet of course, that motivates him, *"Again* you wanna know where *Peter* is?"

I give him a scowl. *"I* don't give a shit where our Lord and savior is. Evangeline was asking for him," I lie, mentally awarding myself with an Oscar for my believable performance, because I actually haven't even seen her either. "I figured since you're *so* obsessed with him, you'd know his every move."

He laughs, holding in a mouth full of sausage and breakfast potatoes that I didn't want to see. "Well, you're famously mistaken with that presumption, Half-Pint." *I think he's presenting himself with an Oscar too in his head.* He shifts in thought, as if the answer that I'm looking for is above him to the right. "Last I saw him he was heading toward the lake yesterday – didn't even see him last night." He shrugs as if it's no biggie, which is the normal case with Finn.

"Assumed he was still takin' a well needed skinny dip or somethin', but I was out like a light before I could hear him come in, if he even did; cause he was gone when I woke up, too." I pick apart the somehow still warm toast on my plate, my normally famished-by-choice stomach genuinely far from hungry. "Though as I've said before, if Evangeline found him, I'm sure he's *just* fine," he says this with a tone that makes any sort of chill in me dissipate, and causes my insides to turn to heavy lead for some goddamn reason...

I reprise my prior acting role and mirror the fact that I don't give a rat's butt. "Why, 'cause she's a slut sack?"

Finneas snorts out his coffee. "Sheesh, Sexton, I know you don't have a filter but cool your jets." Of course, he smiles then, "But yes."

I run my fingers through my hair, my heart thudding and the back of my neck beginning to heat.

Why? WHY?
Why am I sweating over Peter potentially being with that pixie pushover?
Reacting like this when I don't give a shit?
What if something actually happened to him?
He's been gone for three days, it could be something bad...
*Shit, shit, shit...Now I'm **really** worried...*

I don't even notice I am ruthlessly squeezing my bread to mush until Finneas reaches over the table and gently extracts it from my fist.

"Do I need to ask?" He looks at me knowingly, as if he doesn't even have to question what I'm thinking because I am, cursedly, an open book by defect. "Bit more aggy than normal today, are we?"

"No." My eyes find my squished no-longer-toast.

"You wanna take a walk? Burn off those...crumbs?"

Against my better judgment, I eventually agree, because if I don't move from this suddenly claustrophobic table, I might flip it over to find the oxygen that is refusing to go to my head. Finneas and I walk along the grass, allowing nature to fill the silent gaps between us while I think of everything I don't want to say. He pulls out a cigarette, his defense weapon of choice when things go a little too awkward for a little too long, and stops to light it. I don't look at him for the fear he'll read into my soul through my eyes as he so often does, but it's no use.

"It's okay, ya know," he vaguely starts as the cigarette erupts with a small flame. Though it doesn't take a rocket scientist to know what he's getting on about.

I play dumb; one of my favorite defense mechanisms, "What do you mean?"

He pollutes the clean morning air as he speaks the words I was afraid he'd say, "It's okay if you like Peter."

A bit too promptly, due to the fact that I was far too expectant of these irrevocable words and because my demon-Peter-no-show toast is now embedded into my brain, my vindication rises as well as my volume, "I do *not* like Peter! Fuck, I can't *stand* that cocky, callous, inconsiderate, narrow minded, unreliable, *bastard.*" I'm flailing about while talking nearly a million miles a minute, not even looking to see if Finneas is buying what I'm saying – *honestly, I think I'm just trying to afford it at this point.* I keep going, nonetheless, "He's a thorn in my ass, and I've hated him since the day we sat in that goddamned ninth circle of hell when he belligerently exploited me in front of the entire room to fuel his ego, then pretended to care for me just to fuck with my head, *then* continued to do *both* on and off whenever he pleased!

He's a manipulative, no good waste of oxygen; not that he has much left, anyway. Perhaps he's better off dead to these people, because honestly, when it comes to being a hero, he's about as fallible as Cailey was when it came to porn! *My God,* I hope *she's* doing okay..." My heart sinks for the first time at the thought of leaving my only friend behind without a shadow of a warning...without a trace of a goodbye. I dare turn my guilt into more anger,

"Now because of Peter, we've been thrown into a world we legitimately can't get out of! *I don't belong here!* I'm *not* special – neither of us are! No offense..." He holds up his hand as if to say *'none taken'*... he knows what I meant.

"Peter may be a *'Pan'* or *'magical'* or whatever," I continue, "which is wack in itself, but in the end, we're all just fucked up delinquents that had a run-in with coincidence, but now we're *screwed,* and I blame *him."*

Finished with my spiel, I take my first breath in what feels like an hour and my knees wobble like I just ran a marathon, thus I collapse onto the ground in surrender to this dire subject. Looking up, I see Finneas frozen still with a stupid ear-to-ear grin on his face, his cigarette hanging limply from his mouth. He stomps on the dirt excitedly like it's glass at a Jewish wedding before finally plummeting down beside me.

"Well cut my chord and call me sonny!"

I never know what the hell he's saying. "Huh?"

"You don't like Peter."

I sigh. "Thank you. I'm glad I made that clear –"

"You *love* Peter!"

I feel like I'm about to throw up. "Did you not hear anything I just word vomited out to you, Delfinnium?"

"Watch the name calling, Impossible Burgers," he points his finger at me like a big brother as he draws closer, shaking his head. Then his left eyebrow acts as if a string that is coequal to the corner of his mouth, and he decrees, "Just admit it."

Play dumb, play dumb. My stunned tone that involuntarily squeaks doesn't match my eyebrows that furrow. *There goes my Oscar.* "Admit what?"

"You *know* what!" His hands find my shoulders. "You love that Brit! Just spill it – not only to me, but also to yourself – amongst the ears of *nobody* else, that you're madly in love with Benjamin Peter Green! The same copper-headed kid you *'loathe'* with the burning passion of a thousand muddah-fucking suns – that's been more recently patented as Peter Pan!"

My head shakes at his words with the denial I'm so desperately trying to find, and the breeze bites my skin, giving it a chill and doing me a solid by masking the true reason behind the goosebumps riding up my flesh. Finneas' excited brown eyes glisten a honey whiskey color in the sunlight, and I do my best to glare at them to seem more convincing, "You're certifiably insane."

His blithe spirit doesn't falter. "Admit you're absolutely wild about him – dead ass bonkers. Mad, even." He's wildly expressive now, like a kid in a theater performing his favorite scene. "You know the truth. It's eating you alive and for once you *have* a filter? Maya, oh Maya." He shakes his head in disapproval. "Why don't you just say it?"[102]

His words echo in my topsy-turvy head, competing with the ruthless pounding in my eardrums. I don't want to say it – I *never* want to admit it. I've spent this whole time denying every bit of the fact, and I would've happily taken it to the grave...I still would be more than jubilant to do so, but I don't think this fucking hopeless romantic would allow that for a second. My soul surrenders and my voice becomes small.

"Because if I say it, then it will be real."

---

[102] *This was one of the first lil lines I ever shared from Finn. I fucking love it.*

He kneels down now to sit with me, his face becoming teddy bear soft as his voice turns as gentle as if speaking to a child, "And what's wrong with that?"

I stare at his dirty shoes, unable to meet his gaze with confidence after my few failed performances. "I'm afraid."

He lifts my chin gently with the curve of his finger and smiles at me with some of the kindest eyes I've ever seen. "And what's wrong with that?"

🖑 🖑 🖑

Later, Finneas and I sit by the lake where I last saw not only Peter but that heinous mer-thing that I'm not even sure was part of this land. It looked too…well, evil, I guess…compared to the rest of Paragon's purity. The breeze around us cools my sensitive skin and the sound of the still water begins calming my ever-present anxiety minute by minute…However, I resentfully envy Finn's boundless steady breathing, so subtly, I try to match it – *to absolutely zero avail.*

"So?" He finally yet abruptly speaks up, which almost makes my heart attack me.

"Fuck off, Del."

"We gotta talk about it!" He says through laughter.

"We will not now, nor not *ever*, be speaking of it."

"It's just us here, Half-Pint, and I won't tell a soul." He places his hand over his heart in some sort of a pledge of allegiance to me. "Scouts honor."

"Scouts honor my ass, you *sob.* There's no way you were a boy scout, let alone would you keep the honor and not tell your Lord and savior Peter Christ."

"Quit saying that! I do not *worship* the kid!"

"Oh, bullshit! You're more in love with him than I am."

He's silent, but not more silent than I become. I don't for a millisecond dare meet his gloat, though what I said rings in my ears like the most ear-splitting red-alert alarm. I feel Finneas' eyes piercing my skin more intensely than the sun, so I rebuttal without acknowledging them,

"I didn't mean it like that."

"You sure as shit meant it like that. Out of the abundance of the heart, the mouth speaks, Maya W. Sexton."

"What in the everloving fuck does that even mean?"

"It means you love Peter, and even the Freudian slip knows so."

His cockiness is driving me up the wall, but Delfinnium and I both are fully aware my stubborn ass isn't giving in anytime soon. In a sense, I may have partly conceded, but there's no way I am muttering even half of those actual words into Paragon's mystical atmosphere...who knows what the Paragod's – past, present, and/or future – or whatever the hell's will do with them. Knowing this freakshow of a place, the fucking whispering bell flowers will no doubt *actually whisper* and spill all of the shit I've said into Peter's boyish-lookin' ears if they caught wind of even a butt of it.

On the other hand...maybe it isn't such a big deal? It's highly possible I'm just absolutely terrified of the likelihood Peter loathes the concept of affection...or, more so, loathes it from *me.* We do have a mighty set-in-stone mutual bond based on hatred that we both are seemingly content with – that *he* is obviously content with...

But it could be just as possible that the idiot totally feels the same way and is in the exact same boat as I am; caught in a raging storm like I am...one where he simply doesn't think he can express how he truly feels because he too believes *I* loathe *him*...

*That **is** possible, right?*

*Hell, maybe the miscommunication trope in every romance
book known to man is my brutal fucking reality.
How would female book character protagonist Maya Sexton
handle this?[103]*

Another roadblock is that I also know for a sheer fact
that naive idiot doesn't have the slightest clue what love is;
hell, I don't think he even believes in love...*But then again,
do I?* What if we could change each other's minds?...
What if...

"Hot *fuck!*" Finneas once again crashes my train of
thought, scrambling back and nearly performing a backward
somersault at the height of his fear. He points at the water,
"Girlie, did you see that?"

I turn in the direction he's pointing. "No, I –" But
before I can get another word out...

*It's her.
I hoped with my entire being she was a figment of my colorful
imagination...but no.
It's that she-monster again.*

I tug on Finn's arm, "Fuck, Finneas, we have to go."

"Why?" His aghast tone, completely opposite of
mine, surprises me. "She's the most stunning creature I have
ever seen!" He can't keep his eyes off of her, while I can
barely keep her gaze without simultaneously wanting to pass
out and puke.

"Are we looking at the same vile mistress of death?"

---

[103] *Hehe. Look at this power I hold – I guess we'll find out*

His eyes widen. "How could you say that? Shit, Half-Pint, I know you have a brooding jealous bone, but let's not be cynical here."

I'm almost at a loss for words. Either Finneas Scott has the most undeniably atrocious taste in women, or we are not seeing the same thing. I test, "Finneas, tell me exactly what you see."

"I see the most drop-dead, sinister yet divine woman I have ever laid my young eyes upon. She looks like a mermaid – shoot, I think she *is* a mermaid – we are in a town of anything-goes, after all."

I roll my eyes. "Okay, what color hair does she have?"

He narrows his eyes as if it's the dumbest question he's ever heard. "Are you blind? It's a shining, sterling silver. Like that of a stunning sword," his words come out irritatingly poetic. "Why, what do you see?"

"Finn...her hair is a sickly seaweed green."

"What?" He looks at me, then her, completely baffled. "And her eyes...?"

"Terrifying, mustard yellow cat eyes."

"I see iridescent violet wonders."

"Her face?

"Flawless."

"Strange, 'cause I see a scaly she-devil."

At that, the mermaid hisses at me like the demon I keep comparing her to, and immediately after, looks to Finneas like he is the most dazzling thing she has ever had the pleasure to gaze upon.

I grab his arm, "It's a trap, Finneas, let's go."

"No fucking way!" He pulls out of my grasp and begins to be lured into the water. This is all so backward – it's as if *he's* the fish who just fell for the bait, and the fucking mer-thing is the expert catcher – as if she has the fatal fishing hook lodged into this moron's mouth, and is ready to reel in for the kill. "I'm going for a swim," Finn says in a daze, "you go on ahead."

"Del, stop! You know this is wack as hell, we need to get out of here!"

The mermaid screeches at me again with a sound that's worse than any nails on a chalkboard I have ever heard, yet it doesn't phase Finneas in the least,

"Don't you hear her gorgeous siren song?" He shouts backward, "She's singing just for me!"

"Finn, don't fall for it, she's just gonna hurt you!"

"Don't be so bitter, Maya! I bet she has some merman friends for you, now come on!" He waves his hand toward the water, trying to coerce me into following him. Whatever spell this siren is casting is obviously not affecting me in the slightest for God knows why, and I too have no idea how to break it for his sake. I look to the ground and, seeing giant rocks, I figure I got nothin' to lose.

"Hey, ugly ass Ariel!" I pick up the largest stone I can muster *(not the most ideal one of the bunch, but it'll do)*, and throw it in her direction – it doesn't go far, but hey, the splash gets her attention. "Leave Finneas the fuck alone!" She doesn't pay any mind to me, so I go one step further. "Don't bother, *he's gay!"*

The mermaid looks at both of us in utter confusion, and Finneas turns to me with distaste, shaking his head. "Grimy one, chick."

Flicking her tail up and creating a tsunami-like splash to spray me – *I assume she's flipping me off –*, the siren dives back into the lake, swimming away into the unknown. I had no idea if what I said would work or if she'd even give a shit about it considering Finn was all up in her gills regardless…*yes, fishy pun intended*…nevertheless, she conveniently got pissed off at something and scrammed, so *mission completed.*

However, still amongst the glorious high I feel for saving his life, I feel Finneas' stare burning my flesh again, and this time not in a friendly manner. "What the hell, pipsqueak?"

I think he's expecting an apology, but that's never coming. "I'm not sorry, Del. That fish would've eaten you alive. Take my word for it."

"It's not so much that…I'm sure the mer-queen will be back…" his tone is inquisitive as he walks closer, studying me like he's seeing me again for the first time. Finn suddenly stops as if he's scared to get too close to me, and I think I already know what's coming before he says it. He lowers his voice, "Do you know?"

Oh…maybe I didn't know what was coming. I ask genuinely, absentmindedly shaking my head in uncertainty, "Do I know…?"

"For goodness sake, Maya, level with me," he says anxiously through half-gritted teeth.

He's scared to say it…

The decent, humane part of my brain wants to mimic his character from before and comfort his fear, telling him to *'just admit it between us'* and that *'he can trust me'*. Though, the super bitch in me wants to do the exact opposite, and well…*she usually wins*.

"C'mon, Del," my illness forces me to tease, "one admittance for another."

His head sways back and forth, and luckily he isn't easily triggered by my bitchiness. "You're a heatheness, little one, but I ain't got shit to say. You're more than welcome to verbally admit *your* part though. I'm all ears."

"Oh, I have nothing to share, thanks. But, while I'm yapping *now*, would you want me to relay *yours for* you?" I smile facetiously.

He chuckles nervously, "It would be preferred that you didn't."

He hides his hands in his pockets, fidgeting due to the unwanted attention. I see a different kind of apprehension on his face – one that seems to have hoped this moment would never surface, but yet here we are…and he's petrified. For as long as I've known him, Delfinnium has claimed not to be scared of *anything,* and it rings stark true up until now…Honestly, it's unsettling.

Straining for the least intimidatingly condescending way possible, I murmur the words he likely dreads hearing, "You've never said it out loud before, have you?"

He looks down, now all jokes aside, and half shakes his head, "Can't recall."

I mimic the teddy bear tone he used with me before, "So why don't you say it now?"

He smirks cheekily up at me, clearly understanding my tactic. "Because if I say it," he mimes me from earlier, "then it will be real."

"And what's wrong with that?"

He looks at his shoes. "I'm *fuckin'* terrified."

I smile, too short to lift his chin, so I dip under his face to meet his downcast eyes. "And what's wrong with that?"

I toyed with the option of doing this for a really long time. I had a plethora of different ways this was going to go…
Some days I love the concept, some days I hate it…
We find out a bit more details in the next few chapters, though I'm still debating where to go with it (and how strongly) after Book 1. What do you think? I'm curious!

CHAPTER twenty-seven

Peter Pan
Neverland

the imagery in this journal entry is
some of my favorite in the book...
what do you think?
Were you transported to Neverland?

joURnaL EnTRy ~ neVERland

tHis PlacE.. thIs brAND nEw WorLD oF MY oWn...Is EveryTHing ivE evEr dreaMed oF anD morE.

I CAnt evEn begIn to desCRiBE its PUre aND uTTer mAGNifiCEnce, buT hell, iM goNNA trY:

iF yoU imAGINE soMEthING AnD beLIEVE haRD enouGH, youVE goT it. You could say thIS worLD is BASEd puREly oFF oF faITh...ANd i Guess tRUSt as weLL, BuT i WILL adMIT, ThaT One iS GonNA taKE me sOME geTTIng USEd to. It tOOk me nEarly 30 MInutES to conJUre uP waTEr yesTErday, but i sUppOSe We'LL gET theRe. Evangeline has BEEn TEAchINg me so mUCh...TOo muCh...bUT luCKIly, im A quICk stuDy.

If i EVer gET REaLly stUCk, SHe hAs SOmethING tHAT ComEs frOM heR Skin...oR...fRom soMEwhEre, IM sTIll nOT suRe...caLLEd PAraDust. She's menTIOned it A tiME or two, BUt askIng ABouT itS FAcetS waS neVER on My to-DO lisT. basICally, iTS a MAGIC, gLITtery subSTance thAT maKEs thE onE wHO PoSseSSes iT all-PowerfuL Im NOt quITE suRe thE fuLL extEnt oF whaT it CAn Do, noR aM i awaRE of ALL thE terMS anD conDITions qUiTE yet eithER, But i Do KNOw, evidEnTLY aLONg wiTH mY jouRnal, it noT onLY haD a HAnd in creATing thIS world buT ALso thE moSt quENching, puREst waTEr thAT haS evEr hit my LIps – aND I oncE saID thaT aboUT PARagon's...

It aLSO caN aPPArentlY MakE me limiTLess, buT whatEVEr.

The sky is tHE moSt ravISHinG shADE oF royAL bluE i HAVE eVER seEN. IndeeD, i wrOTe abOUT what I thougHt IT should look like, thOUgh NOthinG couldVE prePAREd Me For iTs glorY wHEN it actuALLy apPEAred inFront of My verY eyes. The SUn iS begINNing tO set Now, aND it iS thE moST smaSHinG compOSitION of sherbEt colORs, melTing toGETher tO creaTE oNe exquisITE shADE i canT even exPLain – I wont evEN daRE trY to foR feaR of inSULTing its bEAUty. fURTHermore, I thouGHt PARaGon's clouds weRe unREAl? I canT even BEGin to Describe tHE whiPPEd creAM bliSS of The cloUDS here. Pure whITE, fluFFY, CottoN canDY puFFS oF aRT – i JUSt wanT tO takE a nAP on thEm, aND i HAVE no DoubT in MY miND thaT i CouLD, buT aT THE saME TIme, i NEVER wanT TO closE my eyeS agaiN. It's quiTE jolLy, really, thAT tHE lonGEr Im herE, thE more I see tHAt evEN thoUGH WherE i Am siTTIng it IS spRING, oN All DIFFereNT pARTS of thIS place, iT's a varyINg seasoN – sO If yoU want Summer, WinTEr, Spring, or Fall – yoU caN havE theM all, in thEIr entiREty aNd BEaUtiFUlly DESignATed splEndor.

In adDition tO thIS, tHE dewY GRAss iS SOFT – LIke, VELvety SMooTH...noT aHACKing mY skiN wiTH daGGER–LIke tEXTures, Semi siMilar to PARAgon's, bUT exCeEDinglY More so. THE tallEST trEES oF aLL kiNDS suRROuND ME likE a HEDge oF pROTECtion EveRYWHERE i tuRN – tHEY Move witH ME as ThOugh I owN thEM – as iF Im tHE gOD thAT plANTED theM.

I gueSS mayBE i am?

The freSH bERRy bUSHES, thE pERPEtuaL blOOMIng FLOWERs wiTH shaDEs iVe NEVER seEn ANd scENTS iVe neVER inHALed, tHE serEne crySTAL cLEAR lAkes aND watERfaLLS leadING inTo goRgEOUS laGOOns, thE biRDs AND buGS thaT flY HigH ANd lOW – thEY all do THE same.

iT's like everything here is alive... aNd tO aLL of it – aLL of ThEM... So it sEEms, I am THEiR gOD.

The gRAMarYe I cARRy iS piERcinglY uNMAtchEd tO evERYTHing iN thIS pROVIncE, thUS maKING me feeL...i DOnT kNOw... inFinITE.

I hAVE never felT thiS..imPORtant? tHIS wanTED? tHIS poWERful? thIS...HOME?

I FeeL mORe connEcted To thiS iSland mORe thaN i HAve felT to.. ANything .. asIde frOm maYbe mY moTher.

~~anD maYbe ma~~ dISreGArd *Note: this is not an annotation. It's actually apart of the book LOL.*

iT's aS if mY hearT noT onlY belOngs tO me, bUT dUE to tHe faCT that iTs beatINg, iT alSO means That tHE islanD is Alive. iF my hearT ever Stopped, I feaR thE islaND woULd diE as WEIL...

thEREfore, it'S quite possIBly anotheR thinG to trUly liVe foR.

I keeP stumBLing upoN thinGs oF thaT sort aNd aT firSt, it Bothered ME...now I conSTantly l00k forWard to thE NExt reason tO stay aRound.

I PRay thIS feElinG nEVER EndS.

Oy, That'S why itS naMEd NEVerLAND. :) HaS A wickEd rinG to it, DOn't chA think?

yA KnoW, tHis plACe reMInds ME a lot oF her..My mumma, I meaN. Which I guess WAs EXActly thE kinD of FEeling i desIred iF I evEr got This dreAmlaND to exiSt: SOMEthing tO fEEl cloSE tO her Again. NoW Granted, it's noT entiRELy thE same .. nothiNG ever Will be... buT it'S something. And soMEthing is A hellUva lot bEtter thAn nothiNg.

iVE ONLY BeeN disCOverinG nEVEerland foR a few days, buT Eevee PLans On SHOWIng mE aroUND mOre todAy. She KNows thE in's aND outS as PArt oF her pIXie maGic, alTHOugh whaT She HASn't mentiOned, noR do I fancY askinG abOut...

whaT do I make Of aLL the BAD paRtS of mY jouRNal entRIEs?
There weRE...aMPle.
Do ThOSE noT appLy? ARE they LUrking amongST thE gooDnESS oF thIs tOO-beAUt-To-BE-TRuE dreAMscaPE juST waiTIng to TurN eveRYthinG intO a waKIng nIGhtmaRE...?

wiTH mY luck, tHat seeMS moRE likeLy.
I SUppOSe i'LL havE To crOss tHAt bridGE iF i geT to It...foR now, everY biT of mY limbS arE CRossED iN hopES thaT's juST a comMon negatIVE conNOtaTIOn FroM mY eVer sO lovELy minD.

uGH...sO FUckinG wiLD.
thE whoLE kiT And CAbooDLe - so BLOODY FACKING bOnkers.

EevEE...speaking Of tHAT piXIE bird. I cANT TAKE fuLL CreDIT fOR thIS plaCE. Yes, mY ancesTOrs creaTEd it firsT, and SURe, i deveLOped thE ins anD ouTS oF it wiTH my jouRNAl, whiCH heLD mosT oF the SIGNIficanCE foR thE manUFACturing...BUT As unSTOPPAble aS i fEEl, iF it wereNT for EVangEline, noNE of tHis wouLD eveN exist ouTSIDE of my IMAGinatioNs aND nEARly impOSSIble tO reAD penMANshIP. SHE's BEEn an ANGEl tO mE SINCe we'VE ARRIved in PARagon, aND hoNESTly, i'LL neVER knoW hoW To sHOW my aPPRECIAtion. iLL havE to ASK hoW i Can REPay hER.

I Cant HELp BUT wonDER why Though. WHY diD she dO aLL of THis For ME? sURE iT Was aLL 'prOphetic' anD 'predESTinED' & yaddah yaddah...buT whY ALl thE extrA heLp anD hOSPitalITy? Is iT wronG of me tO think there'S A catCH attachED? shE didnT havE TO agreE to assisT thiS situaTIon...tO menTOR a worLD claSS fuCK up fRom NEW yoRk...hell, i COuld probAbLy figUre ouT hoW To makE my jouRNAl uSEFul for eveRYthing...thOUgh unFORtunately, i fanCY it'S nOT thaT simple. WHy heR? wHY me? DOEs she truLY belIEve wE couLD be omNIpotEnT togEther? iS it BECAuse IM a PAn ANd SHE thinkS shE oWEs mE? iS shE LEttiNG mY MAgiC FESTer jUsT sO shE caN draIN mE OF ALL oF IT lateR WitH sOME sORT of SPell? IS she buTTEring mE uP CAUSE she'S gONNa gIvE ME the fUll reSPOnsiBILity oF SavInG heR HomE anD shE WantS mE To SEe mY DreaM worLD beFORe i DiE?

iS it BECAUse of SOMEthinG else..?
SOmethINg mOrE..?
uGH. No.

ON AnOTHER noTE, i WIsh FINNEas AND MaYa Were HEre to sEE aLL OF thiS. I WONT lIE, i KInDA MISS thosE shithEads a HEllUva Lot. THIS is The lONGESt iVE bEEN sepARated FroM tHEm sinCE we mEt, anD it feEls...ofF. DiscoNNEcted. nOT seCUre...
liKE we'rE bluETOOth sigNALs desPEratEly tryIng to sYNc Up wiTH tHEIr desIGnated paIRings, buT failIng to Find thEM evERYtime...doES thAT MAke senSe?

I DOnt fuCKin' knOW, bUt iT sounDEd cool.
ALL thAT to say, I'LL HAVE to ASk EEvee hOW to gET theM HEre.

It'S alSO BEen 3 daYS sinCe i'vE had a cigARette fOr breAkfast... siNCe thE daY i maDe thaT baRgaIn witH maYA. YES, i'Ve forCEd mysELF to abIDe bY my eND oF thE DEal...mOSTly becAUsE i reaLizEd waY too laTE THat i fLAKed oN tHE breakfaST plAN we Had anD I feEL liKE a cockNut abOUt...i noRMAlly donT, sO thiS iS FResh. i havEnt thE foggIEst if She kEPt HEr deal.. buT shit, I woULDnt exPECT her too. whAT a dicK moVE on my paRT - i forgot all about iT AnD waS tOO cauGHT up In aLL thE maGIC oF mY owN heRE, i FORgot tO tRy ANd giVE soME to heR foR onCe.

shE probABly haTEs me riGHT Now.

~~I kiNDa wiSH shE waS here.~~

CheeRs.

    I look down off the balcony of my new luxurious treehouse home, filled with everything I need, want, and nothing I don't; and scan Neverland as far as the eye can see. The ocean is directly across from my view, and the horizon seems centuries away – it's beyond mad that this is a completely separate realm, yet Paragon is practically right next door, more or less at a simple snap of my fingers.

Though, I'm not entirely sure the way back, if I'm being straight with you…
I've been so caught up in this place I forgot to ask.
And frankly, I never wrote it down because I never thought it'd actually exist…

    I trot down my grand, twisting outdoor staircase that leads me to a dirt ground patched with freshly growing grass that seems to wave at me as I pass, and admire my 'home' *(can I call it my home?)* from the tippy top to the bottom, and from side to side. With everything from fresh, dark oak wood for a rich-looking finish, a playful swing hanging off the side so I can launch into what seems like a forest oblivion, a net hammock built into the balcony's edge instead of a railing so I can lounge hanging off the side – even the inside is the most dreamy, aesthetically pleasing, comfortable home, with dark green interior walls and plenty of space.

It's...perfect.
And it's all mine.
I never, ever want to leave.

Evangeline is situated comfortably on a rocking chair beside the front door, smiling brighter than the Neverland sun when she sees me approaching. "It's about time you woke up."

"Cheeky you would think I even slept. I was terrified I would wake up and this would all have been a dream."

Far too swift for me to react, she reaches out and gives my arm an awful pinch. Caught off guard, I yelp in pain like a little girlie.

"Not dreaming," she titters. "Now c'mon, there's still so much to see, and even more to learn!"

She begins to scurry away, but I call after her, "Wait!" Eevee turns, huffing at me like an annoyed little girl. "There's just one thing – well, not *just* one…but a *specific* thing in particular that's been haunting me…"

"And that is?"

I try to think of something – anything better than the one word, but I can't. "Why?"

"Why what?"

"Why did you do all of this for me?"

"Well, to save Paragon, *no duh;* but also because you deserve it," she still says the last reason as if it's *'duh'* ridden obvious, whilst pointing and briefly placing her finger on my chest.

"Really –"

"You're a *Pan!*" She states before I speak further. "Since clearly, you were the key – *i.e. the only one* – who could even open this portal with that antique journal of yours completing all the details, don't you see Neverland was kinda meant to be yours before time itself? You just needed to get here to obtain it. Then, with a bit of Paradust to assist, of course," she drops a curtsy, "the stars aligned and led you straight home; and you can't argue with stars – stars don't lie.[104] It was just meant to be."

"How is that possible? How did Pétros know someone – *I* – would come?"

"He was a Paragod…" she shrugs, "he knew everything from when the rain would pour to when the wind would blow. He must've known the prophecy would be fulfilled. Granted, no one knew *you specifically* would show up, let alone the journal be the key to completing and opening the realm…but *he* certainly must have known something we didn't, otherwise we would have been left here to die on purpose…But I don't deem him as one to do something of that nature to his people."

"Why didn't you try?"

"To open it?" She spits out in a mocking laugh. "Hell, we did! We tested everything, from spells, potions, riddles, sacrifices…" *I don't pry on that last one, even though it begins to gnaw at my question bank…The look in her eyes gives evidence that it's a bitter subject, and truthfully, it scares the shit out of me to even begin to guess the details anyway.* "We wasted more magic than we could afford by doing so, and that's why Paragon is dying so quickly as we speak. When we used up the power, we couldn't regain it due to no magic flowing in or out of the realm. Paradust could only help so much, but since we weren't able to resupply, we had to use it sparingly."

---

[104] *Another one of my favorite quotes in here.*

"How do you resupply…?"

"Only pixies can – at the Hollow Tree. The dust keeps the tree alive, but once the magic stopped abounding, the tree started to die. Now not only is Paragon losing its magic, but pixies are too. Everything is sort of one giant clusterfuck…*But now, you're here!*" She jumps giddily like a child, and I crack a taut smile.

"And you believed it all this time?" Subtle astonishment oozes off my tongue. "That someone would come and potentially rescue you all, even after *centuries* of nothing? Weren't you afraid of dying?"

Evangeline scoffs. "Of *course* I was afraid, you sob…" I can easily tell she doesn't like admitting that. She sighs then, "But how did the people know Jesus Christ would come and save *them?* Somethings you just have to use a bit of faith on, pixie boy. Believe without seeing."

There's that word again: *faith.* This whole phenomenon has had me digging through every nook and cranny of my innermost being to try and find each wee drop of faith in there…

Let's just say, there ain't much.
Is there a faith tree too I can snag some from?

Nevertheless, I nod at the lass, unable to argue with her logic. I rarely ponder the story of Jesus, though the way she says it makes me reconsider everything I was never sure of.[105] "Okay, so follow up question…" I shift my stance and cross my arms, challenging, "Now that the portal is open and I have all of my hopes and dreams, what's the catch? When's the showdown or the 'quest' to wherever or whomever? How the bloody hell do I get the magic flowing again to even *save*

---

[105] *I always like to give a shout out to the one who made this all possible. Give glory and honor where it's due. - 1 Corinthians 10:31 -*

Paragon? *How do I defeat the Royals?" Shit,* I'm riling myself up to panic again. I take a breath and joke, "Seems like we're just on our dream vacation here."

Eevee smirks at me at the mention of the word *our.* "That's not a bad thing. This *is* your – *our* – dream world, after all. No harm in a little pleasure." She winks, and I roll my eyes, trying to hide the corner of my mouth peaking. "However, I'm glad you asked," there's a hint of confidence in her tone, and honestly, I'm relieved she has the potential answer or even at least an educated guess. She places her feet firmly on the ground as if ready for battle. "We need to train you."

"Okay…No – what?"

"Face it, kid, you're a rookie. A greenie, if you will…pun intended." *Mmhmm. Haven't heard that one before. So fucking original, I'm dying of laughter.* "If you plan on going on any sort of 'quest', which we are – you're gonna need to awaken the hell out of that magic of yours and learn how to control the shit out of it. Conjuring a world through a journal that was already spiked with divination was a cheat start –" my eyes slit, and she winks before mouthing on, "You need to resurrect the alchemy that is buried within your veins."

"Isn't that what Paradust is for?"

"See, that's what you have to realize, Peter…you're stronger than the dust. Though it's in your veins, you're far more powerful, if not just as. The quicker you have faith in that, the faster you too realize you even have the ability to defeat the Royals with ease."

"Me? Evangeline, I don't know if all that dusty-dust has gone to that pretty little head of yours," she slightly pinks at my unintentional chat up, "but need I remind you that Pétros *died* while battling those monsters? Why should I be so confident in my inherited power, if it stems from a man who couldn't use it to clobber the enemy, let alone save himself?"

"Silly ass, *you* have your *own* magic festering in there *along with* your inherited magic. You don't get that you are twice as powerful as Pétros – as any ruler within any of the realms."

"That's undeniably false, pixie chick. Why wouldn't he just *woosh* the responsibility over to someone like you or Gideon? A Peculiar who knows all there is to know about the ins and outs of charmwork and whatnot – why *me?* Why did his last spell have to command a forthcoming *Pan* to do everything?"

"It's simple, really," she states cockily. "Who better than a descendant of the one in which it belonged? He knew no one would be powerful enough, wise enough, let alone *man enough* to take on the task. He needed someone who thinks like him, talks like him, *is* him, in a sense – it was all a part of the plan. Seems Pétros *wanted* Paragon to wait until they had someone who was fully willing to save it by traveling through the forbidden realm to take control of Paratoze and Paradmir, thus bringing the magic back. Suppose he knew only a Pan would be fit for the taking."

Firstly: Man enough? Please. Give me a fucking break. Secondly, though tied for first: Willing is a mighty strong word.

"You must be insane."

"All the best people are. [106]And, like you said, it may be *false* and kooky right now, but not for long. You just need to be educated, and then *become it.* But we don't have forever…Thus, we gotta get cookin', Pan." She chuckles, proud of her wordplay.

---

[106] *A nod to Alice in Wonderland. But we can pretend I made it up for the hell of it since this is, in fact, my book.*

I have to fucking idea if this pixie is a complete and total wind-up, but if I were into conspiracies like Finneas thinks the Earth is flat...then what she's saying makes a bit of sense. And seeing that it's the only bit of *somewhat* sense I've heard in a while, I'll bite.

"Alright, well, if what you're saying is true, I have a lot of work to do. I have a strong feeling I'm not even close to portraying the man, other than devilishly handsome good looks, of course." I run my fingers through my hair and grant her a cheeky simper.

"You'd be surprised how well that works in a fight..." she reciprocates the coyness with a bite of her plump bottom lip.

Fuck me with a pogo stick, I'm bollocks at not accidentally flirting. "Be that as it may," I stifle a smile, "we're also not going down without a fight. Neverland is seemingly pretty safe, at least to what meets the eye – but I was mulling it over...If this world is based on the whole conglomeration that is my journal...there could be nightmares lurking around any corner just for the hell of it."

Her pupils get large with uneasiness for the first time since I've known her. "I...never really thought about that. That's a whole other ballgame that could come into play within the quest...especially regarding *your* entries...God, *dammit,* we *need* to get training."

As uneasy as her panic makes me, for once I very much agree with the pixie chick, because if the *good* can be as magnificent as it is here, I don't want to imagine how *bad* the grim could be. On the other hand, I also can't help but selfishly feel zeal with the pride that I knew something Evangeline didn't for once.

It's the little wins in life, laddies.

I nod, "Yup. We may have created my dream world, but dreams are just nightmares sprinkled in dust,[107] birdie. I've got a colorful imagination, let alone dark history behind me." I inwardly shudder at the not-so-joke and the possibilities of the nightmares that could befall us, but I don't let her see my apprehension. "But it'll be alright," I reassure her...and also myself, "because we don't need to be alone. Finneas and Maya...they're back in Paragon, likely antsy for an adventure or two. Perhaps not this one, particularly...but beggars can't be choosers, as they say..." I let out a breathy, strained laugh before awkwardly clearing my throat as if doing so would clear the tension building in the air too. "Any chance we can get them in on this action?"

"Who?" Her tone is nearly disgusted, causing my eyebrows to furrow, but she quickly begins to laugh. "Your *face!*" She continues to laugh hysterically, as I raise my eyebrow, waiting for the joke to be funny.

Spoiler: It never becomes funny.

Finally, she stops and sighs, "Sure we can go get them. Of course, then we...*I*...have to teach those corporeal dumbasses how *not* to die too...*god's help me...*" I take it she's trying to get me to reconsider, though since she's failing perfectly, she attempts another edge, "Are you positive you want them on *our* dream vacation?"

I cringe a wee bit, though grant her a chuckle that sounds real enough. *I hope her magic doesn't possess a built-in lie detector or some shit.* "How do we leave, Eevee?"

---

[107] *QUOTE OF THE BOOK! Refer to the cover! Fun Fact: I remember brainstorming this quote, my personal prompt being, "what would readers get tattooed? What would stick with them forever? What would they highlight on their kindle? What would make them go "whoaaaaaaaaaaa..." – It changed everything.*

Now her eyebrows furrow. "I don't know, Peter Pan, how do we leave *your* island?"

My stomach drops as my eyebrows rise. "You mean you don't know how to leave?" My voice jumps three octaves. "I only created an escape *to*, not *from...*" my insides quake. "Tell me you're joking, because I sure as hell is liquid lava barely know how I got here –"

"Calm your tits, Brit," she sasses with a roll of her eyes. *She's alright, don't get me wrong, but Maya wasn't far off...Evangeline is a little lairy bitch.* "It's simple: your journal."

"What about it?"

"Write how you want to leave."

"What are you –"

"Ugh! Keep up, will you?" *Little brat.* "Go to a new page in your magical diary and write down with your little pen how you would like to come and go from the island. A bit of Paradust-y dust and *bam!* Done deal."

"Really? That's all?"

"Not everything is as complicated as you corporeals make it. Welcome to the Pararealms, where life is as it *should* be: happy as fuck."

I genuinely laugh, and as I do, her eyes become quizzical yet sanguine. "Wow…"

"What?"

"You have a full set of teeth!"

I give her a curious expression. *Similarly to Maya, yet not quite as violently unhinged, this bird says the most dodgy shit...though, this time in particular I suspect what she's going on about.* "Indeed, I grew them myself," I respond softly.

She gives me that cheeky grin of hers, "I just…don't think I've ever seen you genuinely laugh or smile before. Keep it up, it's a nice dash of color on you."

What a nutty thing to say.

"So hold on," I ignore the exchange, "if everything is that simple, why can't I just write us to victory and we can be out of this shitshow altogether?"

"If only," she half shrugs, sighing girlishly. "The journal only works in regards to world-building, dream sketching, and things of that nature – it seems confusing at first, but I promise you'll start to figure it out in time. Despite you being the one who *technically* created the place, there *are* still rules and regulations…Just a fair warning: do not bend them; you'll pay the price."

"What kind of –"

"Ugh, too many questions! I'll explain later. Get out your thingy."

As I pull out my journal from my jean jacket pocket, I mutter curses under my breath. I know Eevee can hear me with her crackerjack fairy hearing, so the tinkering she produces is expected and presented almost immediately.

OnE mAY enTER aND/oR lEAvE nEVERLand By nIGhT, whETHER trAVEIING tHe sky alONE oR witH somEone THat holDs thE poweR of Flight.

DIRECTIONS THERE AND BACK:
seCOND stAR tO thE riGHT, aND straiGHT oN tiLL mornING.

Fuck you, Colin.[108]

---

[108] *See pg. 21*

I hand the journal to Evangeline and she gapes at it, reading my sloppy handwriting slowly. Not that she needs to, so I assume she's humoring me. "Nice rhyme, Dr. Seuss."

"I prefer Allan Poe, but Theodor was a genius, all the same."

"Who?"

I wait for her to laugh, but alas, she doesn't.
How disappointing.[109]

I discharge a spent sneer, "Are we going to fly or what, uncultured pixie bird?"

In the fashion of a dire necessity, she ties her hair into her infamous topknot, and instead of wrapping her arms around my waist, she lays her palm out flat, blowing straight toward my face as if blowing me a kiss. I close my eyes and scrunch my nose, the sensation of needing to sneeze overwhelming me, and expect anything but what happens next:

As the pixie's earrings jingle while her pointed ears wiggle, I am surrounded by a golden blanket of glitter and a warm, tingly sensation prancing along my skin and coursing inside my veins. Every single time this hullabaloo arises within me, it gets stronger – less foreign. Time after time I encounter it, the less I repudiate it, and the more often I long for it to never end…

The further the desire increases for it to overtake me –
for me to become it…

---

[109] *Maya would've laughed. Just sayin'.*

I Prefer Peter

Evangeline takes my hand, her eyes warmer than hellfire and her tiny palm nearly engulfed in the same heat. Not only does she fly, *but for the first time on my own...more or less...so do I.*

Perhaps one day I won't need Paradust...or her.

Perhaps one day.

Second star to the right, and straight on till morning.[110]

Off to Paragon!

---

[110] *Would it be a Peter Pan reimagining without it? Nope!*

CHAPTER twenty-eight

Finneas Scott
Neverland

I fucking *flew!*
With sparkly, heavy druglike assistance from a
fairy...but still flew, no doubty-doubt.

So Petey hadn't been around for a few days because
he was fuckin' gallivanting around his new dreamworld that
evidently was magically connected to his journal thingy due to
some legendary *Peter-Pétros Pan* shit...but honestly, I ain't
mad. Sure, I lost sleep assuming the kid died or drowned in
the lake by the sensational mer-chick or some horrific shit, but
meh...he didn't and I guess that's all that matters.

Plus, he came back for me.
*Well, **us**.*
So pish posh, problemo tossed.

Flying here was, without a shadow of a doubt, the
greatest moment of my entire young existence. I thought
soaring high *metaphorically* was fun when I hung with all
them druggies, but yeah nah, deadass *literal* flying? Can't get
any better than that.
I marveled at the fiery stars from merely an arm's
length away, danced with the planets as they rotated around
the sun, and got to watch the sunrise with a front-row seat – all
whilst being in the utmost protection of Eevee's pixie shit she
blew out from her skin or somethin'. I know it ain't called
that, I just like to call it pixie shit to piss'er off – she called it
Paradust, and let me just say, it makes you feel on fire in the
most euphoric way possible. *can you imagine that?*

337

If that ain't the definition of feeling alive...
*or, if you've never felt alive...the feeling of **becoming** alive –*
then I don't know what is.

Now after a few days of playing mind-numbing catch-up of all the 'Pan' tea, we'z been game planning the routes to Para*somethin'* and Para*other...I can't ever remember the names, but as long as we survive long enough to get there, that's all that matters anyhow;* training and whatnot to save them Peculiars, their magic, and whatever the shit else.

Yeah...never thought those duties would be birthed outta me.

It's been a hella batshit trying to succumb to all *this* newness after finally starting to get settled into Paragon, so not only was Pan *(ours, not the dead one)* kind enough to poof up a pretty bougie treehouse for every single one of us with his little booky book *(I think it was mostly Eevee, no way Peter knows how to do that Potter hooey yet),* but the rest of this place don't come close to anywhere I've ever been...even them really pretty places...

Neverland is what I imagine Heaven to look like.
Greenie and the angel chick did a swell job.

We had a proper send-off from the people of Paragon and a good-luck potluck...though, to be totally honest, it was sorta morbid as hell...Everyone was lookin' at us as if it were the last time, and who knows...*maybe it was...*But I guess there ain't no going back now. You've seen those TV shows – once the main character finds out they're the chosen one, they gotsta do their chosen one shit, or else there'd be no story.

A few days ago, Eevee went back to Paragon to gather weapons, clothes, and essentials, plus enough of it all to make ourselves cozy for the time being…*however long that may be*…But since there ain't much useful technology or modern artillery anywhere – if any, whether it be here or in that town of strange-o's –; we'z been making do with the learning of proper *Naked and Afraid* survival skills and use of medieval type weaponry – swords, daggers, bows – the badass of 'em. At the moment, the pixie is in the middle of giving Peter another sword and magic lesson, cause the kid's sure got a lot to learn before we set off to hunt for all the whosits-or-whatsits, that's for damn sure…So, after a long day of sparring the best us city folk could (cause we *(she)* ain't gonna pick up the fighting shit very lickity-split), Maya and I casually chill on the Neverbeach right on the ocean's edge – it somehow constantly crashes the perfect length away as if to purposefully never get us wet.

Now, and I can say this on behalf of the both of us – high key, Half-Pint and I ain't special by any means. We gots no powers, no mind-bending techniques – *none* of them what-have-yous. So due to that, we're still not even the tiniest bit sure what kind of help we'll be on the adventures we'z about to embark on, and I know for a damn straight fact Maya is being dragged into the tasks by the hairs on her arm. But, be that as it may, we'll sure as the sun is golden do what we can to not be two bumps on a log. Likely, I'll master a weapon or something…but who knows about the chick. Nonetheless, we'll be here for him, 'cause let's face it – there's no way in the deepest, most inflamed bowels of hell that Petey asked to be caught up in any of this, so we may as well be forced into this fiasco as a team, right?

Though for now, Sexton and I stare out at the horizon, both of us likely thinking nearly the same thing as one another and equally having no clue how to say it, if we want to say it; and if yes, who will go first.

So, I volunteer as tribute.

"Maya..." My voice is steady, but my insides are shakin' like a rattlesnake in Antarctica in the middle of February.

"Finneas." We don't look at each other, but our ears are open more than they ever have been and we both know it.

"I think...I think uh...I'm...a fruity," I clear my throat to make room for the big word. "I think I'm gay." *I wanna throw up and die and explode all at the same time.* "Or something – or...I don't know."[111]

Maya's head shifts immediately from the ocean to me, her lips breaking into the gentlest smile as she takes my hand. "Del, around the time that I first got to Brand New Life, you once stole alcohol on your point-granted night out, relapsed and got wasted, then insisted we all watch you perform a one-man show of the entire *Newsies* Broadway soundtrack instead of having a movie night...*I know.*" At that, I laugh harder than I have in quite a damn minute and accept the small hug the kiddo gives me around my neck with her itty bitty little arms. "It's a shame, though." She lets me go and fake sighs. "I was starting to get a little crush on you there for a second."

"That's *rich*, Half-Pint." I run my hand through my hair as the ice breaks and my 'elephant in the room', who's been living rent-free, finally leaves our surrounding area.

Though just as I think I am forever about to be smooshed by Maya's giant elephant in return, she speaks through a nervous chuckle, "Yeah, I'm just kidding. Cause um – I'm..." she trails off, and I bet she feels like the rattlesnake now.

C'mon, chick, you got this.

---

[111] ¯_(ツ)_/¯

I reach for her hand, and she squeezes mine back impressively tight. Her eyes turn a shiver-inducing blue and her body trembles like she is, in fact, in Antarctica. Maya doesn't look at me as the words tumble out of her mouth, "I guess I don't have a crush on you because...because I may just be falling in love with a boy named Peter Pan."

The tension in the air is like a noose around her neck, and I do my best to cut through its thick chokehold with my devilishly handsome grin and my enthusiasm. "Fuck yeah, you are, kid."[112]

She gives the ocean a sheepish smile, so I wrap my arm around her, kissing her delicate little temple as if I may break her into tiny Maya bits if I press too hard. My little sister from another pisser has always been a pain in the ass, but she sure as hell has a bigger heart than anyone on the planet, and that's a damn straight fact.

finn ♡

"Hey, earthlings!" Evangeline's nasally voice washes up onto the shore and kills our precious heart-to-heart. Maya and I both turn to see her trudging through the sand with her Frankenstein lookin' stompers. "Soup's on if you're hungry."

"Where's Peter?" Maya asks her, and not only does the constant wondering where Peter is make sense now, but I can also nearly smell the jealousy wafting from the pixie's aura.

"Bathing in the lake. Why, hun, did you wanna enjoy the revue or something?"

I can't tell if the Half-Pint's face turns red from rage or near-fatal blushing. She doesn't answer the pixie, and I feel as though that's best for both of their sakes.

---

[112] *FUCK YEAH YOU ARE, KID!!!!!!!!!*

"Well, I'm famished!" I say, squashing the tension with all I got and standing to my feet. I stretch, "Let's feast, shall we? Leave nakey Peter and his...*peter*...alone with his lake. We'll keep his seat warm. Onward now, ladies!"

Who, me? Want tickets to the Pan revue?
Stfu.

◈ ◈ ◈

Shift POV: Peter Pan

Even after a magical dinner, *(literally...I thunk up some fish and chips and that's all there was to it),* sleep feels nearly impossible. Every time I close my eyes, I see something I don't want to see – the siren slicing me open, my mum falling to her death, everyone in Paragon dying and their world being destroyed because of *me*...

So sitting in a garden of what we named moonflowers *(because they glow, tinker, and light up the night path as anyone walks or sits among them),* seemed like a fine alternative.

I fidget, making my bare feet fake fight as the petals light up my toes, illuminating the blisters and fresh cuts from the long hours of training with Evangeline. A small waterfall sounds to my far left, one that leads into a ravine that spreads to the deep blue lagoon and cascades light through the trees. The unseen yet audible critters sing along through the falls, helping me remember I'm a little less alone. Though every haunting thought creeps in still, at least it's with a lush view.

I like Neverland, I do. I am finally getting the hang of simple magic, and I have everything I could've ever dreamed of. I just can't help but think there's something off...something missing? *Something wrong.* Maybe that's just me and my ever-present anxiety that not even the strongest magic can dissipate, or my inability to accept the *good* without waiting for the catch that comes with it...or maybe there *is* a beast about ready to attack.

Who's to say?
Perhaps I'm just scared,
And perhaps that's okay...
Isn't it?

"Couldn't sleep?"[113] Breaking through the mayhem in my mind, Maya's voice is soft and gentle like one of the chittering, ticking bugs keeping the closure's peace. I shrug in response, not wanting to break the ASMR somehow with my tainted tongue and continue to play with my feet. Though part of me wishes she'd leave, the rest of me is thrilled to not be alone with my thoughts anymore. "Mind if I join you?" She sits next to me before I even have a chance to nod my head, and all at once, nature speaks every word we don't. I quite fancy when the itty bitty creatures do that, as starting conversations has never been a strong suit of mine, so the buggies helping me out are much appreciated.

This time, however, I decide to try and give it a whirl. "It's decent, isn't it?

She turns to me, "What is?"

"The island." I don't return her gaze that burns my skin like a sunburn. "It's nice. Quite dazzling, really."

"It is." I feel her smile all over me.[114] "You're quite the knockout architect."

I scoff. "I did nothing."

---

[113] *Fun Fact: You're about to read one of the first pieces of dialogue I ever wrote for the book!*

[114] *Have you ever felt someone's smile all over you? It's a riveting sensation.*

She scoffs back harder. "Don't tell me you're into modesty now, Peter! You created this whole island in that journal all on your own –"

"Pétros created it. Eevee did as well, really. I just provided the fluffy details. I may have written the blueprint, but I didn't build squat shit."

"Oh give it a rest, Peter." I happen to notice then that Maya always says my name in conversations – what a quirk of hers that I don't even think she knows. "Give yourself some credit for once. You're far more special than you think you are."

The bird's voice trails off, and though I am knackered as hell and have had varieties of this sentence thrown at me a nearly humourous amount of times as of late, her words revive a small fire in me that has been fizzling for hours – even days. I smile inwardly so she can't see nor feel it through the dimly lit garden, and refresh the atmosphere with a new phrase,

"Hey, Maya…I normally don't do this, but I wanted to apologize."

Her eyes nearly pop out of their sockets, as expected because my pride is legitimately suffocating and eating me alive from the inside out right now.

"Oh?" She mockingly bats her eyelashes and smirks. "And to what do I owe this wondrous occasion?"

"That whole breakfast thing." I shake my head at the thought of my wrongdoing. "It was careless, and I should've been there for you like I said I was going to be…Did you eat the toast?"

"Squeezed it into oblivion, actually. Pretended it was your head."

I chuckle, "Fair enough." Relieved she isn't as aggressively bitter as I presumed she'd be, it's still rather strange that I even care as much as I do…I still can't seem to wrap my head around *why.* "I refrained from having a cigarette until I felt like I was going to throw up if it's any consolation."

"Good," she says curtly, though her pearly whites shine brighter than the moonflowers at the news of me keeping my word despite the absence. "I'm glad you tortured yourself on my behalf." She lets out a small laugh through her nose, and even though I can barely see it, grants me a wink. She's alright, this chick. It just takes her a bit to crack out of her shell, I suppose.

"I'm a man of my word..." I mutter in more faith than truth, "for the most part," I finish in confession. "I'm trying."

She worries her lip in between her teeth, "Can I ask you a question?"

"Alright..."

"Why now?"

"Hmm?" I hum, my head cocking in question.

"Why all of a sudden did you choose to go with all of this...*Pétros Pan-heir-to-the-throne* shit?" She waves her hand as if to magically gather all of the context regarding the subject toward us. "It just..."

"Doesn't seem like *me?*" I cap her thought.

"Well, yeah," she admits coyly. "When did the black sheep all of the sudden become a wannabe hero?"

Her bluntness never ceases to inspire me. "Well, little bird, I figured if I couldn't save one life that meant more to me than my own, the least I could do with the meaningless life I am forced to still lead is try and save a few others."

Maya doesn't hurl back, ask what I meant, nor does a sassy or cheeky remark slide off her tongue. She just pulls her knees up to her sharp chin and finds my hand in the dark, "I'm proud of you."

And just like that, I'm higher than I've ever been.[115]

---

[115] *If you need me, I'll be in my grave.*

"So…Miss Sexton." I flip the subject and let out the breath I didn't know I was holding for days. "Maya *something* Sexton. I never really got a chance to get to know you."

She returns my prior exhale, and I think I would be able to hear her little heart beating all the way from New York. As usual, she plays it cool despite it. "What about me, Green? Pan? Whatever or whoever you identify as."

I give her a cheeky eye roll and pull out the cigarette box from my sweats. I light it with the flick of my wrist, fire erupting at my command, and it sends heat similar to it up and down my spine. I can tell it impresses her as well.

"How'd your journey at B-N-hell treat you?" I suck in smoke and exhale it through my next words, "Were you able to receive your *'brand new life'* before our grand escape?" I offer her the cancer stick, and though she almost accepts it, she refuses like the good girl she is. Therefore, I take another generous puff in her honor.

"I don't wanna bother you with all the sad-girl details."

"Not a bother if I'm the one who asked."

Accepting defeat, I can practically hear her chest tighten. "Well…considering I was about 90 pounds at 5'4, I nearly didn't even get the chance to try." Maya brings her knees up to her chest and wraps her arms around them tightly. "One day, my heart stopped and I was in a coma for two months…They said it was a miracle I even woke up; and if I didn't seek professional help immediately, I may not wake up next time – thus beginning my adventures at BNL. But I never got much better because…well, I'm scared, I guess? Stubborn? Maybe I don't want to? I don't know. It's complicated." The agony in her eyes is ever-present as she speaks like she's having this conversation more with herself than me. "So to answer your question…no. Through the year or so I'd been there, I don't think much changed, if I'm being honest."

I pretend to inspect my cig. "What pride did you take in that?"

She's taken aback. "Sorry?"

"You didn't learn from your mistakes." I blow out smoke again before turning to meet her gaze. "You said you were stubborn and didn't want to recover. So were you secretly proud of how sick you were? Took pride in the fact that you still needed help? After the coma, your brain told you you were a *'good anorexic'*, did it not?"

I'm not antagonizing her.
I just know it all too well.

Maya's eyes turn a shade of blue I've never seen as the trauma in her soul floods to the surface. I hear it in the way her voice eggshells that she's nearly breaking, perhaps due to the fact that for once, someone understands the way her mind torments her.

"I guess when I woke up I was relieved to hear how sick I still was, yes," she confesses. "I'm more ashamed of it now than I was before, but then again…maybe not enough." Her shoulders bounce, beaten and owning up to her pain, causing my stone heart to genuinely crack a bit for her. The lass fiddles with the flowers around us; her voice becoming smaller than she is, "I've never admitted that to anyone before…not even myself."

The pride and gratification in me swells then, but I too wonder…*Is this a matter to be proud of?* When did I begin to consider it a win to be the one Maya wholeheartedly confides in? *Do I?*
Could it potentially be that she does *not* hate me entirely as I thought?

Or, perhaps now…am I getting too close?

Fuck if I know...
But the main question is:
Why don't I care?
Why is Maya the only girl I am so afraid of, yet willing to fight
my own deep-set boundaries for?

"Are you happy you did?" The words tumble out of my mouth before I have a chance to think, and she puzzles.

"What do you mean?"

"Woke up, I mean. Are you happy you woke up?" Maya nearly speaks, but her aura is so obvious – and I don't know if it's a magical power I have or if she's just as open in the dark as she is in the light –, but I stop her in her tracks before she begins. "And before you recite your pocketed rehearsed answer, remember: I'm not your therapist. You don't have to give me the bullshit mumbo-jumbo you think I want to hear. I won't write you up or anyt hing."

The lass deflates. "Fine." Her eyes dart to and fro from mine, to the serene water. "Sure, it's a miracle I'm alive. But no lie, Peter, I cried when I woke up in the hospital. It meant I had to keep fighting a battle I'm *still* afraid daily I'm gonna lose. It's exhausting to be alive, Peter..." The pain in her tone nearly makes the moonflowers around us burn out. "I'm grateful I woke up, I *am*...not everyone does...But truly, some days I think it may have been easier if I hadn't." She rubs her forehead with her palms, and I can only presume she has never told anyone that before either.

I feel a tinge of guilt when I don't respond. I want to say that I know the feeling to the core – want to tell her she's not alone and that it doesn't have to last forever; *that she's worth it*...But who am I to give lessons on how to live, when I am no different – *if not worse* – in my philosophy of life? Therefore, I'd be a hypocrite at his finest. So instead, I just nod and silently loathe my lack of courage to do any speaking of the sort – to give empathy when I know it's due. Perhaps it's just not in my nature.[116]

"What about you, Green?" She switches gears, and though my guilt still lingers, I respond,

"What about me?" I revert to smoking for comfort.

"I know what you shared in the inferno was minor cockshit. So tell me the solid truth: why'd you get sent to rehab?"

I quickly debate whether or not I should tell her about my dark history with my tainted childhood since she has shared more than enough with me, though I advise against it and kick myself for even considering it. I choose instead to skip to the good part,

"In a fat nutshell, I took too much PCP and overdosed."

Maya's pupils flare as her lips part slightly, "Holy hell, Peter –"

"It wasn't even my drug of choice." I presume my absent expression is infallible, as I say this more to myself and the ground in recollection than to her. "Frankly, I would've rather gone out with a bang from something I was more keen on, like tranqs or some sort of Robitussin trip…nothing's more romantic than dying with your friends, as they say[117]…But nah," I shake my head in…*shame? Ownage?*…and smack my tongue, "got put into a two-day coma after losing a battle with a needle and too much pixie dust," I laugh almost as mad as a march hare at the revelation. "Ironic, isn't it? The substance that saves me now, is the shit that almost killed me then. Oh, the mysterious, serendipitous contradictions of life." I puff my everlasting cigarette and continue speaking until the awkward fade out of my laughter, "You beat me there with your

---

[116] :(

[117] *A brilliant line from a song called "Till Forever Falls Apart" by Ashe feat. Finneas (the singer, not the beloved I Prefer Peter character)*

two-month nappy, though." I give her an ironic thumbs up yet still don't look at her, but truthfully, I don't think she ever took her eyes off me.

"That must've been...so...so...terrifying," she trips over the comforting words she can't quite find.

"I mean, I definitely wouldn't recommend it to a friend." She huffs through her nose at my facetiousness, and I do the same with a smirk. "To be straight..." I finally meet her eyes, "I was scared shitless."

She bites the inside of her lip and nods in comprehension as if to say that she would've been as well. Then, the bird hits me with the same bomb as I did her,

"But are you happy?" I question her with my eyebrows, asking her to elaborate even though I know full well what she's about to inquire of me. "Ya know..." she says delicately, "that you woke up?"

I sigh, already knowing my answer but not wanting to admit it. "Put it this way, love..." I say, semi-reluctantly, "If I hadn't, right now I would – *hopefully* – be someplace serene, free from my own worst enemy which is, in fact, myself. I especially wouldn't have to deal with the fucked up game of life anymore that I can't quite seem to master," I say as I clench my fists and hammer them on my thighs. "I swear someone changed the player mode to expert without my consent." I curl my lip and snicker ironically at this image, rubbing my eyes until I see a kaleidoscope explosion of colors. "If I hadn't woken up that day, I wouldn't have to worry about where the fuck I am, what the fuck I'm doing, where the fuck I'll go..." An angry spark of fire abruptly ignites in my hand, startling me into floppily shaking it as if trying to make it detach from my body. Irritated at the lack of control, I joggle my head, extend my sleeve over the tips of my fingers, and ball my fists around the fabric. I hold back tears I didn't expect to show up then – hold them back for dear fucking life. I muster, "It's funny, really..." It's *actually not 'funny', and*

that's the funniest thing, "Evangeline once told me Paradust runs through my veins, and that the key secret to me flying without her assistance is thinking *'happy thoughts',*" I mock the nasally words of the pixie from one of our private magic sessions. "I figured out fairly quickly that I don't have one...all of them are gone. Tainted. *Dead.* So when death itself becomes your only happy thought..." I direct candidly to myself, "I think the tactic needs reassessing. How does a broken boy learn to fly?"[118] I ask the stars, momentarily forgetting Maya is silently sitting beside me. "How does someone who'd rather *die* than *fly,* revel in the act of waking up each morning, forced to trudge through a new day?"

Because Lord knows if I hadn't...
I'd be with my mum, and as far away from my bastard of a father as possible.
*The fact that we're even on the same earth sickens me every day after what he did...what he claims **I** did...the thing I still can't decipher the truth about.*
*The word **father** still rots in my mouth to this day.*
I wouldn't have this responsibility of saving a planet whose existence I still can't fathom.
Growing up would be automatically canceled.
The pain...the confusion...the trauma...the nightmares...the questions...the noise...
Gone.

Though I battle with my emotions for a few agonizing moments, Maya patiently waits and allows me all the time I need.

---

[118] *Probably the quote that sums up the entire book. A favorite amongst hundreds of readers, as well as myself.*

I finally finish, "So, in other words...no. I can't wholeheartedly say I'm happy. Guess that's something we finally have in common."

Neither of us speaks for a bit but go back to letting the critters do so for us. I realize I haven't told anyone half of this shit before, and it petrifies and elates me all at the same time that Maya has now become the only person who has this information other than me.

Guess that's another thing we have in common.
I don't tell her she's the lucky number one, but something tells me she doesn't need to be told.
She knows.
And she's cherishing it all.

"Well, Peter," her voice is as calm as the nearby water, and I just want to drown in it right about now, "if it's any consolation...I'm glad you woke up." I permit myself to let those words hang in the air around us until they attach themselves to my skin like a leech and seep into my cold exterior. A tear burns in the back of my eye, and I allow it to fall. She doesn't see it, but somehow I feel like she knows.

I just feel like she always knows everything.

"All I have ever been was a massive dick to you," I whisper, and I'm not sure if it was more to her or myself. "And it's fairly clear that you hate me...so why are you suddenly being so goddamn nice to me?"

Though I half expected a snide remark, she takes my hand and squeezes it tightly so I can't pull away – *but I can't say that I even think to.* She runs her fingertips along my scars, and I tense.[119] "Mayhaps, Peter Pan, you hate yourself so much

---

[119] *This is so personal – so tender. I love it.*

that you *assume* everyone *has to* hate you just as much as you do," she mimics her bratty tone from the first therapy circle when she similarly condescended me into oblivion with her theory about my life. "So how about for a change, you just accept the kindness someone is trying to grant you and don't fuck it up, yeah?"

At that, Maya stands and walks away, allowing my hand to slip from her grip and leaving my wrist to tingle where the ghostly presence of her touch still lingers. As much as I want to go after her, I watch as her moonflower-lit shadow stretches more and more until her quick paces cause the light path in her wake to begin to fade as she disappears with the incoming breeze. Just when I think she's gone, I hear her call through the crisp night air,

"My middle name…it's Wendy, by the way!"

Wendy.[120]

I smile at the purest thing I have learned about Maya thus far.

Wendy.

The name sends electricity through my veins, and my hands glow an iridescent blue that mimics a mixture of the grotto in my Neverland and Maya Wendy Sexton's forget-me-not eyes. Hell if I know what it means, but I can't help but confess it feels damn good.

⌇ ⌇ ⌇

When my hands at last return to normal and my overthinking – *though doesn't completely disappear* – but at least unknots itself a tad, I make my way to a door that isn't

---

[120] *wink wink*

my own. I have a feeling I won't be sleeping tonight, and as much as I would prefer to be alone, I don't think I can right now. My heart thuds violently in my chest and my veins surge with emotions I'm not particularly keen on, and as it does, the normally cool climate becomes sticky and humid, and the area around me a haze of heat as if I am walking through a hot oven.

As my rollercoaster of emotions cycles daily here in Neverland, I think I've finally come to register that the island somehow recognizes how I'm feeling, and knows how to personify the emotion within the climate around everyone within it...whether it be sheer anxiety, sadness, joy, anger...it mirrors my every mood.

As if I am the island, and the island is me.
As if I am one with it.
As if I am the island's soul...
Everything I feel, so does...She? He? It? TBD.

With that epiphany now racing in my mind on top of all of the other shit suffocating my brain cells, my unease builds in my throat and dry lightning begins to flash across the sky. Regardless of my will, I've become an open book, and frankly, it's a sheer invasion of my mysterious persona and I loathe that concept *entirely.*

I knock on the wooden door, my hands shaking and glowing red – a color I've yet to emit.

The hinges squeak as they swing wide open, "Well, well, well! If it isn't the weatherman." *Fuck, he caught on hella fast. Finneas has always been pretty plugged-in...There's never much hiding from that one.* "To what do I owe the pleasure?"

I stand in his arched doorway, my hair a tousled mess from a restless, windy hour and I can't imagine my eyes are not red from staring into oblivion.

Ya know, as one does.

"Can we talk?" My voice is uncommonly desperate, as I have been having an ongoing panic attack contemplating for hours whether or not to ask someone, anyone, for company. He looks at me as if he cannot fathom how he got to be the lucky bastard,

"Schlep your ass in here, Greenie."

I do; my fingernails being filed down by my jacked-up vampire teeth because my hand is already scratched raw. I needed another tic before I started to see my bones, but now I'm afraid I need another before I gnaw off my fingers like baby carrots. I slump in the swinging chair attached to the tree bark paneling across from Finneas' bed and refuse to speak for a brutal moment. As my panic attack continues to increase, causing a weird summer storm to brew outside, the voices in my head are going batshit awol…I squeeze my temples so aggressively, that it feels – *and probably also looks as though* – I'm trying to force the chaos to ooze out of my ears.

"Peter," Finn walks over with haste, kneeling in an attempt to meet my eyes. He puts his hand on my knee and shakes it as if the anxiety will empty out of it, "talk to me, what's going –"

I stare into his eyes with despair, "Finneas, I think I like Maya."

FUCKIN' TOOK YA LONG ENOUGH.

Random side note regarding page 345 –
I just didn't want to spoil the tender moment:

Never refrain from telling people that you're proud of them.
It's a direly underused and underestimated phrase
that people need to hear more often.
Tell someone you're proud of them today.

CHAPTER twenty-nine
Finneas Scott
Neverland

At last, the kitty cat's outta the bag!

"Yes…I know," I stand and say when he admits his not-so-deep dark secret to me. "I've been knowin', Petey. Since the moment yee two locked eyes, I knew you'd be fuckin."

"*Whoa there,* keep your hair on, nobody's *fucking,* you numpty."

"Not *yet.*" I hold up a peace sign and wiggle my tongue in between my fingers sensually.

The inner young lad in Peter laughs automatically, but he still can't hide his frustration. "I'm serious, mate, what do I do?"

"Whaddya *do?* Pally, *embrace it!* It's a beautiful thing youz two found each other. It's clear you go together like diet coke and minty mentos – it's an explosion of pure art."[121]

"The *'opposites attract'* bullshit? Really?"

"It's old poetry, Green. Liking her ain't a bad thing."

"It's a bloody awful thing."

I chuckle at his adorably bashful anxiety and cross my arms. "Why is that?"

"Because she's…*Maya…*" He buries his head in his hands. "Not only that, but she normally loathes the ever-living shit out of me, unless it's some sort of year three *'be mean to the lad you secretly fancy'* bit…Oh, *fuck me…ugh!*" He grunts

---

[121] *Have you ever done the diet coke + minty mentos experiment? If not, go now and report back to me.*

in major [amusing] irritation at his riddle-solving. "I just *cannot* like a lass."

I absentmindedly laugh ironically, "Word to, man."

"No, no, not like – wait, *sorry, what?"* His head shoots up so fast that I'm nervous for a split second he broke his neck. He leans in, "What do you mean *'word to, man'?"*

I freeze, nearly certain I said that in my head. I dunno if it's Petey's magic powers kicking in, or if my facetious laugh wasn't subtle enough, but the kid catches on like a life preserver after the sinking of the Titanic. "Apples to oranges, pally. She doesn't hate you, by the way!" I quickly toss in, hoping it'll distract him.

Spoiler: It doesn't.

"Finn..." he stands up, Maya completely dissipated from his memory bank *[momentarily], "I* meant I have too much shit going on to deal with a girl, but do *you* have something you wanna share with the class?"

"No-siree! Plus this isn't even about me, Pan, this is about *you."*

"Nah, we'll get to me in a minute, *pally."* Little prick mocks my tone and damn well too. He places a hand on my shoulder, guides me to sit on the foot of the bed, then proceeds to say a bit too bluntly in a Sexton fashion, "Finn, be honest...are you a fruity?"

I aggressively point at him, "I could beat your face in for callin' me that, Greenie, but imma Jesus-turn the other cheek for now." I rake my hand through my hair and exhale in defeat over this long awaited, constantly haunting subject I never wanted to jumpscare me. "But, I will admit, I sure am somethin' or other, deadass. Been trying to figure it out for a while now."

"How long?"

"Since I met you, *beauty.*" Peter rolls his eyes and rubs them as his shoulders dance with his small chuckles, and I won't lie, this kid is making it easier to talk about shit than any therapist you could pay for just by that eminent smirk of his. It makes any situation less of a shitshow. Thus, I somehow proceed with ease, "Nah, my parents immediately kicked my sorry ass out for it when I was younger – twas quite the palooza. Not quite the coming out party ya hear about on the medias, am I right?" I shake my head as I recall the heinous Winter night they caught me in my room with my best friend Levi[122] at the time very much *not* studying. I was young and stupid as hell…; curious and still figuring everything out…*and they were nosey pricks anyway.*

I absentmindedly light a cigarette to take the edge off. "I wasn't too sure what to make of the realization, let alone if it was *just a phase* like my dad said more times than I could count in the interventions of sorts, so I tended to kinda keep the subject under wraps from my pals and other fam after everything that happened. I felt ashamed for a while…Had secret rendezvouses here and there that meant cockshit, which involved getting high and drunk off my ass in an attempt to mask the ignorance parading my senses…Then coming off alcohol made the facts harder to hide from in the long run. Ignorance is bliss, as they always say, ay? Now here I am, things suddenly wanting to clear up like a summer fuckin' sky, and I dunno if it's my stubborn ass refusing to admit it or if I just really *don't know,* but I won't fib you, kid…I'm still hella mind-fucked about it all."

Peter listens to every word that spills outta my pie hole and hangs on to it for dear life – something no one has ever done for me before without asking for my damn life savings afterward.[123] He sits next to me and taps his knees

---

[122] *My nephew's name.*

[123] *THE TRUTH BEHIND THIS IS DEAFENING.*

with his palms nervously, as I know regardless of his generous ear, empathy still ain't his thing. Be that as it may, whether or not he has 'magic' in his veins, he's definitely got it deep down in that chilly heart of his.[124]

"Well, mate," the kid sighs on my behalf, "I'm not gonna say I know how you feel, especially considering I sort of was just having a panic attack over hardcore fancying a *lady...*" We both laugh at the irony, and it feels damn good. He lets out another breath then, but this time with a consoling smile, "Ah, dammit to hell, Finn. I know I'm total shit at empathetics of any sort – my utmost apologies for that – but hey," he claps my back and his hand rests on my shoulder, "thank you for trusting me. You're gonna be golden, Ponyboy, just give it time."[125] As he loosely quotes our mutually favorite book, my heart of a soldier rests at ease. "In return," he continues, "I cross my heart to not flirt with you and make your road even more difficult to figure out."

There's the insensitive little pricky legend. "Don't flatter yourself, kid, you may not even be my type." I blow smoke in his face, and he breathes it in dramatically, hardly coughing now that he's all ethereal and shit...*So wild.*

He finally chortles playfully as he takes in my *[unrealistic]* snub, *"Poppycock bollocks bullshit!"* he says *so damn* Britishly it's almost offensive. "I'm not daft, lad, I've seen the way you gawk at me. You'd shag me in a heartbeat if I gave you the consent."

I shake my head and snicker, my thoughts in a tornado of new seemingly illegal fantasies at the mere thought, but I do my best to extinguish them. "Don't tempt me with a good time." Peter winks and shines his teeth at me with his tongue peeking out in between – a cheeky, crooked grin, it is –

---

[124] *My aspiration in life is to see people the way Finn does. I created him and yet he's someone I wish I could be...ironic and wild, innit?*
[125] *You already know.*

and I nearly fail to refrain from giggling. I continue speaking before I do, "Plus, between you and Ev-*angel*-ine, I'm having a helluva crisis deciphering which way I swing anyway, so I'll get back to you."

"I will not be awaiting your call, but thank you for your consideration. Best to choose the pixie bird."

"She'd slap me straight *so* hard."

Again, I make him chuckle. That rare laughter.
Fucking melodious.

"Does Maya know?" He asks me, though his mind is now undeniably veering elsewhere at the mention of her name.

"Yep, she knows. Not by choice though...the little mouse solved the riddle before I even told her...her gay-dar is stellar." I put out my cigarette in the ashtray residing on the small wooden kitchen table, and raise my eyebrow. "So speaking of Madam Sexton, what's the story, kid? Ya like the girl?"

His relaxed frame becomes so stiff, I almost feel like I can tip him over and he'd shatter into a million little itty bitty pieces upon hitting the ground like a museum statue. His cheeks heat and his voice turns coarse, "I don't know."

"Yes, you do."

"I don't know."

"Yes, you do."

"Finneas, *I don't know.*"

"Peter, I'm gonna tell you the same thing I told her, only this time with different pronouns to avoid general confusion, and nonidentical wording to spice up my life –" I hardly notice his eyebrows knit at this, as I just assume he's listening intensely to my forthcoming wisdom, "You like her. It's a facto for-sureo, you already said so. So now, just admit you're geedamn wild about her, man. Deadass down bad. Look, I said to her –"

I am to proceed, but now his brows are nearly unibrowed and I gather he hasn't heard much when he stops me, "Hold on…when exactly did you chat with *her?* More importantly, *who* or *what* were you talking about with *her?* "

Fuck big mouth me.

My mouth hangs slightly ajar and I stand motionless as if Christ hit the pause button on me. "What did I say?" I stall.

"You know damn well what you said, Delfinnium; *who* did you give her all this Pinterest wisdo-shit about?"[126]

My face blanks. "Look, I know you're mad, but cool it with the Delfinnium. It doesn't make me wanna do nothin' for your ass."

He glows the same color as his cold stare that cuts into me like four hundred knives, and bites through gritted teeth, *"Tell me…now."*

"Damn…You're a for sure dom, ain't cha?"

"Finneas…"

I laugh, *"You,* ya fucking idiot, we were talking about *you!"*

He draws out a century-long sigh-grunt-groan-*ugh* thing and pulls at his hair, and I will say it's better than the reaction I expected. "So *she* fancies *me* as well then, is that right?" His tone is fully exasperated and I can see sweat beads on his forehead. *Adorable. "Fuckin' hell."*

"You're saying this like it's a bad thing." I reach into my pocket and pull out another cigarette, light it, and hand it to him. He takes it without hesitation. "You like her, she likes you. Happy, happy!"

He inhales the ciggy and blows out more smoke than a fireplace in the dead of winter. "Finneas, I presumed all her

---

[126] *Finneas is definitely a walking Pinterest board.*

recent cheeky chit-chat was pity or something – she *despises* me."

"Well…" I chuckle, "Not anymore."

Peter sucks smoke in again with oodles of anxiety, the *taking the edge off* factor not working, and holds it then in his lips as he scratches his raw hand delicately, "What do I do?"

"Geez, man, have you never liked a chick before?"

"Not particularly, no," he says matter-of-factly.

"That's a real shocker, stunner. That mermaid musta really fucked you up. What about before that?" He shakes his head in response like a little boy who just got asked if he wants his loose tooth yanked out. I'm runnin' out of fuel for this back and forth. "You just gotta tell her, pally."

"I can't do that."

"No? And why is that?"

"I just can't."

"New choice."[127]

"Finneas, I am a guy who hates change." He holds his cig in between his fingers and speaks to me as if he's telling a bedtime story. "However, on account of life loving to attack me with the inevitability of making me uncomfortable, I have had to endure thee most change I have ever had to deal with all at once in the last month of my life. For instance, let's recap:" he takes a puff and says through smoke, "I have been thrown into worlds I'm still finding my belief in, I am filled with a magic, I repeat *magic,* I cannot fathom and am just barely comprehending how to control, and I also have to learn to believe in someone I truly despise – *ME!*" He aggressively points to himself at the word for emphasis. "But oh, believe it or not," he carries on, "these are all just among the tippy top of the list of ailments surging through my garbage chute of a brain, and then *now,*" he throws up his hands, winding down

---

[127] *cough* theater kid *cough*

his vent…I think, "after eighteen years of living and being free of the burden, *I suddenly like a girl. Fuck me in the ass, right?* So if you could be so kind as to assist me and my lack of experience with said subject, I would greatly appreciate it."

I'm smiling with every part of me and he hates it. "You're a funny dude, Peter Pan. Don't worry, it's simple:" I stand up then from the cushy bed and remove his ravenous hand away from the opposite, thrashed, scarred-up one, "you just have to tell her. You're already a master with words – when you wanna be, that is –, and you already have a leg up because…well, she adores you, kid. She always has."

His eyes become a soft sage and the weather outside bites colder, the frost welcoming itself in through the bark of the tree surrounding us. "Really?" He whispers, and I think it's the most tender I've ever heard a word escape his tongue.

"Without question."

He puts out his cigarette and looks in the decorative mirror, pushing his sweat-lined hair back and breathing in deeply. *Wow*…I can't help but wonder if he's ecstatic that he can do that now, or if he hasn't noticed at all, or if he doesn't say a word cause he's afraid to jinx it.

"Finn," he looks at me and I think I see a glisten in his eye. That's the thing about Peter – he only cries when it counts.[128] "I'm terrified."

I step over to the kid and place my hands on his shoulders, looking at him like I did Maya when I experienced nearly the same situation just a few days ago. "Why are you so terrified, pal? Why does love scare you so damn bad?"

I witness his brain switch to a terrorizing thought so fast and unwillingly, that the tears he's been holding back race down his face like rain on a car window. Afraid and assuming it's one of those day terrors of his and despite his hatred of

---

[128] *Probably one of my favorite characteristics about a character I've written…it's so personal and distinct.*

hugs, I engulf Petey before he disintegrates to the ground, and to my surprise, he holds on to me too.[129] He doesn't answer my question entirely, but says what he can,

"Because if I say it, then it will be real."

I mentally smirk and chortle at her majesty déjà vu's reappearance that sends my skin into an erection, and respond the only way I know how, "Yeah…and what's wrong with that?"

He retreats from my arms in a flash, storming over to the far side of the room to nowhere in particular, paces a bit while biting his nail, then halts. "I'm really, really…not ready." He surrenders to a swift sit on the ground, elbows propped on his bent knees, and his hands hiding his wrinkled features. I crawl over and meet him at his level, gently peel his hands from his face, and smile softly at him.

"And what's wrong with that?"

---

[129] *His mother was his first love.*

CHAPTER thirty
Maya Sexton
Neverland

As we sit around the fire for the evening, Evangeline won't shut the hell up about her and Peter's sword training and magic lessons, so I tune her out as much as I can. My mind wanders this way and that, and for some god-awful reason, I can't help but constantly revert back to that wretched mer-thing. She's been haunting my dreams, my daily thoughts, and everything in between – it's like the harder I try, the more she carves herself into the deepest crevices of my brain...I've come to the rotten conclusion that forgetting her demonic appearance is utterly hopeless.

"So, I have a question." I lean forward and say to Evangeline when there's a break in her yapping...*at least I think. I zoned out a while back when she started raving about how Peter's body is developing.*

Like, shut the fuck up, pervy bitch.

"And what might that be?" She snootily challenges back, mocking my movement and placing a hand under her chin, batting her uncannily long, gold-flecked eyelashes at me.

"Do you know anything about a freakishly fucked up mermaid back in Paragon?"

Peter chokes on his tea, and as I chalk it up to him being an idiot, Del ignores him and chimes in, "Fuckin' hell, Maya, she was nowhere *near* freakish! What's hella freakish is that you *think* that, you little bitterbean!"

"Fuck off, Brooklyn!" I snap at him, actually sending Evangeline into a chuckle. *One point for me, I guess.* I proceed back to her, "Finneas saw this luscious, siren goddess, while I basically saw the female devil of the sea. What's that about?"

The pixie shifts her ass on the log she's seated on and plays with the loose strands of hair around her face as she speaks, "That would be Etain,"[130] her voice is uncomfortably hesitant as if the siren is listening amongst the shadows. "She's a nightmare if you get on her bad side, so please, by all means, go say hi."

I roll my eyes and knit my brows. "Why did we see different things?"

"Why did Finneas see a celestial being while you saw an ugly ass fish face? I don't know, bitterbean biatch, why don't you ask yourself again?"

"Hey!" Finn barks, causing me to jump. "Only I'm allowed to call her that, aight? Mind your territory."

Evangeline gives him a derisive apologetic raise of her hands. "Noted, my bad." She groans, as if she really does not want to be discussing this topic but rather gawk about Peter's abs, however, it's been eating me alive, so I couldn't care less about her lust fest. Plus, any chance to irritate the witch is my complete and utter pleasure. "You're not going to believe me if I tell you," she states.

I scrunch my nose in a wry smile, "Try me. I've gotten this far with all your bullshit. What's a little more?"

I catch Peter looking up from his cup with a half-smirk and my tummy twirls.

Dammit.

"Well, if you must know," she says through a bothered sigh again as if she's telling us the sky is blue and the grass is green, "men see sirens how they are. Finneas, what did you see exactly?"

---

[130] *Fun Fact: The name Etain means jealousy or passion.*

"I saw what Ariel *wishes* she could be, man. No cap. Her tail was golden but she had sterling silver hair, purple eyes, tits the size of watermelons, hips that have never told a single white lie –"

"Holy shit…" Peter says under his breath and looks like he's about to barf.

"What? You've seen her?" We all look at him apprehensively, and he looks up like he's surprised to see us. Without saying a word, he nods sheepishly as if he's a child in trouble. Evangeline beats us to talking – *shocker* – before anyone can ask what his deal is.

"Maya, what did you see?"

"Let's just say, I saw a hideous monster with slimy scales and a vicious stare that only begged for her next victim."

"Poetic," Eevee deadpans. "Anyway, the reason why he sees her drop-dead beautiful and you don't is because of your inner self-criticism and hatred."

"Come again?" My anger seethes at her bluntness…*damn, is this what I sound like **all** the time?.*

The fairy rolls her eyes. "Women are generally insecure, right? So if a timid girl, like yourself, should lay her eyes on a siren whose power is fueled by jealousy, she will see said creature the way she *wishes* to see her, not how she actually *is.* All sirens have different powers, and you happened to attract that one. Go figure."

I don't engage with the insult. "And men?"

"See her in her natural form. She has the tantalizing power to lure them to their deaths by her beauty due to men generally being full of lust, so best to keep your distance." With this, her bored stare targets Finneas.

I look at him curiously and he laughs. *Fucking laughs.* "Oops." He shrugs. "Maybe I'm bi."

"Peter," Evangeline says gently as if she's his little comfort whore. "Are you okay?"

"You would know, wouldn't you?" This catches Del and me off guard. "You read my journal. Why don't you tell them what happened?"

"I think it would be good for you if you let it out, don't you?"

"Not particularly, pixie bird." I can't tell if it's the smoke from the fire or even just my imagination, but Peter's throat becomes hollow and desert-dry with these words. He's not one to *let it out* to just anyone, so clearly she must not know him all that well. I want to hug him – want to grasp him around his neck and tell him he doesn't have to breathe out a single syllable regarding whatever he and the pixie are referring to if he doesn't want to – but Evangeline beats me to speaking,

"C'mon, we're all friends here," she insists with that devilishly pretty smile. "Maybe more than friends, I would say." She goes to take Peter's hand, and as the rage in me boils like a pot of molten lava, to my surprise, he doesn't acknowledge the hand but subtly stands, grasping the back of his head anxiously. Evangeline pretends it wasn't an obvious *skirt-skirt* reaction, and I laugh inwardly despite the transition of intensity surrounding us.

"That siren thing..." His voice is miles away and he doesn't look directly at any of us, just at the nothingness that encamps us from outside the fire pit as the wind begins to blow. "I didn't understand it until now...She nearly killed me when I was sixteen back in New York. Well, dare I say *killed,* amongst other things prior. I've seen her a few times in visions...nightmares...I've seen her everywhere."

"Other things, what other things?" I ask, almost aggressively...protectively. Not that I care much about my tone at this point, but curiosity is likely about to murder this pussy into oblivion.[131]

---

[131] *WAY more unhinged and badass than saying 'curiosity killed the cat'.*

"She...uhm..." He looks down, clearly hoping nobody would ask; a flood of shame masking his face as the air around us becomes colder instantly. It's fascinating how Peter was so good at hiding his emotions, and now this island genuinely won't allow that in any sense.

Perhaps it's one of Neverland's nightmares and he doesn't even recognize it.

He attempts a deep breath, promptly clearing his throat out of habit yet producing little to no phlegm for once. I expect his voice to shake, but he stands boldly despite his fear, "You want me to let it out? Fine. She was the first woman to ever touch me – the only one that ever has since. She not only destroyed me mentally but her mark is left on me forever..." Peter lifts his shirt to reveal deep scars that make my stomach twist, as well as abs that make it...*and another part of me*...buzz for other reasons entirely...

Muzzle it, Maya, not now.

I can't help but stand and before I know it, my body is inches away from his. I reach out and almost touch his shoulder, but refrain. "Peter, I – we didn't –"

"I never told anyone. No one was *ever* meant to know." His green eyes are nearly black as they turn toward Evangeline, and as she meets his gaze, hers are full of iniquity.

But does she actually feel guilty?
I choose to think not.

"How did she even get from New York to Paragon?" Finneas asks. "Could she get to Neverland too?"

Evangeline nods and responds, "There are so many things humans of your kind haven't discovered yet, and most of that is what lies beneath the deepest depths of the water. It's said there are portals and some sort of supernatural connection sirens have with other realms, and they can come and go as they wish. Neverland could easily be included now as well."

Peter continues and looks back into the oblivion of his world, quite possibly missing our conversation completely, "I mean, what was I to say?" I can't tell if he's speaking to us, himself, to his past self...or to anyone, really. "Who would believe a kid was sexually harassed and physically abused by an ethereally smashing mermaid in the New York harbor?" He laughs, but I can tell it isn't just. "Not to mention, how I got her to finally piss off was just *one look* and a magical green light appeared and *WOOSH!*" he waves his arms for dramatic emphasis, "she ran away out of shock or terror or whatever...and she was all but a purgatory. Her calling me *Pan* eventually made more sense after I got passed the brutal denial of who I am, but *fuck* – I surely wouldn't believe a bloke if he told me any of that bullshit in any sense – that's pure mental! Fucking lunacy! I was *forced* to keep my mouth shut. Live with it and die with it. An incessant nightmare."

I look at my bare feet, unsure of what to say. "No wonder you're so fucked up."

NO!
NOT THAT!

WHY?!

MAYA,
YOU FUCKING
DUMBASS.

I cannot believe this slides out of my tongue, so much so that I nearly knock myself out when I slam my hand against my mouth. Everyone's eyes nearly explode out of their heads, and Peter's neck turns so fast toward me I have no doubt he got whiplash. I half expect him to yell at me; to slap me in the face or tell me to fuck off and stop being so insensitive…but no. His face brightens, and the weather becomes just a little warmer.

"I know, right?" Is all he says, with that cheeky grin I wish he knew I adore so much.

CHAPTER thirty-one
Peter Pan
Neverland

JOurNAl ENTry ~

I love this entry.

"No wonder you're so fucked up" ...

It'S onE oF thE TRUest tHINgs thE liTTle biRd haS eveR saID, aND foR Once, I whOLEheartEDly aPPreciaTE heR bluNT anD bruTAl honESty. foR yeaRS, whAt seeMed liKE aN omNIpreSenT nigHTmaRE, aLL aT oNce waS washED awaY bY heR <u>quirK</u> – <u>nO, it'S noT heR flaW...</u> as I onCE thoUGht in Such hoSTIlitY; Not HEr IllNess oR thE linGEring disORder thAT crUCifieS heR wiLL and MINd daILy...It'S thE thinG thaT maKEs hER holY – Set aPArt. tHE thiNG thAT maKEs her SPECIAL

AND yes, PERHAps iT doesNT maKE SENSe hOW somETHINg shE saID, thAT tO moST WOUld BE inFINItelY inCONsiDERate iN REgards To SUCh a SEnsiTIve SUBject, someHOW CURed MY torMENt to nearlY a Full extEnt iN ONE MOment...

bUT it's raTHEr sIMPle:

I Prefer Peter

she made me laugh
amid a waking nightmare, she made my lungs dance to a
rhythm they became two left feet in.
she made an open wound seem like damn all in the most
delicate way possible...
and did it all without even trying.

lAUGHTer doeSNt cOME VERY easilY tO me — iT's
forCEd, unCOMFortable...i forgOT whAT It reALLy felT liKE
To sinG A soNG of genUINe lauGHter. anD THEN i MET
HER. evERY laugH i HAVE wiTH HER is so REAl, it'S aS if
I'M leaRNinG WHAt it MeaNS tO laugh AGAin.[132] i Can
ASSuredlY saY thAT i AM glaD i NEver pAid foR anY vilE
yeaRS oF theraPY anD thaT My escAPE froM BNL waS
successfUL, beCAUSe i COULD sweAR on mY LIfe thaT no
doCTor, nO psycH maN, NO tHERapiss off, blOOdy nO ONE
WOUldvE Ever COME up wiTH the PREsCRIPtion i NeedEd
tO heaL — A conCOctiON CONsiStinG of CRYstaL BLue
Eyes, a SMILE thaT couLD swiTCH thE buTTErflieS in YOur
stOMACh inTO a fULL oN bLOODy Zoo, A minD THAt tELLS
tHE resT oF Her BEinG whAT to DO, aND A heaRT tHAT
coNNecTS WIth mINe on A leVEl tHAT i DOnt unDERstand.

mAYBE nevER will.

---

[132] *Pieced together from a poem I wrote — it's published in "i probably shouldnt say this, but..."*

I Prefer Peter

And MAYBE im oKAY with That.

I close my journal and slide the pen into the crevice of my ear. Not being able to fathom all of the sap I just wrote, I set the book away from me in the grass as if it's gonna attack me with even more emotions that I can't handle, and loosely hug my knees as I move on to deciding what to do next.

That siren.

Etain is the only thing that is interrupting my negotiations of what to do about Maya – of what to do at all about anything. Though she has haunted the nooks and crannies of my mind for a little over two years now, it still stings as if it were yesterday…The claw mark scars on my torso and thigh are ever-present reminders that I was almost torn of my innocence before I even had a clue what value it held…the cherry on top to deciding against love entirely. Because of her, any potential touch from a woman that genuinely could ever *mean something* will be ripped at the seams from the getgo – tainted. Perhaps one of the biggest nightmares that came of all of this is that as long as I am alive, I will only see *that* moment when it comes to intimacy.

When it comes to lust.
Longing…
Love?
Whatever that is.
If I'll ever even feel that.
If I ever even want to…

> But what if…

> *What if it doesn't have to be forever like I thought?*

Maybe...just maybe...
It only has to last until tonight.

Neverland is not supposed to be a place of
nightmares, no – it was always meant to be my land of
dreams. *Happy thoughts,* as Evangeline put it.

A place to escape even the harshest realities no matter where
you are.
And I intend to get my island back to the way I created it.
I need to destroy the corruption prowling through **my**
Neverland.

Neglecting to gather the rest of my thoughts for fear I
may pussy out, I stuff my journal into the pocket of my jacket,
grab a water canteen and a dagger for the journey, and make
haste toward the lagoon. I know she'll be there, I feel it in my
bones – through the Paradust in my very veins – that she's
been there before. Etain has been everywhere I've been since I
was sixteen, and I sense she's now followed me here with the
sorcery she's invariably held. I know this, and I didn't even
have to see her.

Faith.
The faith I have in this place is growing.

The longer I'm in Neverland, the stronger it and I
become bound as one, and the more aware I am of everything
from its highest point to its lowest depths. I can practically
feel Etain's unnerving presence looming from the portals
below, preying on me until I willingly succumb to her
halieutics – or so she wishes. To lure me, a Pan, into her trap
would be a priceless kill; a pride-filled trophy of supremacy
under her belt. But as I walk to my confrontation, the epiphany
rises from the pit of my stomach, that perhaps all this time, I

have had more dominion over this nightmarish villain in my story than I ever realized, and I'm just now coming to terms with that fact. Fucking hell, she may know who I am, that vulgar creature, as she said my real name the first time we met before I even knew what it meant…but she knows not quite what I am capable of.

But she will.
Yes, I hardly know…
But I'll be damned if I don't start finding out.
Finding out and taking charge of who I'm meant to be –

PETER PAN.

Now she cannot hunt me and haunt me in mere silence. I am summoning her, and I know bloody damn well she can hear me.

Because now, when I listen closely…
Now I can hear her too.

🏮🏮🏮

"Etain," my bellowing voice echoes across the water, making its ripples animate and dance for me in the moonlight. All is calm, and so I call again, "Etain! Show yourself at once."

When she doesn't appear at my beck and call, I try the tactic we used previously.

Etain,
I call to her through my mind, and with the magic I have inside me, put vast control over my thoughts so she can't unmask my plot.
We need to chat.

Suddenly, the water begins to create wave-like currents, illuminating a deep, uncanny glow of turquoise and glittering orbs of light. The siren appears to me as the same ethereal femme fatale, and my stomach whirls as my cheeks flare, but I stand firm. It's finally time to act – *and I mean that in more ways than one.*

"Darling boy,"
her voice is filled with taste.
"To what do I owe the pleasure?"

Ah, the pleasure is all mine.
I say/think, cocksurely.
I haven't stopped thinking about you –
I've missed you, pet.

"You've grown, Pan.
Your beauty is that of this island you've fashioned."

"And you are as the Neverland sea you inhabit –
simply celestial.
(Yeah...I wanna throw up at that.)
Now, Etain...I've come for...a courtesy.

"Your thoughts are indecipherable
for once.
Do I get to guess?"

I don't think it'll take many.

In the deafening silence between us, I strip off my shirt in one fluid motion, revealing my improved physique. I toss my hair, seductively smirking at the temptress as I know she won't be able to withstand the sight, then gently yet swiftly move my body into the blue and soak in the presence of her. The water would be soothing in of itself, but the siren's aura is pleasant and warm like a bubble bath as her essence seeps into my skin like an essential oil that cures every ailment known to man.

It's been a while, hasn't it, mermaid?
I start.

    "Mermaid – " Etian scoffs, *"so informal, Pan."*

Peter. Call me Peter.

  Her tail wraps around me then; not quite too tight to put me in discomfort, but restraining enough that I'm surely not going anywhere unless she decides. However, my arms are free, so I run them through her soaked hair and then down her bare, scaly shoulders, which are somehow soft as silk. I lean in, letting out a sensual chuckle as my breath catches her ear,

Do you like it when I tell you what to do?

      "You are my master, Pan – "

Peter.

      *"You are my master, **Peter**."*

Good girl.
  ...Lol.

  I feel her tail unwillingly loosen and when her breasts become hard against my chest, I know then I have her exactly where I want her. Though obscenely *yet obscurely* terrified, I cup my hand around her slim waist and slide my hand around to her lower back.

I Prefer Peter

You know what I want you to do next for me, Etain?

> She moans; seduced and surrendered,
> *"Tell me."*

I let the silence ring for a while and guide her body
away from mine, letting the lack of gravity carry us
weightlessly. I reach for her hand and spin her around, and
when her back is facing my front, I snatch the blade with
breakneck speed from within my boot and simultaneously
grasp her long hair with my free hand. I yank her backward
until my chin is within the curve of her neck and bring the
knife to her throat and she gasps,

> *"You treacherous –"*

Shhh, shhh. I think/hiss. *I wouldn't cross me, love.*
I press the blade, sharper than her jaw, gently upon her chin
and trace it down her neck.
You're already treading a fine line.

> She quivers,
> *"What do you want?"*

Firstly, no. I don't want to know why.
I fully read her thoughts for once, answering her question
before it's asked. Dismayed, she freezes, and my expression
stays brooding, though I hide my gut full of pride.
I just want you to savvy, lass, that now, I am in charge.
This land you're in? It's mine.
You will never hurt me. You will never touch me.
You will never damage or lay a hand on my friends, or death
will wreak havoc on your pretty little scaley's.
You work for me.

Do you follow, siren?

She wants to fight back but knows if she moves even a fraction of an inch, this blade will make her tonight's catch of the day. I've never felt such power and dominance – I've never known this side of me, nor do I hardly know what to do with it…but this improv seems to be working. She pleads and agrees, becoming weak and desperate contrary to her usual overconfident demeanor, thus I unwrap her locks from my fist and, conjuring up as much magic as I need, throw her onto the sandy shore.

Her hair is tangled and her eyes are frantic, searching for a way out of my supremacy. I'm out of the water in a flash, meeting her gaze as she looks up at me now oppositely, in complete and utter disgust.

"Now, are we gonna talk like adults?" I cock my head, verbally speaking to her as if to a child, which propels her to spit on my boots. Looking down at her grimy slobber and emitting a wickedly deep snigger, I click my tongue in disappointment, and with one light-speed motion, I viciously tug her hair back again as if she's my puppet so her chin points upward toward the stars that are watching this charade like a reality show. "I asked you a question."

Her shoulders sag, "Yes, Pan," she verbally speaks to me for the first time, her voice raspy and adenoidal.

I smile condescendingly and let go of her matted silver locks. "I'm not gonna hurt you, Etain." I pace back and forth, moxie still soaring through my veins and making me feel like a whole new person. I twirl my knife's hilt in my hand like a drumstick – *I am enjoying this more than I thought* –, "I'm past the point of revenge for what you inflicted over me. However, I *am* a man of bargain."

"What could I possibly want from you, son of the devil?"

I lower my head at her, and she cowers back. Being compared to my father is *not* the way to play. "Your life, cretin." I drop to my heels next to her. "Your life in exchange for answers."

"Answers, what answers?"

I give her a bilious scan and angle my head. "You stalk me enough to know, pet. Don't play daft."

"I –" she stutters, "How did you – I don't –"

I don't have time for this. "How do I get to the forsaken Pararealms?"

"The what?"

I trace the knife along her tail. "God, I hate liars."[133] I shake my head, twisting the hilt of the knife as the tip of the blade nearly breaks her scales. She winces, but I ignore it and instead growl, "I'm gonna ask you again: Where, or rather *what, who, whatever the fuck,* are the keys to the Pararealms and how do I get there?"

"Pan, I don't know –"

At her denial, I push the blade down, and she yelps in pain. *"Alright!"* She gives in way too quickly for fear of tainting her outer beauty. *The inside is clearly already done for.* "The keys aren't physical," she admits, panting. "You must..." she sighs and her shoulders drop in defeat, "you must conquer your greatest nightmares in order to unlock the realms."

I raise my eyebrow, "The fuck do you mean?"

"You found Paragon by not only being a descendant of Pan but by not being afraid to venture into the unknown. You conquered your fear – *'the nightmare'* – of uncertainty...thus gaining entrance to the realm."

Barely conquered it...but I guess there's uncertainty in everything, which is where the adventure lies...

---

[133] *This line always gives me chills.*

Huh.
I guess the fact that I have that mentality says something in the least.
Hooray, character development.

"Go on." I twirl the blade on her tail.

"Now the nightmares…the nightmares that prowl around Neverland…" her eyes never leave the dagger, "they are the ones that infect your subconscious the deepest. The two closed Pararealms are a part of your soul just the same as Paragon was – is –, though they come at a deeper price –"

"Why? Why can't they just be opened with a journal, and/or with a spell and Paradust like Neverland was?"

"Neverland was just a piece of the puzzle to obtain the next part of the journey. A gift, nonetheless, yet also the key to the next steps. It's a haven you will always come home to throughout your perilous journeys through the Pararealms. But to answer your question, if opening all of the realms was as easy as Paradust, you then would not be mighty enough to rule. Your mind, will, and emotions have to be in one accord in order to be the leader Pétros Pan was – the one he knew you would be. If you don't conquer your demons, they will conquer you."

I'm not sure I will ever be intact…
Will I ever be the leader Pan was?
Fuckin' hell…who am I to even try?

But try I must.

I need answers and I can tell this will be a bit longer of a chat than I intended, and Etain will not help me if she suffocates from lack of water and fear. I remove the blade from her scales and place it in my sheath, then pour the water from my canteen down her tail. "Keep talking. But you should know that's all I have, so best make it snippy."

She doesn't hesitate to act. "Journey through Neverland – don't ask the way, you will know; you are The Pan, after all. The more you endure, the more you shall uncover. You will embark on a perilous journey through the vast island, and if you survive, you will happen upon Covera. There, you will discover what to do next."

"What the fuck is Covera?"

"Another dominion grown within your Neverland – it is based off of a dreamland that once appeared in your mind, be it from a daydream, a nightmare, REM dreaming – it merely depends on what the land decided during the creation process – it was part of the prophecy. You may recognize it, you may not – it may all just feel like déjà vu…but that will be your justification. Be that as it may, members of the court there are meant to guide you further."

"Wait, there are other people here? How do they know me – about the Pararealms? Where did they come from? I never mentioned having anyone else here in my entries."

"We can't always control what happens in our dreams, Peter Pan. They are often illusions we scarcely understand…be it good or bad. As you once said: *'Dreams are just nightmares sprinkled in dust.'…*"

"Fucking hell…" I whisper more to myself in sheer astonishment.

She continues, "All of the inhabitants you see are based on your past relationships, or perhaps ones you've seen in passing, mixtures of the like, or what-have-you."

"Literally like the people you see in actual dreams…"

"Precisely. They may be similar, or rather you may not even notice. Neverland is populated, but adhere to my words: you *must* be careful. You may have created this world, but not everyone is on your side."

"Why? I created the world, dammit, shouldn't they all be on my side? –"

"Nightmares, Peter. Keep up." I glare at her attitude, causing her to shrink back. When my gaping eases, I nod, giving her permission to track on, "All that to say, Pan: You must unhinge the locked away parts of your soul to open the Pararealms, and that comes with constantly adventuring into the unknown and embarking on the quests it takes. Once you have done as the universe requires, only then will the realms proceed to be opened."

"How will I know if they are...or when I'm finished?"

"You will just know."

"How do *you* know all of this? Why doesn't Evangeline know, or mention it if she did?"

"The magic around us is stronger than you fathom. As leader of the sirens, I have knowledge of all I need to, precisely when I need to. The pixie doesn't know shit, though is skilled in acting as though she does. She would've set you off on a journey completely blinded to everything secretly skulking around you. She's made of *primarily* magic, but she's certainly lacking in functional information, particularly when it's most vital."

I chuckle ironically and look her in the eyes, to which she freezes at the emeralds that never fail to captivate her. "Funny, as she was helpful in enlightening me about *you...*" Etain's face pales. In a trice, I virtually feel every physical assault the siren did to me once again, and I ask with a sour mouth, "The nightmares. The people against me – my enemies...are you one of them?"

She swallows a barrel of a lump. "I –" she stammers again, "I don't –"

"Do I need to kill you, Etain? Wipe you out with the rest of the nightmares to move on with my quests? Or are you going to obey and help me?"

The mermaid trembles, and I can't tell if it's because she is drying out on this sand from being out of the water for so long, or if she is petrified. She shakes her head, "Don't kill me. I will help. Consider this nightmare defeated…you win, Pan. You have my word."

I move the blade away but keep a keen eye on her every movement. "Talk's cheap, siren. How do I know I can trust you?"

She lifts her hand and goes to place it on my stomach, and I can't help but mindlessly tense, flinching a tad as well when the memory of her brutally labeling me forcefully resurfaces. Momentarily ashamed and pissed the hell off that my dominance was briefly interrupted, I peer down at her frozen gesture with a curious scowl. Thankfully, Etain doesn't mention my minor shift in disposition – *smart fish* – if she even noticed it at all, that is…yet just simply asks, "May I?"

Apprehensively, I nod. The claws that once dug deep into my flesh years prior touch the very same skin, and as her hand makes contact with my scars, a warmth surges through my belly like soup on a rainy day. My skin glows golden as Etain's hand emits a silver light, and once she finishes on my stomach, she moves down and hovers over my thigh and the surrounding area, but doesn't touch it – hardly comes close.

Before long, the telltale scars the siren caused completely disappear. Though the ones tattooed upon my wrists and arms will forever remain, the omnipresence of her insidious markings now will forever cease to haunt me.

"I am sorry, Pan." Etain pulls her hand away. "Your innocence was not mine to take. I left the moment I ascertained –"

"You didn't take it. Not all of it. Not the part that matters." I remind her to empty her pride. "And you never will."

She hangs her head and whimpers, "I'm sorry."

At her apology, I cast the lagoon's tide up to Etain to grasp her and pull her back out into the deep depths of the water. I watch her fade into the sea and when I turn away, I stop dead cold in my tracks to see Maya watching from the cliff above.

CHAPTER thirty-two
Peter Pan
Neverland

"You saw that?" I walk toward the bottom of the cliff and look up to meet her gaze.

"Pretty much the whole thing, yeah."

"Did I look tough?"

She laughs, and I strike a pose by flexing my muscles, causing her to blush. "Yes, very." She runs her fingers through her messy hair. "I almost believed you."

I cross my leg over and bow with a roll of my hand, grinning whilst looking up at her crimson cheeks, "Oh, the cleverness of me."[134]

She motions for me to come up, and though normally I would instinctively choose the stairs, my body intuitively begs for another tactic of reaching her. I feel a pull from my innermost being, and as I fix my gaze on her, I feel a warmth of such solace that it nearly causes me to melt on the spot. The comfort is so uncanny – so unfamiliar, that my brain wants to revolt against it; push it away for fear it isn't real, or that it may be stolen away from me in an instant –

I close my eyes and remind myself of the rule –
Think happy thoughts, Peter.

I think of Maya's face. I think of her subtle skin and her cerulean eyes, and I think of her gentle smile that she tries but fails to hide every time she and I lock eyes. I think of her voice – her laugh – the melodic tones it sends freely through

---

[134] *giggles*

my ear canals and up through to my brain, signaling it to listen to every word she says. I think of her body, so delicate and fragile – the being of the only one I solely feel the dire need to protect and nurture; to keep safe from the darkest nefariousness that dwells within every world we have, and ever will, encounter together.

Together.
I think of us together.

I think of us as one – physically, mentally – thoughts I have never dared think about anyone for fear of...*what? Growing up? Disappointment? Rejection?* Whatever it may have been, I don't feel scared to imagine it anymore. I want to think of Maya. I *need* to think of her. I *crave* the mere presence of her in any form I can grasp. The more I dwell on all she is, the more I want her – *all of her.*

And the more I pray she wants me too.

The longer I let my mind wander, the warmer I become, until finally I feel my feet leave the ground. As I am graciously lifted above the sand, I don't open my eyes until I know for certain when they open again, the first thing that will greet them is the woman centered around my happy thoughts.[135] The most effective stimulant in granting me a better high than any substance – *literally and metaphorically.*

"Show off." Her smile is willingly unhidden at my flight, so much so I can feel my cheeks heat with pride. I shy away so she misses it – though I doubt she does. I look back at her, and her smile never fades; not even a trifle.

---

[135] *This is the first time Peter flies on his own...and it's euphoric. Is it weird that I created him, yet I'm proud of him and his development? LOL*

"Don't act like you didn't…" I trail off, for fear that the next word that involuntarily entered my thought bank may have the power to change everything in an instant. A word that I've never been fond of – a word I've never believed in.

"I loved it," she says so I don't have to. I sheepishly smile, though say nothing. "By the way…" she reaches her hand out, then pulls back gingerly, "you look good…while flying."

I bite the inside of my cheek, my bottom lip, and anything else my jagged sabertooth teeth can reach, "Thank you," is all I manage to say toward the awkward compliment. "You look dashing while watching."

Her cheeks become redder than I've ever seen at my newfound confidence, and it becomes her turn to shy away; though I don't miss anything – for this time I can't keep my eyes off of her, and I do everything in my being not to ask myself the dreaded question of *why.*

"I'm proud of you for standing up to your nightmare," the phrase slides off her tongue like sweet honey. "That was very brave of you."

"It had to be done." I don't look at her, but at the glistening lagoon behind me where Etain still swims freely. "I couldn't go on with that hanging over my head. Unfortunately, there are still plenty more nightmares to wake up from…" I sigh at the terrorizing thought of what's to come, "but at least that one is nothing but a distant memory now."

Maya smiles tenderly and I nearly miss it, but I turn back just in time to catch the end. "So that's how we get to the realms and save Paragon, huh? We have to defeat the evil, enigmatic inner workings of your mind?"

I crack up, "We're so fucked."

She laughs with me and takes my hand, "We'll do it together. None of us are going anywhere, alright?" I grant a slight smile back at her, and we stay silent for a moment, basking in each other's presence and pure gestures until her voice fills the void again, "Peter..." She is hesitant to speak, but the expression I give her tells her it's safe to ask whatever it is that haunts her mind, "I know this may be forward..."

"You don't have to warn me; *forward* is not new for you, darling. Go ahead."

She titters in acceptance and at the use of the pet name, but it stops timidly. "Have you really never been touched by someone who...who is...who –"

"I said *speak,* Maya."

She lets out a tsunami of anxiety in one breath, but I can tell she appreciates the totality of permission. "Have you really never been touched by someone who loves you?"

I don't know whether I want to fly away, scream, throw up, cry, or launch myself back off the cliff. Responding to the personal question, however, is nowhere on that list of desires...though I walked right into this trap with the consent I granted the mouthy lass to ask in the first place, so I must do my part.

"No," I mutter, looking at my wet boots and trousers. "Why?"

Once again, I don't want to answer – I'd rather chew glass than have this conversation, but perhaps it's a part of conquering this nightmare as a whole for good...or even another one entirely.

So, I say as straightforwardly as she would, "There's never been anyone who has loved me enough to do so, Maya."

Her eyes glisten at my truth, then find their way down to my boots with mine. "What if there was, Peter? Would you let them?"

The lassie's voice is hardly audible, and I know now that this moment between us will make or break my perception of what I truly believe in; because what happens next, is based on the answer I give.

*Most of what I said at Brand New Life Wellness Home was
horse shit....*
*But I truly **did** hope Peter would be less of a fuck up than
Benjamin....*
And it's my job to ensure that happens.

I know what Benjamin Green's answer would be next –
But what about Peter Pan's?

"Maybe," I whisper lower than her already nearly
indistinguishable voice. "I think that would depend on how I
feel toward the person who, *supposedly,* loves me." The word
rots in my mouth. Still, having said that, I look up and see she
seemed to have already met my eyes a long time ago.

"How *do* you feel, Peter?"

"I..." I hold her gaze like cherished gold. Licking my
lips, I whisper, "I don't know."

Maya inches closer to me, and as much as I want to
run and avoid all of what could be coming, I keep my feet
firmly planted where I am on the green grass, curiosity
bubbling in my stomach. Her movement stops when it reaches
my body that towers over her, and as her arms wrap around
my bare waist, I peer down and smell a mixture of her classic,
fresh scent mixed in with the smokey embers from tonight's
fire in her hair. I wrap my arm around her shoulders and graze
her back with my hand.

"How do you feel now?" She tries.

"I don't know," I press back, lying and she knows it,
as a consequence of the humid air beginning to flux into a
nippy breeze.

The lass attentively grazes her fingertips up and down
my back – every muscle of mine tensing and adhering to a
touch they've never felt before, though covertly always
desired.

"Peter?"

"Yes?" Our voices are taut.

"I'm scared."

I can scarcely hear over the blood pounding in my eardrums, but I'll be damned if I let her sense that. I do my best to steady my breathing, and voice toward the top of her head, "What is it that you're scared of?"

"The things I feel for you. The things I want...*need*...from you," her voice trails into a desperate plea, all censorship thrown out the window. Maya's body stiffens and presses closer against mine, which responds to her adjacency with an ache and burning heat I faintly recall, though haven't felt this explosively.

The last time I was in a situation like this, feeling even a fraction relative, I was ruined...torn...broken...shattered – for years. The thought of intimacy has always nauseated me – repulsed me to a point of straight loathing and pure malice toward it – as love has long been an illusion, so lust became a mirage just the same.

But as someone who, for the longest time, *knew for a fact* those things were myths, what I failed to be cautious of – and what everyone failed to warn me about – was a woman who could alter my perception of reality entirely. One who could cause a slow burn and create a change in me so vast, that it would convert my morality and everything else I believe in completely. A creature of such beauty, that carries within her a heart that beats on the same level as mine – one that is as if a magnet and I am the metal susceptible to her irresistible pull. Walking, moving, breathing poetry, right before my eyes.

Maya Wendy Sexton.
The darling girl I never expected.

So, contrary to usual, I allow my mind to be right here, right now. I let everything I thought I knew fly away with what I assumed to be true, and with a new, undeniable reality, I accept who I am and finally welcome in the new soul.

I am Peter Pan.[136]

And 'Peter Pan' wants this nightmare to end...
Start all things new –
And that's waking up to a new dream
that's filled with her and only her. *does anyone...smell...spice?*

A surge of new power, stemming from an even younger spout of courage, ignites within me, and I lower my mouth to her ear, "And what might that be, love?" The little bird doesn't answer, but I can feel her heart pounding through her thin skin. I spin her around by her waist like a dance and she gasps at the suddenness, grasping hold of my forearm as I wrap it around her. I sensually whisper again into her ear, "Tell me what you want."

Her knees buckle. "I want…"

"Hmm?" I hum, sending shivers down her spine. "Tell me what you want, Maya, and I'll give it to you."

"I…I want you, Peter."

"Me, darling?" I snicker sinisterly. "Why, I'm right here. What of me do you want? Put me on the same page…Or do I have to guess?"

I run my fingertip along her side and down to her hip, and then delicately lift her shirt upward, petting her pleasantly soft skin. She squeezes my arm tightly as if she's holding on to her innocence for dear life, but I witness her silently give in when I slowly begin to move my hand farther down to her thigh, stroking the surface as if it were the finest glass known to man. Without warning, I squeeze it aggressively and she inhales sharply, desire fueling her gasp.

---

[136] *FUCK YEAH YOU ARE*

"I don't think it'll take many guesses," she spurts out, mocking my words to the siren.

"Is that right?" I question, very well already knowing the answer. "Give me a hint." Unsure yet unbothered by whatever supernatural force is devouring me, I take this coquetry a step forward and kiss her neck slowly, licking it down to the hollowness of her collarbone, sending her into a moan filled to the brim with a need I've never heard any woman want from me.

Maya doesn't play the guessing game – just purrs, *"Take me."*

"Where?" I tease, sending her into a grunt of annoyance at the squib.

"Ugh just *fuck me,* you silly ass."

In one swift motion and without an ounce of hesitation, I bridal-lift her and place her body gently onto the soft, dewy grass – a bed made just for us. I creep up to meet her at her side, my hands finding a place on either side of her stomach. Trembling with either desire or anxiety...*or both,* Maya cups my face in her hands and runs her fingers through my damp hair.

"You should know I've never done this before..." she says softly, almost shamefully.

"Neither have I," I say with the opposite flare. "No one was ever special enough for me." Her eyes close as she lets out a breath that could have seemed like it was held for twenty years. I caress her jaw with my cupped palm and as her eyes flutter open, her pupils grow large at the sight of me so close as if she forgot who was touching her. I gently glide my thumb across her cheek, "We don't have to, darling."

"No –" she protests, almost too quickly and I inwardly laugh. "I want to...maybe just...start slow?"

"As you wish." Ever so largo, I caress her hip with my hand and slide her shirt up, traveling to meet the undercarriage of her breast. I feel her skin as if it's the first and last time, memorizing every inch of her – every bone. She is so small, so brittle like a new leaf in the fall – I don't want to ruin her in any way. "Are you sure? *Really, truly* sure?" I ask with all seriousness, holding my breath.

She nods in response, and I exhale. To be quite honest, I haven't the foggiest if I was asking for her sake more so than mine, but let's just say both for the hell of it.

"You really aren't that horrible, are you?" She says upwardly toward the sky full of stars that light our midst.

I chuckle at the memory of the first time she ever said that to me.[137] "Ask me again in ten minutes."

Well...if I last that long, of course.[138]

Finally, after what feels like a century-long craving, my lips crash into hers. The moment we come together, my entire body momentarily glows a vibrant shade of turquoise from within, and the night air feels like the most perfect summer day from back when I was a kid. Heat soars through me as if my entire being is catching on fire from the inside out, and I know she can feel it too.

Our tongues intertwine, threatening to tie one another in knots as she and I never come up for air but instead hungrily survive off of each other's breaths. I use my hands for leverage as I lay on top of her, but soon give in when I pull the lass close to my chest, rolling over so now I am the one getting to look at *her.*

And my God, is she beautiful.

---

[137] *Pg. 128*
[138] *HAAAAAAHAHAHAHAHA SELF AWARENESS AT ITS FINEST*

"So you're a bottom?" Maya smirks, and I can't help but nearly choke on the phlegm that hasn't attacked me in quite a while. Luckily, it comes out more like a guttural growl.

"Shut up, Sexton. Make your last name useful."

PAUSE, READER.

Apologies for the interruption, as I can practically feel the goosebumps and hairs rising on your skin... But for all of you classy fucks who aren't into the horny details, no worries! Turn the page to skip them – *you're welcome* – but just know...you're skipping absofuckinglute euphoria.
The rest of you smut fanatics, scan here:[139]

We fuck. Passionately, aggressively – like we were two halves of a whole soul meant to be from the second the

---

[139] *I realize this is an acquired taste, but I wanted to ensure everyone had an equally enjoyable reading experience here in I Prefer Peter, so I made the organ rearranging, tongue numbing-ly spicy details optional, which nobody ever does! I wanted to start a new legacy! Hence the QR code. Either way, the story continues more PG-13 (still euphoric, though) on the next page. What do you think? Did you scan? ;)*

universe spewed us out from our mother's wombs without our consent. A golden light emitting from my skin illuminates around us and as she sobs my name into the surrounding air, I crow hers louder into the sky full of stars.

As my innocence dissipates, so vanish the nightmares of intimacy; and all at once I am with the woman who I can fully call *mine.* We catch our breaths, our bodies still connected like a new form of imperishable magic.

"I love you, Peter Pan," she whispers.

My heart stops and I die for an instant. It's at this moment I realize that death is, in fact, the grandest adventure in this lifetime, the next, and forevermore. For the first time, I have experienced the truest depiction of dying to my own self and living for another.

I smile, though I say nothing…
Yet it seems she's okay with that for now as I hold her tight.

But I think I just might love you too, Maya Wendy Sexton.

CHAPTER thirty-three
Maya Sexton
Neverland

I feel like absolute shit today.

Everything after the fire pit last night is a total blur, so I'm assuming whatever drink I must've inhaled went straight to my head, especially considering my lack of sustenance. Evangeline offered us all some pixie pinot or whatever the fuck, and considering I'm not *technically* among the *recovering addicts* part of our trio, I accepted. But what she didn't mention was that I shouldn't have had more than a glass because man, everything is as foggy as the windows of a horny high school couple's Prius.

I wish I had the courage to eat something — anything.
Perhaps in time.
Perhaps not.
Will I ever get my character arc?[140]

The sun is doing a bang-up job sunning today, and normally I would love nothing more than to soak up the warmth of its rays, but at the moment it's just way too much for me…So instead, I curl up in my bed for a bit longer and skip going down to breakfast, socializing, and Paragon in its entirety so I can be with myself for a bit and regroup for the first time since I landed in this pell-mell. Though regardless of whether I want it to or not, my mind drifts here and there, and I can't help but stumble upon the question of whether or not I miss BNL and the mundaneness of it all…

---

[140] *Don't worry, chick, I gotchu.*

You'd think, considering it's my own brain, that I would *know* if I missed my old life – but it's so *damn funny* that no matter what I do; how many old farts with clipboards I pay to try and fix me, or how much I 'grow up', I hardly know myself at all. So much so, that if I were another human trying to get to know me, I'd fucking give up.

I'm just an impossible personified gray area.

I'm a walking paradox. Among the innumerable dilemmas that flock my universe, one crucial ailment is that I have a pretty solid idea of who I've always wanted to be and what I have to do to reach that nirvana…but I don't fucking *do any of it*.

For instance:

In my daily life, I'm fairly content, yet simultaneously, excruciatingly depressed. I want to feel alive, yet *surviving* is the only method of life I ever manage. I'm so batshit in love, though I'm tremendously petrified by even the mere thought that it makes me want to vomit. Contrary to popular belief, I'm truly determined to get better, yet also remarkably unmotivated and scared to death of not only the inevitable but also the things that are *probably never* going to happen as well…I hate being starving, yet have no self-control with constantly feeding this addiction. I trust way too easily, yet I constantly doubt. I want to grow up, yet I'm only good at being young.

I see this beautiful person I long to be every day, yet there is a wall made of scorching flames blocking my way to her and I feel like I'll never be able to extinguish it…

But I am so close…
So close that it is burning me alive.

Be that as it may, the harder I try, the more I face the harsh realization that I shouldn't even have to try…I should just *be*. But then, of course, I get frustrated when I can't *just be*, and then I get frustrated that I'm frustrated, thus I ruthlessly attempt to claw my way into my skull to find the answer as to why I am like this…

When I think the real problem is, in fact, irrevocably me.

How do I fix this?
*How do I fix **me**?*[141]

My brain is running like the wind – as if a million prize-winning horses took its place, and as loud banging on my door jolts me out of the mental races I'm losing pathetically, the salty tears streaming down my cheeks startle me…I don't even remember starting to cry. I wipe my face with my comforter and scurry to the door with it still enveloped around me like a giant cozy shield; my feet numbing at once upon meeting the freezing wood floor.

What the fuck?
It was just hotter than hell…
How long was I in bed?

I slither my hand out from the seemingly one-hundred-pound blanket and open the door to a biting chill and a frosty cold Finneas.

"M-Maya," he shivers, his nose looking like Jack Frost did quite the number on it, "s-something is *mad* off."

---

[141] *Fun Fact: This is derived from a journal entry I wrote in highschool.*

I nod as I invite him in, pulling the comforter back onto the bed, resulting in us unhesitatingly and synchronously diving underneath the covers.

"When did it start snowing?" I ask as we curl our bare feet together to keep warm.

"Half-Pint, your g-guess is as good as mine. We need to f-find Evangeline or Peter lickety-split, 'cause I don't have any winter sh-shit, and low temps in Neverland seem like they mean big f-fat business."

I agree, biting my nail as my eyes catch his cheeks turning a pale rose. Though we claim we're in a hurry, Del and I both stay put, generously letting the blanket and queen-size bed do their jobs to defrost our bodies for a quick bit.

"How are you?" I whisper to him as if the walls are listening, knowing he'll comprehend what I'm referring to.

"Right as rain, sis. Petey knows now, though fortunately for you, the kid is not in love with me." I roll my eyes at that, and Finneas smiles. *God, I love his smile; it gives me the warmth the blanket fails to grant me inside.* He boops my frozen nose, "How are you?"

"I'm okay. Foggy as shit from last night."

"Yeah, you downed that parawine like it was your spankin' new superpower. I half expected to have to send you back to rehab this morning."

I sit up and hold my spinning head, trying to remember something – *anything*. "Did Evangeline drug me?"

He scoffs and places a hand on my back to steady me, "Now why would she do that?"

Why wouldn't she do that…?

"Yeah, you're right I guess. I dunno. Maybe I've just never been hungover before."

"You get used to it," he says way too nonchalantly. "Some Neverland coffee and a good stretch, and you'll be fresh as a Spring daisy. Let's hop to it, kat."

Of course, the former alchy was right, because by the time I have my coffee, I feel a bit more with it and a lot less like the pissed-on bathroom floor of a bar. A Neverland cup of joe seems to have a way of perking you up better than any home remedy…it's like it's laced with something of its own.

Frankly, the more I think about it, I don't even want to know what sort of witches brew Peter concocted to come up with it…
Hopefully, it's just some sort of pixie magic.
No, wait…I actually don't know if that's better or worse…
Well. Fuck. Too late.

As I sip my mysteriously caffeinated beverage, it still irks me that I can't – for the dear life of me – remember going to sleep last night, let alone getting to my room…*Who got me there? Did I say anything stupid? Dammit, I probably did…*but I guess I'm just gonna have to let the coffee run its course and then hopefully, I'll be good as new.

Hopefully.

The air is still like February in Jersey, so I do everything I can to stay warm. My body isn't equipped for this type of cold without the proper multi-layered clothing, so I'm forced to practically jump into the fireplace in my tree house…
Which – *hold up*… can I be honest? A fire in a treehouse freaks me the fuck out and is a total design flaw because of *obvious* hazardous reasons I don't even need to begin to explain…though due to Paradust, it's perfectly

safe…? *So sketchy.* It makes as much sense as Spongebob swimming in Goo Lagoon's ocean.

Finneas kept my sorry ass company and had breakfast with me, and then went to practice his archery. *Fucking archery.* He picked up the bow and arrow as his weapon of choice once we decided to embark on these seemingly unavoidable adventures to be genuinely helpful, and of course, he's a natural. He's hella good at everything. I, on the other hand, am just trying to damn well *survive.* I tried every weapon and fighting technique possible, but I am as useless as a car without an engine…and Evangeline made that clear as day during training too, that winged bitch.

I'm just too weak to hold a weapon, let alone my own self up half the time. I wish Peter could poof me up a healthy body that I didn't hate with every fiber of my inner being so I can make myself useful for once.

Peter.

He has apologized profusely for getting us all wrapped up in this clusterfuck, but none of us can totally blame him…I doubt he wants to be here either.

I wonder if he has something to do with the cold.

I recall the weather changing according to his mood, but I don't have a Blue's Clue what snow means. Peter is a boy of ever-fluctuating emotions that he has a radical talent of hiding, so for all I know, it could mean everything and nothing all at once. What I *do* know, however, is that I need the heat to be turned back on before I get hypothermia.

I grab my trusty comforter, wrap it around my goosebump-covered body, and as I twist the chilled doorknob, run straight into the boy I was about to go looking for and nearly knock him off my balcony.

Dropping the blanket and throwing my arms out to catch him, I somehow end up in his instead – warm and safe. Why I embarrassingly even attempted to save Peter, I have no idea...considering I would've definitely taken the tumble with him, and then in return, he would even more easily have been able to fly us back up here like nothing happened...but it's the thought that counts, I suppose. I go to retreat, but he catches me off guard again when his breath becomes heavy and he sounds like he's doing everything he can to contract a panic attack.

I speak first, doing a shit job of hiding my concern, "Oh, Peter, I'm – I'm so sorry, are – are you alright?"

He pants, "I'm – I'm fine." He's undoubtedly not, but he avoids his inner demon that I just summoned by trying a smile and turning his full attention to me.[142] "Are you alright, darling?"

Darling. The pet name sends a magical warmth through me, so I half-lie, "Cold. Extremely cold."

"Of course...apologies. That's on me."

"What does snow mean?"

His brilliant malachite eyes seize me in a way that no one else ever has, nor ever will. He cups my jaw, his hand brushing my hair back, and Peter Pan kisses me.

---

[142] *If you didn't grasp the meaning, he has a brief traumatic flashback of his mom falling... :(poor guy.*

CHAPTER thirty-four
Maya Sexton
Neverland

Wow.

What...and I can't stress this enough...the fuck?

Not only my stomach, but my entire body fills with butterflies, and the veins underneath my skin fill with the magic that Peter breathes inside me with his kiss. He starts slow, but proceeds to intertwine my air with his; his tongue memorizing every inch of my mouth as he ravenously walks me backwards until I collapse onto the bed. With the spell that emanates from his skin, I forget about the chill from outside, and I am instantly hot.

"Peter, I..." I can barely speak. His lean frame hovers wondrously above me, not too far that I crave him nearer, but still not suffocating my small frame. His hands lift my waist and caress my skin like a fine china doll as I grasp onto his hips like it's the only salvation I have to stay alive. I didn't know how badly I wanted to be kissed by Peter...to be the *one* girl to own his undivided attention...until right now. He pulls back a bit, the sparks between us still ignited and places his forehead on mine, the tips of our noses grazing.

He whispers, "Maya, about last night..."

"Wait, *finally,* what was last night?" I ask a little too excitedly at the possibility of answers, the eagerness in my voice hardly complimenting the flame anymore.

I drop a little more abruptly from the air than I prepare for and onto the bed just below me. Peter descends slowly, disregarding the inconsiderate crash landing he caused, as his knees press into the cushioning beside me.

His face contorts, looking almost...confused? Wounded? "You...Wait. You don't remember last night?"[143]

"Should I? Did I do something stupid – I knew I did something stupid, all that parawine, right?" I cringe, imagining nearly everything possible I could've done to make an ass out of myself. But Peter doesn't laugh...doesn't even crack a smile. The boy in front of me nearly swallows his lips and his eyes darken to a threatening shade of gray. I'm lost, as I seem to have offended him...but I cannot, for the life of me, figure out why.

I can't imagine anyone has ever truly offended Peter.

He pushes off the bed and scoffs as if I made an outrageous joke. "Something stupid, hm?" Peter's boots trace back across the room and stop dead in the middle of it as he peers at me like I'm a mystery he can't solve to save Paragon, and everyone in its lives. "That would be a matter of opinion, I suppose."

I sit up and roll my eyes, "Peter, can you just stop with the riddles and tell me?" He seems to know something I don't, and truly believes I am fully aware too, though trying to pull a fast one...

But for God's sake, I have no fucking clue what happened.

"Oh, *I'm* the one playing games?" He points to his chest and steps nearer to me; his cold, spiteful manner causing me to shrink back. I'm not afraid of him, not even a sliver – but I am taken so far aback by his rapid rise in temper, that I hardly recognize him.

---

[143] *Uh oh...*

"Fucking hell, Peter, I'm not playing any games! I swear, I have no idea what happened last night, or why you're suddenly so damn upset –"

"Because I was right about you!" The volume in his voice raises almost fully now…Peter has never yelled at me before…I don't think he's ever yelled at any of us before.

I don't like it at all.

I look at him with uncertainty and distaste, pleading desperately for an explanation for his brash behavior, but he doesn't meet my gaze. He bites his lip and blows air through his nose, seeming to be in the middle of his own epiphany of some sort, smirking in hot-tempered amusement. He continues flatly, "I was right about you."

"Peter, what –"

"No." His stare meets mine then, and I am silenced. My heart is flat on the ground, and I wish that's where I was too – curled up in a tight ball due to the way he's looking at me. "Too pissed off your boney ass to remember everything we did, all we gave each other – everything you *said…what we said!"* His rage builds and I see from my window the dark clouds roll in wildly; a storm approaching at full speed as the greater storm wells up inside of him. He laughs in disbelief, "It meant nothing. It never does, does it? If you wanted to confirm my prior suspicions and conclusions about *love,"* he spits acid on the word, "then well done. You win."

Peter's feet carry him out my door too quickly for me to catch him in the state of shock I'm in, but I force my legs to race after him anyway. I call, "Peter, stop! Peter, *please* talk to me!"

But he flies away. In an instant, the boy who, just moments ago, was smiling and passionately kissing my frosted lips as if they were the one thing he's hungered for his whole life, is now soaring off of my balcony and taking off into the lightening rung sky that is a personification of everything he's feeling inside...*and it's all because of me.*

❦ ❦ ❦

"It's time!" Evangeline is way too fucking excited to be walking into the jaws of death.

After weeks that felt like years of training, our quest to save Paragon and open the Pararelams by defeating Peter's prowling nightmares is about to embark...

Had someone told me a month ago I'd be saying that, I'd say you were on drugs and should join rehab with me and my loony bin friends.

Just as the siren said, Peter knows the route...more or less, I think *(I hope),* and so he let us in on some of the battle plan information...though not enough for us – *me* – to feel secure in any way, shape, or form. I tried to convey that to him, but to say the least...*he hasn't been in the talking mood for a while now*...so now we're off to Covera.

The bitch *(yes, her)* is clothed from head to toe in the sexiest *(sluttiest)* warrior garments in history, and it physically is making me sick. Peter is eying her subtly, and naturally it's impossible to tell what he's thinking; as well as Finneas, whose mind could be anywhere and nowhere all the same. I honestly can't fathom how we're gonna fight off any nightmares if she looks like that because she's more of a nightmare right now than anything could be out where we're headed.

"Hey, barbarian Barbie," it slides out of my mouth uncontrollably, and frankly, I mentally applaud it this time, "are you gonna be protected in that *inviting* getup?"

She snarls. "At least I'll be remembered not only for my trophies but for looking like a goddess while slaughtering them.[144] You, on the other hand, should just watch and take notes."

"Maya is stronger than you think." At least Del has my back; though I can't imagine he believes a word he's saying. "She'll bring more to the battles we encounter than you'll realize."

Evangeline raises an eyebrow and challenges, "Oh? Like what?"

Finneas shrugs, "We'll cross that bridge when we get to it, yeah?"

Welp. He tried.

The pixie giggles prudishly, looking at me and tossing her hair over her shoulder before turning away to lead us into the forest. I bite my tongue because there's really nothing to be said that will defend me in this situation, and insulting her will just make that more obvious. I can't be angry at Finn, either…he was just trying to vouch for me the best he could. But honestly, what's there to say? I'm useless, and we all know it.

We walk for hours in silence and luckily don't get fatally attacked. I'm not too sure how the nightmares work, but if Neverland is a personification of Peter's brain, journal, or whatever the fuck, they're gonna be total horror movie jump scares, so we have to be ready. That boy has the most unpredictable mind of anyone I have ever met, and that's coming from *me*.

"Go north." I jump at Peter's sudden demand echoing off the trees. He's trailing behind us, guarding our backs with his dagger in hand. His long-sleeved, olive green tunic is only

---

[144] *She has a fairness to this philosophy.*

halfway laced up his chest, and his brown trousers hug his strong legs in all the right places. He wears a belt with a sword hanging from its sheath, and a satchel across his shoulder with God knows what inside – probably the cursed book that got us into this mess, for all we know. His black leather boots trace up his trained calves like they were made just for him, cause well, they were…and the foliage surrounding us affects his eyes in such a way, turning them an identical shade of green that would allow him to practically blend right in if he desired.[145]

That…
He…
is a warrior.
I just wonder if he knows it, too.

Evangeline dismisses him, "I think we should follow the leader, don't you?"

"Yes. And I'm saying to go North." Peter's tone is as cold as when I met him, causing the pixie to sharply halt, turn, and walk straight toward him as if she's rehearsed those exact steps at some point before. She's several inches below his chin, so I don't know what makes her think she's the least bit intimidating.

"You have a bone to pick, Pan?"

"No, pet." *He looks hella annoyed.* "All I'm saying is that you may want to listen to the heir creator of this island, who, mayhaps, just might be more keen on where the nightmares are than you. After all, they came from *my* imagination, did they not?"

Evangeline bites her lip, "*You* created this island?"

"With a little help."

---

[145] *Sexy, I know.*

"A little?" She is comically exasperated. "Need I remind you that *I* created this world for *us?"*

"Did you?" Peter states, his tone staying maliciously even. "Don't suppose your name is Pétros Pan, is it? Furthermore, in what world, real or fiction, did you think in that little pixie head of yours, that this could be *our* world?"

She eyes him, seemingly to be shoving her foot not only in her mouth but up her ass too. "When I realized the infinite power we could have together, Peter." She takes his hands and lowers her voice as if Finn and I aren't there, a fire burning in the pit of my stomach. "We can save all of the realms, bring the magic back, and rule them *together."*

He smirks, the evil tone behind it sending chills down my arms, making their hair rise. "So you opened this – my Neverland – for you? Not to save your home?"

"No –"

"Let me get this wrong, pixie bird..." he pauses her poor forthcoming explanation by lifting one hand, and I wouldn't put it past him to have *literally* muted her speech somehow by the gesture. "My journal happened to be the key to opening Neverland, *and* filling it with awe, wonder, and all that fairytale shit... You coincidentally, perhaps serendipitously, had the same dreams and what-its as I did, *plus* you saw how powerful I was destined to be, thus you took *my* journal, created *my* dreamland for *'me'...you,* and now are expecting us to rule it *and* the other realms *including* Paragon..." he paces back and forth, pretending to gather his thoughts, though we all know far too well he already has them perfectly sorted. Evangeline wants so badly to interject, but Peter denies her the access as he gruesomely proceeds, "Be that as it may, you didn't want it to become clean it was mostly for your own selfish ambition, therefore you came up with a plea to make it *appear* this was a camaraderie-cahoots-kumbaya between two misunderstood outcasts, taught me to fight so I could gain confidence in myself for battle, and have been an *angel* to me since we've crash landed here – but then what? What was your plan after, if it weren't for the guidance of Etain? Oh, right! Nothing, really. We'd proceed to no, not fully *rescue* Paragon, but *overtake* it and the rest of the recovered magic, along with the rest of the realms with this newfound power, thus this story ending with you and I living happily ever after here on the island and flying to and from the realms as we please? Tell me, am I close?"[146]

His summarizing skills, from the therapy circle to now, never cease to baffle me.

The pixie stammers, absolutely discombobulated, "Well, I...I –" she huffs, "Actually, it's –"

"Women," he curses. "They're all the fucking same. They play with you, use you, and when you find them out, deny anything ever happened, and for *what? Pride?* Please."

My stomach twists at his words, assuming his passive aggressiveness is aimed at me particularly, but I rightfully say absolutely nothing. Evangeline pleads,

"No, no, Peter, I –"

"You've always been an outsider, Evangeline – a Peculiar; and yes, perhaps so have I...But you used it against me – you took advantage of me, your home, and this entire situation *completely*. You've always wanted your own world to rule – your own power...So you helped uncover this realm so you could do just that, and use my power for your selfish ambition. You created *my* island for *you. Never for me. Never for Paragon."*

"There would be no Neverland without you, you ass!" She shouts. "Of course, I did it for you – for us! For

---

[146] *I would NOT want to be Eevee right now. Or Maya. Honestly I'm just picturing Finn's face during all of this – it's probably priceless.*

Paragon! This is *our* island, Peter!" She takes his hands, and if I were able to control the weather with my emotions right now, we would all be wooshing and whizzing into a fucking tornado. Evangeline lowers her voice again like this is still some sort of secret, "We can save *and* rule the realms – all of them, *together.* I made this island not only to save Paragon but also for us because we want the *same things.* Can you imagine how powerful we could be?"

Peter's foul spirit lingers around us, making the air foul and blistering without warning. His lip is curled now like a rabid animal ready to pounce at the fairy, and for once, she takes a step back.

He says through gritted teeth, "There will never, ever, be an *us.* I don't need anyone, especially a woman telling me how to run *my* domain. What I need now are allies – an army. That's all. If you can't succeed in that position, you're nothing to me." Evangeline's face turns red with wrath and green envy – she is the personification of Christmas without the jolly. Basking in his ego and as if she disappeared, Peter looks above the pixie's head at Finneas and they give each other a mutual nod, and then he and I lock eyes – the emerald spark igniting the fire in my belly to spread to my entire being. He looks back into the forest, "So, as I was saying: Go North."

And so, we do.

CHAPTER thirty-five

Peter Pan
Neverland

As we walk the grounds of the island, I can't help that my mind is anywhere but on the task at hand. It races from Maya to Evangeline; to Evangeline to Maya, forward and back, then back and around again. I'm getting dizzy from this mental rollercoaster, yet I can't seem to jump the hell off.

Why did Evangeline play me like that?

Am I really as important as she said I am?

Fuck...is this how all women are?

Why is Maya claiming she doesn't remember anything?

*Does she **really** not remember?*

Or did it just mean nothing?

Was I not good or something?

WELL!
Welcome, you newly confident son of a bitch!

...Haha...with those screams? Not possible.

Nightfall is approaching fast, so I suggest to the rest of the group that we make camp for the night in order to build our strength up, that way we can set off again in the early morning. Due to the events that previously unfolded when someone didn't adhere to my command, they don't argue and we do so, making ourselves at home the best we can in the surrounding nature and soft beds of grass. As I lay sleepless and counting the Neverland stars, I think about what may unfold for my allies...*friends*...and me on our adventures.

What types of vile nightmares is my mind capable of creating...?
What will happen when we get to Covera? Or if we don't?
What if one of us gets killed?
What if we all get killed?
*What if we have to kill or **be** killed?*
What's the farthest we would all go to protect each other?
Are we all on the same team one hundred percent?

Boundaries were never discussed, and probably never will be until we are forced across that bridge by means of life or death.

I twirl my knife in my hand, an easy trick I taught myself in a day or so, and when I hear the snap of a twig, I'm up in an instant alongside Finneas. He draws his bow like a badass motherfucking barbarian ready to fight, and after we share a correlative nod, relieved we're not alone yet scared as hell just the same, he and I begin to slowly approach the noise. We let the lassies sleep, as it's been a heavy day and it's safe to presume it'll be even heavier tomorrow, yet still keep a watchful eye on them as we patrol the area.

"Ya see anything?" Finn's whisper is about as level as an average human's speaking voice, forcing me to shush him aggressively.

"No," my whisper is more professional, and I'm hoping he's taking notes. "Maybe it was just the breeze or something. I'm calling it."

But as I go to stash my dagger, we hear it again – louder and closer this time. With our weapons drawn, we inch slowly toward a small line of shrubs along the trees, and as

one rattles and vibrates threateningly, we plant our feet –
stanced and ready. The anticipation builds inside of my chest
like a tidal wave, and as if we are in a comedy sketch I didn't
write, the bushes rattle and the berries parade along the
ground, until at last we are greeted by a small bunny.

Nonetheless, I scream.
And Finneas screams because of my scream.

      The Brooklyn asshat thumps the back of my head,
"What the literal, actual *fuck* is you hollering about, you
pussy?" Despite the insult throwing, I, oh so shamelessly,
cower behind him and extend my arm forward, dagger pointed
at my target. He laughs, "You'z afraid of fluffy bunnies?"[147]
      I couldn't give less of a fuck about his sarcasm,
because I *am,* in fact, *petrified* of the ravenous creatures. Maya
and Evangeline scurry up behind us and simultaneously ask in
various inflections of curiosity, grogginess, and concern if we
are alright and what all the screaming was about.
      "Petey's nightmare has come to play," Finn
enlightens the ladies. "Be careful, I think it can smell fear."
      He points at the tiny critter twitching its button nose,
and on account of the fact that they both are girls, it means
they are bred to attack our ears with an excruciating and
simultaneous
'AWWWWWWWWWWWWWWWWWWWWW!!!'.

And they definitely do.
That's another thing about women:
Put a cutie little animal in front of them, and they all become
the same.[148]

---

[147] *I desperately want to see this scene in a movie.*
[148] *Pfft. Sue me.*

"Peter, how on earth could you be afraid of such an innocent, precious little thing?" Evangeline's voice is raised three octaves, making it more piercing than usual. "Hi, you! Welcome to Neverland! Have you been here long?" She wiggles her index fingers at the mini creature and welcomes it like her newfound next-door neighbor.

I bite a little too aggressively. "I may have written about them in my journal, but I'm not bloody C.S. Lewis…Talking animals was just a tall-tale until your *furry-filled* village." My dagger is still drawn and ready to fucking brawl, but all the same, I answer her prior question, "Long story short, I had a pet and it didn't go well…dastardly little thing was a practically possessed nightmare, so let's just leave it at that, yeah?"

"Wait, a *nightmare?* Peter –"

Exasperated, the pixie bird doesn't…or rather can't…finish, because, before our very eyes, the bunny begins to twitch and glitch like a simulation running out of signal. Its body stretches like taffy and quivers violently, looking about ready to self-destruct. I look over at Eevee, pondering whether perhaps it has something to do with her magic and if she's then unfazed…because it sure as shit ain't my doing…but on the contrary, she's as still as a statue watching the creature perform an exorcism-esque show on itself. I can hear everyone's breathing, including my own, escalate as we gape at the bunny convulsing…and then turning from an adorable puny thing to an enormous, ravenous, mutant beast.

Our eyes lead our heads as we synchronously follow it up…up…up…until it finally stops midway to the tips of the trees, thus having tripled its size, and now towers over us menacingly. Like something out of the most diabolical horror film I never want to see, the nightmare's ears are as tall as I am, its eyes are lustful for murder, and its teeth are the size of daggers – though these are all blade, no hilt…

I Prefer Peter

We are so bloody dead.

"And that, friends," I never take my eyes off what I once thought could never get worse, "is why I hate bunnies."

As if it heard its cue, the beastie roars an ungodly, earsplitting bellow as its razor-sharp claws attack at us with a vicious swing, graciously missing as we dart out of its path in time.

My first instinct is to run – sprint out of these woods as fast as my legs can possibly carry me…Then I think: *fly, Peter, you fucking ijit! Soar unfathomably high like a drug seething through the veins of the sky; avoiding the mass chaos below and imminent death arriving.*

But that is so like me, isn't it?
Once so daring against fear, now unable to look it in the face.
A runner.
A fucking coward.
Well, no more escaping my nightmares.
This time, I have to fight.
This time, I have to win.

I sheath my dagger and draw my sword; my fellow team eying me in shock.

"It's fight or die, mates!" I holler at them. "Pick your poison."

Hearing my command, the three straighten their backs and plant their feet firmly on the ground with mine. Evangeline conjures up balls of fire in her palms and lets them rip straight at the bunny's chest, though somehow they extinguish directly on impact; the monster fully immune to the blows. Cursing in annoyance yet unwavering as if she had a plan B from the start, she shape-shifts into a glowing, zippy, tinkling fairy as tiny as a child's figurine that could easily fit in my pocket.

Huh. I all but forgot she could do that.[149]

The itty bitty Eevee scutters around the beast's head; Paradust parading around it like a mystic powder, so that within seconds, the bunny becomes dazed and drowsy, swaying to and fro like she just performed some gnarly Pokémon shit on it. Taking the moment to his advantage, Finneas draws his arrow and aims it straight in between the giant's eyes, focusing and breathing steadily as if he has all the time in the world –

Calmest motherfucker I know.   *Probably in my top 3 favorite Finneas Scott lines.*

He mutters, "Sweet dreams, fuckface."

Finn lets the arrow fly; the weapon smashing into its target with a heavy, grotesque thud. He cheers with the pump of a fist, and as much as I want to clap him on the back and tell him *'Nice shot!',* the creature hardly wavers yet instead comes more to life, shifting to a frenzied, scorching rage. The demon slopes down to Finneas and bears its violent, wooden staked teeth, snarling and exhaling a putrid odor into his face. Its eyes turn a murderous red as it snatches him in its grip like a useless Ken doll, clutching him so tight that the disarmed kid desperately gasps for air. Its breath attacks all of our nostrils like a poisonous gas, sending us cowering back – though as my eyes spill unwilling tears, I never take them off of my best friend.

For the first time in what seems like forever, I can't breathe, but I do everything in my being to cast out the anxiety

---

[149] ¯_(ツ)_/¯

and panic as I attempt to keep my mind clear enough for a plan to save Finneas. I watch as he flails and curses, using all his wrath and might to pluck himself out of the bunny's grasp, and just when I'm in the middle of helplessly failing my search within every nook and cranny of my brain for a solid rescue tactic, through my hazy eyes, I make out a tiny body sprinting in front of me and into the grips of a death wish.

"Hey, bunny boy! Come at me!"

Maya.
DUMBASS.

"What the blasted flying fuck are you doing?" I nearly deafen myself as my voice screeches; my legs darting after the lass without delay. I lift her by her teeny torso, hauling her ass back toward safety…well, *more or less,* and she flails and thrashes in my arms; her boney body making it nearly painful to try and hold her still,

"Let me go, you dickshit, I'm actually *trying* to help Finneas, unlike you statues who aren't doing a single damn thing!"

Evangeline's tiny fairy frame flutters above my shoulder, shouting obscenities at Maya through chimes and tinkers neither of us can understand. While I'm distracted attempting to make out even a single word of what she's saying, Maya bites my thumb so viciously, that I yelp in pain and believe for a moment she too can shape-shift and perhaps morphed into the ravenous bunnies little kit.

She releases my limb when I instinctively push her off, scowling and pretending my thumb isn't beginning to leak blood. "What you're *trying* to do, you muppet[150], is get

---

[150] *My favorite British insult of all time.*

yourself *and* Finneas killed! So stay the bloody hell back, alright? I couldn't bear to see either of you get hurt!"

In such a vulnerable state, the words slide out like butter on a hotcake. I try not to dwell on how easily they did, or the truth behind them after what happened...what she seemingly can't recall...or simply refuses to...*the ache she caused in me after...*

No. I can't reflect right now.
Move the hell on, Pan.

"If we all just stand and watch," she yells over the starting wind, "he *will* die! If I'm the only one who is willing to risk my life for my friend, then *so be it.* "

Finneas desperately screams for help, kicking and bashing the bunny with his fists for dear life. Maya's long legs make haste toward the scene again, and a paroxysm of passionate rage and terror floods my soul for her. The dire need to protect her engulfs me as she thrashes about, doing everything she can think of to distract the beast with her actions and loud wailing, looking like a total fool to save her friend.

But is a fool who's willing to risk their life for someone they love, more foolish than the one who does nothing at all?[151]

I shake my head at my possible madness, though surrender, lunging at the distracted monster with my sword. I slice and stab its leg with the fresh razor-sharp blade, sending the demon bunny howling with rage and unruly pain. The roars don't cease as it takes its free fist and backhands me full force, sending my body flying through the air and barreling back first into a tree. Oxygen escapes every part of my being,

---

[151] *This is a wise Mia Battaglia quote and I am DAMN PROUD OF IT.*

and I am forced to watch weakly and helplessly as the creature pulls the arrow out of between its eyes. Gore and goo spurt like hellish red rain all around us, and without a moment's hesitation, the animalistic being lodges the arrowhead straight in between Finneas' shoulder blades with all its might.

This time, it is I who produces an ungodly noise, along with Maya's muffled scream from behind her hand, and Evangeline's loud chiming bells that I still don't understand ringing through the commencing rain. Finneas' neck snaps upward toward the black and deep gray sky as his body arches, the tip digging into the top of his spine, breaking skin and tissue until it is no longer seen, but hidden by flesh. My chest heaves as black blood pours out and down his back, his eyes filled with every emotion and sensation he has ever felt, never felt, and then some. The beast drops him like a littered piece of trash, ready to move on to its next kill.

I'll be damned if that's any one of us.

But Maya beats me to it. She lunges at Finneas, her arms grasping him for fear his soul will fly away and her sobs wreaking havoc on the mammoth's ears – yet filling my heart with even more lead. With plenty of traumatic torment left to spare, I scream at the top of my lungs for her to get the hell out of there – to stop being such a bloody halfwit and run away –

Run so far, far away, and never look back – disappear to New Jersey and start over and pretend I never, ever existed – that I never dragged you into this nightmare.
I beg you.
RUN.

I pray to a God that I hope is tuned in for this shitshow, asking that for once he makes her just *fucking listen*...and though perhaps He tries, she doesn't adhere to either of us in the least.

Because if there was ever a creature of habitually doing the exact opposite of what needs to be done in crucial situations, it's Maya fucking Sexton.

She stays put, eyes closed, awaiting the sweet kiss of death. I advance hastily toward her, dread rising in me at the mere image of anything happening to her next –

But I'm too late.

The monster expels another screech and its massive claws slash Maya up her middle; the blow filled with enough force to send her flying back through the night air and plummeting to the ground like a puppet cut from its string.

I can't remember how to speak. My eyes blur and my heart disintegrates – the beating ceasing to exist entirely, as I feel like everything that I just witnessed happen to her, happened to me instead. Neverland freeze frames – my universe going deafeningly silent.

She's dead.
She has to be dead.
She and Finneas – my two best and only true friends – gone in the blink of an eye.

A howling, frigid, tornado-like wind attacks us all then like a blizzard without the snow. Razor-like rain pelts down brutally, and I try to stop it – strive with everything I learned about control in magic lessons to soothe my anger and despair so the uproar in the sky will cease, but it's no use. The storm stirring in me is violent and uncontrollable, and Neverland knows it full well.

With adrenaline, loathing, passion, and every bit of Paradust I have surging through all fibers of my being, I fly. But no, not up, up, and *away* –; alternatively, I dart head first like a fucking pelican after its prey toward the only thing other than my rancid father that I have ever wanted to witness the macabre, lurid death of.

Since I haven't been fortunate enough to receive the latter,
Let's make this dream a reality.

I travel at the speed of light – faster than I ever thought possible –, and as the fury builds within me, I become surrounded by an emerald, blazing sheen that envelops me entirely. Swallowed by strength and courage, all at once, I am indestructible.[152] Before the monster can process my swift, nearly vaporous presence, I hail the trees and command their branches and vines to expand and fasten themselves ruthlessly around every part of the beast, taking it prisoner and stretching out its limbs like taffy until it bellows in agony. The demon bunny's breathing is cutting short, so I make haste to finish the job, with the cutlass of my weapon meeting the thick neck of the foul player and digging into its meaty flesh with a grotesque sever. I slice with all my might, chopping into bone and marrow as blood explodes onto my body, as well as upon everything and everyone around me. I don't stop until its head is my trophy, and the remnants of my former prey are at my feet, lifeless.

My chest rises and falls so heavily that I feel I may pass out and tumble out of midair at any second. It's not until now that I notice my entire being is soaking wet, and so are

---

[152] *I want this tattooed. I want to live by this quote.*

the keepers of the despairing gasps for life toward the earth below me.

Evangeline is consoling and assisting a kneeling Finneas, shedding Paradust on him so his pain will lessen for now. *He's alive...My sweet, good God, he's alive.* Though the arrow shaft is now drawn out of his back, the sharp head somehow snapped and has supernaturally made its way deeply buried beneath the surface of his skin; now protruding out like a massive diamond-shaped tumor.

Strange, to say the least.
A mystery we'll have to unwrap later.
But he's breathing, and that's what's vital.
His face is pale white and caked with sweat,
but he's bloodyfucking alive.

"Finn!" I dive down to him and for the first time, see his eyes filled with tsunami tears. Mine do the same as I grab the back of his hair and place his forehead on mine, "You stay with me, and that's an order, yeah? I swear to you, we'll figure it out," I refer to the arrowhead, tracing my finger gently over the skin it's hiding under whilst pondering how something such as this is even possible...*But I've questioned the impossible quite a lot recently, and it always has something in store.* "We'll figure it *all* out," I resume, "but you *damn* well better not bloody quit on me, you hear that, mate?"

He winces, and my heart bleeds for him. It's never done that for anyone, and I can't say it's a luxurious feeling in any sense...But if my solid cold beater has to bleed for anyone, I'd drain it out for Finneas Scott.[153] "Aye aye, Captain Pan," his voice is trembling and feeble, but a crimson red smile crosses his face like a feared warrior from another dimension. A warrior I swear I'll never be.

---

[153] *I can't describe how undeniably powerful this is.*

Maya lay motionless aside from her sobbing in the dirt, blood staining her blouse and seeping out her corset. I'm by her side in half an instant, lifting her limp body and turning her over promptly, yet still delicately; slicing and tearing out the strings to remove her top and tend to her horrid wound.

I flip her now bare and shivering upper half over onto the wet grass, and she tries to hide her breasts with her arms, breathlessly protesting, *"No,* don't, Peter –"

"The *fuck* do you think I'm doing?" My tone is harsh, as I, to some degree, fucking expect her to bloody well understand I'm not trying to strip her for lustful, sensuous reasons, but *nooo* – she actually tells me to stop trying to save her life.

And so, I repeat: Dumbass.

Disregarding her delusional stupidity, I peel off my drenched tunic and try to soak up her flowing blood the best I can. With belligerence and fear, Maya pushes my hands away like a child and cries, *"Stop,* it hurts!"

"I know, I know," I attempt to be gentler in tone now. "But you *must* keep it pressed tightly for me, alright? Can you do that for me?"

She shoves me, though winces in pain while doing so. "I can do it myself –"

"Please, Maya, for *fucks* sake let me take care of you!" My voice comes out in a riled growl due to the overwhelming fear and worry overtaking me. She complies at last, perhaps at my demanding tone or the fact that her energy is diminishing swiftly – of which, I'm unsure, but I'm grateful, nonetheless. She replaces her stubbornness with more sobbing, and with blood now soaking my hands and wrists, I'm at the end of my rope.

"Eevee, I need your Paradust *now!"* I holler at her through the screaming wind. She pays no mind to me, so I assume she doesn't hear, and I try again, "Evangeline, Maya is dying – *help me!"*

"She won't." She glances at me for a split second, though stays mildly attentive to Finneas, who is now fairly stable though drowsily in a far-off daze from Paradust and unable to follow all that's happening around him.

"Well, what do I do? Can my magic heal her? Can I –"

"You don't have that kind of magic. Not yet, anyway – if ever."

Rage seethes and boils within me. "Okay, well *you do!"* My voice is screeching and frantic, wondering what on earth would propel Evangeline to act this carelessly toward Maya. Sure, they don't always see eye to eye, but fuckin' hell...*she's dying.*

"I don't have enough to spare –"

"Bullshit!" I snap with such violence that thunder roars. "This is crucial, fairy; now are you with me like you oh, so poetically blubbered earlier, or against me like the rest of these nightmares? Make your choice *now."*

Annoyed and with a bratty huff, the pixie leaves Finneas in a small bed of moonflowers to sleep and stomps over, sharply placing her glowing, golden hand straight upon the dying girl's gash. At the sudden unpitying impact, Maya howls like the bunny in agony and writhes beneath Eevee's touch, but forthwith, her flowing, deep red blood slows and begins to vanish into the spell of the Paradust.

I gape at the blinding light beginning to cascade off of Maya's pale skin, one that surrounds her entirely like Heaven has found her and is stealing her away. I keep my curious gawk glued to her, unable to remove it for fear of what I may miss. My eyes burn and see nothing but spots, and at an explosion of blue and gold, I am quickly forced to avert my eyes for, now, fear of going completely blind.

I Prefer Peter

Once I am finally able to look back again, standing there with her arm still outstretched and a crooked glare is Evangeline…

And Maya, fully alive.

CHAPTER thirty-six

Peter Pan

This chapter hurts me.   Neverland

I should be thrilled – elated – practically hopping up and down on one leg and doing flips and twirls at the sight of Maya Wendy Sexton breathing...

But instead, my insides feel like they're frozen solid and violently inflamed all at the same time.
A feeling I've grown too familiar with, nowadays.

I stalk over to her – the one is clearly and rightfully puzzled yet relieved that she is no longer in seething agony or about to meet her Maker –, and as she meets my cross gaze, her expression switches so vastly, that she could easily pass for wishing she would rather be dead.

I tower over her, "What the bloody *hell* was that?" The words come out a mixture of monotonously seething rage and complete and utter shock at everything I was just savagely forced to live through. As I gape at her bare body, I notice Maya's wounds have miraculously disappeared, along with her clothing and all of the blood that poured onto the soggy grass – as if none of it was ever there at all.

She covers her breasts with her arms, "My eyes are up here, perv," she bites, causing me to roll the bloodshot balls lodged within my own head, which are tired of tumbling around all day thanks to her. "I did what I had to do." Though modestly shielding her body, she stands her ground regarding her actions and looks up to meet my eyes with more genuine pride than I have ever seen her carry. "Had I not, you wouldn't have either, and Finneas might've been as good as dead." I let out hot air through my nostrils at the fact, but she pays no mind and turns. **"Now, if you'll excuse me, I'm cold."**[154]

Maya begins to walk back in the direction of where we set camp as if what just happened was a mere *whoopsie* and we can all just move on.

But I can't move on.
Not from what she made me feel before.
Not from what she made me feel just now.
Not from what she makes me feel entirely.

Everything builds like acidic bile inside of me, and with one last push over the edge, it projectiles upon her, "You were so *stupid!*" My insult comes out in a growl, causing the lass to spin around on her heels, eyes rounded.

"I was stupid? While you stood there with your fear of bunnies, I risked my *life* for him –"

"Yes. *Stupid* girl." My temper is uncontrollable – unhinged. "You were *unarmed.* You can't fight, you're not strong in any sense, and you sure as hell would've been history if it weren't for Evangeline, and you know it! We always have to babysit you, and it's pathetic."

The surging pride Maya carries falters, and her eyes glisten with hurt and resentment – *since Brand New Life, this has been a look I never wished to receive from her ever again for as long as I lived...yet here we are, facing the inevitable.* Sexton grinds her teeth and scoffs with hostility, "You honestly think I'm that useless?"

With wide arms, I gesture an homage to the scene that just played out, *"Clearly."* I throw my wrist toward her, and a blouse similar to her last one covers her shivering body. As she adjusts to her clothing, I sigh and attempt to catch my

---

[154] *Badass as hell.*

breath. "You almost died," it comes out strained. "And with another stunt like that, you *will* die next time."

"I – just thought –"

"No, you didn't think."

"I thought you'd be proud! –"

"Proud?" I viciously sneer. "Well, I'm not." I hardly mean it, yet it falls out like a nasty egg full of spiders. "You shouldn't have come if you were just gonna perform shit like that and get in the way. You should've just stayed in Paragon. Or better yet, in New Jersey."

She looks down at her feet, trying to hide tears streaming down her cheek, though failing even in the pouring rain. Her arms flail upwards, then limply back down to her sides again. "You're right, Peter. Maybe I just shouldn't have come. Maybe I should've just politely asked the ravenous, heinous beast to murder me so I wouldn't have to be the problem anymore, right?"

I want to answer. I want so badly to run to her and hold her in my arms, mindlessly expressing to her that the bullshit she just uttered isn't true, and half of the poppycock I said wasn't either. I want to scream through the storm that I'm so bloody damn proud of her fighting; for doing what we were all too frightened to do, even *with* weapons and magic. I want to tell her so badly that the gut-wrenching sensation of watching her helplessly kiss death right before my eyes was so beyond unbearable, that I wished I were the one on Grim's doorstep instead.

But I can't.   UGH.
I don't.

The excruciating misery she spawned on me before – toying with my emotions and my heart, combined with the distress she sprung upon me while she was nearly dying before my eyes, is fueling me with such darkness that I can't contain its dominion. I lucidly look up at her, and I guess that's telling enough.

"So right," a voice perks up behind me, and I am blinded by another bursting, golden beam of Paradust enveloping the area where we stand. I shield my burning eyes, and when the light behind their lids finally darkens, I thrust them wide open to make out that the only lass standing there, with her arm outstretched again, is Evangeline...

But this time, Maya's gone.

CHAPTER thirty-seven
Evangeline
Neverland

I wipe my hands together, "There. Shall we go now?"

Peter's face is in mass hysteria. Poor kid has no idea how to feel all of these emotions attacking him at once, or what to do with the shitshows occurring before him one by one, and I won't lie, I'm eager to see how he handles the even more grandiose charade I just pulled.

"Where…What the fuck did you do?"

"I did exactly what you wanted," I say with a half-shrug, my tone chipper and matter-of-fact. Inside, however, I am seething with heated jealousy at the certainty that Peter is readably hiding a cutthroat panic attack over this worthless chick he is so head over heels for vanishing, even though he rightfully implied the idea.

I just humbly served and did what we all wanted before the journey through the woods even started.

"She was holding us back – you practically said it yourself," I respond. "So now she's someone else's problem to *babysit,*" I mime Peter's previous words, and he gapes at me with such stupid, handsome confusion, that I can't help but giggle.

He doesn't like that.

"Evangeline," my name is thrown like a razor blade off his tongue and pricks me like a rose thorn, "where precisely did you send her?"

"Nowhere far," I say with a wave of my hand, deserving an award for my nonchalant deposition. "She'll be just fine, there's no reason to worry your pretty little mind." I tap him once on the head for each last three words and force a believable, shiny smile.

Lightning strikes above us as he threatens through gritted teeth, "I'm not gonna ask you again, bitch." For the first time, his electrifying green eyes and sadistic tone cause me to pale. "Tell me where she is, or you're on your own with Paragon – fuck the prophecy, fuck it all. Hell, I'll conjure that bunny beast back so fast –"

I press out a gasp, and my bullshit, sunny expression turns to true vexation. "Oh, that is so like you, Peter Pan. Finding any and all reasons to run away from responsibility. Such a *child.*"

"I wouldn't test me, fairy –"

I spit at the 'F' word. "The only thing you need to be fixated on right now, Pan, is getting your sleeping beauty over there," I point to a Para-drugged Finneas...*I hope that doesn't throw his sobriety out the door...*[155] "to Covera to seek medical attention, and to find out the next steps to *your – our* – quest. The fate of Paragon, the people within it, and its pocket realms are *your* priority now, and none of it can be remedied without *you* no matter how badly you want to damn it all to hell. It's too late to back out, and you know it." He bites his lip and scratches his hand. "You can worry about your precious side hustle later, but you and I know full well having her here would have weakened us – all of us. Not to mention, potentially kill her."

This – this right here is the breaking point. His mind entertains the thought of her actually dying in battle; getting fiercely and irreversibly hurt and never again being lucky

---

[155] *You're so fucking lucky I say it doesn't. I literally could kill you off in seconds with my index fingers, bitch.*

enough to be graced by my healing elixir through Paradust...*especially since I'm now running perilously low because of that weakling she-headache.* I can see in his heavy-set eyes that no matter how much he doesn't want to admit it, he knows I'm right – Maya being here isn't beneficial to anyone.

I got him.

Peter turns to look at a sleeping Finneas, then around the forest defeatedly, as if the answer or reassurance he's searching for is hiding somewhere within the trees. I know he loathes himself for giving in – for leaving her to the vast unknown that only I know and can't be bothered to reveal for fear he'll run after her – but I also presume at least a portion of him agrees with me or else he'd be denying it wholeheartedly with that chaotic, stubborn mouth of his.

"She's safe?" He simply asks, his tone crestfallen. The guilt-ridden side of his heart is visibly killing him, but he's pressing it aside. He doesn't want to know where she is because he knows himself too well for once. He'll go after her, thus causing the magic of Paragon to die, and resulting in him failing to save slews of dying people. Therefore, that would add more lives under his belt to mourn...just like when he couldn't save his precious mommy.

I don't need his journal to read him like an open book.

"I pixie-promise," I say with an enthusiastic nod of my head; my wings fluttering on my back and glittering as I grant him a smile. "I made sure of it." I bat my eyelashes at him, and though his trust in me is currently ever so slim, he dips his pretty little head.

"Alright," he says with slight hesitation. When the world doesn't explode, he clears his throat and shakes off every single one of the previously treacherous events that just unfolded. "Let's get Finn to Covera, and we'll figure out where to go from there. Can't imagine what he'll say when he finds out Maya is gone..."

He says this last part more to himself than me, and as much as I want to express the obvious fact that Finneas has much grander issues to worry about...I can fully tell he's not going to stop wallowing over Maya's absence for a stupidly long time, so I choose to refrain from responding for the sake of not opening another can of worms on the subject.

I wake the sleeping Ponyboy, and we begin our journey over again. It's now just the three of us, as it should be; scaling the Neverland forest without Maya Wendy Sexton to break our mighty strides with her sickly, powerless being. Sure, Finneas is slower due to his wounds, but not a dire hindrance in comparison to the incapable, lost girl. Peter doesn't deserve someone of her stature, nor does he need the burden of being weighed down by her. Ironic, isn't it? Someone so frail and meek has the ability to weigh someone down like a house made of cinderblocks.

I think he knows it too – somewhere deep, deep down in that soul of his. He's just too blinded by his *'first love'* to admit it.

He's far too good for her – too divine for her; and in time, I'll make him see that truth in its entirety. Once we get to Covera and Peter discovers more species similar to his own, and when we travel forward from there, he meets more Peculiars in the realms of Paratoze and Paradmir, the kid will realize just how royal he is and forget all about that earthling in a split second.

I'll ensure he becomes stronger; mightier in his ability every day, and soon, surviving in this world and the next will become as effortless as blinking – as easy as breathing has turned out for him.

He'll be shatterproof.
He'll be infinite.
Immortal.
But we have a long way to go…

Poor little Pan. So foolishly in love…So naive.
Wake up, Peter. Things are about to change.[156]

---

[156] *The quote from the back of the book and one of my all time favorites. The first one I ever shared on social media whilst teasing for the book, actually! I knew once I typed it that it was going to be the perfect ending to this chapter. It's crazy…now I have sweatshirts and crewnecks that say it with wicked grand designs on my site. Crazy how time flies…pun intended.*

Epilogue

DeAr MayA,

The love I have for the epilogue could likely be considered unhealthy.

I TruLY hoPE thIS leTTer fiNDs yoU weLL, if aT aLL bY thE shEEr GrACE oF nEVErLAnd. clEArLY, regARdinG Our lAST fEw tIFfs toGETher THAt we nEVer haD The tIMe tO soRT, iM nOt gRAnd...or kiND...wiTh worDs, sO i shALL dO mY beST tO expResS whAT i NEEd tO riGHT herE, righT noW.

I fanCy tHE bESt waY to stARt, IS by apolOGiziNg. IndeeD, I dONt dO thAT ofTEn, aS I onCe saID...buT yOU desERve aLL oF thE apolOgiEs i nEVeR GAVE anyOne iN mY enTIRe 18 yEARs of livING. yOU arE strONger thAN you weRE eveR FORced tO beliEve, anD bRAver tHAn aNY herOInE iN a unIVerse oF suPErs. yoU certAInly aRE my hERo, And i SIncereLy aPOLOGize For doING aboSLUte Shit coNVeyinG iT. iF yOU werE a laSS in a BOOk,[157] i WOULdn'T STop baBBlinG About you anD rOOTinG For yOU paGE afTER pagE. YOU'D bE mY favOrIte fiCTIOnaL charACTEr – thE onE id LOok foR iN everY girl I evER meT – onLY To faiL tO FInd heR becAUse theRE coulD NEveR BE anOTHer yoU.

---

[157] *Lol...she is, and so is he, yet they are so blissfully unaware. Deadass BONKERS.*

bY tHE way, FinN iS DOIng fIne. There'S pOIson IN HIs veINs froM tHe deMONiC bUNNy blOOd and tHE gOOp oN tHE arrOWheaD tHAt goT emBEdDed inTO hIS skIN, buT witH tHE carE proVIDed herE in COverA, i THInk he'LL puLL tHRouGh. He's a gEEdaMn warrIor, tHAt one.

tHE diffErenCe bETwEEn HEre aND PAraGOn is abUNdanT — tHEir oWn advAnced TechNOlogy, poTIons, ArchitecTUre — eveN THe crEAtuREs hERe aRe mOrE exquiSITe. tHEY caLL tHEmselVEs Ethereals, whiCh iS exTREmelY SuiTing. fraNkIY, darLing, You'D fiT rIghT in.

I HAvent tHE foGGiest hOW mY braIN camE uP with anY of THis, buT I gueSS thaT's tHE funNY thiNG abOUT dreAMs...theY maY neVER maKE senSE unLESS you MAke seNSe of Them. IM TRying — FAILING! — buT tryiNG, noneTHEless, to beLIEVe thaT i couLD be caPAble of subCOnsciouslY creATing somEthiNG thIS magnIFIcent. I juST wish yOU werE HEre to seE it.

anYway, lASs.. I'm noT cERTain whAT weNT wroNg thAT nighT — pERHaps tHE paRAwiNE wenT tO youR swEEt heaD, bUT tHE nighT We shARED waS unDOUbtedlY tHE graNDest of mY lifE. ReGArdless iF you dO reMEMber iT oR noT ... i ALwaYS Will. fOr as LONg as I livE, i wiLL nevEr forGEt tHe waY youR snOW whITE skin raDIated iN tHe cLEAr mooNLIght, tHe waY yoUR cryStAl eYEs danCed lIKE tHE iriDEScenT merMAId lAgoon, tHE Way yOUR voiCE expELLed meloDIous souNDs eveN tHE piXies couLdnt rePLIcate – you aRE nEVerland personIFied, Maya Wendy Sexton. If Ever theRe waS a HAPpy thOUGHt tO seND me SoarinG, iTs yoU. iT wiLL AlwaYS be YOU.[158]

So, WITH thaT, I wiLL maKE you THis voW: I wiLL coME baCK foR yoU. iF tHe cONNectIOn i FEel foR yOU goEs boTH wayS, thEN juST alWAYs bE waitING foR me. I foUnD yoU oNCe aFTER danCIng wiTH deATH aND trAVEling TO tHE unKNoWN... *tHE unKNOWn toWN of New JersEy, lol...* aND I wOULd tanGO wiTH tHE devIL himSelf tO finD yoU anyWhere all Over AGAIn. ALl oF thIS haPPENEd beFore, aND so IT shaLL begIn agaIn.

I WIll alWays FInd mY waY baCK to yoU.

IF whAT wE haVE is TRue, tHen i WIll aSk The stARs iN tHE skY tO guIDe mE strAIght To yoU. aND if THEy leaD mE astRAY, I wiLL reWRite THem aND trY agaIN. THEre is nOwhere yOU caN gO thAT i wonT comE searChing. wHAt moSt asSuMEd wAS mY mAGIC bEINg uNCOVEred, I alWAYs knEw You weRe – Are – tHE one thiNg...

tHE MAGIC...

the oxYgEn I neeDed iN thEse patHEtic luNGS tO finALLy begIN feelIng ALIVE – TO aT laSt reaLIZe whAT it wAS

---

[158] *Gut me with a chainsaw.*

likE to fiNALly havE aiR In my lUNgs afTEr suFFocaTIng foR so lONG.

And DAMmit ALL tO HEll, I donT waNT tO forGET How tO breAThe agaiN.

ALL THAt tO saY, i PRay yOU NeveR forGET mE. I PRay To a GOD we'RE STill TRYing TO figURe oUt abOUT tHAT you FOrgivE aLL of THE shit thaT'S haPPENEd, aND we cAN staRT OVer. i'LL mAKe-belIEve iT's aLL oKAy unTil tHE daY i See YOU agaIN.

jUSt alWAYS Be WAitinG foR me.

by The wAy...
fUCk, aM I prOUd of yOu.
sO uDeniABly prOUD of you...
aNd I LOve yoU, mAYA wendY SextOn – thE daRliNg girL oF mY happIESt tHOughts.

sinCerEly,

Ugly sobbing. SO fucking UGLY SOBBING.

PetEr PaN

I slam the journal shut with an appalled scoff and look out of the ceiling-high infirmary window that overlooks the dystopian city of Covera. I always concluded hidden cities were a myth – more of a wish from the hopeful people of

Paragon and beyond to stumble upon one day, but no. It's more real than anything I've seen in quite some time.

My eyes shift from the view back down again to the tethered, leather-bound book I realize I'm aggressively white-knuckling,

"Maya Wendy Sexton, the darling girl..." the words are sour on my tongue and erupt my skin into a sickly green glow, "give me a fucking break." Without hesitation, I tear the pages of the mawkish, nauseating letter out of Peter's journal, and hold them tightly in my grip. With the Paradust at my fingertips, I smoothly fly the journal across the room and easily slither it back under his pillow.

¯_(ツ)_/¯

Of course, I said I would send the letter...

I didn't say *where.*
Combusting into ashes in mid-air?
I didn't say where.

Peter sleeps soundly on the cot beside Finneas, both boys being provided obligatory fluids and treated for their many battle wounds. The bond they have is strong, indeed...but that's one more alliance Pan has with someone that is foreseeably about to be tainted, due to the poison spreading through Finneas' veins as we speak...

Brynasyth Bane? That shit changes people.
Poor guy.
Peter, I mean.
Finneas too, I suppose.

A wicked smirk creeps upon my face. I guess that's one hidden power of the pixie in me I didn't even know I carried, and what's more, something I can do without even trying:

Demolition.
Because let's face it, the only one Peter needs is me.
And I'll see to it I'm the only one he has.
And I will be perfect for him.

Oh, dearest Peter. Resting so soundly, likely dreaming of his precious, helpless, little duckling lassie. I scrunch my nose at the foul thought, and at this point, I could light the city with my burning, viridescent infuriation.

I glance at the letters one last time before crumbling them within my fists, casting fire through my heated palm and watching them singe and burn to ashes.

"Poor, poor, Wendy bird," I say, tossing the dust into oblivion and watching what was once paper disappear. "Your sweet Peter Pan is never coming back for you. Not if I can help it."

I sit gently on the side of Peter's bed, softly stroking his bare skin which is still slightly tight and damp from his recent shower. I welcome the few drops of water on my hand, and slick back the flyaway hairs from my messy topknot bun.

I gaze up and down his bare, titillating top frame slowly rising and falling, and reminisce of the night he and I shared when that lusty chest of his expelled crows, moans, and growls for *me*.

Yes, me.
While he was screaming her name, seeing her face – it was me he was giving his all to, and I to him in return.
Pity he thinks Maya, the tiny house mouse, could be so confident...
Seductive.   ¯_(ツ)_/¯ BITCH
Sexy.
He should've known it was the devil in disguise.

The sensitive place between my inner thighs throbs, and my skin crawls and tingles with goosebumps. Though Pan doesn't know yet that it was I, his shape-shifting pixie bird, that he gave his innocence to that beautifully enchanted night, he soon will. Of course, it will bring wrath-ridden questions, like *'why?'* and *'how could you do such a thing, you little pixie bitch?'* – but Peter will understand soon after that it's because he *needs* to be with me...is *meant* to be with me...

That together, we are invincible.

I did this for us.
All of it.
And he will accept that in due time.

"It's time for Peter to grow up, Maya darling." I stand and gape at my small frame in the mirror growing ever so swiftly, little by little, as we Fae do when with child. "He forgot to mention in his charming little love letter that he's going to be a father."

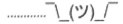

I BET YOURE READY FOR BOOK 2?
Dont shit your britches, it's COMING SOON!

ACKNOWLEDGEMENTS

I don't even know where to begin…

I think *Thank You* would be a safe place, right?

THANK YOU to everyone who made I Prefer Peter possible, and also to those who encouraged and supported me through this awfully big adventure. The last two years held wild amounts of starting, stopping, rewriting, deleting, giving up, and getting back in the race again…

Because: 'That's life!'
As Sinatra put it best…
> *Hehe.*

But if I didn't have the people in my life who believed in the magic of this wacky, *'confusing'* idea from the start, let alone their faith in me to bring it to life through this lil book, I wouldn't be writing this right now.

Zachary St. George…my luv : Thank you for being the muse I never knew I needed. Not only is your vivid, clever brain my bff, but also, this is a special thanks to your beautiful face – you make a better Peter than Peter does. Thank you for being my forever happy thought.

To my momma : Thanks for telling me to stop complaining about what I wish the 40+ Peter Pan Retellings I've read had within their pages, and to just write my own dream book, *letting my soul and imagination run wild.* Without you, this would've been merely one of those *'maybe I will…probably not'* situations I constantly find myself in. I love you.

Jessi Ramey : Without your brilliance and the Stolen by Pan series, I wouldn't have discovered the magic of fairytale reimaginings. *CHEERS* to you for bringing my favorite characters to life in such a monumental way; leading your work then to inspire me to create my own story. Thank you for being an encourager and a friend to me since the beginning – I admire you more than you'll ever know.

Most importantly, thank you Lord : Without You placing this gift inside of me and Your Holy Spirit guiding me from the first sentence to the last, this would've been downright impossible. But all things are possible with you, and *I Prefer Peter* is sole proof of that.

TO ALL OF YOU :

Thank you for your support and never-ending love. Keep living life as one awfully big adventure, and stay as golden as ever.

THE FUTURE IS BRIGHT, AND THE BEST IS YET TO COME!

Mia Battaglia

About the Author

HELLO! My name is Mia Battaglia. I live in sunny Southern California, and whether it be music, writing, baking, theater, art, adventuring, or whatever whosits or whatsits – I am all for it. Doing what lets me fully create from my heart, is the sole reason why I'm alive. I self-published my first poetry book, *"i probably shouldnt say this, but…"*, in 2021, which means the world to me & is available on my website, Barnes and Noble's site, and Amazon; and I also have my own small local baking business, called tinyBAKER, which is ALWAYS accepting orders for any and all occasions!

Peter Pan is also my everything if you haven't been informed. I have read over 40 Peter retellings, and I plan to read even more as I continue the I Prefer Peter series, which owns my heart.

To God be the Glory. Stay Gold.
Socials: @miabattags, @ohitsmiagic, @_tinybaker
authormiabattaglia.com

The moment you doubt whether you can fly,
you cease forever to be able to do it.

- J.M. Barrie, "Peter Pan"

Made in the USA
Las Vegas, NV
12 October 2024

96704296R20246